HALL OF MIRRORS

Gradually Jason's eyes were becoming used to the moonlit darkness. He could make out Glen, spread-eagled on his bed, naked. On top of him was a man, a big man, muscular and hairy, also naked. The man's hands clutched and clawed at Glen's shoulders, his toes dug into the bed, his buttock muscles contracted and relaxed and his whole body rolled in a smooth rocking-horse motion, up and down, up and down, planing against Glen's smooth torso, his cock grinding across the youth's stomach.

After a while the man dropped lower down the bed. He was nibbling at Glen's balls, biting and stretching the ball-sac with his teeth. He popped first one ball then the other into his mouth. The man's tongue snaked out along the underside of Glen's scrotum, back towards his dark crack, then forward again, up the underside of the boy's cock, lingering where shaft met head.

HALL OF MIRRORS

Robert Black

First published in Great Britain in 1997 by
Idol
an imprint of Virgin Publishing Ltd
332 Ladbroke Grove
London W10 5AH

ISBN 0 352 33209 3

Cover photograph by Trevor Watson Photography

Typeset by SetSystems Ltd, Saffron Walden, Essex
Printed and bound in Great Britain by
Cox & Wyman Ltd, Reading, Berks

SAFER SEX GUIDELINES

These books are sexual fantasies – in real life, everyone needs to think about safe sex.

While there have been major advances in the drug treatments for people with HIV and AIDS, there is still no cure for AIDS or a vaccine against HIV. Safe sex is still the only way of being sure of avoiding HIV sexually.

HIV can only be transmitted through blood, come and vaginal fluids (but no other body fluids) – passing from one person (with HIV) into another person's bloodstream. It cannot get through healthy, undamaged skin. The only real risk of HIV is through anal sex without a condom – this accounts for almost all HIV transmissions between men.

Being Safe:
Even if you don't come inside someone, there is still a risk to both partners from blood (tiny cuts in the arse) and pre-come. Using strong condoms and water-based lubricant greatly reduces the risk of HIV. However, condoms can break or slip off, so:

* Make sure that condoms are stored away from hot or damp places.
* Check the expiry date – condoms have a limited life.
* Gently squeeze the air out of the tip.
* Check the condom is put on the right way up and unroll it down the erect cock.
* Use plenty of water-based lubricant (lube), up the arse and on the condom.
* While fucking, check occasionally to see the condom is still in one piece (you could also add more lube).
* When you withdraw, hold the condom tight to your cock as you pull out.

* Never re-use a condom or use the same condom with more than one person.
* If you're not used to condoms you might practise putting them on.
* Sex toys like dildos and plugs are safe. But if you're sharing them use a new condom each time or wash the toys well.

For the safest sex, make sure you use the strongest condoms, such as Durex Ultra Strong, Mates Super Strong, HT Specials and Rubberstuffers packs. Condoms are free in many STD (Sexually Transmitted Disease) clinics (sometimes called GUM clinics) and from many gay bars. It's also essential to use lots of water-based lube such as KY, Wet Stuff, Slik or Liquid Silk. Never use come as a lubricant.

Oral Sex:
Compared with fucking, sucking someone's cock is far safer. Swallowing come does not necessarily mean that HIV gets absorbed into the bloodstream. While a tiny fraction of cases of HIV infection have been linked to sucking, we know the risk is minimal. But certain factors increase the risk:
* Letting someone come in your mouth
* Throat infections such as gonorrhoea
* If you have cuts, sores or infections in your mouth and throat

So what is safe?
There are so many things you can do which are absolutely safe: wanking each other; rubbing your cocks against one another; kissing, sucking and licking all over the body; rimming – to name but a few.

If you're finding safe sex difficult, call a helpline or speak to someone you feel you can trust for support. The Terrence Higgins Trust Helpline, which is open from noon to 10pm every day, can be reached on 0171 242 1010.

For Azeem Zakria

Prologue

R ain at night, beating on glass, driven by the wind. His favourite sound.

Jason Bradley peered through the tiny upstairs window, out into the darkness. Over the road a woman scuttled across the orange pool of a street-light, collar turned up against the downpour, hugging the wall for what little shelter it might offer.

He was glad to be indoors tonight. Too many nights he had been out there, clinging to walls like one of his mum's bloody creepers or huddled in doorways like a bag of rubbish, shivering in the wind and rain.

His favourite sound. Provided he was on the right side of the glass.

Around him the house breathed and sighed and settled, hunched and warm, snoring with the gale.

Using only his feet he eased off his trainers and socks in slow, fluid movements. He heaved his heavy, hooded top over his shoulders, over his head, and let it fall to the floor. He was naked now to the waist; naked except for the tight leather cord which never left his neck, a small silver spider the size of a thumbnail perched against his throat. He stood and stared, posing and flexing, in front of the long, narrow mirror which was the only piece of furniture in the tiny space he had carved for himself out of the attic room. He unbuckled his belt and slipped his hand expertly down half-a-dozen metal buttons. Jeans and pants slid to the floor around his ankles.

The candle at his feet threw dancing shadows up the length of his body. He was in good shape, he noted with satisfaction. Other twenty-year-olds he knew were already sagging in the gut from too much beer night after night, or still fighting the terrible teenage battle with acne. Not Jason. His body was smooth and firm, lean and toned in spite of the fact that he took no exercise to speak of. He had always hated organised sports. He had always hated organised anything. Then again, his teenage years had been anything but sedentary . . .

With his index finger he traced a scar which ran for several inches down his inner right arm. One of many he had picked up over the years. He traced another – short, faded almost to nothing with time – on the back of his hand. Childhood trophies.

With both hands he bunched his hair, straight and full, dark blond, letting it fall in great fronds through his fingers, down over his face. It was ages since he had had it cut. Through the tousled layers of gold, two eyes, as deep and blue as lakes, stared out of the mirror at him. A scar, tiny but deep, at the edge of his left eye, pulled the point of the eye out slightly. It gave his face a very subtly Chinese cast. People said it looked sexy, and he wasn't about to argue. He liked the way he looked.

He ran his fingers across his full, arched eyebrows, ever-so-slightly meeting above the ever-so-slightly upward tilt of his nose.

He drew his thick, elegant, almost feminine lips forward in a languid pout.

He let his hand fall, brushing across the lips, down over the hillock of his chin, down his neck, past the silver arachnid clinging to its leather web, and on to his chest. He liked the way he felt, too.

He let a finger play with each full nipple. He ruffled the thin band of hair that cupped each dark teat and then, meeting at the breast-bone, cascaded in a delicate column like the sand in an hourglass and thickened and piled around a heavy, uncut cock.

Somewhere deep in the house he heard voices.

He smiled to himself. The others had laughed at him when he

had grabbed the mirror and dragged it away into his little nest. Christ, what a narcissist. He should get himself a man, not a mirror.

Spider had always taken the piss out of him for that, too. Posing in front of mirrors.

Spider . . .

The thought was dismissed almost instantly. Jason dropped to his haunches and wriggled into his sleeping-bag, drawing a sharp breath, shuddering as the sheer flaps slid, bitingly cold, around his naked form. It was a glad shudder of anticipation. Almost immediately the heat from his body began to infuse the nylon cocoon. He drew the covering up to his neck and hugged it tight around himself, half-closing his eyes, half-watching the crazy shadow-patterns which danced about the walls of his candle-lit cave. The massive curtain which sectioned his little world off from the rest of the room swayed slightly in response to some undetectable movement somewhere else in the house.

The rain beat time on the window.

He was almost afraid to allow himself such enjoyment of his surroundings. It might all end tomorrow. Any day. This was a squat, and squats were by their very nature unpredictable. It wasn't even *his* squat. He was at best a guest. It was good of Glen to let him partition off a part of his room, but he couldn't imagine Glen wanting this situation to go on for ever.

Footsteps on the stairs. Smiling slyly to himself, Jason turned onto his side and stationed his eye at the narrow chink in the curtain. He often watched Glen from inside his hide, silent in pretend-sleep as his friend stripped for bed. Usually Glen would walk around the room naked, stopping in front of the large window which looked out over Mauritius Road, London SE10. There he would exercise, full-face-on to the street, slowly and deliberately flexing his muscles, the moonlight warm on his honey-brown body, letting his cock grow large as he posed. Glen was big down there. He knew it and he didn't care who else knew it.

He heard voices. Glen had company.

Quickly Jason licked his fingers and pinched the wick of the candle. The flame died with a furtive fizz. Glen had no inhibitions,

Jason knew, but it probably wouldn't do for his guest to discover him there. Reluctantly pulling the curtain tight he lay back in his sleeping-bag and closed his eyes.

The door creaked open. Mutterings, whisperings. Some kind of scuffling sound. A match being struck.

A giggle. Heavy, muffled breathing. A deep, long kiss, by the sound of things.

Murmurings; breath irregular now. Little grunts of pleasure.

Jason sniffed – Glen had lit a joss-stick. Its heavy, musky perfume snaked between the folds of his tent. He could hear, gently at first, the random creakings of his friend's bed.

Jason let the perfumed air wash over him, the gradually coalescing rhythms of sex seduce him. Jason's resolve to resist the urge to watch his friend making love was evaporating fast. Delicately he pulled the curtain slightly apart again, and stationed his eye at the tiny aperture. He shouldn't be doing this . . .

At first all he could see were shadows, which he strove to marry up with the sounds he was hearing. The rasp of zips unzipping. Belts jangling and clanking as they plummeted to the wooden floor. The sigh of cloth sliding away from skin.

Low voices. *C'mere . . . Mmm . . .*

Gradually Jason's eyes were becoming used to the moonlit darkness. He could make out Glen, spread-eagled on his bed, naked. On top of him was a man, a big man, muscular and hairy, also naked. The man's hands clutched and clawed at Glen's shoulders, his toes dug into the bed, his buttock muscles contracted and relaxed and his whole body rolled in a smooth rocking-horse motion, up and down, up and down, planing against Glen's smooth torso, his cock grinding across the boy's stomach.

After a while the man dropped lower down the bed. Jason could now make out his face. He looked to be about forty, with short, neat hair and a trim brown beard. He was nibbling at Glen's balls, biting and stretching the ball-sac with his teeth. He popped first one ball then the other into his mouth. The man's tongue snaked out along the underside of Glen's scrotum, back towards his dark crack, then forward again, up the underside of the boy's cock, lingering where shaft met head.

Jason was hard by now, his eye still fixed on the chink in the curtain. His hand drifted almost unconsciously to his cock. He began rubbing it with long, loose strokes, drawing the skin slowly backwards and forwards, careful to make no sound.

The man swung himself round on the bed. Jason could see his member clearly now, silhouetted against the moonlit window – not as big as Glen's monster, but still some serious meat, long and thick. The man was straddling Glen, his mouth open to receive the boy's huge cock, craning up towards him from beneath. Glen angled his own head slightly to catch the man's cock in his mouth. As he did so he thrust upwards with his pelvis, pistoning into the man's mouth. The man did the same, driving down with his cock into Glen's wide-open mouth. They fell into a rhythm, synchronising their upward and downward strokes, like a well-lubricated flesh-and-bone machine.

Jason's own stroke was getting faster now, his cockhead swollen and starting to release its clear juices. He extended his index finger and thumb above the end of his foreskin to rub the delightfully slippy seepage into the super-sensitised head. A tiny squelching noise now accompanied his stroke. He didn't care – the couple on the bed were far too engrossed in one another to notice.

There was sudden movement from the bed. The man rolled off Glen and onto his side. He was staring past his partner, directly into Jason's spy-hole. Jason froze. Had he noticed?

'Turn around,' the man said quietly to Glen. 'Straddle me.'

Glen hoisted a leg over the man's muscular, barrel-like torso and sat as if astride a horse, his balls nested in the thick mat of hair which coated the man's chest. Smiling, the man reached up and began pumping Glen's cock with one hand. His fingers barely met around the monster girth. Glen responded with little shufflings of his hips. Jason could hear the rustle of skin against chest-hair.

The man released Glen's cock. From somewhere he produced a condom, which he rolled blindly, expertly, down over his shaft. He clamped a hand on each of Glen's buttocks, lifted Glen from his chest and eased him backward, down on to his waiting cock.

Although they had never made love, Jason had listened to Glen having sex on more than one occasion. He recognised the short heavy exhalations of breath he associated in his mind's eye with this moment – his friend being penetrated, relaxing, opening up to a large, eager prick. Glen lowered himself onto the man, who began pushing upwards with his hips, drilling the boy's arse as the boy sat like a cowboy on a bucking bronco, his mouth open, a smile playing about its edges. With one hand he rubbed the man's thick chest-hair, squeezing and pinching his nipples. With the other he worked on his own cock, increasing his speed and ferocity as the man's motions got faster and more frantic. Jason recognised the quiet, strangled gasp that announced that Glen was about to come.

Jason, too, was approaching orgasm. He slipped a finger of his free hand into his own arsehole, bending and flexing it inside himself. He couldn't stop himself from crying out slightly as his seed spurted forth, covering his hand, his belly, the inside of his sleeping bag.

The couple didn't notice. A moment later Glen's jism erupted in a great fountain, cascading down over the man's chest and face. From the look on that face Jason could see that the man was coming too.

The couple collapsed in a heap on the bed. The man was chuckling to himself.

'That was great,' he whispered. 'We'll sleep for a bit now, yeah?'

Sleep. Jason let his head fall back onto the pillow. The room was drunk with perfume – the thick scent of sex mingling with the musk of the joss-stick. His eyes felt heavy. Sleep eased over him.

Sun, wind, and all the Newcastle day below them. They stand on the parapet of the world, holding tight to each other. The wind hammers them, tugging at their hair, tugging at their clothes, tearing cloth away from skin. From this height the city is tiny, clean and ordered. It turns in a graceful wheel far below.

No, it's they who turn. They spin, their now-naked feet doing an elaborate sabre-dance, in and out, in and out, foot leapfrogging foot, around, around. One false step on the narrow rampart, and . . .

Falling, now. Still clinging on to one another. Jason feels Spider's cock swelling against his leg. Spider is laughing. Spider is always laughing . . .

The city snaps up around them. Buildings close in. They can hear the traffic now. The sound of voices. Dogs barking.

Spider isn't laughing any more.

They're in a place of darkness. It's like they're buried alive. It's so, so hot.

And then, from out of the darkness, the dog. Pitch black, its mouth red and raw, its eyes in flame, it thrusts its massive head into Jason's face, biting, snarling . . .

One

T he thin, chirpy music was carried far across south London on a blustery late-March wind: a barrel-organ, or at least a recording of a barrel-organ, amplified and piped through the fair's old tannoy system. It sounded pitifully out of place, the archaic optimism of the music, echoing thinly between the huge metal drums of the gasworks, snaking under the derelict railway arches, ebbing and flowing across the flat expanse of mud, rainwater and oil-seepage which separated the two.

Gasworks, railway, mud. And in the middle the source of the music: Gamlin's Fair.

Dwarfed by the massive grey gasometers the fair looked faintly absurd. It was small and it was old: brightly painted in the way fairs used to be brightly painted in the decades before they started plastering their rides with images from *Star Wars*. There was nothing like that here: here was all fancy lettering, pretty, abstract swirls, rows of coloured bulbs edging the cheery, carved wooden panels or strung between the rides, creating muddy avenues of broken colour, rainbow-reflections which splashed and recombined vividly underfoot.

Tom Jarrett stood beside the Big Wheel, not yet bothering to call his pitch, get the punters rolling up. It was early. There was hardly anyone here yet. And of course it was raining.

Maybe it would be a quiet night. Tom didn't care. He wasn't

in the fair game to make money. No one in their right mind did this for the money. Tom loved the travel, the never-standing-still. He loved the new faces emerging each night out of the dark, the banter, the way it was possible to share with the punters a sort of intimacy born of anticipation, of mock fear – an intimacy nurtured by the peculiar, magical atmosphere of the fair itself, an intimacy made easy by the fact that by the end of the night the faces would have vanished, to be replaced the next night by new ones, the whole magical process beginning again. It wasn't so much that the life of the fair was rootless; it was as if they gathered their roots and carried them with them. The fair was sufficient unto itself: it was a sort of family, he supposed, nurtured not by any one place or by any extended, static community, but by this endless flow of passing strangers.

A wry grin broke out on Tom's face. For some of the guys that was quite literally true – on its travels the fair provided an almost inexhaustible supply of brief, sweet sexual encounters. Tom enjoyed watching the fervour with which they would often compete with one another. Occasionally they would get quite analytical about it – which towns provided the most arse, which towns provided the best arse, where you had to be careful of rough types, where you were most likely to pick up a dose of something nasty. Jack, who ran the Tunnel of Love, and who approached the whole business of getting laid like an exact science, had even compiled charts of this sort of information.

Tom regarded the whole thing as strictly a spectator sport. He fired the motor controlling the Wheel and gave the huge, creaking structure a spin. Automatically it began wheezing its old tune, a queasy, reedy cadence laid neatly over the similar strains coming from the other rides. None of the rides at Gamlin's blasted out dance or rock music. It would scarcely have been appropriate – the Big Wheel was about as exciting as things got at Gamlin's. All of the rides had their themes, but all of the themes were similar, all barrel-organ-based and all combined to produce a whole which was to Tom's ears both seductive and eerie. Welcome to another world, it seemed to say.

He stood on the ride's painted platform and felt the wind as the empty Wheel whistled past his nose. He tensed himself to spring.

In contravention of all the rules he applied to the public he jumped and caught the spinning infrastructure. It yanked him off his feet and hauled him like a rag doll up into the evening sky.

You could cut the atmosphere under the railway arch with a knife. At one end, Jason stood with his back to his companions, occasionally shooting them a sulky glance over his shoulder. Towards the centre of the tunnel a group of four youths was crowded on an abandoned sofa. In between Glen hovered uneasily.

All six were drunk. One of the sofa crew passed Glen a half-empty bottle of cider. He clamped his lips around the mouth of the bottle and jerked his head back, drinking deeply, shuddering slightly as the sweet bite of the drink hit home. He pulled the bottle from his lips and, with an uncertain glance back at the sofa, offered it to Jason.

'Jase . . .'

'No,' came the sullen reply. Jason wished he was somewhere else. He scowled at the group messing around on the sofa, scuffling and trying to push each other off into the mud. As usual, Nige had the upper hand. Nige always had the upper hand in every-thing. He was well over six feet tall, sharp-featured, pale and gaunt. Skinny, yet as tough and wiry as steel cable, and with a personality to match. Soon his rivals for the sofa were sprawling in the mud at his feet. Nige stretched his long arms across the back of the saggy old piece of furniture and casually fended the others off with his feet. The king on his throne, holding court as usual.

Nige was very much the boss back in the squat. He and Jason had never really got on. And early this morning – before the sun was even up – they had had their biggest bust-up to date.

Nige had given Jason an ultimatum.

'You won't do rent,' he had ranted, 'you won't rob . . . This gaff costs, you know. And now you're starting to fuck it up for the rest of us!'

Jason had been screaming in his sleep again. Fuck it. His own memories of last night were vague, still tangled in the remnant coils of sleep. He remembered raised voices – Glen, pleading, apologising; Glen's client, shouting – *Fucking madhouse . . . Why*

*didn't you tell me there was someone else in the room . . . If you think
I'm paying for this shit . . .* – Footsteps thundering down the stairs.

He'd been screaming in his sleep again, and had woken Glen's
client. The poor man had been petrified.

Nige, when he found out, had been furious.

So here they were. This was Glen's idea, to pacify Nige. Jason's
chance to redeem himself. His last chance.

Nige was on his feet now. He strode across to the end of the
tunnel where Jason was slouching, his face like thunder.

'Don't forget,' the king said, 'seventy-five quid. That's what
you cost us last night. That's what you've got to make up. Let's
go.'

He turned and, with his entourage in tow, strode out into the
drizzle, pointed nose to the wind, following the sound of the
spindly fairground organ.

The fair receded sickeningly beneath Tom Jarrett. From up here
it appeared as a tiny splash of colour against an expanse of grey-
brown flatness. Ranked behind the spread of tawdry attractions, in
a tight line like a makeshift wall, were the big old trucks which
carried the fairground equipment from one venue to the next, up
and down the country in an unending circuit. In front of the
trucks were the win-a-prize stalls – the Coconut Shy, the Duck-
Hunt, an ancient Aunt Sally stall, darts, hoop-la. The Big Wheel
itself stood at right-angles to the row, with the food stalls – Mavis,
the hot-dog and candyfloss woman, 'Willie Wonka' the sweet-
man – behind it. Across the middle of the ground were a
miscellany of rides – the Bumper Cars (*not* dodgem cars, Crash-
Annie, who ran the cars, would insist: the whole point was to
bump into each other as much as possible – none of this going
round in an orderly circle rubbish), the Merry-Go-Round, the
Waltzers. And at the furthest end of the fair, screening off the
huddle of tatty caravans in which the fair-folk lived, were the
Ghost Train, the Tunnel of Love and the Hall of Mirrors.

Standing now in a swaying car on the Wheel, Tom felt the
ground surge up again to meet him. He bellowed a hello to Rex
who ran the Test-Your-Strength machine as he shot skyward once

more. From the top of the Wheel his fellow stallholders seemed like wind-up toys in some too-brightly-painted model village. Most of them, as far as Tom could make out, had been with the fair for decades. Some, he knew, had inherited their stalls from parents or uncles. A few had come from other fairs or from the circus. Rex was a former circus strong-man who still sported the waxed moustache and – when the mood took him – the leopard-skin leotard, and who would still rip apart the occasional phone book to relieve boredom and amuse the punters. By and large, though, the men and women of Gamlin's didn't have much to do with the other fairs which toured the country. They were a community unto themselves, ignored by and ignoring other travelling shows. They had their own unwritten rules and codes of conduct and their own invisible ways of determining who was a part of the family and who wasn't. Tom had been with the fair less than two years. He still wasn't sure whether he was an insider or an outsider: fated to remain a part of this travelling fraternity for life or one of the many transient figures who passed through, usually at the instigation of old Piper, spending a few months, a year or more perhaps, travelling and working, before disappearing back into the real world. At the moment Tom didn't care. At the moment he was enjoying life.

Tonight Jack was running the Tunnel of Love – a job he fought for covetously and usually got – and his French friend Laurent was running the Hall of Mirrors. Tom could see the two of them, shoulder to shoulder, whispering and conspiring and scanning the thin crowd 'for meat', as they invariably put it. They were part of Piper's gang – that endlessly variable crowd of young men who seemed to gravitate around the old man like planets around a dark sun. Piper owned the rides Laurent and Jack were working on, as well as the Ghost Train. Tom could see him now, sitting just out of the rain beneath a huge painted skeleton, puffing on his long pipe, shaking his head slowly and gravely at a group of giggling girls. Tom knew the routine: 'I shouldn't go in there,' he would warn punters approaching the Ghost Train in his best mad-old-man voice. 'It's haunted.'

'Hey, Rex!' Tom bellowed from on high. 'Bring me down, would you?'

The former strong-man loped across to the Big Wheel and cut the motor. The fairground was starting to fill up. Tom could see a group of youths sloping in across the waste ground, passing a bottle between them. Time to get his feet back on the ground. Time to get active.

By the time the group reached the fair Nige's good humour had been restored. He, Tony, Mitch and Andy were tumbling and crashing into each other, laughing and swearing, trading oaths and insults. Glen and Jason walked a little way behind, silent and thoughtful.

'You don't have to do this,' Glen said suddenly.

'Yes, I do. You know I do,' Jason replied bitterly. 'Otherwise I'm out on my arse.'

Glen lowered his head.

'Nige may be a cunt, but he's right,' Jason continued. 'Until I get my head sorted out, sort out these dreams and shit, I can't sleep in a room where you're turning tricks.'

'It's not like I do it a lot, Jase.' Suddenly Glen sounded defensive. 'None of us do. It's just for a few extra quid now and again.' He paused for a moment, weighing his words with care. 'It wouldn't do you any harm to turn a few tricks, Jase. It's OK. Most of the punters are quite nice . . .'

'No!' For a moment Jason sounded almost savage. Instantly he regretted his tone. 'I can't, Glen. I just can't.'

He stopped and placed a hand firmly on his friend's shoulder, turning him and looking deep into his gentle brown eyes. 'You've been so good to me, Glen . . .' His voice was choked with emotion. 'I don't know what I'd have done . . .'

It was true. Jason had left Newcastle with a rucksack on his back and next to nothing in it. No money. No job. No home. And no idea of how to cope with living rough in this giant of a city. He had wandered around for a day, getting progressively hungrier and colder. He had tried and failed to spend the night in Leicester Square tube station. Down on the Embankment he had been robbed of his rucksack and sleeping-bag.

He had crossed the river and wandered most of the night,

finally collapsing in Battersea Park, frozen, hungry and exhausted. Glen had found him curled up on the Peace Pavilion overlooking the river, at the feet of the great bronze Buddha, shivering in the dawn. He had taken him to a hostel, found him a bed. Glen had been on the streets several years already. He was only a couple of years older than Jason, but seemed so much more worldly. Born in north London of a white mother and an unknown but undoubtedly black father, Glen seemed to have used London in much the same way Jason had used Newcastle – as his own personal adventure playground. He seemed to like it out there – even sleeping rough.

Glen had stuck with Jason for the first couple of months, vanishing and reappearing every few days, showing him the ropes – where to beg, how to sign on, where to find a dry bed for the night. Somehow he would always find Jason again after his disappearances, wherever in London the Newcastle lad happened to be dossing.

'You can't escape me, boy – I got your scent,' Glen would joke in his best mock-Jamaican accent.

As Jason had struggled to become more streetwise Glen's absences had grown longer. Jason hadn't seen him in nearly four months when, a couple of weeks ago, Glen had appeared out of nowhere and announced that he was living in a house – a squat just south of the river, close to the Greenwich Marshes – where Jason could, if he wished, join him. Glen's arrival had been timely – street-life had been gradually eating into Jason's health and his luck. Truth to tell, he wasn't very good at it – finding decent dosses, begging, steering clear of the trouble-makers. He had been badly beaten up on more than one occasion. Glen's reappearance had been a kind of salvation. Shame it didn't look like it would last.

'Come on,' said Jason. 'Let's get on with it.'

'What if we get stuck up there?'

'I'll just have to climb up and rescue you.' The man in the white T-shirt winked and grinned at the clutch of giggling teenage girls clustered around him. He looked born to this. His T-shirt and jeans were tight. The rain had plastered the strained cotton and denim to a lean, muscular body. To Jason he looked to be in his early thirties, a swarthy, weather-beaten complexion, a ruggedly handsome, chiselled face, a shock of untidy black hair.

Grinning, the man took the girls' money and held their hands as they climbed into the car. A large queue, dwarfing that for any other ride, had already formed at the base of the Wheel. Half-a-dozen places back in the queue Glen looked up at the creaking, towering structure, then leaned close to Jason and whispered, 'It doesn't look all that safe to me.'

Jason smiled. He knew Glen hated this sort of thing. Only last week Glen had returned home to Mauritius Road in the evening to find him perched on the roof of the house in a ferocious gale. Glen had had a fit. Jason couldn't see what all the fuss was about. Up above the world, that was where Jason felt safe. Up above the city, up above the crowds, the bustle, the aggression, the dog-eat-dog . . .

They edged nearer the front of the queue. As they approached the guy in the white T-shirt Glen nudged Jason and nodded towards the box at his feet. A plastic sandwich-box, already filling up with money. Jason said nothing. They paid their two quid apiece and climbed onto the wheel. Slowly, as the wheel filled up, they inched into the air.

Finally, with a lurch, the Wheel began to spin properly. Screams of exhilaration rose from the other cars. Next to Jason, Glen groaned as they plunged earthward. Jason smiled. Poor Glen. He was rigid, clinging to the bar which held them in the rickety seat. Jason sprawled in the seat, relaxed, not holding on to anything. He was once again in his element. Up here nothing could touch him.

Below them he could see Nige and his cronies clustered around the Test-Your-Strength machine. He saw Nige heft the mallet overhead and bring it down on the peg. A moment later he flung the mallet to the ground in evident frustration. The others were laughing at him. Jason smiled. Serve him right.

The rain had finally stopped.

Three times in succession Jason rode the Wheel.

'You're mad,' Glen told him. 'We're supposed to be on the rob here. There's no point in nicking our own money back.'

A furious volley of barking rose from below. Jason saw the tiny figure of Nige, facing off against a huge black dog which was tied to the side of the Ghost Train. The dog was straining at its leash, trying to get at Nige. Some distance off, Nige's cronies egged him on. He picked up a large stone which was lying, half-buried in mud, in the middle of the fairground. To the cheers of his little gang, Nige hurled the stone at the dog. The dog snarled as the rock bounced off its flank, then resumed its fearsome barking.

An old man shuffled around the side of the Ghost Train, fists raised.

'You fuckin' leave that dog alone!' Jason heard him shout. 'He'll 'ave you! He'll not forget this!'

'Fuck you, grandad!' Nige shouted, to howls from his supporters.

'I'll set 'im loose if you're not careful,' the old man bellowed. Nige had already begun to walk away. 'He'll drink your blood, boy!'

Finally Jason allowed Glen to drag him from the Wheel. They shot rifles at a belt of metal ducks, pelted the gaudy, grinning Aunt Sally dolls with wooden balls, ate hot-dogs to soak up the cider. They spoke little to one another: both were preoccupied with what they had come here to do.

From the other end of the fairground their movements were being watched.

'Which one do you want?' asked Jack, operator of the Tunnel of Love.

His friend Laurent shrugged and pouted. 'They're both gorgeous,' he replied.

'Hold it,' said Jack. 'They're coming this way.'

The little French lad cast a sidelong glance at his friend. Jack knew that, to Laurent's mind, he took some terrible risks. He stepped forward as Jason and Glen approached.

This was all starting to get on Jason's nerves. He was running out of money, losing at everything he tried – the coconuts, the guns, the darts. The Merry-Go-Round was out of order, and Glen, having virtually lost his lunch on the Wheel, had point-blank refused to go anywhere near the Waltzers or the Bumper Cars. They were just killing time. They had to wait, Glen had said, until the stalls had had a chance to make a bit of a profit.

'Gentlemen . . .'

Two boys of about Jason's age, standing next to each other, grinning.

'. . . Care to take a ride on the Tunnel of Love?'

The pair paused. Jason shot a look into Glen's eyes. Glen's mild, brown, cowlike eyes. His soft, gentle face, manly yet compassionate. That warm, understanding smile. Jason had never even allowed himself to contemplate . . .

'You hesitate,' the lad continued. 'I would be more than happy to accompany one of you . . .'

Jason smiled to himself. Only now did he realise the audacious recklessness of the offer. Who was this guy? How did he even know they were gay? Did he and Glen look like a couple?

'. . . Or perhaps a turn about the Hall of Mirrors with my friend Laurent here . . .'

Jason appraised the two fairground boys. The one who was speaking was around the same height as Jason himself – five feet ten, say – with a long mane of brown hair tied back in a pony-tail and a broad, cheeky grin. The other – Laurent, apparently – was altogether smaller, his skin pale and smooth, yet rosy-cheeked, his facial features delicate and boyish, his hair thick, dark and tousled.

Glen was digging him in the ribs.

'You hear that?' he said. 'Hall of Mirrors.'

He turned to Laurent. 'He loves mirrors.'

There was a commotion coming from the Waltzers. Raised voices, swearing, insolent laughter. The two fairground boys were silent now, peering beyond Jason and Glen, trying to see what was happening. Jason spun around.

Bloody Nige. Who else?

He and his men-at-arms – Andy, Mitch and Tony – were crammed into a Waltzer made to hold two people, and were engaged in trying to push one another out into the path of the rotating arms which carried the cars round in their manic dance. A man was balanced on one of the arms, shouting at them over the top of the music. He appeared nimble and agile – he was navigating the rotating arms with evident experience – but he was middle-aged, slight and only about five feet six. If one of the toerags should have a pop at him whilst he was balanced there the result could be fatal.

More fairground people were approaching the Waltzers now: the tough-looking roustabout from the Big Wheel and the burly guy with the ridiculous Kaiser Wilhelm moustache from the Test-Your-Strength machine. They looked pissed off. The little guy in charge of the ride was now trying to dodge the kicks suddenly being aimed at him by Nige and his drunken coterie. Mitch was standing up in the car, hands on hips, jeering and laughing.

Jason took a step towards the Waltzers. He felt a restraining hand on his shoulder.

'No,' said Glen. 'Leave them. Come on.'

Flashing a parting smile at the two would-be suitors, Jason allowed himself to be led away by his friend around the back of the Waltzers, trying his best to become lost in the thin crowd. The music from the Waltzers died. Jason saw out of the corner of his eye the cars judder to a halt and Mitch go sprawling, head-over-heels, into the mud which surrounded the ride. The guy from the Big Wheel was standing over him, a look of unrestrained fury on his face. He hauled Mitch to his feet. Mitch seemed to be pleading with the guy. Nothing doing. A fist came down hard on Mitch's face. Blood spurted from his nose and he hit the deck once more.

Jason took a deep breath. This was the man whose ride he was going to rob. Ahead of them the Big Wheel was still spinning, unattended, filled with screaming people. The sandwich-box, now overflowing with money, still sat at the edge of the boarding-platform.

'You wait here,' Jason said to Glen. 'It's me who's got to do this.'

Hoping he looked less guilty than he felt Jason attempted to saunter nonchalantly up to the Wheel. Christ, he thought, I'm practically whistling. He dashed the last few yards, lunged forward and grasped the box in both hands.

'Hold it, sonny.'

He attempted to turn. Suddenly his neck was held in a choking grip. He couldn't breathe; he couldn't move. A bony arm was clamped across his windpipe; someone's cheek was pressed against his. The smell of a woman's perfume filled his nostrils. Perfume and stale cigarette-smoke. He thrashed, first one way and then the other, trying to break her grip.

'Now don't make me hurt you,' the woman crooned in a soft, husky, forty-a-day voice. 'I could, you know.'

Jason didn't doubt it. The bitch was old, he could see from the corner of his eye, but she was strong. He was held fast. He could see the gypsy in the white T-shirt lumbering back across the mud. He was still holding the box. He let it drop to the ground. Five-and ten-pound notes were carried away on the wind.

'I caught this little bastard trying to pinch your take,' the old witch croaked.

The man stooped and gathered up the money.

'Take this, Annie,' he said.

She released her grip on Jason and reached for the box. In a split-second he was running, heart and legs pumping. The man was just behind him; he could sense it. Seconds later a blow to the small of his back sent him sprawling to the ground. A boot planted hard on his shoulders drove his face into the mud. He felt his wrists being grabbed, clamped together, hard. The man was dragging him across the fairground on his belly. He kicked and wriggled like a landed fish. Mud and stones and discarded rubbish splashed and bounced against his face, caught in his hair, worked their way inside his clothes. He could feel the march of the mud down past the waist-band of his jeans, seeping and squelching through his pubic hair, around his cock. It felt good. Ridiculous. Amazing. Here he was being humiliated in front of a fairground full of people, dragged to God knows where for a probable beating, unable to do anything to help himself, and he was getting a hard-on.

They were passing between the Hall of Mirrors and the Ghost Train. He could see the two fairground-lads – the little one called

Laurent and his pony-tailed friend – looking on, shocked, giggling. The old man, bent and whiskered, sitting on the side of the Ghost Train, puffing on a long, thin pipe, eyed him intensely, unblinking, as he was dragged past. And next to the old man the dog, huge and black, sitting, staring at him through baleful eyes. The dog growled as Jason was dragged past.

His captor stopped at the door of a small caravan. He opened the door, hauled him to his feet and threw him inside.

'Stay here,' he ordered. 'I'll decide what to do with you later.'

He slammed the door. Jason heard a key turn in the lock.

Tom returned to the Big Wheel in a black mood. The little swine wouldn't be able to escape from the caravan, and now he had a lot of custom to make up. He reckoned the kid had cost him a good forty or fifty quid, lost to the wind. Profit margins were already skin-tight on the show; he couldn't afford such a loss.

What a night. First the business on the Waltzers and then this.

The Wheel was still spinning. Its occupants had been going round for an age. He slowed the huge machine down, stopped it, and started helping the riders off. Some of them looked nauseous.

It was raining again, heavily. The wind had an icy chill to it now. Tom thought about his little caravan. The roof leaked and it had no heating. He hoped the thieving bastard was as cold and miserable in there as he was out here. The crowds were starting to drift away in the sudden squall. Tom guessed they would soon be shutting up for the night. Only one more day in this dump then they were due to start moving north again.

Two hours later, tired and hungry, Tom Jarrett trudged back to the caravan. He was thinking about a hot shower and something to eat. For the moment he had forgotten that his little house on wheels was serving as a holding-cell. He turned the key in the lock and pushed the door inward.

All he saw as he entered the van was a flurry of arms and legs flying at him, striking fists, clawing nails, a savage head, snarling, biting. Tom's reaction was instant and automatic – his open hand shot out, the heel of his palm catching the boy a breath-stopping blow to the chest. The boy cannoned back across the little caravan, skidding over the single bed and colliding with the wall. Instantly Tom regretted the force of his counter-attack.

Coughing and choking the boy pulled himself to his feet. He looked a state. His entire front was covered in mud. It was caked in his hair, it was all over his clothes, it stained his face. Tom wasn't sure whether the streaks of skin he could see through the mud on the boy's cheeks were where he had attempted to clean himself up or where he had been crying. He suspected the latter.

The boy looked pitiful.

Tom placed his plastic money-box on a shelf inside the door. There was no way the kid was going to get his hands on that again.

'Look . . .' said Tom.

He got no further. With a low growl the young captive again launched himself at Tom, fists flailing. This time Tom's response was more measured. Almost without effort he gripped and immobilised the boy's arms. The boy started to kick. Tom twisted. The boy's body buckled and he collapsed to the caravan floor. Immediately Tom dropped on top of him, straddling him, the whole weight of his body across the lad's groin and upper thighs. For a moment he lost the boy's hands. Again the boy began pummelling his tormentor, crying tears of bitter frustration. Tom didn't flinch as the blows struck his chest and sides. In a matter of seconds he had the boy's wrists again. Leaning forward he pinned his arms above his head.

'Calm down,' said Tom, no longer able to feel any anger in the face of this pathetic display. 'I'm not going to do anything to you. But you shouldn't have tried to rob me. You've cost me a lot of money. I just wanted you to know that.'

The boy's sobs had receded now to the occasional sniff. He was staring up at Tom, unblinking, his cobalt eyes still wet with tears. Tom looked back, a hint of uncertainty creeping across his face. He didn't know what to make of that stare.

Tom felt movement below him. The boy was hard down there. He began grinding his pelvis determinedly against Tom's perineum, forcing his cock against the downward pressure of the taut cord of muscle between Tom's wide-apart inner thighs.

'No . . . Wait . . .' Tom was taken aback. He recoiled, relaxing his grip on the boy's wrists, rolling his body away from the bucking of the boy's hips.

For a long moment the two men held each other's gaze: Tom's eyes twin mirrors of shock and uncertainty; something altogether less readable in the lad's – something of fear, something of longing.

In a flash the moment of contact, of almost-understanding, was broken. The boy was wriggling like an eel to free himself from the grip of Tom's muscular legs. He scampered to his feet and scrabbled at the door, yanking it open and lurching into the darkness.

Tom slumped back onto his knees, his mouth hanging open, a firestorm of confused and conflicting thoughts sparking across his brain as he watched the boy through the swinging door disappearing into the rain-soaked night.

Two

Tom slept late the next day, and awoke sweating.

Damn. He hated missing his early-morning exercise routine. It was too late now, there was work to be done.

The wind and rain had abated in the night, but the canopy of clouds still hung heavy over south-east London – great bruises of moisture which obscured the sun and lent the day a cloying, oppressive heat. Tom heaved himself from his single bunk and padded naked across to the tiny kitchen – just a pair of gas-rings, a tiny fridge and sink, and a kettle, really – which occupied one end of the little caravan.

He stooped to peer out of the window and across at the dormant rides and stalls, forlorn under that slate sky where last night they had been gay. The day's jobs were tedious. There was the litter from last night's punters to be picked up and disposed of, breakages to be mended, safety checks on the Wheel to be run. But first there was the money to be counted. Tom lifted the plastic box from its shelf. As was his habit, he dropped to the floor, legs crossed, still naked, and sat the box in his lap. Deftly he began sorting through notes and coins.

Tom worked in silence that day, ignoring the cracks and questions of his young colleagues Jack and Laurent. The situation was worse than Tom had thought. He had a rough idea how much money he ought to have taken last night. Even taking into account the sparseness of the crowd he reckoned he ought to have had seventy or eighty quid more in the box.

Tom was struck with a sudden thought. Stupid! The kid might have robbed him. He returned to the caravan and opened a drawer at the side of his bed. This was where he kept his most personal possessions. It was also where he kept the only thing of material value he owned. No – it was there. He lifted the heavy gold medal and felt its weight. Regimental Boxing Champion, 1995.

The drawer, like the rest of the caravan, was uncluttered and ordered. Everything seemed to be as he had left it – four-square and regimented. But no, Tom knew things had been moved. The pile of letters was slightly ragged about the edges, as was the neat stack of photographs.

Why would he have done that – gone through his stuff and not taken a solid gold medal?

The kid. He kept thinking about him. That strange obsessive look in his eyes . . .

By mid-afternoon the air was leaden. In the caravan he shared with Laurent, Jack was sitting cross-legged on the floor. Like Tom several hours earlier he was assessing the damage of the night before. He had spread a large map of the British Isles in front of him. Next to it was a fat, open accounts ledger. His forehead was creased into a frown. He chewed restlessly on the end of a biro. He shuffled uncomfortably in the muggy atmosphere. His sweat-shirt was plastered to his back and the crotch of his jeans felt damp and rough and uncomfortable between his legs. At least it was his day off, he reflected. At least today he didn't have to do any of the mundane daytime jobs which the running of the little fair demanded.

He leaned back against the big wardrobe that jutted into the middle of the caravan, dividing the floor-space roughly into two domains. Jack's bed was against the far wall in one of these little territories, Laurent's against the far wall in the other. In between was a chaos of piled books and clothes covering most of the floor and every available surface. Even the little shower-cubicle was full of junk. Jack sat in a bare circle he had made for himself in the middle of the debris on the floor.

The door of the caravan opened and Laurent entered, looking flushed and exhausted. He booted Jack's map lightly with his foot.

'I do not know why you bother,' the French boy said. 'All these times you try. Your system is shit. It never works. You said last night was – how did you say it? – a dead . . .'

'Cert,' said Jack flatly. 'It was, for Tom.'

Laurent grinned. Both boys had watched Tom dragging his struggling captive back to his caravan and locking him in.

'Just like the Sheikh of Araby,' Jack had quipped with a theatrical sigh.

Both had felt a combination of surprise and amusement, shot through with just a pang of jealousy. This was Tom. Tom who never did anything. Tom who didn't seem to be into men or women.

Tom the Ice-Maiden, Jack had dubbed him at first. Somehow it hadn't seemed accurate, though. It wasn't that Tom was frigid. There was a kind of sadness about him. There was almost something penitential in his demeanour, and in the simple way he lived his life at Gamlin's. He worked hard, he ate, he slept. He didn't drink, he didn't smoke, he rarely left the fairground – wherever it happened to be at a particular time – for anything other than show-related business. He maintained a polite, amicable distance from the rest of the show-people. He never spoke of his life before he came to Gamlin's.

'Tom,' mused Laurent. 'It is such a waste . . .'

He sauntered fully into the caravan and, kicking a path through the debris which littered the floor, slumped onto his bed.

'Ah well . . .'

'I don't know what happened last night,' Jack mumbled, his pen still clamped between his teeth. 'My system never fails . . .'

'I told you,' said Laurent petulantly, 'your system is shit.'

He rolled over onto his stomach and buried his head in his pillow.

'Ah well,' his muffled voice floated up, 'only one night more in this shithole.'

Jack blew the pen from between his lips. It sailed through the air and jabbed Laurent in the arm. He batted it away, irritated.

'No, Jacques,' he complained, raising his head. 'It is too hot today. Too . . . muggy.'

He let his face fall back into the pillow. A moment later there was the brief, warm thrum of a just-flicked ruler vibrating against air, and Jack's pencil eraser bounced off the side of Laurent's head.

'Fuck off, I said,' the French boy snapped. '*Merde.*'

Jack sprang to his feet with a bored sigh. 'There's a swimming-pool a few streets from here,' he announced. 'I'm going there to take a shower. One that works.'

He cast a glance towards the shower-cubicle-turned-cupboard in the corner. Fishing a towel from deep in the rummage-pile that was the floor, and a bar of soap from on top of the telly, he swung out of the door and into the heat of the afternoon.

The pool had seemed slightly more impressive when they had driven past it on the way to the show-ground. It was one of those 1930s municipal jobs, small and in poor repair. Still, it suited Jack. It only cost fifty pence to get in, and provided the showers were hot . . .

He handed a coin to the old woman at the reception desk. She gave him a wire basket for his clothes and a locker-key on a wide red rubber band, on which was stencilled a number. Zero one.

'Many in?' Jack asked.

The woman shook her head.

'Not since they built that new leisure-centre down the road,' she said. 'Been dead as a doornail, this place, the past six months.'

She looked at her watch.

'You got an hour,' she said.

Jack wandered through into the changing area. Deserted. The wall at one end was entirely covered with numbered lockers. The rest of the room was taken up with low wooden benches, each surmounted with a horizontal metal bar from which hooks jutted every foot or so. Jack hung the wire basket on one of these hooks and proceeded to wriggle out of his clothes. Hair band, off and into his pocket. He shook his head and the long, straight curtain

of dark brown hair billowed out around him. Sweat-shirt, off and
in the basket. Trainers, he stooped and prised from his feet
without undoing the laces. He flicked open the button at the top
of his fly and pulled the zip apart. Trousers, off and in the basket.
Pants . . .

Within a moment he stood naked in the empty, tiled space. He
swung the basket from the hook and placed it in locker number
one. He locked it with the key and slipped the red band around
his wrist.

A corridor led towards the pool. Off the corridor was the
shower-room – a large communal sink into which six shower-
nozzles continuously pumped steaming water.

Bar of soap in hand, Jack padded, slim and pale and elegant in
his nakedness, past the shower-room, towards the rippling blue of
the pool itself. He half-fancied a dip. He didn't have any trunks
with him, but if the pool was deserted anyway . . .

He stopped. From where he was standing he could now see the
figure of the pool lifeguard, sitting high on his stool, his back to
him, trunks, T-shirt and a mane of long, dirty-blond curls hanging
down between his shoulder-blades – almost as long as Jack's own.

From behind he looked nice. Muscular arms and legs, a toned
back.

Jack drew in a pensive breath. It was his dream to be a scientific
prophet of sexual opportunity. According to his calculations –
based on area-by-area demographics, personal experience and
word-of-mouth – he ought to be able to pick *something* up in this
part of London. And on first appearances this was considerably
more than a mere *something*.

He smiled to himself and turned his back on the pool. Who
was he kidding? Laurent was right – his system was shit. Just like
his football pools system before it. Gossip, guesswork and wishful
thinking. If he tried it on with the lifeguard there was every
chance he'd just get beaten up.

He stepped into the shower-room and let the hot water jet
over him, pasting his hair to his scalp, neck and shoulders, blinding
him, slooshing down his face, over his practically hairless chest,
the delicate indent of his belly-button, down into the rich fuzz of
his pubes. Brushing droplets from his eyes he watched the water

gather into a slow jet and pour as if from a spout off the top of his heavy, slightly engorged cock. Jack stood there for perhaps five minutes, letting the torrents of hot water drench him, then languidly he began to soap his torso. The soap-suds were practically invisible against his smooth, porcelain-white skin. He massaged the suds into his pubic bush, caressed his cock and balls with soap-slippy hands for several minutes before running the bar of soap down his slim, graceful thighs.

He heard a slight noise behind him.

Before he could turn around he felt the gentle pressure of a hand – not his own – snaking round under his right arm to clasp his chest, slowly squeezing and rubbing the soapy pectoral. Another hand traced a gentle line down his spinal column and into the crack of his arse. A broad smile spread across Jack's face as an exploring finger probed his arsehole, sliding soapily into the tight pucker.

'I thought maybe you could use someone to hold the soap.'

Laurent.

The little Frenchman clamped his lips against Jack's neck, sucking hard and biting down with his teeth. Jack winced slightly, arching his head back, smiling with pleasure. He pressed back against Laurent, feeling the French boy's hard-on against his buttock. Laurent continued to work Jack's arsehole with his left hand. Slowly, in, out. Jack winced slightly – Laurent's nails were a bit long for this. One finger became two, and then three, working apart the soft tunnel of flesh. His other hand slid down from where it was pinching and massaging Jack's nipple, playfully tweaked his belly-button and then dived into his pubic hair. Laurent's fingers skirted around his crotch and came at his balls from underneath, cupping them, testing their low-slung weight, pulling at them slightly. He ran his hand up the shaft of Jack's now-erect cock, thick, long and gently curved, building to a great bulb of a head, barely wreathed by foreskin. Around this head his fingers now closed, squeezing, skinning back the hood, wet, soap-slick, and throbbing.

As Laurent pumped on Jack's penis with one hand, the other was still working his friend's butt-hole. Three fingers pumped, penetrated, kneaded from deep inside. Braced now, partly against the wet, white-tiled wall and partly against his naked friend, Jack was responding to the dual stimuli, front and back, with little jerks and buckings of the hips. He thrust a hand behind his back. Blindly his fingers closed on the gobstopper-cheek of the French boy's arse; his nails dug into the firm flesh. His breath was ragged, fast and shallow.

'You are coming . . .' Laurent whispered teasingly in his friend's ear.

He was right. Jack let out a low moan. He jerked his pelvis forward. His cockhead, red, spasming, spurted its load in great gobs, snatched away into the torrents of falling water.

Laurent didn't release his grip on Jack's cock until his orgasm had burned itself out. Slowly Jack turned around, wiping hair out of his eyes. The little Frenchman stood in front of him grinning, his cock − smaller than Jack's, straight, cut and hard − jutting playfully from his dark groin. Laurent was generally smaller than Jack − all toned, pert, concentrated sexual energy, a pale yet strangely ruddy complexion, a mat of thick, black hair springing from his head, more than a dusting of dark hair on his arms and legs, his chest and his butt. Like Jack, Laurent was naked but for a single rubber band around his left wrist, from which a key dangled. Laurent's band was blue. The number on the band was zero two.

'Very good . . .'

A voice out of the steam and spray. Laurent spun around. Jack peered past his little friend, towards the phantom speaker.

The lifeguard, standing at the entrance to the shower area, beyond the sheet of water. How long had he been standing there?

'You know you're in trouble, don't you? Big trouble.' An Australian accent.

Neither lad spoke.

'Against the rules, that sort of thing. Against the law, too − somewhere like this.'

'Christ,' said Jack, 'you're not going to call the police, are you? I mean, over something like this . . .'

'Well . . .' Jack was sure the lifeguard was enjoying this. '. . . I guess that's up to you, matey-boy.'

He paused, obviously mulling over his next words.

'Back when I was a kid, out in Adelaide,' he said, 'I was with a friend in my dad's barn doing the kind of thing you two're doing now. The kid from the farm down the road – he was four or five years older than me and my friend, and he was a bully – he caught us, just like I've caught you. He threatened to tell my dad. I was shit scared of my dad – he'd have had the skin off me if he'd thought I was a faggot – so I begged him not to. He said I had to do whatever he told me to from then on. Anything. Or he'd tell my dad.'

Jack shot an uncertain glance at Laurent. Maybe this wasn't going to be so bad after all.

'You see,' the lifeguard continued, 'I figure this is kind of a similar situation.'

'What exactly did this kid . . .'

The lifeguard walked forward, under the sheets of water, into the shower. The water soaked through his white T-shirt, gluing it to his skin. Both boys could see at the front of his tight, blue Speedos a large, upwardly snaking bulge.

'This,' he said through clenched teeth.

Swinging suddenly to face Jack he grabbed his arm and twisted it hard behind his back.

'Walk,' he ordered.

Not for a second relaxing his vicious arm-lock, the lifeguard frog-marched Jack out of the shower and back into the changing area.

'You didn't think I saw you watching me earlier, did you, matey-boy?'

'You had your back to me,' Jack winced as he walked.

'I saw your reflection in the window, fool. On the other side of the pool. Standing there, watching me, butt-fucking-naked . . .'

Only when they were standing, facing the low wooden changing-benches did the lifeguard release Jack. Jack stood, trying to massage some life back into his arm, staring half-nervously, half-expectantly at the bully. He was about twenty-three, Jack guessed, big-boned and strong, but with the classic swimmer's build – the muscles lithe rather than bulging. His off-blond curls fell in messy ringlets over his face and neck. Beneath the hair he was a dark gold colour, his antipodean tan crowned with an array of dirty freckles.

'Turn around,' he ordered.

Jack did as he was told.

'Now . . . where's your little friend got to? Call him.'

'Laurent . . .' Jack's voice was uneven.

He saw his friend pad nervously around the corner into the changing area. The Frenchman's cock was small now. His balls were tight against his body.

'Come here,' the lifeguard said. 'Give me your wrist-band.'

Laurent slipped the heavy rubber band from his wrist and passed it to the lifeguard.

'Put your hands behind your back,' the lifeguard snapped at Jack, 'where I can get at them.'

One of Jack's wrists already sported his own red band. Now the lifeguard slipped Laurent's blue band onto his other wrist.

'Lean forward,' the Australian voice barked. 'Grab the bar. Assume the position.'

Jack let his fists close around the horizontal metal pole which ran the length of the benches at head-height – the bar for the clothes-baskets. The lifeguard grabbed first his left wrist, then his right. One after the other he gave the rubber bands a twist, so that they were painfully tight, and wrapped each around one of the hooks which sprang from the bar. His arms were painfully stretched out, the hooks which held him nearly six feet apart. His feet were barely touching the floor, now slippery with the water their bodies had shed.

From behind, the lifeguard jerked Jack's legs apart and out from under him. Jack groaned at the pain in his wrists, at the sudden pressure on his shoulder-joints – now bearing the whole weight of his body. He heard the rustling sound of material – the lifeguard's trunks being discarded – followed by the tiny crackle of latex. Then he felt a familiar driving pressure between his thighs. Jack gasped as the lifeguard's cock began to penetrate him. It was thick and it was long. Stroke by stroke it inched deeper into Jack until he could feel the Australian's balls slapping against his cheeks.

Jack could see Laurent, hovering about the exit, watching, his look of uncertainty gradually giving way to one of open interest. He seemed unable to tear his eyes away. His cock was starting to swell as he watched his friend being force-fucked. Slowly – he seemed barely aware of what he was doing – his hand strayed to the rigid pole. He began running his fingers up and down the shaft in loose, slow strokes. Finally they closed upon the circumcised cockhead and began pumping hard and fast.

Jack was wreathed in sweat. The lifeguard continued to pump his arse; his feet continued to slip and skid. His arms felt as if they were being pulled out, his sphincter was working at full stretch, flexing and relaxing around the thick cock.

And in front of him stood his little friend, naked and aroused, the steam of the shower still rising from his bare shoulders. Laurent, watching him being taken. Watching and masturbating. In spite of the pain, Jack's own cock, so recently brought off by Laurent, was fully hard again.

The lifeguard's strokes were becoming harder and faster, accompanied by deep guttural grunts from far back in his throat.

Laurent too was approaching climax. Beating himself hard he drew close to Jack and knelt down before the bench. Jack's erect cock danced in his face, its purple head jutting past the sparse foreskin. Laurent leaned across the bench and sunk his mouth over it. The rhythm of the lifeguard's thrusts forced Jack's cock hard against the back of Laurent's throat, again and again.

Jack had never felt so powerless, so deliriously out of control.

'Jesus . . . I'm coming,' the lifeguard croaked, slamming into Jack. In Laurent's mouth Jack could feel his own cock starting to spurt for the second time. A moment later he felt his French friend shudder as he came, splashing the bench and floor.

Like a piece of fairground machinery all three men juddered to a halt at the same time. Drained, the lifeguard pulled out of Jack and dropped into a squat. Jack hung from the bar like a piece of meat. Laurent grinned up at him.

'I was right,' Jack whispered breathlessly from his hooks. 'I knew we'd get some action around here. It's just like I predicted.'

By mid-afternoon the preparations for that evening had all been completed and the heavens had opened. The fair-folk were taking their customary afternoon siesta, isolated, canned, napping or relaxing with their thoughts in tin caravans lashed by the rain.

Tom lay on his bed and listened to the irregular, bead-like drumming of rain on his roof. He gazed vacantly out of the window. Jack and Laurent were crossing the soaked waste-ground, grinning like naughty schoolkids, nudging and splashing each other.

Piper was sitting in the shelter of the Ghost Train, puffing on his long clay pipe and watching the rain bounce off the stalls. The old man nodded almost imperceptibly as the two lads passed him, and said something which Tom couldn't hear, waggling his pipe in the air to illustrate a point.

Everybody else had fled to shelter.

He was still thinking about the kid. Homeless, probably. That would explain a lot. Poor bastard, out in weather like this.

Swinging his legs to the floor, Tom pulled open his bedside drawer. Everything looked in order. A tour schedule for Gamlin's, charting the fair's forthcoming progress back into the heartlands of England, lay folded beside the pile of letters. The medal in front of the photographs. Everything in its proper place. He lifted out the pile of photographs and flicked quickly through them. They were old ones of his family. Mum and Dad. Brother . . . He put them back. Too many memories . . .

He straightened the medal ribbon. He still couldn't understand it. The kid was a thief. He knew it and the kid knew he knew it. Why go through the drawer and not take the medal? Why take such pains, having gone through his stuff, to put it all back exactly as he had found it?

He closed the drawer and slumped back onto his bed, once again allowing the rain-tattoo to fill his head.

Away north of the river the pre-storm heat still hugged London.

Jason stood with his back to a wall. Somewhere on the other side of the wall were Nige, Mitch and Andy. They were on Hampstead Heath. Public toilets. This really was Jason's last chance.

He had returned to the squat the night before to face Nige's fury. He had known what to expect: Nige, humiliated on the

Waltzers, hung-over on cider, denied his tribute from Jason. For a moment Jason had thought that Nige was going to hit him. Then the cunt had gone all quiet and broody. He had disappeared back into his room, emerging ten minutes later with a new plan.

'If you won't do rent, you won't do rent,' Nige had said. 'But you can fucking well do some clipping.'

That was the plan. Jason would pose as rent; when a customer approached him he would take that customer into the toilets, and play out the little charade until the others emerged from hiding in the cubicles to relieve the customer of his money. One hit, then they would all leg it.

Unconsciously Jason's hand went to his throat, searching for the silver spider which always clung there, searching for reassurance. But there was none to be found. Ashamed, he had removed the talisman for the first time in two years — for the first time since Spider had given him the little love-token — and hung it over the mirror back at the squat.

Jason hated this, but what choice did he have?

He hadn't long to wait. A man in late middle-age, smartly dressed in a leather overcoat, white shirt, open at the neck, blue flannel trousers. Neat, greying hair; chiselled face, ruggedly lined. He slowed his walk as he passed the little brick building, and smiled at Jason. Jason, feeling a gnawing emptiness inside, smiled back.

'How much?' the man asked.

'Depends what for,' Jason replied in a voice scarcely louder than a whisper. Nige had tutored him on what to ask for. 'Twenty for a hand-job, forty for oral . . .'

'That'll do,' said the man, and, resting his hand lightly on Jason's arm, led him inside.

Jason was grateful for the coolness inside the little brick-and-porcelain enclosure. There were three cubicles: two of them occupied, the middle one empty. The man gently pushed him into the vacant central cubicle and, following him in, closed the door behind them.

There was little space. Jason tried to turn and face his client, and in doing so lost his balance. He half-fell over the toilet bowl. His shoulder was jammed against the high cistern. The man moved fast – he thrust his mouth against Jason's, his tongue probing deep. Jason, caught off-balance and off-breath, spluttered and tried to free himself. The man pressed harder against his lips.

OK, relax. Nige and the others would be there in a few seconds. Jason put his hand to the back of the man's head. The man was fumbling with the belt of Jason's jeans. Jason gasped. Panicking, his eyes flashed to the door, around the cubicle. Where were they?

The boy's belt was undone now. The man was tugging at his flies, roughly squeezing his cock through the material of his jeans. In spite of everything, Jason felt himself getting hard.

He pulled back as far as he could in the cramped space. He could see the man's erection clearly outlined through his flannel trousers. Now the man tore at his own flies, and pulled his hard cock from the folds of cloth.

'Forty, you said . . .'

He placed a hand on Jason's shoulder and gently but firmly pressed him down until he was sitting on the toilet seat, facing him.

'Uhh . . .' Jason stared about the cubicle in desperation. He didn't want to be here. Where were they?

He heard a scuffling from one of the cubicles. A stifled giggle. So that was their game.

The man didn't seem to have heard anything. His hand was on the back of Jason's head now, steering it down onto the swollen purple cockhead. He was strong, and the cock was practically as thick as Jason's fist. Jason couldn't pull away. He closed his eyes and opened his mouth. The thick cock filled him. He heard the man's sigh of satisfaction as his cock touched the back of his throat. He could smell his powerful musk. The man was thrusting now, piledriving his fat member in and out, painfully stretching Jason's jaw. Jason felt himself gagging. He couldn't breathe.

He wrenched his head away.

'Guys . . .'

Raising his eyes he saw the three of them looking down into the cubicle, grinning – Nige and Andy to his left, Mitch to his right.

The man pushed him away and thrust his cock back into his trousers. His eyes darted about the little cubicle.

Jason could say nothing. There was a sudden scuffling as his three accomplices scrambled from their perches and attempted to rush the cubicle.

The man was ready for them. As the door was kicked open he swung his fist and caught Mitch on the cheek. Mitch fell backward with a cry. Slumped on the floor, cradling the side of his face, he began to whimper.

There was a sudden silence. Nige had pulled a knife.

He and Andy stood, blocking the doorway. He was grinning, almost snarling. The man stood facing the pair, tense, alert. Jason sat behind him on the toilet seat. This wasn't right. Jason would have preferred to do the rent properly. Anything but this . . .

Nige took a step forward.

'No . . .!'

Jason surged from his seat and dived around the side of the man. He cannonballed into Nige and sent him and the knife flying into the opposite wall of urinals.

The man made the most of the opportunity. He jabbed his fist into Andy's stomach. The boy doubled over, gasping for breath, and sank to the floor.

'Thanks for nothing,' the man shouted to Jason as he ran out and away.

Nige and Jason rose to their feet at the same time. Now Nige was pointing the knife at Jason. His voice was low and threatening.

'You're fucking dead for that . . .'

Winded, Andy was struggling to speak. 'We've got to get out of here, man,' he gasped. 'That cunt'll probably call the pigs.'

Nige's gaze flickered between Andy and Jason. Reluctantly he closed the blade on the knife and secreted it in his pocket. He kicked Mitch, still whimpering on the floor, in the back.

'Get up,' he said.

The king cast a final look back at Jason as he marshalled his tattered army away.

'You're dead,' he said quietly.

★ ★ ★

Showtime.

The storm had spent itself, the clouds had moved on.

Suddenly it was like a summer evening. There was a lightness, an uplift to the air in the wake of the storm: the jungle-strings of cheap, coloured bulbs seemed to twinkle magically in the early-evening light; light danced off the rain-flecked surfaces of the stalls and the trembling pools on the ground.

And then came the people. The crowds. As big as any Tom Jarrett had seen since he had joined the fair. Sometimes they seemed to Tom like shy, wild creatures, emerging from their burrows and hibernations, creeping from shelter in the wake of the rains, sniffing and nuzzling around this strange, magical, many-coloured place.

A line of girls giggling with nervous anticipation, and young men eager to impress them with shaky displays of iron nerve, had formed at the foot of the Wheel. One by one, two by two, they filed past Tom, giving over their money, climbing gingerly into the cars. Tom sensed the by-now familiar thrill, an undercurrent like static electricity, which ran backwards and forwards along the slowly advancing line. He loved it – that thrill of expectation. He fed off it.

This was as good as it got for Tom. Right now the wasteland, the gasometers, the railway line, shops and houses and lives, nothing beyond the glow of the lights and the wheeze of the music existed. He gunned the Big Wheel into life.

Jack and Laurent, conspiratorial as ever, had been watching and gossiping where the edges of their rides met since the show opened. Now they were having to think – and talk – fast. A group of pissed, amorous twentysomethings was trying to sweep them off their feet.

A group of pissed, amorous, *female* twentysomethings.

One of them sidled up to Jack. Her fingers brushed his arm.

'Quid a ride, ladies.'

Suddenly Jack was alone. Suddenly Laurent was earnestly attending to a loose panel on the side of the Hall of Mirrors.

'You what?' one of the girls queried.

'Quid a ride . . .'

Go away. Go and have a toffee apple or something . . .

'I'd pay more'n a quid for a ride with you . . .'

Giggles from her friends.

'Look, d'you want to go on or not?'

Oh pleeease fuck off . . .

'Well, it's the Tunnel of Love, isn't it? I can't go in there on my own . . .'

The girl took Jack's arm. He flinched.

'You know,' she said, slurring her words slightly, 'you remind me a bit of Keanu Reeves. Dead sexy.'

'Shy type, retiring, librarian possibly, or primary-school teacher. Lots of repressed sexuality needing to be teased out.'

Jack shot an angry glance at Rex, who had deserted his post at the Test-Your-Strength machine to come and watch the spectacle, and who was now standing at his shoulder, whispering earnest advice into his ear.

'Woo her . . . then strike!'

He winked conspiratorially at Jack, his mouth set and serious under the waxed moustache.

The little crowd of girls was shepherding Jack towards the entrance to his own ride.

'It's all right,' called Laurent, now standing arm-in-arm with Rex, both of them now unable to contain their laughter, 'I'll operate it.' He scampered out of sight and into the control booth which regulated this most romantic of rides. Behind him Jack was being more or less corralled into one of the floating, bobbing cars. A girl plopped herself into the seat next to him. Laurent set the joyride in motion.

'Don't fight it, Jack,' Rex called after the hapless beau as he and his lady disappeared through the romantic arch and into darkness. 'It's like a tide . . . Give in to it!'

'Right,' Tom called to the faces shining out of the darkness, 'who's next?'

They paid and filed aboard, and Tom prepared to send them to the top of the world.

He stopped.

Away by the coconut shy, staring at him, was a face he

recognised. It was that damned kid, he was sure. The kid from last night.

'Oy, mister . . .' a voice whined.

A customer was waiting to board the Wheel – a greasy-haired, late-twenties squirt in a PVC jacket. Tom shot him an irritated glance, then directed his gaze back to the coconut shy. In the second it had taken Tom to acknowledge his impatient customer the boy had vanished.

Tom snatched the money from the man and pushed him into the car. Absently, he continued to take money and wave his customers vaguely into their seats, barely acknowledging them, neglecting to give them change until prodded, all the time scanning the crowd.

There he was again. It was definitely him.

Tom's eyes shot to his money-box. That was safe, practically out of sight under the levers which controlled the ride.

Why would the little bastard have come back? Last night's grand finale – the boy's peculiar behaviour and dramatic exit – played about his mind. Barely aware of his actions he sent another cohort of screaming, shouting patrons spinning through the sky.

The night – and the Big Wheel – rolled on. The boy was there throughout, watching him. Circling, never coming close, like a scavenger beast. Like a jackal.

No, that was unfair. But there was something about the boy's stare – those frighteningly clear, unblinking eyes – that unnerved Tom. Beneath that gaze Tom felt naked.

He tried to ignore it. He tried to get on with his work, chatting to the customers, taking their money, starting and stopping the ride. But every time he looked out into the crowd, somewhere the boy would be watching him.

At last the fullness of night covered London and the last of the crowds went their way. Tom stopped the Wheel and killed the lights. Big day tomorrow – they were packing up and getting out of here. A new pitch, north of London, getting on for the Midlands. Somehow, in spite of the bounties of that night, Tom felt relieved. Gathering up the cash-box, Tom made for his caravan. He passed Rex and Laurent, laughing together outside the caravan the French boy shared with Jack. Jack, it seemed, had taken to his sick-bed and was refusing to let anybody in.

He turned towards his own van, and stopped dead in his tracks. There, standing in the shadows, between Tom and his metal home, was the boy. Motionless. Staring.

Tom opened his mouth to speak, but no words emerged. Mutely he raised a hand in the boy's direction.

'Hoy, Tom,' Laurent called out behind him, 'your date's waiting for you.'

Tom took an uncertain step forward. The boy turned on his heels and ran.

'Wait . . .' Tom called feebly after him. But once again the night had swallowed him.

Three

S hit. Why had he gone back there?

Jason didn't know this part of south London. He had run blindly into the darkness, and now he was lost. He had been walking for much of the night. Not going anywhere, just walking. Knowing he couldn't return to the squat, he had nevertheless walked south from Hampstead Heath. The fairground had seemed like a beacon, guiding him to its gaudy heart. But once again he had fucked up. Once again he had run.

He was lost. He stopped at the base of a tall building, perhaps twelve storeys, of brown stone. An office block of some kind. Classy-looking. It reminded him of one of the buildings back home in Newcastle.

Back home? He didn't have a home.

He looked up the great cliff-wall of the building for a moment, then jumped onto one of the lower window-sills.

He hadn't done anything like this in nearly two years.

He looked about him for a handhold. The building was constructed out of big stone blocks. Where each block abutted the others, above and to the side, there was a straight groove, perhaps a centimetre wide and two centimetres deep. Good enough. He grasped for the highest groove he could reach and sunk his fingertips into it. He swung himself out and up, his trainers urgently seeking a toe-hold. It was a precarious climb, but he'd done worse. Slowly, clinging to the rising grid of narrow grooves, window-sills and air-vents, he made his way upward.

They used to do this practically every day, him and Spider. Newcastle had been their playground, its buildings and building-sites and bridges. They had climbed the lot. It was how Spider had earned his name. It was perfect. His last name was Mann. And Spider Mann and Jason Bradley had ruled the rooftops.

He had lost track of the number of times the Newcastle police had dragged him home to his despairing mother.

He was in an awkward position. The tip of one foot was balanced on a high window-sill; the fingertips of one hand held the window-frame. With his other hand he reached for a distant cornice. He felt himself slipping, his grip weakening. He lunged for the cornice, catching the edge of the jutting stone with his flailing fingers, and swung there, six floors up.

Spider had saved his life once, in a situation like this. It was only about the third or fourth time they had climbed together. Each had a reputation – and Spider his name – before they actually met. Rivalry was inevitable. Although Spider was a year younger than Jason he was marginally the better climber. Jason was trying hard to impress. Then, like now, he had overreached himself and had found himself hanging in space from a loose overflow pipe, easily forty feet up, his grip failing. Spider had somehow – it had been an incredible feat – worked his way across the wall, grabbed Jason's wrist and hauled him to safety.

But there was no Spider now. He spotted a vertical drainpipe, four feet away. He began to swing by one agonised hand from the cornice, slowly at first, then faster. Every swing took him closer to the drainpipe, but not close enough. Every swing loosened his grip on the stone. Finally he hurled himself out across the wall. He released his grip. He was sailing through the air, beginning the plunge downward. After what seemed an age his fingers closed around the metal pipe. He drew himself into it, clutching the wet metal to himself, gasping for breath, eyes closed.

He had done it. He had done it without Spider.

The day Spider saved his life had also been the first day they made love. They had made the flat roof of the building and lain there in the sun. Spider had been wearing jogging bottoms.

Nothing underneath them. Spreadeagled on his back on the asphalt roof, with only a thin cotton covering, his boner had been all too obvious. Not that he was making any attempt to disguise it.

'What you looking at?' he had demanded of Jason, grinning.

Jason had blushed and looked away from his friend's bulge. Shit, it was more than a bulge – you could see every vein, the swelling at the knob-end, his ball-sac, loose in the heat.

'Anyway,' Spider had continued, 'what d'you call that?'

He nodded towards the crotch of Jason's jeans. Jason too was hard, his cock straining beneath tight denim.

Spider had reached across and playfully punched the bulge.

'Fuck off,' Jason had snapped.

So Spider had done it again.

'Fuck off, I said!'

Jason had tried to roll away, but Spider had leaped on top of him, pinning his arms with his knees, his back to Jason's face, and begun mock-pummelling the denim-covered hard-on.

The denim-covered hard-on which would not go away.

'Right,' Jason had said, and reached around Spider's side. Through the stretched cotton pants his fist had closed roughly around his tormentor's cock.

'I'll twist . . .' Jason had threatened. 'I'll twist this fucking thing off.'

'Mmm . . .' Spider had sighed. 'Fuck, that feels good . . .'

So Jason had started moving his hand up and down the rigid shaft. Spider had moaned with pleasure, arching his head back, his dark, tousled mop of hair swaying in the sixty-feet-up breeze.

Spider had reached forward and eased Jason's jeans off, then begun pumping his cock. They had rolled apart and squatted, facing each other, each watching the other undress. For the first time Jason had gazed upon Spider's dark, almost Mediterranean-looking body, revealed bit by bit, as the boy peeled his clothes away. Jason was aware of Spider looking at him in exactly the same way, scoping his body as it gradually emerged from its coverings.

That had been the first time. Making love on the rooftops had become their obsession. Soon they were inexpressibly in love with one another, their constant search for physical danger adding an adrenal buzz to their lovemaking. It bound them ever closer to one another. So many near misses. So many brushes with death . . .

Jason looked above him. Suddenly the rooftop seemed hopelessly far away. The drainpipe to which he clung was wet with night-dew. He could feel his grip beginning to fail. Forty feet up, he began to slide down the pipe.

This was bad – a drainpipe should be easy, but the pipe was wet and Jason hardly had any strength left in his hands. Gradually he was gathering speed. He couldn't slow his downward momentum. His feet were all over the place, kicking at the air and the wall. He bellowed in pain as he hit a bracket in the pipe, which chopped at his hands, breaking his grip. He was falling freely now – the pavement rushed upward. He grabbed for the pipe again. He felt his arm wrench and he swung hard into the wall. His grip failed and he dropped.

He crashed to the pavement ten feet below. His old instincts kicked in – he tried to land lightly, rolling with the jarring impact. He lay there on the pavement, too shaken to move. Above him the building loomed and laughed.

He couldn't do it any more. Not without Spider. Without Spider he was nothing.

He picked himself up slowly. His body ached, but mercifully everything seemed to be intact. Dusting himself down, he began limping down the deserted night-canyon.

He had been walking for hours. The roads were completely empty at this time of night. His footsteps echoed in the stillness. He ached all over. He was desperately tired. He had eaten nothing all day. This silent, stately, orange-lit world seemed to shimmer on the edge of unreality. He passed under a long, harshly lit railway bridge. The river was to his right. Ahead of him was a large traffic roundabout, covered in flowers. And beyond that . . .

He knew where he was. His first night in London he had fetched up here. Battersea Park.

He ran across the empty road, over the roundabout to the park gates, and began hauling himself over the railings.

The park was dead quiet at this time of night. Even the animals in the little zoo seemed to be asleep. The birds on the lake, ducks, swans, even the insects seemed to be asleep. The park felt unnaturally still to Jason.

Quietly – his trainers making almost no sound – he padded past the dark café and up into the jungle-like corridors of dense foliage which enfolded the paths in this section of the sprawling park.

Quite suddenly he became aware of movement everywhere: small, night-bound animals scurrying under the trees. Gradually as Jason became accustomed to the jungle-stillness the park came alive around him.

He stopped, facing a gap in the trees. Through the gap, beyond the trees, a man was standing in a small clearing, bathed in a pool of moonlight. The man was looking at Jason, staring directly into his eyes. He looked odd – Jason couldn't remotely pin down his age. His face was dark and deeply lined. His eyes were wide and dark under a pair of dense eyebrows which met above a proud nose. His hair was jet black, and long – longer than any Jason had ever seen on a man. It trailed far over his shoulders and chest, its ends lost in the darkness. He wore a long, black, leather coat open and bleeding, like his hair, into the shadows of night. He held Jason's gaze in his.

At the periphery of his vision Jason could see that beneath the coat the man was naked. His body was covered with a down of black hair which seemed to shine in the moonlight. His cock was exposed and erect. He was masturbating. Jason resisted the urge to break eye contact and focus on what the man was doing below his waist. The man would know he was watching. That was what the man was waiting for.

Jason could no longer resist the downward drift of his gaze. The man's balls were low and heavy. His cock rose at forty-five degrees to his stomach, seven or eight inches, curving forward slightly, slender and unusually red. A thick mat of dark hair clung about the base.

With his left hand the man was stroking and fondling his balls and perineum. His right hand he ran in a steady motion along the upper half of his cock, letting the fingers run back and forth over the ridge of his swollen helmet.

The man was pumping himself faster now. He must be close to

45

coming. Still he stared at Jason, and Jason stared back. Suddenly the man's eyes narrowed; his face took on a pinched, pained expression. A low growl seemed to be coming from his throat. His left hand tightened around his balls, tugging and twisting; his cock bucked and surged in his right hand, and exploded in a thick jet of spunk, up and out, splattering to earth in the little clearing.

A noise somewhere behind Jason made him turn his head. There was a vehicle. He could see headlights. The parks police. He threw a panicky glance back towards the clearing . . .

The man was gone. Impossible.

Jason slipped off the path and into the clearing, crouching low to avoid the lights from the police van. The sound of the vehicle receded to nothing. His eyes scanned the great, silent shadow-trees. Where could the man have gone? He couldn't have just vanished – not that quickly and quietly. The uneasy notion that somehow in the moonlit darkness he had merely imagined the man was starting to play in Jason's mind. It had been the weirdest of days. He was dog-tired. He didn't understand what had just happened.

Still squatting, Jason's hand brushed the damp grass. Something sticky. An arcing trail of spunk, silvery in the moonlight, curved away in front of him. It seemed to directly follow a line of tiny toadstools. He was in the middle of a fairy-ring.

Suddenly he wanted to be away from the silent forest and its hidden eyes. Wearily he picked himself up and trudged back to the path. The man – if he had ever been there – and the police had both gone. He was alone now.

Christ, he was alone.

Blinding light. A motor, chugging up the Thames.

Concrete, hard against his back, damp and cold.

It was dawn. It took Jason a moment to get his bearings. A wide, open area. The river . . . the park . . . And, smiling down at him, one of the four bronze Buddhas which looked benignly over this part of London from under their elegant, oriental canopy. He was lying curled on the concrete at the feet of the four outward-facing bronze deities in the Buddhist pavilion. He had no recollection of wandering up to this end of the park.

He heard a footstep. There was a figure around the other side of the statue. Suddenly Jason remembered, dreamlike, the encounter of the night before.

The figure rounded the open pavilion's central column.

Glen. A surge of warmth spread through Jason's body. He hauled himself to his feet.

'Christ,' said Glen, 'you look bloody awful.'

Jason didn't reply. He didn't know what to say in reply. He merely stood, swaying slightly, looking at his friend and grinning inanely.

After a moment he spoke, wiping his nose with the back of his hand.

'How did you find me?' he asked.

'I told you before,' said Glen, smiling, 'I got your scent. I can find you anywhere.'

'You remember the last time we were here . . .?'

This was where he had first met Glen. In almost the same way. Then, too, Glen had found him asleep at daybreak at the feet of the Buddha. That had been the dawn of Jason's first full day in London.

Fitting, then . . .

The jumble of emotions fighting for dominance in Jason's mind finally became too much to contain. His face crumpled, his eyes closed, he practically fell forward into Glen's arms, tears cascading from his eyes.

His friend held him. Glen's strong arms were all that was preventing him collapsing to the floor of the pagoda. He buried his face in Glen's neck. His arms squeezed tight around Glen's shoulders and upper torso, pulling him close as if both of their lives depended on it. His lips brushed the skin of Glen's neck, then anchored themselves, making a seal, drawing a kiss. Another. Soon Jason was covering his friend's honey-brown skin, his neck and cheek, his lower jaw and the outer edge of his lips, in wet, sensuous kisses. His hand went to Glen's crotch and began kneading his cock through the thick denim of his jeans. Jason felt it begin to swell under the pressure of his palm.

Glen gently placed a hand on either side of Jason's head and drew Jason's face away from his neck. The two were facing each other now, tears drying on Jason's cheeks, Glen smiling tenderly, a compassionate light in his eyes.

'You sure you want to do this?' Glen asked.

Jason didn't answer. He didn't want to think about consequences. All he was aware of was this one moment and his sweet friend in whose arms he was now standing, and how long it had been since he had held anybody like this.

Spider . . .

He pulled Glen close to him, lips meeting lips, crotch grinding against crotch, tongues smashing and twining together. He ran his hand feverishly up and down Glen's back, tracing and retracing the channel of his spinal column, dipping into the crease between his firm, high buttocks, squeezing and pinching buttock-flesh, finally bringing his hand round again to meet Glen's now fully erect penis, bending and bulging and straining inside his jeans.

Jason dropped to his knees and attacked Glen's belt with fumbling fingers. He prised apart the front of his friend's trousers. Tight white pants. The front of Glen's briefs seemed to thrust themselves forward as his huge cock fought for release. It was dark – almost black compared to the honey-brown rest of him – and far too big for those little pants. Jason had seen Glen's cock many times – his friend had been nothing if not an exhibitionist in the room they shared – but never this close. Easily ten inches, bent slightly to one side. A tight foreskin covering a big purplish-pink head. Almost reverentially Jason drew the foreskin back. It really was tight – it drew itself in at the base of the head and showed no signs of wanting to come forward again.

Jason sunk his mouth over the huge organ. The smell of his friend's musk filled his nostrils. He ran his tongue about the purple bulb; he allowed his bottom teeth to scrape gently at the frenulum – the sweet, sensitive junction where the underside of the cockhead met the shaft. Finally, willing his throat to expand, he took Glen deep into his mouth, feeling him collide with the back of his palate, the soft flesh of his throat. Glen let out a long, appreciative breath and gripped Jason's head, his fingers twisting through the dark gold mane.

Glen was dribbling now. Jason could taste his lubricants seeping out into his mouth. He felt a tugging at his hair. Glen was pulling him to his feet.

'That was nice,' said Jason. 'You were leaking.'

'Let me taste myself,' he said and clamped his mouth against Jason's, stabbing deep with his tongue.

Expertly, his mouth never leaving Jason's, Glen loosened and dropped his friend's jeans. Jason's cock jutted urgently from a pair of white Y-fronts. Glen unhooked the pants and pushed them down Jason's thighs. He cupped Jason's full balls, squeezing hard. Jason let out a sharp breath of pain and pleasure. In full view of the river and the elegant houses on the opposite bank the two boys stood there, clenched to one another, mouth against mouth, hard cocks clashing together. The Buddha smiled down upon them.

'Fuck me,' Jason whispered hoarsely to Glen.

'What . . .' For a moment Glen seemed taken aback.

'Go on . . .'

Trousers and pants around his ankles, Jason swung around, presenting Glen with his back. Glen stepped out of his own trousers and pressed himself close to Jason, kissing his neck, biting and sucking on his ears, breathing in his hair. He ran his big cock up and down the crack between Jason's buttocks, letting the head catch slightly on the hole. He stooped and plucked a condom from the pocket of his jeans. 'Gotta do this right,' he said.

Jason tensed as Glen's cock felt its way into his tight opening and pushed slowly upward. Jason gasped as slowly Glen worked his cock deeper and deeper inside him.

'No . . . You're too big . . .' Jason whispered.

Glen kissed him on the neck.

'Relax, darling,' he said. 'Just open up to it. I'm nearly there . . .'

At last Jason could feel Glen's full balls and soft thighs against his buttocks. He was completely in. Gently Glen started a sickle-motion with his pelvis, little more than a sort of rhythmic twitching at first, short strokes, getting longer, getting bolder, nuts slapping on cheeks.

Jason leaned forward. His cock was hard. He gripped the feet of the Buddha for support, gazing up into the infinitely wise, loving eyes of the long-dead Indian prince.

Glen was breathing short and fast now. He was close to coming, Jason knew, pumping his cock fast in and out of his arse. Glen gasped hoarsely. One mighty thrust of his pelvis was followed by an ecstatic stillness, Jason's friend deep inside him, groin pressed hard against him. Another single thrust. One more.

Glen was done. Sheathed in sweat, panting for breath, he slowly pulled out of his friend.

The two companions sat, side by side on the concrete, backs to the Buddha, looking out over the Thames. The early-morning boat-traffic was starting to build up. For a long time neither spoke.

'I can't go back to the squat,' Jason said eventually.

'I know,' Glen replied. 'I brought this.'

For the first time Jason noticed, leaning against the statue, his green rucksack.

So this was it. It was to end where it had begun. They fell silent again. For another hour they sat in sad, friendly silence, holding hands, staring out across the water.

Finally, 'I can't stay in London,' Jason said. 'It's doing my head in.'

'You can't keep running, either.'

Jason didn't reply. A vague idea was forming somewhere in the back of his mind, but he had yet to put it into words, even to himself.

'It's coming to rain,' Glen observed.

Jason let out a fatalistic sigh, and got to his feet. Glen did the same. Jason ran a hand across his friend's cheek.

'Will I see you again?' Jason asked.

'I got your scent,' Glen smiled, choking back a tear. He kissed Jason gently on the mouth, turned and descended the pagoda's steps, down into the park below.

Jason watched him disappear into the green expanse, now scattered with people and dogs. He slid a hand around to the tight back-pocket of his jeans. From it he pulled a crumpled play-bill. Tour dates. A couple of days here, a couple of days there, always heading north. Gamlin's Fair.

★ ★ ★

Frankly, Tom Jarrett was glad they had left London. Coming from the other end of the country himself, he retained at some deep level the northerner's mistrust of the south-east in general and of London in particular. It wasn't that he was narrow-minded or particularly parochial – he had travelled widely with the army, been to all sorts of places, seen all kinds of cultures – it was just that . . .

'What?' Rex wasn't having any of this. He was a Londoner – *Blackheath, old boy!* – and proud of it.

'Well . . . they're all mad, Londoners,' said Tom. He was only half-joking.

He and Rex hefted a huge section of the Big Wheel out of the back of one of the lorries. It was the hardest part of fairground life, breaking down the rides, loading them into the trucks, driving them across country and reassembling them. Sometimes they had a day off, a short breathing-space between pitches. Not this time. They had arrived at a field outside Harpenden, just north of London. They were setting up there and then, and would open tonight.

'I mean,' Tom continued, 'take the night before last. There was that business on the Waltzers, then that kid tries to rob me. I half-suspect the two things were linked. Sort of a diversionary tactic. Then when I try to confront the kid, first he attacks me and then he gets . . . well . . . fresh.'

'Fresh?' Rex was suddenly all ears. 'What, you mean . . . sexual?'

Tom grinned. Rex was as bad as Jack and Laurent, at least in theory. Rex never did very much, but he was insatiably curious, voyeuristic, and gossipy. Such waspishness on one so physically macho never ceased to amuse Tom. Tom was tough, he was strong, but he wouldn't like ever to have to take on Rex in a fight.

'I mean mad,' he said. 'Londoner.'

The evening drew on, and with it the storm clouds. They had gone on ahead of the fair, and had been waiting over the horizon when the little convoy of elderly trucks arrived. By the time the fair was open for business they were practically low enough to touch, dark, sagging, heavy with flood. You could carve your name on the evening miasma.

The town lay in the distance; the fairground field was bounded on one side by a caravan park, on another by a motorway slip-road. Town, fields, caravans, all the elements in the landscape jigsaw were lashed together by criss-crossing high-tension cables, flying through the air on steel pylons which were stuck in the earth like giant holding-pins.

Tom stood at the foot of the Wheel, looking dubiously skyward. Small groups of people were wandering into the fair. In the distance there was a flash. The first of the thunder rolled around the horizon. Anticipating the storm, he had arranged for Jack and Laurent to head the queue, to take the first ride and reassure the public. Now they were having decidedly cold feet.

'No way,' said Jack. 'Anyway, I've got work to do.'

Laurent merely shrugged his shoulders and smiled ruefully and followed his friend back into the thin crowd.

'All right,' Tom barked, with considerably more enthusiasm than he felt, 'who's going to ride?'

Another flash of lightning. A clap of thunder, nearer, louder.

'No fear,' someone muttered. 'I'm not going up on that, not in this weather.'

What queue there was for the Big Wheel – less than a dozen people – began to melt away.

'Anyone . . .' Tom pleaded.

'I will.'

Tom turned. It was him. The boy. The thief.

'I'll go up.'

Momentarily confused, wholly at a loss for words, Tom didn't even try to take the boy's ticket money. He released the restraining bar on the first of the Wheel's double-seated cars and let him climb aboard. Nobody would join him.

Tom watched him as he rode the Wheel alone. How had he found them? What was he doing here? He looked rough. He seemed to be wearing the same clothes as yesterday – dirty jeans, hooded top, puffa-jacket – his hair was a knotted mess, his face was streaked with dirt.

But what struck Tom more was the expression on his face as he was carried through the air, silhouetted against the lightning, the wind dancing through his hair. He seemed to be neither enjoying the ride nor frightened by it. His lips moved in a silent, invisible dialogue. He seemed to be somewhere else entirely.

People were watching him. The queue had started to re-form. Slowly Tom brought the Wheel to a halt.

'Good,' said the boy. 'I'll stay on.'

This time the Wheel was half-full. The next time it was two-thirds full. By the time the boy dismounted – Tom had lost count, but he reckoned he had been around perhaps a half-dozen times – not saying a word, just melting into the crowd, it was full. The wind was driving the clouds west, and with them the thunder and rain.

A good night, in spite of the poor start. Tom hefted his plastic money-box, testing the weight, and nodded with approval. Switching off the power, bidding goodnight to his fellow-stallholders, he turned in the direction of his little caravan.

He cut behind the Tunnel of Love. Giggles from the caravan Jack shared with Laurent. He slowed as he approached his own van. A figure was lurking in the shadows.

'Who's there?' He clutched the money-box tighter.

He took a step closer. The boy was standing next to the door of his caravan. As Tom approached he shot an uneasy glance towards the road.

'Look, don't run,' Tom blurted out. 'I'm not going to hurt you, OK?'

The boy didn't reply.

'I, uh . . .' Tom felt oddly nervous, awkward in front of this silent stranger. 'Thanks . . . for doing what you did on the Wheel tonight. You did me a favour.'

They were close together now. Tom fumbled for his key.

Why didn't the boy say anything? He just stood there, staring at Tom with the same expression he had worn that first night, when he had lain pinned on the floor of the caravan beneath Tom's iron thighs.

'Yeah, like I said, thanks,' mumbled Tom, opening the door of the little van. 'G'night.'

He climbed inside and began to close the door.

'I haven't got anywhere to sleep,' said the boy.

Tom stopped. Jesus. Why him? What was it about this kid that unnerved Tom so?

'I, uh . . . Christ, uh . . . Come in,' he finally managed to say.

The boy stooped and fished a rucksack from under the van. 'I put it there for safe keeping,' he said.

That accent . . . 'Uh . . . sit down,' said Tom, gesturing towards the bed.

The boy sat.

'Where are you from?' Tom asked.

The boy looked furtive for a moment. Guilty. 'Newcastle,' he said.

'I thought so,' said Tom. 'Not a Londoner, then.'

'What?' the boy asked irritably.

'Nothing . . . Just a conversation I was having earlier. Which part?'

'What?'

'Which part of Newcastle?'

'Jesmond,' the boy interrupted.

'Jesmond. I'm from over the water. Gateshead.'

The boy nodded.

'What are you doing down here?'

'Long story,' said the boy flatly.

'Not much of a talker, are you?'

The boy didn't reply.

Tom smiled. 'Neither am I. Don't worry about it. There's plenty of people round here never shut up. What's your name?'

Again, that look of guilty uncertainty on the boy's face.

'Jason.'

'Tom Jarrett,' said Tom, holding out his hand.

Jason shook it peremptorily.

'Look, uh . . . no offence,' said Tom, 'but . . . when did you last have a bath?'

'I know I stink,' said Jason. 'I'm sorry.'

'It's just that, somewhere as small as this . . . Look, that's a shower. Why don't you dive under there while I knock up something to eat? Nothing fancy, I'm afraid. Just some leftovers . . .'

After a pause Jason nodded curtly. He rose from the bed and clomped the two or three paces that separated the semi-translucent cubicle from the rest of the caravan. Tom watched him in silhouette through the door as he removed his clothes. The door opened a crack and a hand appeared, dropping them in a pile on the floor.

Tom lit a gas ring on the little built-in stove and manoeuvred a pot onto it. Slowly a semi-congealed casserole bubbled into life.

Idly Tom watched the pink silhouette through the shower door, soaping itself from head to toe. Hair − no messing about with shampoo − face and neck, shoulders and arms. A Geordie oath as he dropped the soap. He bent to pick it up; his buttocks pressed against the plastic wall of the cubicle − two vivid, fleshy circles. Tom smiled to himself. His back, sides, chest and stomach, all duly lathered. His backside. Tom watched as he ran the bar of soap up and down the crease between his buttocks. Round to the front. Soaping up his pubes, his balls, his cock. It seemed to Tom that his hands lingered a little too long in this area. Then down his legs to his feet.

The pan was boiling. Snapped from his idle and unintentional voyeurism Tom knocked the gas off, fished two bowls from a cupboard and poured the contents of the pan into them. The shower door opened.

'Got a towel?' Jason called.

Tom plucked a towel off a shelf and tossed it towards him. Jason leaned out of the cubicle to catch it. His limp, heavy cock flopped dully around the door for a second.

'You'd better have this, too,' said Tom. He took a white dressing gown from a hook next to the bed and hung it on the edge of the cubicle. 'To spare your blushes.'

Tom was still thinking of the boy's behaviour that first night.

They ate their meal in silence − Tom because he couldn't think of anything to say; Jason because his mouth was never empty. Belt-feeding the food in, he demolished his bowlful in minutes. Poor sod probably hadn't eaten in days.

Suddenly and unexpectedly Tom yawned. Fuck taking a shower. He could do that in the morning.

'I'm going to turn in,' he said. 'I suppose you'll need some blankets . . .'

'I've got a sleeping-bag,' Jason replied, delving inside his rucksack.

'OK . . . 'night.'

Somewhat self-consciously Tom killed the light in the caravan and undressed in darkness. He was aware of Jason doing the same. Naked, he crawled between the sheets and closed his eyes. The last thing he heard was the shift of nylon as Jason slipped into his bag. He was asleep almost immediately.

Thunder in the sky, but it can't touch them . . .

They stand at the top of the Wheel, and it's huge, millennial . . .

Below them — far below — the town twinkles. The car swings, but they are unafraid. They hold each other in the gale. Jason and Spider. They kiss.

There is a grinding of machinery. The Big Wheel is moving. Turning. Too fast. They plunge earthward. They fall to the floor of the car. Jason reaches for Spider. He turns his head, but Spider is gone.

In his place is the Dog. The great black Demon Dog, its jaws pink and slavering. Growling deeply, its razor-teeth sink into Jason's face . . .

Jason awoke screaming, banging his head on the floor of the caravan.

Tom sat bolt upright in the bed with a shout.

'What the fuck . . .'

He looked as if he had seen a ghost.

'I'm sorry,' Jason said sheepishly. 'Nightmare . . .'

Tom was pale and shaking. Why was he looking at him like that?

After a few moments the older man's expression relaxed. He smiled a strained smile.

'That's OK,' Tom said. 'You just startled me. My kid brother used to get nightmares. Always used to end up sleeping in with me.'

'Could I . . .'

Tom exhaled flatly.

'You'd better keep still,' he said. 'David used to kick me black and blue. Come on then . . .'

Jason crawled quietly into bed next to the burly roustabout and lay, motionless, for long minutes. Tom, naked, muscular, turned away from Jason, onto his side. Moments later a slowing down in the man's breathing told Jason that he was asleep. Gently Jason brought his face to rest against the sinewy back. He breathed deeply, smelling the sweat of the day, dry on Tom's skin. He let his nose and lips travel around Tom's shoulder-blades, tracing patterns up and down his spine, snuffling the rich, aromatic loam of his armpits. Jason edged closer, letting first his chest, then his stomach, his crotch, his legs and feet, press softly against Tom's sleeping form. He breathed as Tom breathed. He sensed their heartbeats moving into synch. He felt his cock growing, riding up the crack of Tom's arse. He brought an arm over Tom's side, fingers cupping the great bole of his chest, snaking down his ribcage, down past his belly-button, down, down . . .

His hand came to rest in the pubic bush that surrounded the sleeping man's semi-erect cock. Jason twisted the hairs gently between his fingers for a few moments before easing his hand around the base of a chunky dick. It twitched slightly as his fingers closed around it. Tom shuffled in his sleep. Jason tucked his head into the crook of Tom's neck and, still holding the man's cock, as a baby might hold a comfort-blanket, drifted off into blessedly dreamless slumber.

Four

Jason awoke to find himself curled, mouselike, in an otherwise empty bed. He looked at the clock on the wall. Eleven-thirty. This lot had probably been up for hours. Wasn't that what they did, fair-people, get up an hour before sunrise? Or was that farmers? Or pixies, or something . . .

He swung out of bed and groped around the floor of the caravan for the clothes he had shed the night before. He sniffed his pants and winced. He fished about in his rucksack and extracted a new pair of white briefs, T-shirt, socks. His old jeans and top would do.

He emerged to a day of litter and mud. Mud, it seemed, accompanied the fair wherever it went. A couple of kids – a boy and a girl – were chasing each other muddily around the little Merry-Go-Round and laughing. The fat old crone who had been frying up all last night as 'Mavis's Fine Hot-Dogs' pushed past him, shouting unintelligibly at the kids, who completely ignored her. She still smelled of fat and fried onions.

In the shadow of the Big Wheel a crowd of people was gathered. Jason could see Tom among them, along with the moustachioed freak from the Test-Your-Strength machine, the little guy from the Waltzers, and other faces he had hitherto only seen by coloured fairground-light. A woman was standing in the middle of the crowd, a clipboard in her hand. Her hair and the pages on the board flapped about in the stiff spring breeze. Everybody's attention seemed focused on her. The little fat, red-faced man who had the previous night been wearing a peach-coloured tail-coat and matching hat and selling sweets and candy-floss to kiddies was now shouting at the woman and waving his fists in the air.

Jason approached the circle with caution. Near enough to hear; not near enough to look conspicuous.

'I'm sorry,' said the woman. 'This land has been subject to a compulsory purchase order. You will have to move on.'

'But we've been coming here for years,' one of the crowd spat. Jason recognised her as the woman who had caught him robbing from Tom that first night.

'Centuries,' someone else added.

'Where's Piper?' The French boy. Laurent.

'Yes, where's Piper?'

The crowd began, as one, to murmur the question, as if in invocation.

''Scuse me, son.'

A figure pushed past Jason and shuffled into the body of the little crowd. The crowd parted like a sea around him.

It was the old man who always seemed to sit on the edge of the Ghost Train, puffing his pipe and scowling at passers-by. He was wearing the same clothes – ancient, faded, stained tweed jacket and trousers that might once have been grey or brown but were now a sort of grim mixture of both – as he had been wearing the night before. And the night before that. And the night before that.

'Wha's goin' on?' he mumbled.

'Are you in charge here?' the woman asked.

'Well, I dunno about in charge . . .' the old man replied. He looked about the crowd. All their eyes, all their expectations, were now on him. '. . . But I suppose I'll 'ave to do. Wha's all this about?'

'I'm afraid this field is no longer common land. It's earmarked for development. You're not supposed to be here, Mr . . .'

'Piper. We've been coming 'ere for . . .'

'Years and years, I'm sure . . .'

'Centuries. Longer.'

'Well, if you have some documentation establishing . . .'

59

'There ain't no documentation. This fair's been comin' here since the dawn of time. There weren't no documents in them days.'

She laughed. 'The dawn of time. Really, Mr Piper . . .'

She was a lawyer, Jason was sure. He'd encountered the type before.

'Come with me,' Piper cooed. 'I'll show you what I'm talkin' about. History, miss. Not just the history of the fair. Not just the history of the area. I'm talkin' about a tradition – a strand windin' up and down, up and down the country, goin' way, way back. A strand we're all joined to. It takes us into the past, miss. And it takes us into the future too.'

Jason saw her flinch as the old man took her arm. He led her through the circle of onlookers, which instantly began to break up into its constituent parts. Talking all the time to her, Piper led the woman across the muddy field. Jason scanned the rides. Suddenly everybody was somewhere else – either tinkering with prize-displays and motors or closing the doors of their caravans. Piper and his companion had paused outside the Hall of Mirrors. To Jason's surprise the pair disappeared through the mirrored doors and into the world beyond.

'So . . . I think you are travelling with us now?'

Laurent, the French boy, was standing at his shoulder. Jason was startled by the voice.

'Well, I don't know . . . I . . .'

'You've spent the night here.' The other boy, the one with the pony-tail, wandered around the side of the Aunt Sally stall, carrying an old cardboard box. 'With lucky old Tom. It's settled. You'll be travelling with us. Everybody who stays overnight does. I'm Jack, by the way. This is Laurent.'

'Uh, Jason.' This was all happening a bit fast. 'Look, maybe I should talk to the old bloke about the possibility of . . .'

'Oh,' Jack replied, 'Piper will talk to you, when he thinks the time is right. He'll completely ignore you until that time, of course . . .'

He began to walk back in the direction of the Tunnel of Love, followed by Laurent.

'What are you doing?' Jason asked as they departed.

'Changing bulbs,' Jack replied. 'All anyone ever does around here is change bulbs.'

The French boy reached into the box as they walked. Bulbs. Coloured light-bulbs. Extracting a handful, Laurent began casually to juggle, throwing the bulbs high into the air, catching them faultlessly.

Jason watched the two of them depart. He felt awkward, at a bit of a loose end. He had no purpose there. He wandered across the ground looking for Tom.

Tom was halfway up the Big Wheel, a canvas satchel slung about his neck. This, too, was full of coloured bulbs. Wedged close to the hub of the great Wheel, propping himself between spokes and struts, he unscrewed a bulb from one of the Wheel's thick, painted iron spokes and dropped it into an empty pouch in the satchel. Deftly he replaced it with a new one and, muscles flexing, swung himself out onto a horizontal beam and stretched himself across a fifteen-foot abyss, his fingers straining for a distant, dead bulb.

He was in a curiously light mood. He had slept well last night with Jason curled up beside him, and had dreamed gentle, long-ago dreams of family holidays at the seaside, his parents sitting on deckchairs, mum with a thermos, dad reading the paper, trousers rolled halfway up his pale calves, he and David splashing about in the waves.

He could sympathise with the boy's tortured nights. At the end of the day Tom relied on exhaustion to drive him to often-restless sleep.

He could see the boy now, approaching the Wheel, looking up at him, again with those eyes. This time Tom stared back.

A bulb slipped from his hand and plunged earthwards, shattering on the Wheel as it went down. It was enough to startle Tom out of his reverie. He was halfway up the Wheel, for God's sake. Fifteen feet up. Focusing his gaze on the line of lights ahead, he leaned out again across the drop.

The day dragged for Jason. Everybody seemed busy; no one was paying him the slightest attention. He had ambled about, watching the sweet man replenishing his wares, the darts woman patiently pinning up a new pack of cards in target rows, a fairground-hand straightening the rather small out-of-order notice on the Merry-Go-Round. Christ, he was bored. He had wandered into town, had a McDonald's and wandered back. The old man – Piper – was sitting in his customary position on the steps of the Ghost Train, pulling on his pipe. Jason made to approach him. A deep growl made him stop. It seemed to be coming from somewhere inside the Ghost Train. Jason took a step further. Another growl. Piper was looking at him, motionless. He seemed to be grinning through his pipe-and-whiskers mask. A scuffling sound, and Piper's big black dog crawled out from under the ride and stood, bolt erect. A short, thick rope tied the dog by the neck to the ride's superstructure. Master and dog, side by side, regarded Jason as one of their customers might study a prize goldfish in a plastic bag of water.

Rude old cunt.

Jason was suddenly distracted by a flash of movement from the Hall of Mirrors. The late-afternoon light bounced off one of the mirrored doors and arced across his eye. The door swung open, and a woman emerged.

She looked confused. Her hair was conspicuously out of place. She hovered in the doorway for a moment. It was the woman from this morning – Jason was sure it was her. Her clipboard had vanished, as had her lawyerly composure, but it was definitely her. She had been in there over four hours . . .

Jason watched her walk across the fairground, glancing around in apparent bewilderment. He looked at Piper. Piper too was watching her, inscrutable as ever, still chewing on his pipe. Growling, the dog lurched in her direction, straining at its rope, choking itself. She walked on, oblivious.

Jack and Laurent, arm in arm, were approaching from the caravan park, talking and grinning furiously. They said something to the woman as they passed her. She stopped, obviously confused, smoothed her hair and walked on. Jason made to approach the two boys. Laurent should be told that someone had got lost or stuck in his ride. Without noticing Jason the pair turned into their caravan, shut the door and drew the curtains.

★ ★ ★

The evening was long in coming. The punters would be there soon. Jason didn't know if he could face another night moping about the fair on his own. He sat down on the side of the Waltzers and opened a can of coke he had pinched from Willie Wonka's unattended sweet-stall. He recalled the old film. Charlie had pinched the everlasting gobstopper. At the film's climax his conscience got the better of him and he returned the gobstopper to an apparently indifferent Willie Wonka, thereby unwittingly inheriting the whole chocolate factory.

Jason opened the can of coke and gulped the contents down.

'Are you just going to mope around all night?'

A voice from the Bumper Cars.

It was the woman who had half-strangled him that first night. He got a better look at her now. She must have been pushing fifty, slight of build and brown-skinned. She wore jeans, but from the waist up was dressed a little like a gypsy – her cheeks heavily rouged; bright scarves and wraps and gold jewellery hanging all about her. Her hair was full and black and bunched loosely on top of her head, tied with a red ribbon. Her voice was low and hoarse.

'Or do you want to do something useful? Make up for your stunt the other night.'

'I don't know, I mean . . . yes, I mean . . .' Jason stammered. '. . . like what?'

'Ride the cars,' said the woman. 'There's never time in between rides, so you jump from one car to another taking the money off the punters. I normally do it, but I'm a bit run down at the moment. Change of life.'

She beckoned to Jason with a long, beringed and painted finger.

'Come on,' she cackled, 'I won't bite.'

So Jason rode the cars.

It reminded him of one of the stunts he used to pull as a kid, back home. On their skateboards they would bomb up to cars just pulling away at road-junctions, grab on to the back bumper and be towed along, crouching beneath the level of the driver's vision, until either they fell off or were spotted by the irate motorist or managed to go the distance. Sometimes they reckoned they'd get up to fifty or more miles per hour. It was hideously dangerous, and more than once Jason had lost large amounts of skin to the road.

It had been an exhilarating sensation. It had always given Jason the most ferocious hard-on. It was on one of his skateboarding outings that he had first started experimenting sexually with his mates.

Sweet, sinful, innocent days. Life had been simpler then. Safer, if you discounted the ever-present possibility of road-death. Of course, this was before he met Spider – before his life had changed for good.

He had a hard-on now, thinking about the past, springing from one narrow back-plate to another, swinging on the pole which connected the bumper-cars to the lethal matrix of wires criss-crossing the ceiling of the little arena. A couple of girls had already noticed and commented on it.

'That'll be two quid, mate.'

There were two men in the car. The passenger reached back, two pound coins in his hand. He half-turned, then spun fully round in the car, his eyes fixed on the bulge at the front of Jason's jeans. The man allowed his hand to brush against the bulge.

'Sorry,' the man said, not at all convincingly.

He looked to be about twenty-eight, chunky, with an open, friendly, somewhat square face and pale grey eyes. His hair, cut short, was sandy-brown and tightly curled. He wore a green and white striped rugby shirt, open at the neck to reveal wisps of chest-hair.

'It doesn't seem to want to go away, does it?' he continued.

He allowed his hands to brush against Jason's crotch-bulge again. This time his hand lingered, risked a gentle squeeze. Another, more vigorous.

Jason closed his eyes. He was skateboarding again, with his friends, Matthew and Paul. Matt was Jason's age, Paul a year younger. Jason could picture them clearly – both dark-haired and slightly foreign-looking, Paul with a cracked front tooth. They were brothers who lived in a posh house on a long, steep hill, on the outskirts of Newcastle. A really long, steep hill. They'd christened it The Drop, Jason and his friends. It was the day the three of them first did The Drop. They had been building up to it for months, taking their skateboards on steeper and steeper runs, going faster and faster. Now the three of them mounted their boards at the top of the fearsome Drop and plunged. Jason didn't know what speed they reached that day, but he had skated for grim death, trying to stay in the centre of the camber, riding the lightning curves, the road a blur beneath the board. He had only vaguely been aware of Paul yelling as he flew from his board and hit the road pinwheeling. He saw Matt flashing glances behind him, trying to see what had happened, wholly unable, as was he, to halt his descent.

When the hill had levelled out and the boards had slowed sufficiently, he and Matt had managed to stop, and raced back up the hill to where Paul was sprawled in the gutter, sobbing. Petrified that their mother should see them – she had specifically banned them from trying to ride The Drop – Matt had ordered that Paul be carried into the garden shed, shielded from the house by a lawn and a line of trees. They had deposited the now-sniffing boy on the floor of the shed and attempted to find out how bad the damage was. Happily it was superficial: he had skinned some of his thighs and his groin area.

His brother had painfully peeled away Paul's trousers and pants whilst Jason had wetted a handkerchief under the outside tap.

'Urgh,' Matt had said. 'I'm not doing that!'

So it had been he, Jason, who had dabbed the wet cloth gently over Paul's grazes, every so often accidentally nudging the boy's flaccid cock. And as Paul's sniffs had subsided, so had his cock swelled, pointing up at Jason, hard and straight. Matt had started chortling and calling his brother a faggot, and Paul had pulled his trousers and pants up and gone indoors in a sulk.

As the two remaining friends had sat in the gloom, slumped against the wall of the shed, Matt had started to laugh out loud.

'We did it, man!' he had said. 'We did The Drop.'

The exhilaration was starting to return to both boys, and with it something else – the residual, alluring memory of Paul's embarrassment incensed the atmosphere. Jason had a hard-on, and he could see that Matt did too.

They had sat in mutually aware silence for a while, and then, 'Christ, I'm horny as hell,' Matt had said.

He had begun rubbing himself through the front of his jeans. Mesmerised, Jason had begun doing the same. Then Matt had reached into his trousers and eased out his young, engorged cock. Again, Jason had done the same. He and Matt had sat almost primly against that wooden wall, fully clothed, flies undone, each flogging himself and watching the other until both came, almost together, shooting white wads into their denim laps.

The next time had begun as before, again in the shed, after they had enticed one another in there by some flimsy pretext, each knowing exactly what was on the other's mind, each saying nothing. Again they had sat against the wall, and again the cocks had come out. After less than a minute Matt – always the ringleader – had said, 'I'm going to take my clothes off.' Without waiting for a response he had shrugged off his shirt and eased his open trousers and pants down around his calves and then off and onto the shed floor. Jason, of course, had been only a few beats behind him. A minute or so more had passed, each naked boy partially turned towards the other, then 'Let me do you for a bit,' Matt had said, 'and you do me.' They had scuttled like crabs towards one another, across the wooden boards on bare backsides, each awkwardly wrapping his legs around the hind quarters of the other, leaning forward, heads almost touching. Matt had reached out and touched Jason's cock. For the first time Jason had felt the sensation of a hand other than his own running up and down that painfully sensitised shaft, massaging the bulb, sending his head spinning. He had himself reached out and for the first time wrapped his fingers around a cock other than his own.

The dam had burst. Blow-jobs then fucking had followed. Other friends had got involved. Even Paul, Matt's younger brother, caught spying on four or five of them giving each other blow-jobs, had become involved: they had made him blow them all as his punishment. The garden shed had become a crucible of secret, innocent sexual pleasure.

The images flickered across Jason's memory like an old home-movie.

Lost in another world, he continued to ride the back-plate of the car. The big, friendly faced passenger continued to squeeze and rub his cock through his jeans, harder now, and faster.

Still locked in the garden-shed of his memories, Jason felt the old familiar build-up deep within his balls. To his surprise he was close to . . .

There was a jolt as the car drove into a pile-up in the middle of the arena. The man's hand slipped from the front of Jason's trousers.

'Whoa . . .' the friendly faced passenger boomed. 'I thought I told you to avoid collisions.'

'It's you!' the driver replied. 'You're putting me off.'

Still clinging to the steering wheel he craned his neck to see Jason.

'He's always like this,' he complained. 'Even when we're doing eighty down the motorway.'

Jason felt a sharp crack across his still-bulging crotch. He flinched with momentary pain. The bloody woman who ran the ride sailed past him on the back of another car, waggling her smarting hand.

'Take a break,' she said. 'You look hot and bothered.'

Flashing an awkward grin at the amorous passenger Jason jumped from the car and trotted to the side of the arena. The two men in the bumper-car watched him go.

'You two,' the woman barked, mounting their back-plate, 'keep your eyes on the fucking road.'

By the end of the night Jason was exhausted. Between the two of them, he and the woman hopped relentlessly from back-plate to back-plate for five hours. Shouting over the wheeze of the music and the crackling of the cars she introduced herself as Crash Annie. By the end of the night she had thumped one man and Jason had been propositioned by fourteen women and three blokes, and had his cock massaged the once.

'So you're travelling with us,' Annie said to Jason as they watched the last of the punters leave.

'I guess so,' Jason replied. 'Everyone seems to think so. That old man hasn't said anything to me . . . Anything at all, really.'

She laughed.

'Piper will talk to you when he's ready. When you're ready . . .'

Jason suddenly remembered the events of that afternoon.

'The Hall of Mirrors,' he said, 'is there anything . . . odd about it?'

'Depends who you listen to, love,' Annie replied. 'Old Piper reckons so. Have you been inside?'

'No,' Jason answered.

'I only went once. Years ago, that was. You start off in this passage – it twists all over the shop, so you lose your sense of direction – and it's all mirrors. Distorting mirrors. Horrible things. Then you go through into the centre, where the mirrors are all flat. Perfect reflections. They're worse than the others. It's like a maze in there, only you can't see the walls. You're everywhere, coming at yourself. Piper says the distorting mirrors shake you loose of your outer shell, so that when you go through to the inside it's the real you you see. I didn't like it. I see as much of myself out here as I need to see, thank you.'

'So you reckon there is something wrong . . .'

'No, love, it's just an old woman being daft. Dozens go through there every night. Most come out smiling.'

'Most . . .' said Jason.

They were interrupted by a stage-whisper, off in the darkness.

'Jason . . .'

It was Jack.

'You run along and play now,' said Annie. 'You've earned it.'

Piaf was playing inside Jack and Laurent's caravan as Jason and Jack approached it.

'Private party,' Jack said. 'Very small affair.'

'I don't know . . .' Jason rarely felt much of a party animal nowadays.

'Stay as long as you like,' Jack said, 'and go whenever you want.'

He ushered Jason up the little flight of steps and through the door.

The first thing which hit Jason was a soft wall of incense and candle-smoke. No wonder Piaf sounded choked. Coloured drapes, tie-dyes and Moroccan rugs had been thrown over everything – floor, furniture and the sprawling ranges of inexplicable hillocks and escarpments which seemed to spring up everywhere in the small caravan. Here and there these had erupted from under the drapes – untidy piles of books, clothes, empty wine bottles.

At one end of this candle-lit cave sat Laurent, semi-recumbent, sipping wine from a glass. The caravan was otherwise deserted.

'Some party,' said Jason, secretly relieved.

'Please, have some wine,' said Laurent, reaching for a bottle. 'From my grandfather's vineyard in Bordeaux. I always steal several crates when I visit him.'

Jason sat himself down on a large cushion on the floor and allowed Laurent to pour him a glass. Jack sat towards the other end of the van in an imposing red-leather swivel-chair.

'It used to belong to a judge, this chair,' he said. 'Piper gave it to me. God alone knows where he got it . . .'

The three sat and drank steadily, saying little. Smells of jasmine and sounds of Piaf washed the atmosphere pebble-smooth.

'Laurent,' Jason asked after a while, 'how long have you been working the Hall of Mirrors?'

The French boy shrugged. 'It is nearly a year, I think, since I came here. Why?'

'Have you ever noticed anything funny going on in there?'

'Funny . . .' He shook his head, slowly. 'I do not understand.'

'If it's fun and games you want you should check out the Tunnel of Love,' Jack interjected. 'Sometimes things get so steamy in there I just have to stop the ride and watch.'

There was a tap-tapping at the window.

'Our other guests,' said Jack from his judge's chair. 'Come in!'

The door of the caravan swung open and two young men entered.

'Welcome,' said Jack. 'Do sit down. This is our friend Jason. Jason, this is . . .'

Jack smiled apologetically.

'I'm sorry,' he said, 'I have a terrible memory for names.'

'Matthew,' said one of the men. 'Jason and I have already met. On the Bumper Cars.'

He stepped into the candle-light as he spoke. Jason recognised him as his broad-shouldered, square-chinned, amorous passenger.

Matthew. Jason remembered his daydream of a few hours ago and smiled at the little coincidence.

'. . . And this is Paul,' Matthew said, gesturing towards his companion and former driver.

Jason then got his first proper look at Paul. He was shorter than Matthew, and lacking his rugby-player's build. He was younger, too, by about three years: Jason put his age at about twenty-five. His hair was darker and straighter, smartly cut and side-parted. His face was slender, almost girlish, his cheekbones high beneath large brown eyes, his mouth small and sensuous.

He flashed a sweet smile at Jason as he sat next to him.

'You're not . . . brothers by any chance, are you?' Jason asked hesitantly.

'Brothers?' Matthew exclaimed. 'Christ, no.'

'Matthew and Paul are staying in the caravan park,' said Laurent. 'We met them last night.'

'Wine,' said Jack. 'Drink.' Another bottle was produced, glasses were filled, the music was changed.

'Bit of a funny place to come on holiday, this,' said Jason. To his mind caravan sites belonged next to beaches, not in the middle of this bland, landlocked tract of countryside.

'We're not really on holiday,' said Matthew. 'It's more of a dirty weekend we're on.'

He wasn't looking at Jason as he spoke; he was facing the other way, his hand under Laurent's sweat-shirt, squeezing and caressing the French boy's chest. Laurent was now laying fully on his back, his hands behind his head, his knees raised and his legs wide apart, eyes shut and a lazy smile draped across his face.

The room had fallen silent, except for the sounds of muted Mozart now lilting from the cassette player. Jason watched as Matthew eased Laurent's sweat-shirt up his body, exposing his stomach, his ribcage, his pink nipples. Matthew's great, broad hand with its long, thick fingers and down of sandy hair seemed almost to cover the little French boy's chest. With his other huge hand Matthew opened Laurent's jeans. Laurent raised his buttocks, allowing Matthew to drag his jeans and pants to his knees in a single movement.

Jack was sitting, motionless in the chair, his hands folded in his lap, watching intently as his friend writhed under the heavy caress of the big man. Jason swung his gaze to Paul. Paul too was staring, but not at Matthew and Laurent. Paul's gaze was fixed on Jason himself. Jason felt himself shuffling somewhat awkwardly under Paul's scrutiny. He turned back to watch the spectacle unfolding in front of him.

Laurent's trousers and pants were around his ankles now. With a grunt Matthew heaved his great frame on top of the little Frenchman. Fully clothed still, he began rubbing his crotch bulge against Laurent's small but hard, circumcised prick. He reached back with one hand and hauled his rugby shirt over his head to reveal a knotted, sinewy back and a pair of the broadest shoulders Jason had ever seen.

Jason felt a hand on his leg which made him jump slightly. Paul was gently rubbing his inner thigh, his fingers edging higher and higher. Jason threw a panicky glance at Jack.

'Welcome to Gamlin's,' Jack said in a soft voice. 'This is our present to you. Laurent's and mine.'

Paul was easing open the buttons on Jason's jeans now. In a swift movement the boy swivelled round and sunk his head to the level of Jason's waist. His teeth nipped at Jason's erect cock through the taut, white lining of his pants. He began running his lips and teeth the full length of the ridge of stretched, virginal cotton which bulged from beneath the denim.

Jason's head was swimming. The wine, the candles, the thick incense-smoke was making the whole thing seem surreal. Almost unconsciously his hand strayed to his throat. The silver spider was not there, of course. It was lost in south London . . .

Closing his eyes, fixing his mind somewhere in the past, Jason let his head fall back, enjoying the cotton-softened sensation of Paul's nibbling teeth catching at the underside of his foreskin, the boy's muffled lips playing around his swollen helmet.

He raised his hips to allow Paul to pull his trousers out from under him. He felt his pants being peeled away from his cock. He felt his balls, suddenly freed from their tight prison, relax and hang. He felt the wet kiss of Paul's lips on his cockhead, before they stretched themselves around the thick shaft. Jason smiled to himself – that delicate mouth hadn't looked big enough to do this. Paul's hands were roving wildly as his mouth moved rhythmically up and down – massaging Jason's flat belly, tweaking his navel, pinching and stroking his nipples.

He opened his eyes to see, next to him, Matthew on his knees before Laurent. Laurent lay on his back, naked now except for his sweat-shirt, bunched up under his arms, and a pair of white socks. As Jason watched Matthew lifted Laurent's legs and wrapped them around his neck like a scarf, letting them drape down his back. His shoulders on the floor, his neck bent, Laurent was suspended, upside-down, from Matthew's mighty shoulders. Holding Laurent by the hips Matthew slowly inserted his cock – as big as his frame suggested it would be, heavily ridged and veined beneath a rubber sheath – into his tight butt-hole. He began to grunt as he pumped hard into Laurent's upside-down arse. The French boy's eyes were tight shut. His face twisted into a grimace which seemed to reflect both pain and pleasure. His right hand began moving urgently up and down the length of his own cock.

Below Jason's waist Paul's neat brown hair continued to bob up and down, his mouth making occasional slurping noises, his teeth every so often escaping the dam of his lips to catch the ridge of Jason's glans. Jason responded to these sharp, sweet punctuations with little twitches and gasps of his own.

Sedate in his red leather chair Jack, still fully clothed, continued to watch. Slowly he rose and walked across the caravan. He knelt next to Jason's head and stroked his tousled blond locks, smiling down at him. Stooping, he pressed his lips against Jason's. Jack's tongue slipped into Jason's mouth, running along the wall of his teeth, jousting with his own tongue. He kissed Jason long and deep, before lifting his head to continue watching as Paul's pretty, girlish, contorted face rose and fell along the length of Jason's hard cock.

Jason watched as Jack shuffled around on his knees until he was in a position to remove Paul's trousers and pants, careful not to disturb the boy's mouth-rhythm on Jason's prick. Paul's cock, Jason could just about see, was long and slender. Out of the corner of his eye Jason could see Jack's hand begin to tickle the boy's balls, occasionally delving back to trace the crack of his arse before finally closing around his slim shaft.

Matthew was on the balls of his feet now, half-squatting, half-standing. Laurent was still suspended by the legs from Matthew's great shoulders; Matthew was still fucking Laurent hard. Jason watched as Matthew's hand landed on one of the piles of dirty clothing that spilled out across the floor from under an old crocheted bed-covering. His fingers closed on a pair of discarded underpants. He leaned forward and thrust the pants into Laurent's face, spreading the stained crotch across the boy's nose and mouth. Laurent spluttered and tried to speak. Matthew's great shovel-hand closed over the pants, over the face of his little fuck-buddy. The French boy kicked and spluttered. He was powerless to break the rugby-player's grip. His head pinned to the floor, he struggled for air as Matthew continued to pump his prick in and out of him. With his hand he continued to masturbate himself furiously.

The pair came almost simultaneously. Matthew gave a strangled roar as he drove home into Laurent's tight butthole. His hand remained firmly clamped over Laurent's face as the French boy shot a great, shuddering fountain of spunk onto his own chest and face and Matthew's sinewy inner arm. Matthew lifted the pants from Laurent's face and tossed them to one side. Laurent lay, drawing in great gulps of air, laughing at the same time. He mumbled something to himself contentedly in French.

Jack had succeeded in removing the bulk of his clothing without ever losing his stroke on Paul's prick. He was down to his T-shirt and pants now, his long hair loose and free. He reached into his pants and freed his adamantine cock, stroking it in time with the beat he was playing on Paul.

Matthew rolled away from the still-breathless Laurent and turned to face Jason. He smiled his amiable smile, leaned down and began licking his neck, shoulders and chest. Idly Jason reached up and began playing with the young Goliath's mat of sandy chest-hair. As Matthew's head worked its way down Jason's body, so Jack peeled Paul away from his duties on Jason's cock and spun him around, plunging his tongue into that dedicated, delicate mouth. He lassoed Paul's slim cock with one hand and drew it against his own. The pair knelt, facing each other, mouths interlocked, cocks held together by Jack's pistoning fist.

Matthew closed his mouth over Jason's cock and pulled hard, drawing him in deep so that Jason was slamming against the back of his throat, then pulling tightly away again, making little effort to shield his teeth. He turned on all fours until he was straddling Jason, the crook of his knees interlocking with Jason's armpits, his calves under his shoulders. Matthew's hairy barrel-chest slapped against Jason's lean belly as his head went up and down.

Slowly Matthew lowered his great buttocks down onto Jason's face. Jason's nostrils filled with the heavy musk of sweat and spunk; the beard that clung to the underside of Matthew's balls and trailed all the way back and up into his arse-crack tickled him. Matthew's loamy brown ringpiece descended like a dark rosette over Jason's mouth. He spluttered − like Laurent before him he could barely breathe. OK, relax. Enjoy.

He inhaled deeply of the rich anal odours. He wriggled beneath Matthew's rough, toothy blow-job. He felt fingers − Paul's, Jack's, maybe Laurent's, he didn't know − clawing their way under his buttocks, feeling their way towards his own arsehole, entering the tight ring.

He couldn't see, he couldn't move, he couldn't breathe. The sharp new odours unlocked by sex mingled with the old − incense and burning wax. He pushed his tongue up into Matthew, tasting the rugby player's soft, bitter arse-flesh. He felt probing fingers up his own arse − the delicious nipping of slightly too-long nails. He felt the fingers withdraw. Two hands, four hands, clamped his buttocks and thighs. They lifted his buttocks from the floor. Matthew, still sucking roughly on Jason's cock, shifted his weight back to accommodate the lift. His arse settled tighter over Jason's face.

Buttocks suspended, Jason felt his legs being spread, invisible fingers again probing his hole, pulling the cheeks apart. He felt the pressure of a prick − whose, he didn't know; he couldn't see − slowly pushing forward, prising him apart, followed by the slap of someone's pelvis against his buttocks. The cock started thrusting; short, fast strokes. A finger drilled its way into Jason's arse beside the pumping cock. Matthew's teeth still raked up and down

Jason's own cock. His massive buttocks still sat heavily over Jason's face. Jason was drawing in hard, musky breaths. He had never felt so much of his body being worked at once. He felt out of control, wonderfully powerless in the face of this sensory overload.

They all seemed to come within moments of one another. First Jason felt the hot splash of Matthew's jism on his stomach. The big rugby player bit down hard on Jason's cock. Jason cried out in pain, but at the same time felt himself coming inside Matthew's mouth. By the time his spasms of orgasm had receded Jason could feel his unknown penetrator – Paul, Jack, Laurent perhaps – heaving and straining against him as he shot his wad with a great gasp.

The finger up inside Jason withdrew first, followed by the softening cock. Someone came with a little cry, his seed splashing against Jason's legs. At last Matthew lifted his arse from Jason's face.

All five men sprawled about the floor of the caravan, saying little, wiping the juices of sex from their bodies. Matthew and Paul exchanged a glance, then began to climb into their clothes.

'Early start, tomorrow,' said Matthew. 'Back to work. Fuck.'

The two holidaymakers said their goodbyes and left. Laurent poured another round of drinks.

Jason drank with trepidation. The atmosphere was still thick with smoke and sex. Jack was again sitting in his judge's chair, still naked, looking at Jason with a satisfied smile on his face. Jason was starting to feel weirded out about what had just happened. Who had fingered him? Who had fucked him? Now that normality had returned the room was beginning to spin . . .

Unsteadily he rose from his seat and teetered through the door. He ran to the edge of the caravan line. If he was going to puke, he wanted to do it out of the way. He stood and looked along the endless corridor of holiday caravans in rows, all identical. Order. He'd always hated it. Well, here he'd found Pandemonium. Naked, drunk, covered in the unguents of love and about to puke, he stared up the neat avenue. He'd made his choice, and his stomach had better start getting used to it.

★ ★ ★

'We thought you'd died.'

Jack, fully clothed again now, had returned to his leather chair. He was rapidly shuffling and reshuffling a pack of cards.

Jason shrugged. 'Too much wine,' he said. 'I haven't drunk in a while.'

'Nothing to do with nearly being crushed by Matthew's arse, then . . .' Jack put down the cards. 'Tonight was interesting,' he said. 'I wanted to see what you were into. You're . . . fairly passive, aren't you?'

Jason didn't reply. Laurent lay on his narrow bed and snored loudly, still naked, his cock limp and a wine-bottle clutched in his hand. Like Jack, Jason was now fully clothed.

After a moment's silence he asked, 'Is this what you do all the time?'

'Yeah,' said Jack.

Jason felt obscurely guilty as he stumbled tipsily through the darkness back to Tom's caravan. In his hand he clutched a part-drunk bottle of wine from Laurent's stock. A peace offering? What? Part of the problem was that he had made no formal arrangement with Tom about staying with him beyond that first night. They hadn't discussed it at all. Others at the fair – Jack, Laurent, Annie – had all seemed to make the assumption that he would be travelling with them. Tom had said nothing at all on the subject.

As quietly as he could Jason opened the door of the pitch-black caravan. At least the door was unlocked – that was something. He could hear the slow, measured breathing of the sleeping man as he tiptoed across the floor.

Something was wrong. Where the fuck was the bed? Jason felt his foot catch against something. He sprawled forward, crashing into the toilet cubicle, and hit the floor hard. The caravan shook; the wine bottle rolled across the floor, noisily shedding its contents.

He must be more drunk than he thought.

Tom was awake, he could tell. There was a long, expectant silence, then Tom's voice cut through the darkness.

'Are you all right?' he said blandly.

'I brought you some wine,' Jason replied lamely.

Another pause.

'No,' said Tom. 'Thank you.'

'Jack told me you wouldn't,' said Jason.

'You've been with Jack.'

Was there an edge to Tom's voice?

'Yeah, so what?' Jason snapped defensively.

'Jack's obsessed,' said Tom. 'That's all.'

'Obsessed? With what?'

'If you've spent the evening with Jack you already know the answer to that, Jason. He tried it with me when I first came here. Look what he's turned Laurent into. Jack's a sexual obsessive.'

Suddenly Tom sounded tired.

'Seems to me everyone around here's obsessed by something,' Jason sneered. 'Even you. Jack told me – you live like a fucking monk. You don't drink, you don't smoke, you don't shag . . . Look at this place!' – Jason gesticulated into the darkness – 'You never leave the fucking fairground!'

'I've got my reasons for being here,' said Tom evenly. 'Like we all have. Go to sleep.'

Jason sat motionless on the floor. He heard Tom turning over in the bed. After a moment Tom grunted, 'You can get in if you like.'

Drunkenly self-conscious, Jason struggled out of his clothes and climbed into the bed. This time he lay with his back to Tom, careful that their bodies should not touch. He lay there for hours, staring into the blackness, waiting for unwilling sleep to come.

Five

_____

The fair stayed three more nights in the field outside Harpenden. Three more nights of steadily improving spring weather
and steadily dwindling audiences. Matthew and Paul had gone; in
fact there seemed little at all to satisfy Jack in his ongoing shag-
quest.

'Are you any good at painting?' Jack asked Jason on the morning
of their final day there.

'Not bad,' Jason replied. 'Why?'

Somebody had taken a spray-can to one of the side-panels of
the Tunnel of Love. A huge, stylised cock-and-balls.

'If only . . .' Jack lamented, casting his eyes skyward. 'Somebody
up there's taking the piss.'

The Tunnel of Love was painted, predictably, with hearts and
ribbons and flying cupids, all on a baby-blue background. Jason
grinned. The addition of a great, crude phallic totem, around
which the cupids now fluttered, seemed refreshingly honest to
him. He would paint the tricky bits; Jack would fill in the
blue.

'Yeah,' he said, applying the first touches. 'I used to be pretty
good at this in school.'

'I was expelled from school,' said Jack. 'Public school. Very
high morals.'

'Don't tell me . . .'

'Oh, I was caught in too many compromising situations,' Jack said, smiling nostalgically.

'I thought that's what all the kids did in boarding school,' said Jason.

'Ah, but it wasn't just the kids. If I'd stuck to the other kids I'd have been all right. But no . . . Teachers, the odd groundsman . . .'

Jason shook his head, laughing, and carried on applying the paint. They worked together in silence for a while.

'So how did you end up here?' Jason eventually asked.

Jack shrugged.

'Much like you, I guess. I just turned up one night. I met Rex. We ended up in bed together.'

'Rex?'

'Oh, Rex – if you believe half his stories – used to be quite something,' said Jack. 'Back in his circus days he claims to have slept with crowned heads of Europe . . . He claims to have caught clap off a survivor of the Russian Imperial family. He's full of shit, of course. Now he generally describes himself – and here I think he's on the level – as a burned-out old queen.'

Jack slapped a great glob of sky-blue paint carelessly on to the wooden board.

'We only slept together the once, but somehow – you know what it's like, Jason – once you've got a taste of this place you end up staying. It was three years ago I came here. There have been others who've come and gone in that time. Some are always popping in and out, travelling with us a few months, disappearing, reappearing . . . None ever seem to leave for good . . . We're the Lost Boys, Jason. This is our home.'

'And what about Tom?'

'Ah, Tom . . .'

Only half-concentrating on his work, Jason was aware of Jack's burning gaze and knowing smile beside him.

'Tom's a real dark horse,' said Jack. 'He turned up about a year and a half, two years ago. I tried to get off with him, of course – a matter of principle, really – but I got nowhere. Now that might just mean he's straight – '

'Or it might mean he doesn't fancy you,' Jason cut in.

Jack adopted a haughty expression.

'As I was saying,' he continued, 'Tom . . . I don't know very much about him. I know he had his problems in the army . . . He doesn't really talk to anybody, except Rex, and it's pointless asking him. He'd just make up something lurid and cheesy. No, I've given up trying to figure Tom out. He eats on his own. He works. Most mornings he exercises himself stupid before anybody else is out of bed. I tell you, he's a raving Muscle Mary! He does press-ups on the base of the Wheel, sit-ups and all that stuff, then he climbs up the Wheel and does all these pull-ups, all this gymnastic stuff, twenty feet up. Then he goes for a run, then he works like a bastard all day. It's a mystery to me.'

The paint from Jack's brush dripped steadily onto the ground and his shoe. Jack didn't notice. He was struck by a further thought. 'Have you seen that film, with Jeremy Irons and Robert de Niro and loads of pretty Red Indian boys? *The Mission*. The bit where de Niro is climbing the mountain, hauling this huge net full of junk behind him as a punishment, a penance. He killed his brother in a duel, or something. That's who Tom reminds me of. Maybe something really bad happened to him in the army . . . Maybe he was in some war. Maybe he was gassed . . . I don't know. You're sleeping with him, for fuck's sake. *You* tell *me* what his problem is!'

But Jason couldn't. It was strange. Each night after the fair closed Jason would return to Tom's silent caravan and bed to sleep. They shared the same bed, but seldom spoke. By day each went about his tasks, more or less ignoring the other. But Jason watched Tom all the time. He had an air about him which, whilst not hostile, seemed to say Keep Out. Jason was curious, but relieved.

'And what about you?' Jack asked. 'What's your story?'

Jason immediately looked away from Jack. Suddenly the paint-job demanded all of his attention.

'Nothing to tell, really,' he said. 'I was homeless.'

'Jesus,' said Jack. 'You're just as bad as Tom.'

By the time they were ready to move pitch Jason had become quite adept at hopping from car to car with Crash Annie. They made a good team, he and the feisty old dear. After a hard night's work, when Tom retired to his solitary suppers and Jack and Laurent were engaged in trawling the town for action, Jason was becoming accustomed to dining in the caravan shared by Annie and her brother Doug, the dapper little man who operated the Waltzers, and who had had the run-in with Nige and his cronies that first night.

Their caravan was a delight to enter. You felt as if you were stepping into an east-European fairy-tale. Longer than most, the caravan was divided down the middle by a wooden rail from which hung a huge array of clothes. The rail served as a wardrobe for both Doug and Annie, who seemed to have endless variations on their customary theme: practical jeans and shirts (Jason couldn't tell which were his and which were hers) hung among shawls, scarves and lace, embroidered waistcoats, braces, even a pair of lederhosen. The rail also split the caravan into two distinct domains – his and hers. Annie's half of the little house-on-wheels resembled a tent – every inch of wall- and ceiling-space was hung with embroideries which swayed gently whenever a breeze blew in through the wholly hidden windows. Fresh flowers curled everywhere around these lush tapestries, and ornate china dolls stood in vigilant rows on shelves and tables. There was even – Jason had to stifle a laugh – a crystal ball on a stand next to her bed.

You had to step under the clothes-rail, which ran the full width of the caravan, to reach Doug's half. This was just as striking. Jason immediately thought of Gepetto's workshop in the old Disney film. Doug was responsible, it seemed, for the carved woodwork which edged many of the rides and stalls. Apart from the narrow bed which ran along the far wall, his space was dominated by a large workbench. Elaborately worked wood lay everywhere – abstract swirls and curves, evidently destined to edge one or other of the little fair's attractions, beautifully lacquered wooden boxes, a half-finished chess set. Screens and shutters obscured the walls and windows just as effectively as did Annie's tapestries. It was on the mighty workbench that the three of them, Annie, Doug and Jason, would take their nightly supper.

Doug and Annie, it seemed, had been with Gamlin's for longer than just about anyone, with the exception of old Piper. They were twins. Watching them sitting together, eating together, Jason could see the striking resemblance between them. They were about the same size, with the same bright, beady eyes, berry-like complexion and hair so dark it looked dyed. Their voices were the same – husky with the continuous chain of cigarettes they both smoked.

They were friendly, but reticent when it came to discussing the personalities who made up the little fairground community. Jason asked them, of course, about Tom, only to be gently rebuked for his curiosity.

'Everybody comes to Gamlin's for a reason,' Annie said to him over a rich stew. 'Sometimes they don't even know what the reason is when they come here. Everybody here has their secrets, whether they realise it or not. You should respect that. Gamlin's is a place of secrets.'

She reached across the workbench to Jason and stroked his ear. He felt something cold and metallic. From inside his ear Annie had produced a pound coin. The oldest trick in the book – but then, that was Gamlin's. Nothing was very new here.

'Don't forget, this is a fair,' she said. 'It's a place of illusion. You've got to accept it at face value. It's always a mistake to go digging around in fairground dirt. And what is true for most fairs is doubly so for Gamlin's.'

The fair moved north. The morning of the move was probably the hardest of Jason's life. Tom shook him awake at seven in the morning. Christ, seven! The big man rolled out of bed and writhed into a tight T-shirt, pants and jeans. Jason watched his rippling back and arms through half-sleeping eyes.

'Why d'you do this?' Jason mumbled. 'I'd get a proper job if I could handle this shit.'

'This is a lie-in for me,' said Tom. 'See you at the Wheel. Five minutes.'

Breaking down the heavy equipment, lashing it together and loading the trucks was the most work Jason had ever crammed into a morning. Nobody spoke much – everybody was channelling all their energy into the work. Only Tom seemed to enjoy it.

By midday they were ready to leave. Jason – still horribly hung-over – just wanted to go back to bed. He sat up next to Tom in the cab of the truck which carried the Big Wheel and towed Tom's caravan.

'Is that legal?' Jason asked as he climbed aboard.

Tom merely shrugged.

For half an hour they drove in silence. Jason was becoming hypnotised by the broken white lines streaming out of sight under the big old vehicle.

'This is fun,' he said pettishly.

Tom didn't reply.

'What is it with you?' Jason said, after a pause. 'Silent order, is it?'

'What?' asked Tom irritably.

'Jack and Laurent call you the Mad Monk. Among other things. It's like you gave up living for Lent.'

Tom pursed his lips in irritation.

'You're not in the army now, you know,' said Jason.

Tom shot him an angry glance and pushed his foot down on the accelerator.

'Why'd you leave the army anyway?' Jason asked. 'Not miserable enough for you? Not enough discipline? You should join the Foreign Legion.'

'Maybe you're right,' said Tom. 'People join the Foreign Legion to forget. Just like Gamlin's.'

He swerved to avoid something in the road.

'Christ, slow down!' snapped Jason.

The truck was going too fast, rattling and rolling along the road's too-tight bends. In his wing-mirror Jason could see the caravan swinging alarmingly from side to side behind them. Tom showed no sign of slowing.

'Look, I'm sorry!' Jason was becoming alarmed. He was a lousy road-passenger.

'I'll shut up, OK?' he said. 'Just slow down!'

He was shouting now. 'Fucking slow down! I'm going to be sick!'

With a heavy exhalation of breath Tom eased his foot back on the accelerator. The vehicle steadied itself. He brought it to a halt at the side of the road. Jason scrabbled for the handle. He practically fell into the gutter.

'You OK?'

Jason nodded, steadying himself against the side of the vehicle.

'I just . . . I . . .'

'It's OK,' said Tom. 'You don't have to tell me.'

Jason climbed back in and Tom pulled into the road again.

'Thirty,' said Jason. 'OK?'

Tom nodded, saying nothing, slowly shifting up the gears. It was some minutes before he broke the silence.

'Why all the questions suddenly?'

Jason was taken aback. It took him a moment to answer.

'It's just . . . Well, you seem to say less and less each day. You get up before dawn, exercise, work, hardly eat, never talk to anyone. I'm not the only one who's noticing it. People are starting to blame me.'

It was true. The previous night Rex had asked him, half in jest, what he was doing to 'poor, sweet, innocent Tom'. Even the punters, it seemed, were noticing Tom's growing reticence. One had asked Rex what was up with his colleague.

'You remember the first night you stayed in my caravan?' Tom asked.

'Of course,' Jason replied.

'I was asking you about Newcastle. You as good as told me to mind my own fucking business. Remember? Yeah, I was a soldier. I'm not any more. End of story. OK?'

He swung a right off the main road

'Some other time, maybe. But not now.'

'OK.'

They stopped on a patch of wilderness outside Northampton, close to a lake dotted with the sails of windsurfers. By the time they had set up the equipment Jason was exhausted. He had helped with the erection of the Wheel, the Bumper Cars and the Merry-Go-Round.

'What . . .?' Jason gasped. Doug was carefully hanging the out-of-order sign on the Merry-Go-Round. 'You mean it's still not working? Why the fuck have we just spent two hours putting it up?'

'Can't have a fair without a Merry-Go-Round. The punters wouldn't come. It's traditional. It's lucky. Piper reckons the whole fair sort of revolves around it, like a pivot.'

'So why the fuck doesn't someone try to fix it?'

Doug shook his head slowly, drawing in breath through his teeth.

'Death trap,' he said, and walked away.

Jason couldn't be bothered to argue. He was too knackered. Too hung-over, still. He felt ill. He sat down heavily on the side of the Merry-Go-Round.

'The day's barely begun, boy,' said Annie, approaching him. 'Showtime in less than an hour.'

'Annie . . . I don't know if I can do it tonight. I feel fucking awful,' Jason replied. 'Can you manage without me?'

'I did for nearly a decade, love,' the woman replied.

Jason limped off to Tom's caravan. Tom himself was tinkering with the engine of the Wheel. Once inside Jason closed the door and collapsed onto the bed.

He liked Annie. No nonsense. She reminded him of his mum.

He hated his mum.

Everything was so confusing round here. Tom especially. What did he want from Tom? What was he after? Jason's attempt to prise some information out of Tom in the truck had gone badly awry. He'd spazzed out in front of him, for fuck's sake. Inadvertently, Tom had hit on Jason's Achilles heel.

That was what he would have to do with Tom. Expose a few nerve endings. He reckoned he knew how to do it, as well.

He waited until he saw the fairground's coloured lights wink into life and heard the night's first barrel-organ strains. He rose from the bed, drew the curtains on the caravan's windows and locked the door. Then he squatted in front of the little bedside cupboard and opened the drawer.

He had searched the drawer that first night when Tom had locked him in the caravan. He had found, among other things, a pile of old family photos and a stack of letters. He hadn't read them at the time. Since then he had noticed how solicitously Tom opened and closed the drawer whenever he had occasion to take anything from inside it.

Carefully Jason extracted the letters and began leafing through them. Some were from his parents. They followed Tom the soldier from posting to posting, HMSO number by HMSO number, around the world. Germany, Gibraltar, Belize . . . The letters didn't say much – they were uninteresting, and largely whining in tone. Annoyingly they seemed to allude to old family matters, without actually naming names or stating facts.

Towards the bottom of the pile were the most recent communications, all from Germany. Here the tone was notably darker. *Coping with the tragedy, taking each day as it comes . . . Maybe you should think of leaving the army . . . Perhaps you should see a doctor . . . Counting on you to be strong . . . How can you expect us to cope with this, on top of everything else . . .*

At the bottom of the pile was a formal letter on stiff paper. It was official notice of Corporal Tom Jarrett's discharge from Her Majesty's Armed Forces. Dishonourable discharge by Court Martial.

The door-handle turned.

Jason's heart lurched. He dropped the letters clutched in his hand. They sailed to the floor.

A key was turning in the lock.

Frantically he scraped them back into a pile, thrust them into the drawer and slammed it shut.

The door opened.

'Jason . . .'

Laurent.

'What d'you want? How the fuck did you get that key?'

Relief and annoyance vied for precedence in Jason's voice.

'Most of the caravans here are rubbish,' said Laurent. 'You can open them with any key. I have a message from Jacques.'

It was cute, the way Laurent always pronounced his friend's name.

'He invites you into the Tunnel of Love with him.'

'What?'

'*Ah, non.* Please, you misunderstand me,' said Laurent hastily.

'He wants you to go and sit at the top of the stairs with him. Perhaps you will enjoy it. *C'est très interessant.*'

'Yeah . . . why not?' Jason replied. Suddenly the caravan seemed too small. Suddenly it would be a relief to get out. 'Give me five minutes . . .'

'OK, said Laurent. 'But don't be too long. You do not want to miss the show.

'Side door,' he added as he left.

Somewhat puzzled, Jason turned his attention back to the drawer.

He took the letters out again and straightened the bundle. He flicked quickly through the photographs. He removed one that he was sure was of Tom – a much younger Tom – and his family. He gazed at it for a moment before putting it carefully inside his shirt.

Then he straightened and closed the drawer for the final time, and walked out of the little caravan.

The Tunnel of Love was lit up like the Big Rock Candy Mountain. Jason cut through the crowd and slipped around the side of the gaudy, bulky structure to where a thin rectangle of light in the wooden wall indicated a door. Slowly he opened it. A bulb-lit flight of wooden steps led up into shadows. Jason slowly ascended the staircase.

'Come in.' Jack's voice floated languidly down to him.

Reaching the top of the stairs Jason stopped. The area in front of him looked as if it was lit by moonlight. Flooded by moonlight.

'Welcome to the observation deck,' cooed Jack.

Jason found himself standing on a broad wooden platform, extending out perhaps eight feet on either side of him and ten feet ahead. It was bare except for a single item of furniture: a chaise longue, perched close to the furthest edge of the platform, on which Jack was reclining.

Jason moved forward. The moonlight was flooding up around the platform. It seemed to come from below.

Reaching the edge, Jason gasped. Fifteen feet below him lay the Tunnel of Love – an absurd, impossible love idyll in a huge box. A stream wound its way around green hills clustered with trees. The whole tableau was silver-lit with artificial moonlight. The moonlight seemed to come from everywhere, throwing the fake trees into stark silhouette, their flat, shadow branches writhing together like snakes.

Along the stream little boats bobbed idly, one by one, each just out of sight of the others, behind some hill, screened by trees or just around some turn in the stream. Barring the peeping prow or just-disappearing stern of another lazy boat, the couples who clung and kissed and squeezed in the boats were completely alone in this paint-and-plaster paradise.

The effect was compelling. The Little-Bo-Peep vista seemed to go on for ever. Jason stepped right up to the edge.

'Careful,' called Jack. 'The net's not as strong as it used to be.'

For the first time Jason noticed the net which stretched loosely over the drop, hanging, swaying slightly, between their platform and the paradise below.

'I always think it's like gazing at Eden through the bars of a cage,' said Jack mournfully.

He waved an arm in Jason's direction. He was handing Jason a spliff.

Shit. Jason hadn't done too much of this stuff recently.

But who can ever refuse? Jason plucked it out of Jack's fingers, pursed his lips around it and took a deep draw. He coughed, then took another toke.

'This is my little treat to myself,' said Jack. 'I come up here, smoke a little, drink a little' – he lifted a practically full bottle of malt whiskey from beside the chaise longue – 'and watch the show.'

'Hang on . . .' Jason passed the joint to Jack. 'If you're up here, who's operating the ride?'

'Oh, that's covered,' said Jack with a wave of his hand. 'Kevin and Willow Simpson are doing it.'

'Who?'

'You know. Mavis's grandchildren.'

'Kevin and . . . those kids!?' Jason exclaimed. 'What are they? Ten? Eleven?'

'Kevin's nearly twelve,' said Jack defensively.

'So you let a couple of babies run this huge machine every night.'

'Good God, no!' Jack exclaimed. 'No . . . Just once in a while. Just on . . . special nights.'

'Special nights . . .?'

'Oh yes,' said Jack, warming to his theme. 'It all depends whereabouts we are. Since I first came to Gamlin's I've been keeping a chart of the best pulling-grounds up and down the country.'

'And this is a good one?'

'Have you seen out there tonight?' Jack squealed. 'The whole place is crawling with poofs! It must be some kind of poof holiday!'

'So . . .' Jason didn't understand.

'So whilst Willow works the controls, Kevin juggles the crowd, pitches to the gay couples, gets them to come on in a bunch if he can. Then, when they're in the grotto Willow will slow down or gradually stop the water-pumps. The stream will stop flowing and the boats will glide to a halt. Then the magic takes over.'

'And you . . .'

'Oh, I just watch. This is my night off.'

He handed Jason the whiskey bottle.

'Make yourself at home,' he said.

Jason glugged on the bottle's neck.

'By the way,' said Jack, 'Kevin and Willow are sworn to secrecy. I'd rather nobody else in the fair knew about this. Laurent knows, of course.'

Jason looked around the platform. 'What is this place?' he asked.

'It's supposed to be for storing stuff,' replied Jack. 'That's why the net is there – to catch anything that falls. Trouble is, the net's so knackered that we daren't keep anything up here. There's a proper store-room below. We're on the roof of it, if you like. And below that is the engine. That's why it's so warm up here.'

He was right. It was unusually warm.

'Sit down,' said Jack. 'Make yourself at home. Sorry there's no furniture.'

He lay back on the chaise longue and sucked on the reefer.

★ ★ ★

'When does the show start?' slurred Jason.

The bottle of whiskey was nearly empty. Spliff-butts and tight nodules of ash lay scattered across the wooden boards.

'That's down to the kids,' said Jack. 'Any time . . . There!'

The lightbulb on the stairs had gone out.

'That's the signal,' said Jack. He swivelled around on the chaise longue's smooth, hard leather surface and craned his neck over the edge of the platform. Jason sat on the bare wooden planks next to the elegant sofa and peered over the drop.

Below them they could see three boats, bathed in moonlight. In each boat sat a couple. All men.

'Kevin's done well,' Jack whispered.

'How d'you know anything'll happen?' Jason whispered back.

'This is the Tunnel of Love,' Jack replied. 'In here you can have your heart's desire, and who can resist that?'

The couple in the first boat were holding hands and whispering sweet nothings to one another.

The second boat's occupants were a little further gone. One man was practically on top of the other. They struggled and wrestled, their mouths locked together in a long, deep, breathless kiss.

One man sat alone in the third boat, his legs spread, his arms wide, his head lolling backwards against the boatframe. No – he wasn't alone. A head of dark hair bobbed into sight in the man's lap, then disappeared into the shadows again.

The music. For the first time Jason noticed the music. Sensual, almost subliminal, ghostly chords and deep bass pulses.

The slow boats seemed to be getting slower. Gently they bobbed to a halt. A whispered consultation, then the first couple climbed from their boat on to one of the artificial hillocks. They were a tall, lean, well-toned man, probably in his forties, with a handsome, smooth face and severe grey hair, his partner shorter, bulkier, heavily muscular, about thirty with a crew-cut. Holding each other close, they strolled among a group of a half-dozen little trees.

The second couple, only about eighteen – expensive trainers, jogging bottoms, one in a baseball cap (worn backwards, of course)

– were also out of their boat. They were sprawled on the river bank, one on top of the other. As Jason watched they tore at each other's sweat-pants, wriggling together as they dragged them downward, briefs and all, until they tangled round their Nike-clad feet. The one on top hitched up his puffa-jacket to reveal a tight, round arse, which rose and fell in a smooth, rolling motion as the boy rubbed his cock up and down along his partner's rigid pole. The boy underneath, knees apart, arched his back upwards, raising his buttocks from the ground, bringing his hard cock up to meet his partner's groin and belly.

Only the third boat was still occupied. The couple, both hastily naked, were attempting to perform an elaborate sixty-nine on the padded seat of the little craft. One looked Scandinavian – tall and lanky, with white-blond hair and pale skin – whilst the other was black, lithe and stringy. The blond boy was perched upside-down, his shoulders on the seat, his head hanging, his buttocks against the seat-back and his legs lolling in the air. Half-squatting in the boat, the black boy was facing him, his cock moving rapidly in and out of Blondie's mouth, whilst his own mouth was wide, and half-swallowing Blondie's cock. The love-boat teetered alarmingly beneath them.

Jack tapped Jason on the shoulder. He was waving another joint at him. Christ . . .

Shuddering as he did so, Jason took another heavy pull. The drugs and booze had definitely shifted the moonlight up a gear. Now the light seemed almost crystalline – everything glinted icily, almost tangible points of light came off corners and curves.

He took another drag and offered the joint back to Jack.

'Finish it,' Jack mumbled. He was sprawled on his stomach on the chaise longue, still craning his neck over the edge. His jeans were rumpled and baggy around his buttocks now. His trousers were undone, and slightly down. He was rubbing his crotch rhythmically against the chaise longue. Between his bucking body and the couch Jason could catch glimpses of Jack's cock, rigid and red and burnished as he ground it into the hard leather.

Jason was wasted. He felt a warm, static glow all over. He moved as if through treacle, sliding across the rim of the platform until his shoulder was practically pressing against Jack's ear. He reached down and began stroking himself through the thickness of his jeans.

Below them the lovers rolled in clover. The first couple were undressing each other frantically, clutching and ripping at each other's clothes and discarding them across the branches of the trees. The older man's shirt was open; his penis jutted upward and outward from the front of his trousers. His burly partner – tanned, naked except for a tight white vest – dropped to his knees and sunk his mouth over the jutting member.

Still largely clothed, the second couple – the teenies – were on all fours. One was pushing his mouth between the buttocks of the other, his tongue snaking out to probe the boy's dark crevice. Slowly he slid up his young partner's back, pushing his sweat-shirt up as he advanced. Then, looking down the length of his body, he took hold of his prick and eased it into the spit-wet crack. He began a gentle sickle-motion with his pelvis, gradually increasing in force and speed as his cock slid in and out of his friend's arsehole.

The third couple had tumbled from the boat and crawled ashore. Blondie lay on his back whilst his black friend sat astride his thighs. The black guy had both cocks in one hand – the one, long and slender and oh-so-pale, the other thick and dark, with a swollen purple head. Blondie's neck was arched, his head craning back so that he could watch, further along the bank, the teenagers, one astride the other like a pair of young dogs.

Sitting cross-legged, on the furthest extremity of the wooden planks, his knees over the drop, Jason vacantly rubbed his crotch through his jeans. Soon his hand slipped between the buttons of his fly and loosed his cock from its moorings.

He barely heard Jack's murmur of approval at his ear. His mind was elsewhere. The grotto reminded him of distant memories. The time he and Spider went out to the country, way outside Newcastle. They had run and played like kiddies, dodging among trees, tumbling over bracken. It had been a hot day. They had come upon a fast-flowing stream and had stripped naked, giggling like shy children at the familiar sight of one another's fit, slim bodies and swelling cocks. Spider had dived into the stream. Jason had followed. For the next hour they had thrashed about in the water, wrestling, trying to pull each other under, their wet bodies slipping and sliding off each other like eels. They had invented a game called Cock-Diving, where each had to, by swimming under the water, grab the other's cock whilst preventing his opponent doing the same to him.

At last they had climbed from the stream and lain naked on the grass in the sun. Spider had been still for about a minute before springing to his feet and, still naked, swinging up into a massive oak tree. He had sprawled on his back in the huge, shallow crook formed where the thick lower branches grew from the trunk.

'Why not come up here and dry off?' he had asked.

'Jason . . .' Jack groaned as he came. From the corner of his eye Jason saw spunk squeezing up between the leather saddle of the chaise longue and Jack's T-shirt.

Jason was swaying slightly as he sat, his hands still in his lap, staring into the far corner of the grotto.

The trees seemed bigger there. Not the flimsy cardboard things under which the happy boaters frolicked. There was a fourth couple, whom he hadn't noticed before. They were lying on their backs on the grass, naked. They looked to be in their mid-to-late teens. The light seemed to glisten wetly on their skin. Suddenly one of them sprang to his feet and, reaching up, swung himself into one of the trees. He voiced something down to the other one.

The other one shinned up the tree and slid on top of his friend. They lay like that for a while, wriggling and writhing, their movements gradually getting harder and more rhythmical, more deliberate.

It seemed to Jason that, even at this distance, he could make out every detail of their bodies. The one underneath – the one who had first ascended the tree – sported a shock of black hair and a deep, natural tan. An appendix scar sat on the left side of his lower abdomen; other scars criss-crossed his arms and shoulders. He pressed down with his feet on the body of the tree, arching his back and raising his buttocks, spreading his cheeks with his hands. Slowly the boy on top eased his cock into the other boy's exposed hole.

The boy on top . . . Dirty blond locks that hung in straight fronds about his face. Scars to rival those of his partner.

Something fell from the knot of bodies and caught on a branch below. It glinted in the moonlight – a leather thong, with a silver spider hanging from it.

Mouth open, eyes staring, Jason was watching his youth as if on an old home movie. He could feel Spider's buttock cheeks, tight around his cock . . .

Letting out a moan, Jason pitched forward on the edge of the platform.

'No . . .!' Jack called, distantly, somewhere behind him.

He was falling. The floor of the ride below was suddenly rushing towards him. He spread his arms and legs, flailing wildly. Then suddenly he was caught in something, bouncing in mid-air.

The net wrapped itself around his arms and legs and held him there, a human spider on its web, suspended above the world.

Jason bobbed helplessly in the net. Feebly he tried to free his arms and legs.

He could hear Jack shouting behind him.

'Get off there! I told you the net's not safe!'

Jason could hear a distant ripping, wrenching sound. The net lurched under him. It dropped several feet. The ripping sound got louder and more urgent.

Suddenly the net collapsed beneath him, carrying him down towards the fake fields below. It bounced to a stop perhaps eight feet down, then dropped for the final time, depositing Jason in the artificial stream.

The water was real enough, shallow and warm and greasy. Jason spluttered and thrashed. His head went under before he managed to orientate himself and haul up onto the bank. He could hear scuffling noises around him. He had broken the spell. Like the startled woodland creatures they were, the couples were disappearing behind hills and trees, grabbing handfuls of clothing as they fled.

He could hear a big dog, somewhere outside, barking itself into a frenzy.

'Jason!' Jack called from the sky.

He didn't answer. He stumbled towards where he thought the entrance ought to be. He could hear the usual fairground music now, faint but getting gradually louder.

There was a distant snarling, and then the dog fell silent.

Jason practically fell out of the front of the Tunnel of Love. Young Willow Simpson was explaining to an impatient line of customers that there was a temporary breakdown which was even now being repaired.

A woman shrieked as Jason appeared from the mouth of the tunnel, staggered about, suddenly confused, and bumped against the painted backboard (yet more gently painted hills, spring lambs frozen in mid-gambol). A man shouted as he stumbled through the line of boats waiting to carry off the next contingent of lovers, fell down the steps and ploughed through the waiting line.

He barely noticed.

Laurent's voice shouted something from somewhere. He had no idea what he was saying. He stumbled past old Piper, sitting on the steps of the Ghost Train, ignoring his customers and watching Jason intently.

His dog was gone. The rope which usually restrained it lay limp on the ground.

Jason stumbled across the crowded fairground with no idea where he was going. Annie moved to intercept him, a look of concern on her face. She reached out a hand. He heard himself laughing horribly. He staggered past her and ran blindly on.

In here you can have your heart's desire – why did everyone in this fucking place talk in riddles? He had seen Spider! He had felt him!

He stopped, breathless. He was in the woods beyond the fair, close to the lake. It was very dark here. The fair twinkled and wheezed in the distance.

He heard rapid movement up ahead.

Relax. It's a wood. Of course there's going to be movement.

As a city boy he'd never quite got used to green spaces at night.

His head was still spinning. Images loomed out of the darkness. He tried closing his eyes. They still came. Somewhere in the mix were Spider and himself, still tree-bound, making love. In a wood much like this.

He heard a dog barking. There had been a dog on that day, too, a distant farm-dog whose voice had somehow epitomised the lonely, lazy summer's afternoon. Jason had climbed up the tree next to Spider and crawled on top of him. Their naked, wet bodies had squirmed and slipped against one another. Spider had a beautiful body, small and slim and lithe, Mediterranean skin (rare in Newcastle), and a shock of loose, curly black hair. His dark eyes twinkled like coal; his wicked smile rarely left his face.

Their hard cocks skidded together. Jason slid down Spider's body until his friend's slim, beautiful cock was level with his mouth. He traced the outline of Spider's cock, running his tongue up one side of the shaft and over the bulbous head. A single drop of clear fluid appeared at the end of it. Jason took the droplet up with his tongue. His mouth folded around Spider's bulb, his lips sucked their way down his shaft.

Spider turned on to his side, forcing Jason around. Without removing his cock, Spider swivelled through a hundred and eighty degrees, hanging for a moment between branches. He settled himself in position and took Jason's cock in his mouth. The two boys sucked and squirmed until each could feel the other's hot come splashing in his mouth, balls tight, bellies bucking in orgasm.

Jason felt a cold draught against his hard cock. For the first time he realised that it was poking out of his jeans. He had taken it out on the platform with Jack, just before he had fallen.

It had been hanging out all this time. He must have stumbled through the fair with it out . . .

He reached to tuck it back into his jeans, but instead found himself squeezing and stroking it. He crushed his helmet in his fist, pulling the foreskin out slightly, then drew his hand slowly back, peeling the foreskin away to reveal his bright, peeping bulb.

Somewhere out there Spider still swung in the trees. Jason looked down through the darkness at his hand pumping his cock. He liked watching himself wank. He came quickly, spattering a gorse bush with spunk. He wiped his cock on some leaves and tucked it away.

His vision was still popping with mini-hallucinations, but the images were more jumbled now, occasionally breaking the surface before sinking again in a sea of shape and colour.

He heard a low growling somewhere in front of him. He felt his panic rising. He turned and tried to move away from the sound, but stopped. It still seemed to be coming from in front of him. The beast was circling him. He turned again, choosing another direction. He started to run.

He stopped in a clearing. There was something there. Breathing, panting. He took a step forward. In the gloom he could just about make out a shape, low in the grass in front of him. He moved closer, his eyes straining to cut through their own insistent slideshow of images and into the darkness beyond.

It was a man. He was on all fours, facing Jason. His hair was long and black, hanging down over a sharp, leathery face, deeply grooved. He wore a long leather overcoat, the ends of which trailed the dark ground. He stared up at Jason through big, black eyes surmounted with heavy brows.

Jason was sure he'd seen him before.

His coat was open. He wore nothing underneath it. Craning forward on his knees, he used one hand to support himself. The other was pumping at a long, slender, red cock. The man opened his mouth wide, revealing a line of sharp, irregular teeth. From deep in his throat an animal snarl emerged.

Jason couldn't handle this. Not now. He turned and ran. Deeper into the trees. He heard the dog's low growl again, once more from the direction he was heading.

This thing was sending him in circles. He didn't know which way to run. He slumped against a tree and buried his head in his hands.

Christ, what was happening to him?

He began to grope his way slowly back to where he hoped the fair was. The growling seemed distant now, and behind him. He was surprised, emerging from the trees, to see how far from the fair he had strayed. It sat on the horizon like some gaudy, plug-in Christmas ornament. By the time he reached the huddle of caravans the last of the customers had gone and most of the lights had winked out.

'Evenin'.'

Jason stopped and turned. Piper, sitting as ever on the steps of the Ghost Train, had just spoken to him.

'Wha . . . Uh . . .' Jason spluttered.

The old man rose creakily from his seat, arched his head back and gave a piercing whistle. In the distance a dog barked.

'Old Black Shuck,' the man chuckled. 'Off about his business.'

'I . . . think he's in the woods somewhere,' said Jason.

'Maybe,' said the old man. 'Maybe. Could be anywhere, from that bark. He's got a hell of a bark, has Black Shuck. No, he goes where he will by night. '

Piper drew long and hard on his tobacco-pipe.

'I keeps him tied up by day . . . but by night he's his own master. By night he goes where he will. He goes his way and I goes mine. Which is generally to bed.'

The old man turned and shuffled in the direction of his caravan.

The fairground was deserted now. Ahead of Jason the giant skeleton of the Big Wheel loomed over the rest of the attractions. Behind him the lit windows of the clustered caravans shed pale light on the darkness.

He wandered across to the Tunnel of Love. Painted cupidons winked out of the darkness at Jason as he drew close. He tried to see it for what it was – a charming, childish piece of whimsy. Pure romantic escapism, a quid a go.

Why did so many of the rides give the impression that they concealed something more – something above and beyond the simple lure of the painted boards and coloured bulbs?

He thought again of what Annie had said. *Gamlin's is a place of secrets.*

She had warned him not to go digging around in fairground dirt, but more and more Jason was feeling that he was standing still, that it was the ground beneath him that was shifting, and he was being slowly sucked down into it.

He remembered a film he'd once seen, set in a fair. A disused fair, at night. An eerie carnival where the worlds of the living and the dead met. His eyes roved around the ghostly, unlit rides. Fairs were made for people; laughing, shouting people. They were strange places when the lights were out and the people gone.

Maybe that's what was getting to him. Maybe that's all this was: what was left, slumbering in the dark; what became at night of the great illusion, the magic of the fair.

Six

D^{ear Glen,} he wrote.

Hey, dude, how's it hanging?

He crossed that out.

I'm not sure I can hold this together, he wrote. *It's late and I smoked a load of gear and drank a bottle of whisky earlier. I hope you're still at the squat, cos otherwise this will never ever reach you. You'll never guess what I've done. Don't laugh — I've run away and joined the fair. You know, the fair we went to the other week. I'm travelling with them now.*

It's a bit weird here. It's like another world, and I don't know whether I like it or not. The other day I saw a woman go into the Hall of Mirrors and not come out for four hours, and when she did come out she looked as if she'd been lobotomised. Then tonight I had a weird one in the Tunnel of Love. I don't want to say what it was, but it was some kind of hallucination. It nearly made me break my neck.

There's a guy here called Tom.

He crossed that out.

The people here are OK I suppose. Most of them are nice, but they're a bit weird too. There's an old girl called Crash Annie, who I work with on the Bumper Cars most nights. She's cool, and a couple of the young blokes here just live for sex. But I sometimes feel like they're all in on some kind of joke at my expense. Some kind of conspiracy. God, I sound paranoid.

Anyway, if this letter reaches you I hope you will be able to reply to me, although I don't know how you will manage this, as we're on the move all the time. I miss you, Glen. I miss your sanity in this bughouse.

Look after yourself, and I hope to see you soon.

Love, Jase.

XXXXXX

Jason was woken by a tapping on the window over the bed. Eyes crusted shut with sleep he sprawled and stretched across the narrow mattress. He could feel from the empty space that Tom was, as usual, already up and about his simple devotions. It had been late the previous night when Jason had finally crept in, his mind still rushing about in confusion. He had tiptoed to the far end of the caravan, anxious not to wake the sleeping Tom, switched on a little table-lamp and written a letter. He had waited long for his head at last to start winding down and fatigue to overrun him.

He flexed his still-sleeping muscles, stretching his arms and legs, feeling the bed-covering slide from him to the floor. He lay there, naked, his semi-engorged cock flopping heavily against his belly.

The tapping came again. He opened his eyes.

Annie was peering down at him through the glass, smirking slightly.

He rolled from the bed on to the floor, his heel crumpling the letter to Glen which lay discarded at the foot of the bed. Wrapping the night's blanket around him, he got up and opened the caravan door.

'Come in,' he said, wincing. The day seemed awfully bright.

'Headache?' asked Annie.

He nodded, wincing again as he did so.

'I've no sympathy,' she said, smiling mischievously. 'You sit down, I'll put the kettle on.'

She clattered about in the little sink. Jason lay back on the bed and put a pillow over his face.

'Were you drinking last night? Or was that something else you were on?'

Jason didn't reply.

'I can't tell you the state you were in when you dodged past me.'

Jason knew only too well.

'You said something strange ... You said something like *Where's the spider?*, then you laughed horribly and ran off.'

Jason eased the pillow to one side.

'Is this place haunted, Annie?'

She sat down on the edge of the bed.

'Oh, not this again. Who've you been talking to? Piper? That old Ghost Train yarn of his?'

'No.'

'Jack, of course ... You were coming out of the Tunnel of Love, weren't you?'

'Everybody seems to want to warn me about Jack.'

'Jack's all right,' said Annie, 'but he's a hedonist. He has a self-destructive streak.'

'Who doesn't, around here?'

'Well, I don't, for a start,' said Annie. 'I'm happy with my life here, thank you.'

'Yes, but you're a woman. Women are ... I don't know ... stronger. Softer ...'

'Christ, you make us sound like bog paper.'

'You know what I mean, though. All the men around here are so extreme. So ... brittle ...'

'Women suffer in silence,' said Annie. 'They bear their crosses better than men. That's the only difference. Now, d'you want to talk about last night?'

Jason chewed his lip. He couldn't answer. He felt the urge to cuddle her, to lay his head on her chest and unburden himself. Just like he'd never done with his mother. He cast his eyes to the carpet.

There was a soft rapping at the door.

'Annie?'

'Piper!' She sounded surprised.

The old man craned his scrawny neck into the caravan.

'I've come for the boy,' he said.

★ ★ ★

He wasn't up to this.

Annie had left the caravan without another word, ignoring Jason's panicky glances.

'Get dressed,' the old man had said. He had then parked himself on the edge of the bed, lit his pipe and looked unashamedly at Jason as he tried to slip from his blanket-wrap into his clothes without giving the old letch a free peepshow.

Once Jason was dressed, the old man had risen from the bed without another word and exited the caravan. Jason assumed he was to follow. He smoothed out the letter he had written, folded it and placed it in an envelope: *19 Mauritius Road* . . .

He caught up with the old man at the line of trucks. Piper climbed into the driving-seat of an old, open-backed wagon and opened the passenger door. Jason climbed up beside him.

Piper engaged the engine and steered awkwardly out of the truck-line, with much pulling on the wheel and forward and reversing and swearing. In fury he pounded on the horn. Rex's head appeared round the corner, followed by Jack's. They stood there, watching and laughing as Piper cursed and wrestled with the old truck.

Jason closed his eyes. He was feeling too fragile for this. Two nights on the trot . . .

Finally they pulled away and bucked and lurched over the rough ground to the narrow road that led to civilisation.

'Where are we going?' Jason asked.

'Into town,' Piper replied. 'I've got to see a man about somethin'.'

'What about me?'

'Oh, I thought you'd like a trip into town,' the old man said.

Jason swore under his breath.

Piper began mumbling a song to himself. Jason couldn't make out the words – they didn't sound much like English. It was difficult to tell – the old man's accent seemed broader now.

What was his accent? To Jason it sounded a bit like the country accents you found around parts of Northumberland, mixed up with something else he couldn't put his finger on.

'Where are you from?' Jason asked.

'Me?' the old man replied. 'Oh, I've lived all over. I've travelled most of me life.'

He hauled suddenly on the wheel, narrowly avoiding a parked car.

'Bloody drivers,' he said.

The roads were getting bigger and busier. The old lorry didn't seem capable of doing more than about twenty-five miles per hour. The engine groaned dismally. Piper pounded on his horn as he cut lumberingly in front of another motorist. The other motorist blared back.

'Northampton's got one of them one-way systems,' he said. 'We never needed 'em in my day. Didn' 'ave roads in my day.'

'Is the fair very old?' asked Jason. Keep talking. Try to ignore the travelling conditions.

'Old? Aye. Some say the fair goes back to the oldest of times,' said the old man. 'It used to be called the Redemption Fair. And it had other names before that. It weren't like other fairs, ever. It has a bad past. Very bad past.'

Jason smiled to himself. He'd been waiting for something like this.

'Lots of shiftless types used to be drawn here,' the old man continued. 'Poor friars used to come a-beggin' alongside the fair, and crank preachers would follow it and preach to the crowds.

'They say King Richard himself travelled with the fair when he come back from the Crusades. Him and Blondel the minstrel, his bit on the side. He travelled in disguise, but people recognised him, they say, and came to him with their troubles, and he dispensed judgement. And after that the fair used to travel from town to town, a bit like an assize. People would come to sell and barter their wares, and to dance and wrestle and have fun, just like at other fairs, but they had stocks here, and they had witchfinders, with their books and their ready pyres, and they had cunning men and wise women to judge people in what they did. Any man might accuse his neighbour of a wrong, an evil, and they could come to the Redemption Fair to be judged. The whole town would turn out. And any man judged upon by the Redemption Fair, they'd be delivered by the townsfolk straight up, so feared were the people. This were in the old days, as I said. Lawless times. And there'd be floggings, and there'd be duckings, and there'd be burnings. Of course, once the old kings and Parliament and that, once they started to establish the laws of the land, proper, there weren't no room for the Redemption Fair, and they did their best to put a stop to it. Oh, but people was scared of it, all right.'

The old man grinned broadly.

'Course, that were before my day,' he said. 'How old Gamlin come by it, I don't know. The Gamlins was old and dying when I knowed them. Old Gamlin, he taught me my craft.'

Awkwardly he swung between lanes and swiped at the indicator arm.

'Craft?' Jason winced as another car-horn blared.

'Aye. I were a professor, many a year. A Punch and Judy man. But there ain't much call for such a simple morality tale no more.'

In spite of his barely controlled car-sickness, Jason grinned. Piper looked a bit like Mr Punch.

He was being driven to his death in an out-of-control truck by a senile ex-Punch and Judy man.

'So I give up Punch and Judy. Got to change with the times, right?'

'Sure.'

He decided not to tell Piper that Gamlin's Fair didn't look as if it had changed in a century or more.

'What's with the Merry-Go-Round?' he asked.

'Traditional,' said Piper. 'Got to have a Merry-Go-Round. Important.'

'But it doesn't work,' said Jason, 'and no one ever tries to fix it.'

'There were an accident,' said Piper. 'An accident on the Merry-Go-Round. Nasty, it were. A while ago, now. So we closed it down. It were too dangerous. Dangerous things, Merry-Go-Rounds.'

'When was this?' asked Jason. He was amazed there weren't more accidents on the rickety old rides.

'Oh, a while back, now,' said the old man. 'Seventeen forty-five. The year old Prince Charlie Edward come over to claim his throne.'

'Seventeen . . . Yeah, very funny. Even Gamlin's rides aren't that old.'

'Hee hee hee,' the old man chortled.

'How old are *you*, Piper?' Jason asked after a pause.

The old man let out a spitty cackle.

'Old enough to know better,' he said.

They had been travelling a long time. Piper's driving had settled down, and they were now chugging along what seemed to be the same endless roads at about twenty miles per hour.

'How much longer?' asked Jason. He wished he was still in bed.

'It's this damned thing,' said Piper, 'this one-way system. I don't know how to get off it.'

'I'm sure we've passed that church before,' said Jason.

'We have,' said Piper. 'Twice.'

'Where d'you have to meet this bloke?'

'Some posh hotel.'

Great.

'Is that the address he wrote down for you?'

The old man didn't seem to hear him. He juddered to a halt at some traffic lights.

A woman was shuffling across the road at an oblique angle, approaching the truck from the front. She was old, enormous and filthily dressed. Her shoes were hopelessly worn and broken. In each hand she clutched a dirty old carrier bag which appeared to be filled with other dirty old carrier bags. She stopped and leaned for breath on the fender of the truck.

'You's'll not break through the circle like that, father,' she bellowed at Piper. 'You's got to go widdershins.'

She hitched up her enormous flabby frame and shuffled on.

'She's right!' shouted Piper. He stabbed at the accelerator and swung a U-turn, straight into a stream of oncoming traffic. Jason closed his eyes. He couldn't take much more of this. Brakes screeched and horns blared around them.

'That's better,' said Piper, straightening the truck and accelerating alarmingly.

'There,' he bellowed almost instantly, and pulled the truck into a sudden left turn, mounting the pavement. 'This is the way.'

He cackled to himself.

The hotel was impressive – a big, old building with massive, modern glass doors set into the elegant portico. Piper parked the truck on a double yellow line opposite the hotel and climbed down from the cab.

'Well,' he said, 'you comin'?'

Self-consciously Jason climbed down and walked a pace or two behind the old man, towards the doors. Piper hadn't dressed up for the occasion – wearing the murky jacket and trousers he always wore, he didn't look a million miles from that mad, fat old bag-lady. He had crowned the look with a filthy, battered old trilby, jammed on to his white-downed head at an awkward angle.

Jason saw the horror register on the face of the smartly uniformed bellboy standing at the doors as he caught sight of Piper. He saw the look set into one of determination.

The bellboy extended an arm to prevent the old man entering the hotel. Piper grasped bellboy's hand gently and whispered something to him, then sailed past him, unmolested, into the plush lobby beyond. Jason followed.

Quiet, tinkly music suffused the plush lobby of the hotel, floating unnoticed between chairs you could drown in.

'You wait here,' said Piper. 'I'll be through there.' He turned towards a wooden door, surmounted with a painted sign: OLD NICK'S HEAD, LICENSED BAR.

Jason sunk into one of the comfy chairs and closed his eyes. Time to sleep off the morning, the hangover and the journey.

Jason was woken by a waitress carrying a broad silver tray.

'The . . . gentlemen in the bar asked me to bring you this,' she said.

'Uh, thanks,' he said. Good old Piper.

His face fell as she set the tray down. It had once obviously contained ranks of neatly cut sandwiches. Now all that remained were debris and leftovers – a few triangles of bread and a scattering of cheese, cress, the odd tomato slice.

Oh well. He set about assembling a workable sandwich or two out of the mess.

Actually, there was more here than was first apparent. Reasonably refreshed, Jason stretched himself and rose to his feet. Beyond the reception desk a broad flight of crimson-carpeted stairs rose in a gradual curve to the floors above. It was a while since Jason had been anywhere as posh as this. He decided to go for a wander.

The hotel reminded him of one in Newcastle. It had been a favourite climb for him and Spider. Often they would find a window open and enter the premises, at night and in secret, experiencing all the thrill of illegal entry, of moving about under the noses of the legitimate residents without their ever suspecting intruders in their midst.

'Morning.' On the first landing a chambermaid scuttled past Jason carrying a pile of clean linen. Jason nodded, and padded down the quiet corridor of numbered doors.

He stopped. Room 106. From behind the door came the unmistakable sounds of sex. Sex in the afternoon.

A mischievous smile played across Jason's face. He was remembering a particular climb he had done with Spider. Six storeys up on the outside of a hotel, on a summer's night in Newcastle, they had found themselves on a wrought-iron balcony by some open French windows. Inside, by candle-light, a young straight couple had been fucking on a four-poster bed. The man had been lying on his back, naked, prick in the air. The woman had been in her wedding dress. As Jason and Spider had watched she had hitched up the voluminous lacy skirts. She was wearing nothing underneath except a blue garter.

'D'you reckon she went to the church with no knickers on?' Spider had whispered to Jason.

She had lain next to the man, and he had rolled on top of her, seeking her bridal cunt with his prick. He had driven hard into her, gasping with every stroke. Her long hair, caught up in an elaborate flower-garland, had broken its moorings and spread across the pillow. The flowers had disintegrated. Her dress had rucked and creased and bunched around her midriff, heavy breasts spilling over the lace top, knees drawn up around her husband's pelvis.

'I think we should share their wedding night with them,' Spider had whispered. 'Their most intimate, personal moment.'

Squatting on the balcony, peeping around the glass door, he had wrenched his cock from inside his trousers and began rubbing it hard. Jason had done likewise. Spider had moved around behind Jason – so that they could both watch the spectacle – and tugged his jeans and pants down. Lying on his side, watching the fuck-show through the glass, Jason had felt Spider enter him, parting his soft arse-flesh, moving his pelvis in and out. He had reached around to Jason's cock and begun squeezing and pumping it in time to the rhythm of his hips.

Fucking along with the newly-weds, the two of them had come at almost exactly the same time as the squealing bride and groaning groom. Jason's seed had splashed hard against the glass door.

It was no good – Jason couldn't resist it. Quickly scanning the corridor, he squatted next to the door of Room 106 and pressed his ear against it. A regular creaking, thumping sound was coming from the bed, punctuated with a woman's moans. He pressed his ear tighter against the door. He could hear a slow, steady slapping sound, accompanied by gasps – breath drawn in pain.

There was a click, and the door swung slightly open under the pressure of Jason's head. He panicked for a moment. No. Spider wouldn't panic. Spider never panicked – he'd just go with it. He eased the door open another inch or so and peeped round it.

A man lay naked on the bed; a woman – also naked – sat across him, impaling herself on him, riding up and down his prick. Her breasts swung and bounced as she rode him; she raked the painted nails of one hand across their undulating contours. As her buttocks rose from the man's thighs he swung his hand around and slapped them hard and rosy.

'Darling,' he gasped as he slapped her, 'oh, darling!'

Accidentally Jason nudged the door. It swung inward, creaking slightly. He reached to steady it, but it was too late. The man had seen him. He arched his head up.

'What the devil do you think you're doing?' he spluttered.

The woman screamed and pivoted off the man, grabbing a

pillow and clutching it to her front. The man scrabbled for the bedsheet, only to find it was on the floor.

'I'm calling the management,' the man said, locating his trousers and scrabbling into them. 'I'm calling the police!'

Jason felt a hand on his shoulder. He flinched. Silent as time, Piper had somehow found him and now stood next to him.

'Afternoon,' Piper said to the couple on the bed, raising his hat and bowing low. 'Come, boy,' he said, straightening up and turning back towards the staircase.

Jason followed Piper down the stairs, out of the hotel and across to the truck.

The old man stood in front of Jason, swaying slightly and grinning. His breath stank of booze.

He leaned over the bonnet of the vehicle and pulled a parking ticket from behind the windscreen wiper, crumpling it into a ball and tossing it into the gutter.

'Now, I've had a bit too much to drink,' he slurred. 'D'you reckon you can drive the wagon?'

The journey back was traumatic. Jason had done his best to persuade old Piper to drive – he didn't even have a licence, for God's sake – but the old man was having none of it.

'Course you can,' the old man had harangued him. 'All you young 'uns can drive. Didn' you ever nick cars when you was growing up?'

Piper had hauled himself into the passenger seat and promptly gone to sleep. Jason had been forced to navigate the one-way system and find his way back along unfamiliar roads in a frankly clapped-out old wreck of a vehicle which was far bigger than anything Jason had ever stolen during his youth. Beside him, Piper had snored loudly throughout the journey, only waking up when they were pulling into the fairground.

Jack and Laurent, Rex and Doug and Annie were enjoying a midday break when the lorry halted and its occupants disembarked. Even Tom was contenting himself with only light duties, repairing a broken shoe.

'Had a good morning?' Jack asked as Jason sat down next to him.

'Mmm,' said Jason. 'Not bad.'

'D'you know what I've been doing all morning?' Jack asked. 'Mending that fucking net, that's what.'

He watched as Piper disappeared between the rides, heading for his caravan.

'What was Piper doing this morning?' he asked. 'He never goes into town.'

'He met some bloke in a hotel,' Jason replied. 'That's all I know. He didn't say much.'

He thought about his morning, and the strange old man.

'Where does Piper come from?' he asked. 'What's his accent?'

'I don't know,' Jack replied. 'I think there's a bit of rural Berkshire in it. Not far from where I come from.'

'Dear boy, he's a Londoner,' Rex cut in. 'A cockney, more or less, I'd swear.'

'Breton,' said Laurent. 'Yes, I think there is some Breton in his voice.'

'Bollocks,' said Jack. He rose to his feet and stretched himself. 'I'm off to the lake,' he announced.

Annie snorted.

'To sketch some ducks,' Jack said defiantly. 'Anybody coming?'

Nobody moved.

'Laurent?'

The French boy shrugged and shook his head.

'Jason?'

Jack chatted inconsequentially as they picked their way through the wood.

'Great town, this,' he kept saying. 'Great, great town.'

'Seems a bit of a dump to me,' Jason replied.

It was a bright, blustery afternoon, and soon Jason was sweating. He removed his sweat-shirt and tied it round his waist. Bare-chested, he followed behind Jack until they arrived on the strip of shingle that separated lake from forest. Jack belly-flopped to the ground. Jason sat down next to him.

'So where are these ducks?' Jason asked.

Jack gestured towards the water. No birds were visible, only the brightly coloured sails and wetsuits of perhaps eight windsurfers.

'Let's hope they're in season,' said Jack.

Jason groaned.

'Tom's right about you,' he said.

'What?'

'You're a sexual obsessive.'

'I'm a connoisseur,' Jack replied, a touch of hurt in his voice. 'A scientist. A collector.'

'Yeah? What do you collect?'

'People's sexual chemistry,' Jack replied. 'I only wish I could bottle it and sell it. I love knowing what makes people tick sexually. Now you . . .'

'Hold it,' said Jason.

'I couldn't figure you out at first,' Jack continued, ignoring the warning. 'You seemed quite fucked-up about the whole thing. You came across like a swimmer who once nearly drowned, and who's clinging on to the side for dear life. You want to let go, to get into the water, but you're scared. Then when you do let go it's mad.'

'Seems to me everyone's mad around here.'

'Just remember,' said Jack, 'there's two kinds of sexual obsessive. Those who can do it and those who can't.'

'What are you getting at?' said Jason, bristling.

'Now don't get offended,' Jack said hastily. 'Anyway, I think I've sussed you out now. I found this in the Tunnel of Love this morning.'

He reached into his pocket and extracted a crumpled piece of paper. It was the photo Jason had taken from Tom's drawer. A youthful Tom, his parents, his kid brother, all romping in the sea.

'Give me that!' Jason barked, lunging for the photograph.

Jack snatched it out of his reach.

'*Jason lo-oves To-om* . . .' he sang at the top of his voice, springing to his feet and dancing away from Jason.

Jason scrambled up and lunged again. Jack was quick – he dodged behind a bush and ran, laughing, into the trees. Jason followed.

'So what is it you and Tom get up to at night?' taunted Jack, dodging and weaving to avoid his pursuer.

'Nothing,' growled Jason through gritted teeth. 'Give me the fucking photo.'

'Ah, 'twas ever the way with fair Tom.' Jack sighed theatrically.

Jason's jumper loosed itself from around his waist and dropped to the ground. He didn't care. He dived towards Jack again.

'*Olé!*' cried Jack the matador, trying smartly to sidestep his raging-bull friend. He miscalculated. His foot caught on a tree root, and he went sprawling. Instantly Jason was on top of him, grabbing for the photo.

'OK, OK,' spluttered Jack. 'You win.'

'Prick,' spat Jason, carefully folding the picture and putting it in his own pocket.

'Seriously, though,' Jack said quietly, 'I'd forget Tom if I were you. There's nothing at all going on in his trousers, believe me. Let go. Have fun. There's a lot of nice, sexy people out there.'

'You don't know what the fuck you're talking about,' said Jason sulkily. 'You . . .'

'Sssh!' interrupted Jack. 'Listen.'

Through the trees Jason could hear voices, chatter, laughter.

'We're here,' Jack whispered.

He rolled onto his stomach and crawled through the undergrowth towards a clearing. Jason dropped to his stomach and did the same.

At the far end of the clearing was a low wooden chalet-type building, standing alone in the shade of the trees. Windsurf-boards were stacked along one side of it. Barely six feet away from the two hiding boys a pair of wetsuited youths were pissing into the undergrowth. Jason guessed they had to be in their mid-twenties. Both were tanned; one had hair that fell in brown ringlets over a red wetsuit, the other, blue-suited, a chaotic spike of peroxide blond. Jason could see the water of the lake glistening on their suits, hair and skin. The blond punk's suit was a one-piece; it was unzipped at the front from neck to crotch, revealing a thick triangle of light-brown, undyed hair over a large cock with a long, loose foreskin. His companion's suit was in two pieces. He had pulled the skin-fitting red trousers down at the front and hooked them under his balls. Big balls, Jason noted. Hairy balls, and a thick brown mat sprouting up his lower belly and disappearing under the top half of the suit. Average-sized cock, nicely shaped, circumcised. Each was disgorging a thick stream of piss against the base of a tree.

'I've been here before,' Jack whispered.

'So have I,' said Jason flatly. He was thinking of the morning, in the hotel. He was thinking about the Tunnel of Love. 'Let's go.'

'Did you say something?' Blue-Suit turned to his companion. His cock swung as he moved, spraying drops of piss against Red-Suit's leg.

'Hey, watch it,' Red-Suit laughed. 'That fucking foreskin of yours. Makes you piss like a woman.'

'Yeah?' Blue-Suit turned and swung his cock upward, releasing a piss-jet over the legs of his friend.

'Right, fucker,' said Red-Suit, turning to do battle, 'prepare to drown!'

He aimed his jet high, catching his friend on the deep V of bare flesh where his wetsuit was unzipped, throat to cock.

'Bastard!' Blue-Suit shouted, dodging backwards, trying to target his friend's exposed belly and balls.

They danced a manic dance around the clearing, golden streams of piss clashing in mid-air, their cocks beginning to fill out and rise into the air.

'They're a frisky lot here,' whispered Jack. 'That's their clubhouse back there. Like I said, great town.'

There was a rustling in the bushes behind them.

'Well, well . . .' An American accent.

Three more windsurfers were standing, watching them.

'Spies,' the American said. 'Get up.'

He was well over six feet in height, broad and muscular, with a brown crew-cut. He too wore a red suit, a one-piece, the top half of which hung down behind him like a shed skin.

Jason glanced nervously at Jack.

'Relax,' Jack whispered. 'I know what I'm doing.'

They were marched into the clearing. 'Coupla peeping toms,' said the American to the pissing pair. Their duel stopped instantly.

'I reckon we could all use a piss,' the American said. 'Strip.'

'What?' Jason couldn't believe this.

A smile flickered momentarily across Jack's face. 'Don't argue,' he said, already hauling his T-shirt over his head.

'Hang on . . .' said Jason.

'Strip!' the American barked.

Reluctantly Jason fumbled with the buttons on his jeans. Jack was already down to his underwear.

'Don't I know you?' the American said to Jack.

'I . . . uh . . . don't think so,' said Jack.

'Yeah, I think so,' said the American. 'You were here last spring. I caught you spying through the window that time. You remember what we did to you then? Down on the floor.'

Almost eagerly Jack dropped into a squat. Shedding the last of his clothes, Jason sat heavily on the coarse grass.

The windsurfers were standing in a semicircle – the big American, the two piss-gladiators and two black-suited windsurfers. Naked, humiliated, Jason watched in horror as they began to unzip their wetsuits, as their limp or semi-erect cocks emerged from the rubber folds. He closed his eyes as the first warm, wet streams began to splash against his chest and arms, his neck and face. He could feel piss running down into his pubes and over his cock. He opened his eyes to see Jack, his cock hard, rolling in the golden rivulets. Five cocks fired their thick, steamy piss-jets over them. Even the two gladiators seemed to have found extra reserves of piss. Jason was drenched.

When they had just about pissed themselves out, the American stepped forward.

'On your feet,' he ordered.

Jason obeyed, wincing as the piss cooled and dried on his skin. They were marched into the long, low wooden cabin, concrete-floored and devoid of any furniture except a large wooden table and a handful of stools. Around the walls were scattered piles of clothing, kit-bags, wetsuits, boards.

Jason and Jack stood in the middle of the room, Jason silent, naked, wet, Jack babbling like a fool.

'Nice clubhouse,' he said. 'Very smart.'

The American pulled his one-piece wetsuit down his muscular

legs. His cock, hard now, sprang up and out as it came free of the rubber suit. It was long, thick and veiny. He stood naked in front of Jack.

'What about you?' one of the others said to Jason. A redhead, sinewy, heavily freckled.

The redhead moved behind him, pressing his rubber-suited body against his back and legs. Jason could feel the rough contour of his cock bulging through the rubber, pressing against his buttocks. A hand reached around and fondled Jason's limp cock.

The American reached forward and grabbed Jack roughly by the balls, pulling him close. He jammed his face against Jack's, his tongue thrusting into Jack's mouth. He released his grip on Jack's balls and pushed him down to his knees. Gripping the back of his head, the American forced Jack's mouth over his cock. Jack made a slight gurgling noise as the immense pole disappeared between his lips.

'You're good, buddy,' the American said, slipping a finger and thumb along the shaft of his cock and into Jack's mouth. 'Better'n last year, even.'

The first pair of windsurfers they had encountered – Red-Suit and Blue-Suit – once again had their cocks out, not pissing now, but wanking as they watched Jack going down on their crew-cut American friend. Blue-Suit grabbed Jack by his long hair, lifted his head from the American's cock and pushed it down onto his own erect meat.

The redhead tugged hard on Jason's cock, stretching it painfully, whilst continuing to crush himself against Jason's back and buttocks. The final windsurfer in the party pressed himself against Jason's front. He was pale, his head shaved entirely bald. Each of his ears was pierced with an ascending row of metal rings and studs. A chain linked his right earlobe with his right nostril. He too wore a black rubber suit. Jason stood sandwiched between the two black-clad rubbermen. They clasped arms and squeezed together, crushing Jason, rubbing their hard, pliable body-suits and bulging rubber crotches into his skin. The bald, pierced youth paused and pulled his erection from inside his wetsuit, grinding it against Jason's still-limp cock and balls. He opened his wide mouth and extended a long tongue. Jason caught the glint of a large metal stud, driven through the tip of the tongue. He pushed it between Jason's lips. Jason felt and tasted the cold tang of metal against his tongue, clattering on his teeth. He sensed movement behind him, and felt the redhead's cock, now out of its rubber housing, rubbing up and down his arse-crack.

Jason could see the other three windsurfers, now standing in a line, Jack on his knees, alternating between them, moving his head from cock to cock. The tall, naked American pulled Jack to his feet and pushed him, face first, against the wall of the cabin. Red Suit rummaged in a drawer beneath the wooden table and fished out a packet of condoms, which he tossed to the American, who caught it deftly. Jason watched as the American broke open the packet and rolled a latex sheath over his huge, veiny cock.

'You ready for this, longhair?' the American drawled. Not waiting for a reply, he lined his cock up with Jack's hole and drove in hard. Jack groaned and braced himself against the wall.

The redhead moved around to Jason's front and rubbed his head against the metal-lined face of his friend. He too thrust his tongue into Jason's mouth. His face was covered with stubble, which itched and scraped along Jason's chin and cheeks. Inside Jason's mouth two invading tongues jousted with his own.

Between the two of them, Jason's black-clad suitors lowered his naked body to the cold concrete floor. The unshaven redhead scraped and kissed his way down Jason's neck and chest, pulling hard at his nipples with his teeth, working his way down past his belly-button and into his pubic forest. He caught up a mouthful of hair and tugged with his teeth. Finally his lips closed about Jason's cock.

He was still limp.

'This one doesn't seem to like me,' the redhead said.

Braced against the wall, Jack looked across at Jason. 'Remember what I said,' he urged. 'Get into the swim. Go with it.'

Jason closed his eyes, let his mind go blank and gripped the red head of curls with both hands. The youth sucked and nipped at Jason's cock; Jason felt it swell inside the warm, wet mouth. To one side of Jason the metalhead slid out of his rubber suit and stepped across Jason's chest. He sat down hard and began pumping on his thick, pale cock, leaning forward over Jason's face. Each of his nipples was pierced with a metal ring. A chain, like that running between his ear and nose, swung between his nipples. Jason craned his neck forward, grabbed the chain in his teeth and jerked his head back.

'Oh yeah,' the shaven-headed youth gasped as he wanked. 'Oh yeah . . .'

Jason jerked again on the chain. His head struck the concrete floor.

'Harder!' the youth shouted. 'Tug harder!'

Jason jerked again. He lost his grip on the chain. The youth slid his arse up Jason's chest until his cock was close to Jason's mouth. It, too, was pierced, a studded ring piercing his frenulum and emerging from the eye of the bulbous cock. Jason caught the metal ring between his teeth and tugged. The youth hissed his pleasure.

The redhead's rough chin continued to bounce off Jason's balls as he worked his mouth around Jason's now fully engorged, painfully sensitised cock.

From the corner of his eye Jason could see the rhythmic jerks of the American's arse as he continued to drive into Jack, all the time taunting with 'You like that, huh? You like that, longhair?'

For once, apart from the occasional sharp intake of breath, Jack was silent.

The former piss-fighters, the only ones still in their wetsuits, were watching the show and masturbating each other. The red-suited one with the mop of curly brown hair was working his fingers under the voluminous foreskin of his peroxide-blond friend; the blond punk was pumping hard on Red-Suit's circumcised prick. They moved in tandem towards Jack and the American.

'Give someone else a go,' said Blue-Suit.

The American pulled his prick from Jack's arse. Blue-Suit rolled a condom onto himself and moved to take the American's place. He slid into Jack, still braced against the wall, and began a rhythmic rolling of his hips.

The American, still hard, strode over to a battered surfboard and dragged it out from the wall. It fell to the floor with a crash. He turned, reached into a canvas bag and extracted something.

He began doing something to the board – smearing something across its surface. He mouthed something to Red-Suit. Both of them grinned and nodded.

Still straddling Jason's chest, the shaved-and-pierced youth pulled his cockring out from between Jason's teeth. 'You like the taste of metal?' he said, and drove his cock between Jason's lips, the cockring's studs hard and rough on his tongue and the roof of his mouth.

Jason's heart was racing. He bucked his hips and teased his cock in and out of the redhead's lips. He was close to coming. The redhead was massaging his own cock furiously now. As Jason arched upward his cock slipped from the redhead's mouth. The redhead sought to catch it again, but he was too late. Jason hit orgasm, shooting a great spurt of jism over the redhead's face. The redhead licked his lips, his eyes closed, his face creased and knotted as he too began to shoot.

Still wanking, Red-Suit tapped the head of his bald, pierced friend.

'Lift him up,' he said. 'Get him onto the table. Face down.'

Metal-dick grinned and pulled out of Jason's mouth. He climbed off Jason and took some lengths of nylon rope from one of the bags. He then gripped Jason under the arms.

'What . . . No!' Jason began to struggle. Ropes. This was becoming too much. He couldn't break the windsurfer's grip. Red-Suit seized Jason's kicking legs, and they lifted.

'Fuck off, I said!' Jason shouted, his head darting back and forth in confusion and fear. He was deposited on his stomach on the wooden table. Metal-dick pinned him down as Red-Suit looped ropes around his ankles. He moved around the table and did the same to Jason's wrists. Jason lay over the table, face-down and unable to move, tied by all fours to its legs. Red-Suit slid a condom over his cock and moved behind Jason again. Jason felt the hard smoothness of the red rubber suit against his legs and back. He felt Red-Suit's hand slip between his buttocks, wet with spit, rubbing around his tight hole, fingers slipping into the pucker. He felt the youth's hand withdraw, to be replaced by his cock. It slid up and down his buttock crease, the suit creaking and slapping against his back. Slowly, Red-Suit inserted his cock into Jason.

'Oh, what – Wait a second – What have you –' Across the room, Jack was babbling again. He too was flat out, pressed against the surfboard, held in position by the American and the blue-suited, blond punk. The American reached for one of the discarded wetsuits. With the sleeve of the suit, he began lashing Jack across the buttocks. Jack howled.

Metal-dick moved to the head of the table. 'Where were we?' he said to Jason. 'Oh, yeah.'

Standing, knees slightly bent, he pushed his cock once again into Jason's mouth. He and Red-Suit, working Jason from both ends, clasped hands high in the air. Twin cocks plunged in and out of Jason, one orally, one anally. Jason gagged and writhed, feeling his tunnel walls being forced apart, feeling his mouth filled with hard flesh and metal, quite unable to move.

Jason could just about make out Blue-Suit and the American, play-fighting to get at Jack's exposed arsehole. Blue-Suit got there first, flopping onto Jack's prostrate body and ramming his cock home with a grunt. After a few minutes the American hauled him off and took his place, only to be himself dislodged after a few minutes more. This time Blue-Suit was staying put. His thrusts became faster and more frantic. He sunk his teeth into Jack's shoulder and let out a long moan as he came.

He flopped down on top of Jack, only to be unceremoniously kicked off by the American. There was to be no relief for Jack – the American sunk his huge cock into the boy, grabbing his long hair as if it were the reins of a horse.

'You sorry you spied on us, longhair?' he grunted as he drove his prick home again and again. 'You learned your lesson?'

Jack could only moan.

Jason's mouth tasted of metal polish. The pierced cock continued to bang around inside, rasping against his tongue and teeth. The rubber suit of his other lover planed along the length of his back. He could smell the rubber. Both men came within seconds of each other, Red-Suit shuddering and digging his fingernails into Jason's shoulders, Metal-dick holding his head tight as his jism sluiced down the back of Jason's throat.

Jason and Jack lay across the room from each other, breathless.

The windsurfers dressed, chatting and bantering among themselves, completely ignoring their sexual playthings.

'Guys,' said Jack. 'Guys . . .'

'You hear something?' queried the American, looking around the cabin. The others shook their heads. 'Probably mice,' he concluded.

They packed their wetsuits away and left the cabin, discussing wind-speeds and tidal swell.

'Jack,' said Jason as the cabin door closed behind the windsurfers, 'can you get up and untie me?'

'No,' said Jack curtly.

'What d'you mean no?' Jason snapped.

'They put something on the board,' said Jack. 'I'm stuck to it. I can't move.'

They lay there for a while, contemplating their situation.

'What shall we do?' asked Jason, beginning to panic.

'I spy,' said Jack, 'with my little eye . . .'

It was dark – Jason had no idea what time it might be – when they were finally discovered. There was a loud knocking at the door of the cabin. Jason and Jack remained tense and silent.

'Hello?' Annie's voice. 'Is anybody in there?'

'Annie!' Jason called.

'What are you doing?' Jack whispered frantically. 'They can't find us like this!'

'We're in here!' Jason called.

There was a rattling at the door, followed by a brief conversation. Suddenly the door groaned under a heavy impact. Another, and it flew inward on its hinges. A figure stumbled into the unlit room.

'Find a light-switch,' a voice ordered. Tom. Shit.

The room was suddenly flooded with light. Jason screwed up his face against it. Standing, facing them, were Tom and Annie. Doug and Laurent stood behind them in the doorway.

'Jesus,' said Tom under his breath. He strode over to Jason, stooped and tugged angrily at the ropes which held him. Reluctantly they came away.

'Thanks,' said Jason, massaging his wrists and ankles.

'Get dressed,' grunted Tom, turning away.

Laurent and Doug were crouched around Jack's naked, prostrate body. Doug leaned his head forward and sniffed the surfboard.

'Some kind of epoxy resin is my guess,' he said. 'We should be able to peel you off. It'll be just like removing a plaster.'

'No way!' howled Jack. 'I'll lose every hair from my body. It'll hurt like hell.'

Doug sighed.

'I've got something back at the workshop which should dissolve this stuff,' he said. 'We'll have to carry you back, though. Tom?'

Still staring at the wall, Tom swore under his breath.

'Careful!' Jack whined.

They were stumbling through the wood in darkness, Tom carrying one end of the board, Jason and Laurent the other, Jack still stuck to its bright surface, his sweat-shirt, stained with grass and piss-splashes, draped over his bare arse.

Annie was following, carrying the rest of his clothes. 'We should carry you upside-down,' she said. 'You deserve it. It's gone midnight. You pair missed the show entirely. We had to cover for you. You've pissed a lot of people off tonight.'

'Plus I've now got to spend God knows how long getting you off this thing,' said Doug.

'Well, I'm sorry,' said Jack. 'Believe me, I didn't plan this.'

Jason and Tom said nothing.

They parted company at Doug and Annie's caravan, leaving Jack and his board lying on Doug's workbench. Tom stomped back to his caravan, Jason following him at a safe distance.

Tom went inside and shut the door. Jason stood in the darkness, not knowing what to do. After a moment the door swung open again.

Gingerly Jason stepped inside. Tom was sitting on the bed, hunched forward, staring at nothing in particular.

'D'you want me to move out?' Jason asked after a moment's painful silence.

Tom shrugged his shoulders. 'Is that what you want?'

'No,' said Jason quietly.

'I warned you about Jack,' said Tom.

Jason said nothing.

'You should have listened,' said Tom.

'Jack's all right,' said Jason quietly.

'All right? You call tonight all right? You could have been hurt! Killed! Poncing around like a couple of fucking tarts! Christ!'

He thumped the wall, making the little caravan shake. Jason had never seen him this angry.

'I'm tired,' Jason whispered. 'I'm really tired, Tom.'

'OK,' Tom sighed. 'Bed then, I suppose.'

Jason sat down on the bed and began tugging at a shoelace. Awkwardly Tom put his arm around him. A great, unexpected sob forced its way up from Jason's gut. His eyes filled with tears. He buried his face in Tom's broad shoulder. Woodenly the big man held him as he cried.

Jason slept. Tom couldn't. He lay awake hours looking at the sleeping boy.

Kids. Why did they always have to go too far?

He thought of his brother. Why did this boy remind him so much of David? They didn't look alike . . . How many mornings now had he lain there before dawn, just looking at Jason, pondering that very question? How many times had he wanted to reach out and grasp him, hold him close and say how very sorry he was. Sorry he had failed David. Sorry he had failed everybody.

Seven

Northampton, Coventry, Leicester, Derby; Gamlin's Fair continued its slow passage through the Midlands, always heading north. An agreeable rhythm crept into Jason's days. The work was varied and interesting – as often as not he would help Tom on the Big Wheel in the mornings, climbing among the lights and struts, painting and repairing, and at night, when he wasn't working alongside Crash Annie, he was starting to learn the difficult business of dancing in and out of the Waltzers with her brother Doug. Jason was quite in awe of the way the dapper, middle-aged man weaved and jumped, balancing on the rotating arms as he collected the money. He avoided working on the Hall of Mirrors and the Tunnel of Love, remembering Tom's comment about the Foreign Legion – he was trying to put the past behind him, and anxious to avoid the possibility of any more treacherous memories.

He and Tom seemed closer now. They still said little to one another beyond day-to-day fairground chat, but a tangible bond seemed to be growing between the two men – a bond based on mutual, undisclosed sadness. For Jason, as for Tom, the running of the fair seemed to fill the gaps left by past emotional upheaval. Often they could be seen thirty feet in the air on the immobile Wheel, Tom – if he was familiar with whatever town they happened to be in – pointing out landmarks and explaining their history.

'The Germans flattened Coventry during the war. They had to rebuild it. That's why it's all so modern. There's the new cathedral.'

'How d'you know all this?' Jason had asked.

'I left home early,' said Tom. 'Moved around a lot. I didn't get on with my family.'

A brief, awkward silence had followed, and then, 'Over there's the statue of Lady Godiva.'

Sharing a bed at night with the strong, quiet man Jason felt strangely comforted. Most nights, as on the first night, he would wait until Tom was asleep and then wrap himself around his naked, muscular frame, hugging his great chest, shaping himself into the curve of his legs, before drifting off into easy slumber. Only once, during sleep, had the dreams returned and Jason got the screamers. He had woken in Tom's arms. Tom had held him, whispering words of comfort, talking gently about nothing in particular until sleep had overtaken him once more.

More than anyone else, Jason talked to Annie. He told her about his past, his wild years, his time with Spider.

'He sounds wonderful,' said Annie. 'You should get back with him.'

Jason shook his head sadly. 'No . . .' he whispered.

He even told her about the dream. The heat and darkness, the flames, the great black dog. She hugged him to her chest and kissed him on the forehead.

'Dreams fade,' said Annie. 'One day you'll wake up and realise you haven't had that dream for a week, a month, a year. And it will all be over. It will be just another childhood memory.'

She told him stories from her young days. She and Doug had encountered Piper when they were children and he was still doing his Punch and Judy routine. It had been an inspirational moment for both Annie and Doug. As soon as she was old enough Annie had taken up fortune-telling, with a seasonal stall at Great Yarmouth. Doug had followed her. That year, in a break in its normal routine, Gamlin's had called at Great Yarmouth. The twins had met Piper again and he had invited them to join the fair.

'It's what every child dreams of,' Annie said. 'Running away and joining the fair. You're just the latest – Gamlin's is full of runaways.'

'Why didn't you have kids?' Jason had asked on one occasion. 'You'd have been such a good mum.'

Annie had sighed.

'I'd have loved kids,' she had said. 'There were ... complications.'

She had looked sad for a moment, then said, 'Anyway, look around you. There are plenty of kids here. Even the adults are kids here. I have my hands full with you lot.'

Occasionally Jason would fill in for Piper on the Ghost Train. The old man's absences from the fair were becoming more frequent. He said nothing about where he went or what he did on these occasions, and Jason's fellow crew seemed to avoid any speculation on the subject. Even when he appeared in a brand-new business suit, no one other than Jason saw fit to comment. He mentioned it that same evening over supper to Annie and Doug.

'Piper's been with the fair longer than anyone,' was Annie's only comment. 'He does what he does.'

'But he looks so stupid in it.'

The suit fitted Piper badly. Still unwashed and unshaven, he looked like a tramp who had burgled a gent's outfitters.

The Ghost Train itself, to Jason's relief, fell far short of Piper's fairground-spiel. He had always been slightly contemptuous of such rides as a kid – they had seemed a feeble thrill compared to a really good roller-coaster – and the cardboard skeletons and painted ghosts of the Gamlin's ride were every bit as cheesy and unconvincing as every other ghost train he had ever been on.

'Yeah, well,' the old man sulked when Jason told him, 'it's neither 'ere nor there what you think. The Ghost Train's not for you.'

The only thing about the Ghost Train he didn't like was Black Shuck. The dog seemed to sense Jason's fear – every day it was there, tethered to the ride's metal chassis. Even if it was out of sight under the ride, it would crawl out whenever Jason approached, unleashing a volley of barks and tugging at its rope.

'Don't be scared of old Black Shuck,' Piper told him. 'By day he's all bark. Just go right up to him and whack him on the nose. That'll shut him up.'

Yeah, thought Jason. *Right*.

Jason received a postcard from Glen. It was addressed to *Jason Bradley, c/o Gamlin's Fair, Derby*, and was waiting for him when the fair arrived in town. Jason was surprised – the photo on the card was captioned *Tintern Abbey, Wye Valley*. Glen was a city-boy; more even than Jason.

Dear Jase, the card said, *I was very happy to receive your letter. It came at a time when I was really down. It's lucky it got here when it did. A couple of days later and it would have been too late. I've left the squat. Nige was just getting to be too much. Even Mitch and Andy were starting to turn on him.*

I decided to take a little holiday, so here I am. It's great, this countryside lark. Who knows, you just might see me up there. I've got a couple of bits and pieces of yours which I found after you'd gone.

I hope this reaches you. I miss you too. I hope you're happy at the fair.

Love and kisses,
    Glen.
    XXXXX
P.S. Happy Easter.

Jason hadn't even realised the Easter holiday was upon them. It was one of those occasions which always seemed to pass unmarked at home. He had awoken early – Tom was already out exercising at the Wheel – to see a large, beribboned chocolate egg sitting on the table. He had loped out of bed and picked the egg up. A card had fluttered to the table. *To Jason, Beautiful Dreams and All Good Things, Love, Annie.* He had sat down and breakfasted on the rich chocolate.

On their second day on the outskirts of Derby, a huge, American-style mobile home trundled across the rough ground that separated the fair from the city suburbs, towing a trailer behind it. It arrived blaring Italian opera from a hi-fi system, punctuated by regular fanfares on a horn which played the Star-Spangled Banner.

'What the fuck's that?' Jason asked. He was on the Wheel with Tom at the time, inevitably replacing shot light-bulbs.

'That's Luigi,' Tom replied. 'He turned up about this time last year. He's an old friend of Piper's, I think.'

The massive vehicle halted and the music died. The driver's door opened and a figure emerged. Emerged? Squeezed out. The man was as outlandishly oversized as his vehicle. Well over six feet in height, he must have weighed in excess of twenty stones – a pear-shaped giant in a white vest and the biggest pair of track-suit bottoms Jason had ever seen.

The man lumbered across to Piper, fat, tanned arms at full stretch, and clasped the scrawny little man in a crushing bear-hug which seemed to knock the wind out of him. Piper staggered back against the side of the Merry-Go-Round, coughing. The fat man looked around him, beaming all over his face and patting his belly.

A door towards the back of the mobile home opened and four boys trotted out, all of them under twenty. Two of them danced around each other, sparring like boxers, jabbing and feinting.

'Luigi runs a boxing booth,' Tom said in a clipped voice.

'Didn't you used to box?' Jason asked.

'Who told you that?' Tom flashed.

Jason blushed. No one had told him – he had seen the army boxing medal whilst rifling Tom's drawer.

'Who are the kids?' Jason asked, anxious to change the subject.

'Ringers,' said Tom.

'What?'

'This is prize-fighting,' said Tom. 'He'll have a champ with him. The kids will take on the champ first. The champ will go easy on them, let them come close to winning – maybe even let them win – to encourage members of the public to have a go.'

'A bit like me on the Wheel, that night during the storm.'

Tom grinned, remembering Jason's unexpected appearance that night. He ruffled Jason's hair.

'Come on,' said Tom. 'Let's get down.'

That afternoon Jason watched the young boxers extract a variety of paraphernalia from the trailer. The weather was hot and soon all four were working bare-chested. Though young, each already displayed the lean physique and compact musculature of the boxer.

Jack wandered across to where Jason was lounging on the edge of the Bumper Cars.

'Not introduced yourself yet?' queried Jason.

Jack scowled at him. He had been unusually subdued since the night in the windsurfers' cabin. Removing him from the board had been a straightforward, if lengthy, process, but had not been without its costs.

'I'm bald from the neck down,' Jack said in a leaden voice. 'They're all yours.'

Jason was aware that it had taken Doug much of the night to unstick Jack, and that throughout the process Annie had harangued the boy about his sybarite lifestyle. Jack had resented her lecture, but it seemed to have hit home. He had even told Laurent – who had told Rex, who had told the rest of the fair – that he was contemplating a life of celibacy. 'I'll have a word with Tom,' Rex had announced, unable to resist making a great play of this to Jack, 'and try and set up a few tutorials.'

Jack was scarcely speaking to Annie.

The young boxers, amid much playful scuffling and fighting, were assembling a boxing ring in the middle of the show-ground. This completed, they unfurled a large, gaudily coloured rectangular tent and erected it over the ring. Then all four of them vanished inside.

Curious, Jason waited a few moments then sauntered across to the tent. Inside, two of the boxers were already in the ring. Jason watched them sparring for a while. It was an interesting match: one boy – pale-skinned, sandy-haired, dressed in red silk shorts – was relatively tall, with a long reach. His opponent – in black shorts – was shorter, densely muscular, and South-East Asian. He was working elegant and effective kick-boxing manoeuvres into the fight, constantly trying to move in under the rangy punches of his opponent with sharp jabs and lightning-fast kicks.

Luigi, their enormous patron, appeared under the tent-flap and began shouting encouragement and instructions to the lads.

'You box?' he said suddenly, in a thick Italian accent.

For a moment Jason didn't realise the man was talking to him.

'Uh . . . no,' Jason replied.

'You should box,' the man said. 'All young men should box. In ancient Greece and Rome, all young men boxed. It is how they conquer the world. What do you do?'

Jason shrugged his shoulders. 'Nothing much,' he said.

'You should box,' the fat man repeated, turning his gaze back to the ring. 'Boxing keep the mind of a young man from unclean thoughts. Boxing keep a young man pure.'

Jason could hear voices and laughter coming from one of the canvas walls of the tent. Jason noticed a flap in the wall leading to a section screened off from the boxing area. Luigi's attention was now fixed firmly on the sparring partners. Jason twitched the flap and stuck his head around it. He was looking into an area perhaps half the width of the boxing arena itself. Along the cloth back-wall stretched a long, low, wooden bench. The area was strewn with the stock-in-trade of the boxer – a heavy punch-bag, a small, bulbous speed-bag, a selection of medicine-balls and skipping ropes.

Of the two remaining boxers, one was gloved and slamming his fists into the heavy bag, whilst the other stood behind the bag and held it with his full body-weight. Jason watched as the twin columns of muscle which flanked the boxer's spine jerked, tautened and relaxed as he drove his fists home. He was black, and his skin glistened with sweat. His white silk trunks gleamed and stretched as his buttock and leg muscles pumped with the rhythm of the blows. Stopping to rest, he turned and flashed Jason a bright, toothy smile.

'You want a go?' he asked.

Jason shook his head.

'Give him a pair of gloves!' Luigi was standing behind him.

'I don't –' Jason began to protest.

'Boxing is an instinct!' boomed the fat man. 'Tobias, give him your gloves!'

The black boxer tugged at the laces on the gloves with his teeth and, shaking them from his hands, passed them to Jason.

'They're a bit sweaty, man,' he said in a broad east-London accent.

Self-consciously Jason put the gloves on and allowed Tobias to lace them up. He squared up to the bag.

'Ready whenever you are,' said the boxer, still holding the bag.

Jason aimed first one, then another punch at the bag. Then another, and another, his blows growing in force and confidence.

'Not bad,' Luigi said when he had been punching for about ten minutes. 'You got talent, boy.' He turned to Tobias. 'Put him in the ring against Michael.'

He walked out. Jason let his arms drop.

'You heard the man,' said Tobias.

'Who's Michael?' Jason asked.

'I am,' a voice piped from somewhere. A gentle, well-spoken voice. A head of golden hair in a neat, pudding-basin cut, a fresh, wide-eyed face of about eighteen appeared around the punch-bag. 'You pack a good punch,' the boy said shyly, lowering his eyes.

He walked over to the bench and began untying his shoelaces.

'Hurry,' Luigi called through the tent-flap.

Michael slipped his jogging bottoms off and stood there in a pair of tight red briefs.

'Come on,' said Tobias to Jason, 'don't bother to take the gloves off.'

He tugged Jason's T-shirt out of his jeans and hauled it over his head and shoulders. It came over the gloves with difficulty. Tobias stooped and rummaged in a cardboard box on the floor. He drew out a creased pair of black shorts, a jockstrap and what looked like a crash-helmet for a midget.

'What's that?' asked Jason in alarm.

'That's your box.' Tobias grinned. 'Protect your nuts.'

With a worried smile Jason tried to unbutton his jeans. The boxing gloves made it impossible.

'Come on,' said Tobias, his grin broadening, 'I'll do it.'

He unhooked Jason's fly-buttons and lowered the jeans to Jason's ankles. Using only his feet Jason shucked off his trainers and socks. He stepped out of the jeans. Tobias inserted his thumbs into the elastic waist of Jason's pants.

'No!' Jason cried, crossing the boxing gloves over his groin.

'Hey, don't worry,' said Tobias. He slid his thumbs back and forth slightly under the elastic, his nails lightly tracing across Jason's skin, and eased the pants down.

Shyly, Michael raised his head. For a moment his eyes lingered on Jason's cock. To Jason's horror it was very slightly starting to grow. Michael shot Jason a bashful yet knowing glance and, bending, removed his own pants in a quick movement. He straightened up and stood for a moment, fully naked, facing Jason. Jason's eyes fell to his cock. It nestled like a snail beneath a thin, neat crown of golden hair. As Jason looked it twitched minutely and then, like Jason's, seemed to relax and swell very slightly.

Blushing, Michael pulled on his jock strap. Tobias was urging Jason to step into his. He pulled it up over Jason's knees and thighs and hiked it high around his waist. Flashing his cheeky, toothy grin he tucked Jason's cock in. Then he snatched up the box and scooped it under Jason's cock and balls, wiggling it slightly as he fitted it into place. He passed a thick, padded strap around Jason's waist, and another between his legs, under his balls and up the cleft of his arse. Buckles tightened, he picked up the shorts and slid them into position.

When both of them were fully prepared, Jason followed Michael into the arena. The other two boxers had gone. They climbed into the ring and squared up, moving around one another in a slow circle. Tobias, a towel draped around his neck, squatted in one of the padded corners.

Michael was small – smaller even than the young oriental kick-boxer – but he was fast. Jason could scarcely keep up with the boy as he buzzed around him like a fly, easily evading Jason's guard and landing jab after jab, just hard enough to register the hit. Jason swung wildly. Michael was already feet away from him.

Luigi shouted advice and encouragement from the ringside, darting along the ropes with surprising speed, his voice rising and rising, dropping into Italian to signify any particularly inept move on Jason's part.

The combatants wove about the ring for nearly ten minutes. Occasionally Jason managed to connect with his opponent – or at least with his gloves – but most of his strikes went wild. Jason was out of breath and sweating. Michael seemed as fresh as when they had begun.

Luigi turned and walked out of the tent, shaking his head and muttering in Italian.

Michael lunged forward. Jason thrust out with his fist, catching the boy squarely on the chin, with much more force than Jason had intended. The first thing he was aware of was Michael skidding across the canvas; the next was a sharp pain in his back. He winced.

'Are you all right?' he asked, stooping over Michael. The boy grinned and got back to his feet. He shook his golden head vigorously.

'Good punch,' he said.

'Lucky punch,' Jason replied, wincing again.

'Hey, you OK?' Tobias called.

Jason nodded. 'Just a twinge in my back,' he said.

'OK, that's enough,' said Tobias. 'Come out, and I'll take a look at your back.'

They returned to the changing area. Michael slipped his shorts down and unbuckled his box. He removed the jockstrap, again allowing Jason a brief but full view of his cock. It was hanging low now, the veins becoming visible.

'Hey, Michael!' Luigi's voice, coming from outside somewhere.

Michael dressed quickly. 'See you,' he said and skipped out of the tent.

Tobias unlaced Jason's gloves and pulled them from his hands.

'Lose the box and lay on the bench,' he said.

Jason did as he was told, stripping down to his jockstrap and stretching out on his stomach. Tobias's fingers began prodding and probing the muscles around his spine.

'A good massage will sort you out,' he said.

From somewhere he produced a bottle of oil, which he spread all over Jason's back and buttocks. He then starting kneading his tense flesh, working his fingers deep into Jason's muscles. Shoulders, ribs, small of the back.

'We do this for each other,' said Tobias. 'It keeps us supple.'

His fingers edged down the oiled surface of Jason's skin, crossing the elastic waistband of the jockstrap. Slowly he squeezed the firm, fleshy mounds of Jason's buttocks. Inside the close-fitting pouch Jason was getting a hard-on. His cock was bent painfully between his body and the hard bench. He shifted position to let his cock extend upward. The little strap offered no modesty. Tobias's grin widened. He ran his fingers up and down the cotton strip which ran between Jason's cheeks, joining waistband to pouch. His fingers slid under the strap and played up and down Jason's crack.

'Sometimes we do *this* for one another, too,' he said.

He eased one slippery finger into Jason's sphincter, wiggling it around as it wormed its way in. On his stomach on the bench, Jason squirmed with pleasure.

'You like that?' asked Tobias. 'How about this?'

Jason felt the finger withdraw, to be replaced by two of them. He felt them parting his soft tunnel-flesh, working backwards and forwards. He twisted slightly on the bench and reached for Tobias's white shorts, straining to contain his erect cock, and pulled them down at the front, hooking the elastic waistband under the boy's heavy black balls. His cock stood, thick and proud, not quite as big as Glen's, but close. Jason reached back and cupped Tobias's balls, squeezing and stroking. He traced the tubular underside of the boy's cock and closed his fist around the dark purple head, drawing the foreskin back.

'Oh, yeah . . .' Tobias whispered.

The fingers were withdrawn again. Tobias bent forward and, parting Jason's buttocks with his hands, lowered his face onto Jason's soft arsehole. Slowly drawing Tobias's foreskin backwards and forwards over his glistening knob, Jason felt the black boy's nose and chin coming to rest between his buttocks. He felt Tobias's generous mouth form a seal around the sphincter, his hot breath against him, his tongue oozing and slipping inside his hole.

'Turn over,' Tobias said after a few minutes.

Jason turned. His cock was jutting around the side of the jockstrap. Tobias wrapped his hand around it. The two of them stroked each other's cocks in unison.

The tent wall quivered behind Jason. A head appeared under the wall and looked up at them, grinning. It was the oriental boxer. Jason immediately pulled away from Tobias and drew his knees up.

'Don't worry,' said Tobias. 'Chen's seen it all before. Come in.'

Chen scrambled under the tent wall and bounced to his feet. His cock was hard under his jogging-bottoms. Grinning as widely as Tobias he whipped his T-shirt off and pants down and stood facing Jason. He had a compact body, practically hairless except for the small triangular bush around his neat, delicate, upwardly curving cock. He ran a single finger along the underside, playing with his own frenulum with a fingernail, squeezing the head between his thumb and forefinger.

Still pumping Jason's cock, Tobias reached out with his left hand and shooed Chen's hand from his prick. He replaced it with his own, stroking both men together. Chen reached for Jason's balls and began squeezing them, tugging at his pubic hair. Slowly his hand crept upward, dislodging Tobias's. Jason felt a slight break in the rhythm on his cock, and then a new, different, but no less pleasurable stroke from the oriental boy's hand. The three formed an unbroken chain, Jason lying on the bench on his back, Tobias and Chen standing next to him, wanking each other's cocks in the cool tent.

'Let's try blowing each other like this,' Chen said.

'Wicked!' Tobias enthused. He dropped to the floor and lay on his back. Chen dropped down next to him. Jason rolled off the bench to join them.

Tobias plunged his head into Jason's lap, immersing his cock in his soft, wet mouth, expertly drawing his foreskin back with his teeth. Jason felt the delicious sensation of Tobias's tongue running up and down his shaft, tracing around the ridge of his helmet.

Chen opened his mouth wide and sucked up Tobias's big black cock. Jason watched his head bobbing up and down on the great pole. Jason scuttled around until he could reach Chen's cock. His own boner twisted and slid pleasingly around in Tobias's mouth. He craned his neck and nipped at Chen's foreskin. Chen's elegant cock twitched slightly. Jason swallowed it whole. He felt it tickling the back of his throat. His lips brushed against Chen's small, neat pubic bush.

The three sucked for a long time, hands exploring each other's bodies. Glen's big hands, still slippery with oil, tugged at Jason's balls and probed his arsehole. He in turn ran his hands up Chen's smooth torso, pinching and pulling at his nipples, then moving on to tickle Tobias's hairy balls.

Chen was close to coming. He began jerking his hips frantically. He pulled loose from Jason's mouth and fired a great geyser of spunk over his face. Jason caught the spurting organ between his lips. He was coming too, firing his hot seed down Tobias's throat. Tobias let out a great groan as he too began coming in Chen's hugely stretched mouth.

The three lay there, breathless, their cocks softening in one another's mouths. Outside the tent they could hear Luigi holding forth about something or other. One by one they began to laugh.

Jason spent the rest of the day with the young boxers, messing about on the fairground rides. They rammed each other in the Bumper Cars, rode the Waltzers, chucked wooden balls at the big, painted Aunt Sally dolls. Tobias talked continuously; Michael listened and said little, content to soak up the happy atmosphere. Jason was developing a soft spot for the small, shy young man.

Chen, who was from Thailand, and Finn, the fourth boxer, who was Irish, traded good-natured insults with one another without respite. All four displayed a boisterous camaraderie and an irreverent affection for their employer.

'Luigi's an old woman,' Tobias laughed. 'He fusses about what we eat. He won't let us drink or smoke.' He lit a cigarette. 'He won't let us near women before a bout.'

'So that's why . . .'

'Yup.'

They were sitting on the long bench in the tented area, preparing for the imminent evening's work. Chen was tossing and catching a medicine ball.

Jason fingered the bench, still stained with body-oil.

'So does he know about . . .?'

'Nah. He just lives for boxing. He'd go apeshit. *Boxing keepa da young man pure in heart,*' Tobias mugged in mock-Italian. 'Sometimes he thinks he's that old blind geezer out of *Kung Fu.*'

'But *he*'s the geezer out of *Kung Fu,*' said Finn, gesturing to Chen.

Smiling, Chen dropped the medicine ball on Finn's foot.

Luigi bustled in in a state of high agitation. Hastily Tobias stubbed out his cigarette, but Luigi seemed too distracted to notice. His prize-fighter hadn't turned up, and the fair was about to open.

'I kill him!' he bawled in his thick Italian accent. 'No-good army motherfucker! I kick his fucking teeth in!' He sat on the edge of the boxing ring with his head in his hands. 'You know how much he is costing me?'

'Let me go in,' said Finn. 'I'll do it.'

'There is a saying,' said Luigi. The young boxers groaned.

'Attributed to Alexander,' Luigi continued. 'The best swordsman in France need not fear the second best swordsman in France; he should fear the worst.'

Finn's face closed in incomprehension.

'I am not sending any of you in the ring against a load of amateur sluggers,' said Luigi. 'Look what happened to Michael this afternoon. One bad, lucky punch' – he patted Jason on the shoulder – 'and this guy's quite good!'

Jason chewed his lip thoughtfully.

'You need a boxer,' he said, 'someone tough, to take on the public?'

'You know someone?' demanded Luigi.

'Maybe,' said Jason. 'Maybe . . .'

'Hang on,' said Tobias. 'Why would Alexander the Great be talking about French swordsmen? Man, the French were still shit-kickers when Alexander was around.'

'Look, what is it with you?' Tom was pissed off. Sometimes he wanted to smack Jason one. 'Why d'you do this sort of thing, Jason?'

He clattered angrily about the caravan's little kitchen, an old tea-towel clamped in his fist.

'I thought we agreed not to rake up –'

'It's just this once,' Jason interrupted. 'Their bloke hasn't turned up. You'd be paid.'

'I'm not interested in the money,' Tom snapped. 'You should know me better than that.'

'How should I know you better than that? You never fucking say anything!'

Jason lowered his eyes. Tom exhaled sharply and shook his head. He didn't want to fall out with the kid, but he did have a knack of dredging things up. Almost as if he knew . . .

'If you don't do it, Luigi'll have to send one of the kids in,' said Jason. 'He doesn't want to, but . . .'

'What, those four? Any half-fit full-grown man would murder them.'

'I know,' said Jason. 'That's why I'm asking you. You were a champion . . .'

It was true. Regimental champ. He'd come close to winning the big inter-regimental championships.

'I haven't boxed for two years,' he said.

'But you're still fit,' said Jason. 'You're the fittest bloke I've ever seen.'

Tom sat on the bed, forearms on his knees, the old tea-towel slung around his neck. Only then did he catch his reflection in the tiny shaving-mirror. He looked like Rocky, sitting there.

'I said I'd never box again,' said Tom, already knowing he'd lost the argument.

The night was not a success from Luigi's point of view. Tom spent a half-hour warming up on the punch-bags whilst the Italian stood outside the tent calling his pitch. Fifty pounds for anyone who could last three three-minute rounds with The Destroyer. A fiver a go.

A reasonable crowd assembled in the tent. Tom fought first against Finn, and then against Chen. The fights were slick, but stagey. To Jason, watching from the ropes, the whole thing looked a bit fake. The crowd seemed happy, though. Tom put Finn down in the second round – the result was prearranged; the boy overdid the dive, Jason thought – and allowed Chen to go the whole distance. The Thai lad's kick-boxing particularly pleased the audience, who carried him at shoulder-height in a lap of honour around the ring.

Then the real fighting started. One by one a queue of hopefuls climbed through the ropes to pit themselves against The

Destroyer. Almost all of them, good or bad, were still on their feet after three rounds. Tom danced and punched, but seemed incapable of inflicting any real damage on anybody. Luigi's shouts from the corner were becoming more and more agitated as the night wore on and his money disappeared in reluctant fifties. Eventually he retired to his mobile home in despair, with orders that only those punters who had already handed over their fivers – there were about three standing in a line – were to be allowed to box, then the stall should be closed for the night.

'I am ruined,' he muttered to himself as he left the tent. 'Ruined.'

A man entered the tent a few minutes after Luigi's departure and made his way through the thin crowd of spectators. His arrival caused the crowd to stir. He was in his thirties, over six feet tall, with a shaven head, a broken nose and a body like an anvil. This should be a fight . . .

Except that the man didn't seem interested in fighting. He stationed himself close to Jason and punctuated the contest with tuts, hisses and derisive laughter. His arrival had a noticeable effect on Tom. He suddenly seemed tense, self-conscious. His moves became wooden and clumsy. The crowd started to slip away. By the end of the last fight there were barely half-a-dozen spectators left. As Tom climbed from the ring the tall skinhead bruiser walked slowly towards the exit, all the time staring at ring, staring at Tom.

Jason entered the caravan he shared with Tom with some trepidation. The big roustabout was lying on his bed, on his back, his hands behind his head. He still wore the black silk shorts and boxing shoes he had been given for the night. The light was on; Tom was staring, unblinking, at the ceiling.

'Sorry,' said Jason. 'You hated that, didn't you?'

Tom didn't reply. He swung an arm out from behind his head and held it out to Jason. Jason lay on the bed next to him and rested his head on Tom's chest, feeling his slow breathing, listening to his heart. Tom drew his arm back in around Jason, hugging him to his side, his eyes never leaving the ceiling.

Eight

Tom awoke, as usual, just as the sky was lightening. He listened to the first of the dawn chorus and looked long and hard at the sleeping boy next to him. He stroked Jason's hair gently. He looked so peaceful in sleep.

He heard a distant, distinctive creaking sound. The Wheel. He looked out of the caravan.

He was there again, the big skinhead. He was hanging by his arms from one of the cross-struts of the Wheel, his body straight, his legs held at forty-five degrees to the ground, ankles together, toes pointed, lifting and lowering himself, lifting and lowering in rapid, economical movements. Pull-ups, the army way. He was duplicating Tom's every-morning routine exactly. No surprises there – it was the army routine. The Wheel creaked rhythmically as the man's momentum worked its way through the steel arms.

Tom dressed in vest and jogging pants and slipped out of the caravan. He set his face away from the fair and began running. A good run would help him think. Too many cans of worms were breaking open around him.

Among the usual tasks which occupied the fair-folk that morning, Jason noticed Jack and Laurent erecting a long trestle-table in the space between the caravans and the fair itself. The weather had

140

improved sufficiently, it seemed, to allow meals to be taken communally, in the open air.

Tom was missing. He was usually hard at work on the Wheel by this time. Nobody, it appeared, had seen him all morning.

The big skinhead was there still, just hanging about, scowling and sneering at anyone whose eye he happened to catch. Rex was quite smitten.

'He looks so nasty,' Rex sighed. 'So evil. Imagine getting a moment of tenderness out of that. It would be like finding a seam of gold.'

He was wearing his leopard–skin leotard. He walked theatrically up to the Test-Your-Strength machine – he called it Bertha – swung the hammer overhead and brought it down hard. The bell clanged.

'Don't mind me,' said Rex to the half-dozen faces which turned in unison at the sound of the bell. 'I'm just trying to draw attention to myself.'

He opened a wooden box which was built into Bertha's base. Inside was a stack of telephone directories. He lifted one out and, with a mighty roar, ripped it in two.

There was a slow, ironic hand–clapping from the skinhead.

'Be still, my beating heart,' Rex sighed.

Tom appeared close to midday, flushed and sweating. He went straight to the Wheel and started the engine, staring hard into its oily workings and talking to nobody. Jason watched him with concern. He seemed convinced that the engine which drove the Big Wheel sounded wrong. Jason couldn't hear anything.

'Who was running this last night?' he asked. 'Bob, yeah?'

Bob was a general hand who had turned up at Leicester – one of Piper's many gaff boys who attached themselves to the show from time to time then vanished again. Piper seemed to have such people everywhere.

'That's the last time I let anyone else get their hands on it.'

Tom's speech was clipped and sullen. Across the fairground the skinhead looked on. His eyes never seemed to be off Tom. For his part, Tom worked with even more furious concentration than usual, studiously avoiding the skinhead's gaze.

'D'you know him or what?' Jason asked.

Tom ignored the question at first, staring into the aged motor. At last he said, 'He was a soldier. A boxer. Not in my regiment. I never fought him – I never actually spoke to him – but he had a nasty reputation, in the ring and out of it.'

'Destroyer!' The door of Luigi's mobile home flew open and the Italian thundered out in nothing but a pair of enormous Y-fronts. He ran across the fairground to where the skinhead was standing and clapped him hard on the back. 'Where the fuck were you?' shouted Luigi. 'I was nearly ruined last night.'

'I saw,' said the skinhead loudly, looking across the ground, directly at Tom.

Lunch in the open air, served by Annie and Doug, consisted of a huge vat of stew eaten with lumps of coarse bread. Jason sat between Tobias and Michael. All the boxers – and Jason – were stripped to the waist, chests bared to the sun. Tobias and Finn were arm-wrestling. Jason watched, his chin grazing Tobias's taut shoulder. He could see Jack, a few places away at the table, watching them with the unmistakable longing of the addict, trying to reform but suddenly brought face-to-face with his vice.

Jason couldn't resist milking the situation. Catching Jack's eye, he challenged Michael to an arm-wrestle. The two of them locked hands and strained against one another. It was a close match, but Jason managed with effort to master his opponent. As Michael finally gave way, the two of them collapsed forward and lay in a sweating, laughing heap on the table, sweat mingling with sweat, their chests pushing hard against each other as they strained for breath.

Tom sat some distance away, ignoring the fun and games, scowling and speaking to no one.

Piper approached the head of the table. With him was a laughing, chattering, gesticulating Luigi and a silent, smug-looking skinhead. Luigi made a speech – largely ignored – about what a pleasure it was to be back among his friends at Gamlin's, what the great Homer had said about the pugilistic arts, and his new boxing sensation, The Destroyer.

They sat down to eat. Luigi continued chattering to Piper,

every so often turning to point to some muscle on The Destroyer's upper body, illustrating some point or other. Piper ate messily, stew dribbling down his whiskers and suit, and didn't appear to be listening.

Presently The Destroyer leaned down the table towards Tom, who was staring into his empty bowl.

'I saw you in the ring last night, Jarrett,' The Destroyer said. 'I was surprised. The rumour was you'd sworn never to set foot in the ring again.'

Tom's head snapped upward; the two men's eyes locked.

'You were ring-rusty,' The Destroyer continued. 'You'd lost that spark. That thing that gave you the edge – marked you out as different. That . . . killer instinct.'

Slamming his fists on to the table, Tom surged to his feet. The whole assembly fell silent at a stroke, all eyes on Tom. The Destroyer smirked up at him.

Jason suddenly noticed Piper. The old man's stare was blazing down the table, flashing between the two protagonists. Suddenly Tom seemed to become aware of the attention he was attracting. He blushed and lowered his head, stepped back from the table and strode off into the fair.

Jason caught Annie's eye. She was watching him steadily. She seemed to know what was on his mind. He wanted to go after Tom. She shook her head slowly and slightly. *Let him go*, she mouthed. Jason felt almost relieved.

The conversations around the table struggled to resume their flow, but the atmosphere was muted now. Only Luigi seemed oblivious to the mood, and chattered as before, shovelling in great mouthfuls of stew between sentences.

The arm-wrestling started again, but in the changed atmosphere it didn't really work. What had begun as friendly rivalry with much laughter was turning serious. An aggression had crept into their bouts.

Michael did very badly. The fit and fast but small boy was beaten by everybody. Jason was beaten by everybody except Michael. He sensed that the boy was a little upset with the drubbing he had received. The communion was starting to break up. People were returning to rides or caravans. Tobias, Chen and

Finn disappeared into the tent, their good humour returning. Michael lagged behind, getting up slowly and trailing unenthusiastically in their wake.

Jason called after him, 'Michael, d'you fancy a wander into town?'

The boy turned, and a shy smile crept over his face.

The fair was on a recreation field close to the centre of town. The pair ambled easily about the busy streets, got lost and separated in the picturesque old market, met up by the long sweet stall, ummed and ahed among the enticing glass jars and finally bought a gobstopper each.

'Ruigi hakesh ush eaking gish shork og skukk,' Michael mouthed from behind the gobstopper. Jason could only nod in semi-comprehension. They sucked in silence for a while.

'You're kind of small for a boxer,' Jason said when his mouth regained its feeling.

'I used to get a lot of shit at school,' Michael replied. 'So I started boxing. I joined a gym. That's where I met Luigi. Things weren't too good at home either, so when he said he was getting this tour together I thought *Why not?*'

Another runaway, thought Jason. Another Lost Boy.

'D'you fancy a drink?' asked Jason. It seemed ages since he'd been into a bar.

They wandered from the market until they hit upon a street pedestrianised for shoppers. They passed along the dazzlingly ordinary array of shops. There must be somewhere to get a drink around here. Mothercare. Argos.

The row of shop-fronts was broken by a narrow alleyway. Halfway down it Jason saw a sign. The Nautilus Bar. Splashed across a pink triangle.

'Oh,' said Michael, 'I don't know.'

'Why? Because it's a gay bar?'

'Yes, sort of . . .' Michael replied shyly. 'I mean, I've never been in one of those before. I'm not queer . . . um . . . gay.'

Jason raised his eyebrows.

'But you know about Tobias and Chen. And I dare say Finn.'

'Um, yes. I don't do much of that stuff myself . . . I mean . . .

the odd circle jerk now and then, but that's about it. I had a girlfriend before I joined the fair.'

Jason smiled nostalgically. 'Haven't we all, mate, at one time or another. Come on, it'll be OK. You're a boxer. Anyone bothers you, just lay a haymaker on them.'

As they moved down the alley, Jason could hear the strains of some disco diva or other coming from behind the black door which sat under the sign. This was nice – he hadn't been in one of these places in ages. He pushed open the door and slipped in through it. Michael followed close behind him.

A bar ran the length of one wall. At the far end of the bar was a small stage, on which a six-foot woman – endless legs and black hair, lips like fruit, sparkling in a sheer, gold-leaf dress – gyrated to a high-energy backing tape and moaned love into a microphone. Jason smiled. He had a soft spot for drag-queens.

There was hardly anyone in the dimly lit room. Jason rummaged in his pocket – he only had a few quid on him.

'I'll get these,' said Michael. He was practically standing on Jason's feet.

'Relax,' Jason laughed. 'We're not fucking Siamese twins.'

Michael ordered a couple of beers. Jason wandered towards the stage.

'Jason!' A deafening stage-whisper of panic from the bar. 'Where are you? Jason!'

'I think your friend's lost,' the drag-queen boomed down the microphone. Jason stopped and turned.

'Don't worry, little boy,' the booming, teasing voice continued. 'Come up here. I'll look after you.'

Jason laughed – in spite of the clothes and make-up, in spite of the obvious deception being worked, there was something refreshingly open and honest about drag. He patted Michael on the shoulder. 'Look, relax,' he whispered. 'If anyone asks, we're together, OK?'

He led Michael to a table close to the stage. The tall, willowy female impersonator had hauled some poor sod up from the audience – a bloke about Jason's age, stocky, with dark hair. From the shadows a friend egged him on, clapping and shouting. The lad was obviously a bit drunk. He was pressed close to the drag-queen, his hips swivelling as hers did, in time to the music. Jason could tell he had a hard-on, which he was trying to press against the front of her gold dress.

'Cheeky sod!' the drag-queen shrieked in mock-outrage. 'I wanted someone pure and innocent up here.'

She pushed him off the front of the low stage.

'You!' she boomed.

She was pointing at Michael, who blushed furiously into his pint.

'No? OK, relax, honey, the table ain't gonna swallow you up. How about your friend?'

She leaned from the stage and grabbed Jason by the lapel.

'Never mind your goddam beer,' she said. 'You can drink anytime. Dance.'

Self-consciously Jason began to shuffle in time to the beat of the music. He had never been a dancer – he and his friends had scorned such mundane pursuits. From the stage he could see directly into the alcove where his on-stage predecessor now sat close to his loud supporter. Their mouths were locked together in the gloom. Their legs were intertwined; the hand of the dark-haired stocky boy was inside the trousers of his taller, slimmer friend, squeezing and rubbing. Did they think they were shielded from prying eyes by the little table in front of them? He practically had a grandstand view from up here. As he watched, the tall boy fumbled with the fly-buttons of his mate and slipped his fingers inside.

Jason looked across at Michael. The boy's eyes flashed between the stage, the alcove and his pint.

'Hey,' the drag-queen scolded him loudly in his ear. 'Pay attention. Ignore them two. It's a disgrace. At it like monkeys. This early in the day, too. *Ooooh . . .*' Her gruff voice attempted to soar into 'I Feel Love'.

Jason's eyes returned to the alcove where the two boys, still kissing passionately, masturbated each other inside the dark, cramped folds of their trousers.

'*I feel lo-o-o-ove, I feel lo-o-o-ove* – keep in time – *I feel lo-o-o-ove . . .* try not to tread on my feet, darling . . . *I feel lo-o-o-ove . . .*'

It was turning Jason on, the secretive way they were bringing each other off, as quietly and with as little movement as possible and the way Michael's curiosity was struggling to overturn his conscience. His eyes were staying longer and longer on the alcove. One of the lovers started to jerk uncontrollably, his face creased as he came, his cock – and his friend's hand – still inside his trousers. Jason could picture spunk with nowhere to go coating pants, fingers, mingling with pubic hair. As he came he yanked the other boy's cock, swollen and livid, from its cramped cave. It too started to spurt, shooting a great jet of spunk over the little table.

The drag-queen stopped in mid-gyration.

'You dirty sods!' she exclaimed.

Jason pulled away from her. She planted a wet kiss on his cheek.

'Thanks, love,' she said. 'You go play with your friend.'

Jason emerged from the bar smiling. Michael too was grinning his shy grin.

They'd better get back to the fair. Jason turned towards the main shopping street.

A group of four youths, all leather jackets and boots, stood at the end of the alleyway, blocking their exit. They strode towards the pair, standing uncertainly under the lit pink triangle.

'Look,' he heard one of the lads say, 'he's got lipstick on his cheek. He's been snogging with one of them trannies.'

The tallest of the boys reminded Jason of Nige. Same boney face and sallow complexion. Same arrogant, nasty expression.

Jason and Michael backed slowly away from the group. Jason shot a glance behind him. The alley ended in a blank, high wall.

'Come on!' he shouted.

He turned and ran at the wall, jumping to catch a hand-hold. If ever he needed his old climbing skills . . .

No good. The wall was sheer. He felt a hostile hand on his shoulder. He swung around into the stale breath and sadistic grin of the tall boy. As his friends watched, the youth drew a flick-knife from his jacket.

He could see the other three youths clustering around Michael. Michael had his guard up.

There was sudden movement behind the group, and a volley of savage barks. A dark shadow lanced into the huddle. Black Shuck.

The dog's teeth ripped into the left shoulder of the boy with the knife, piercing the thick leather shoulder-pad with ease and dragging the boy to the ground. He screamed.

Jason cowered against the wall, more frightened of the dog than the youth. His accomplices stood, paralysed, staring at the dog.

More in panic than judgement the boy brought his knife-hand round hard. The blade bit into the dog's neck. It howled and snarled.

A piercing whistle seemed to freeze the moment. The grey figure of Piper was thrashing at the dog's back with his open hand. The old man dragged the dog off the sobbing boy.

'There now,' said the old man. 'No harm done. He'll not have broken the skin. I caught him in time, you see. Another minute and he'd have ripped your fuckin' head off.'

Black Shuck lurched away into a corner and licked casually around its neck, seemingly unperturbed by the wound and enjoying the taste of its own blood.

The boy on the floor scrambled to his feet and backed around Piper, his eyes flashing between the old man and the dog. He backed towards his friends.

'Oh, ah, wait up,' said Piper. 'C'mere.'

Blinking, as if suddenly confused, the boy stepped towards the old man. Smiling, Piper leaned forward, whispered something into his ear and kissed him lightly on the cheek.

The youth's expression turned instantly from confusion to scorn, then to revulsion and to fear. He thrust Piper away and began to run back up the alley. Confused, his friends followed him.

'Thanks,' said Jason. 'How did you find us?'

'I didn't,' said Piper. 'Old Black Shuck here got loose. I just came lookin' for him. I reckon he's gettin' to like you.'

'What did you say to him?' asked Jason, jerking his head in the direction of the rout.

Piper shrugged. 'Oh, I reminded him of somethin',' he said casually. 'Somethin' in his past. Somethin' he'd forgotten.'

'You know him?' Jason's voice registered his scepticism.

'When you've travelled about as much as I have, you get to know practically everybody,' Piper replied. 'I know his type.

What makes him tick.' He winked at Jason, suddenly grinning all over his face. 'I know your type too,' he cackled.

Suddenly his face became serious. 'I do, too,' he said. 'Go careful.'

A protest greeted the opening of the fair that night. A local vicar and a parade of men in cardigans and headscarved women was standing outside the boxing booth.

'This is barbaric,' the vicar chanted. 'It's medieval, and we don't want it in Derby!'

Peaceful, law-abiding Derby, thought Jason. He was standing at the Wheel with Tom. Luigi was dancing around the protesting crowd, waving his arms and shouting.

His classical composure had quite deserted him.

'I fucking kill you!' he ranted. 'I fucking punch you vicar's head down you fucking throat!'

'He's right,' said Tom. 'It is medieval.'

There was a loud hiccup, and Piper swayed around the side of the Wheel, a gin bottle in one hand, a toffee-apple in the other. He appeared very drunk.

'Course it's medieval, Tom. This is Gamlin's, and you know what they say about Gamlin's. They say however it wanders about, there's only one place the fair's ever goin'. Into the past. Always into the past. Maybe my past for a bit, maybe yours, or yours . . .'

He suddenly guffawed loudly. 'We're headin' for Newcastle,' he said gleefully.

He turned unsteadily in the direction of the crowd. 'Pain in the fuckin' arse,' he shouted. 'God squad . . . I'll feed 'em to the fuckin' Ghost Train . . .'

He stumbled away, toffee-apple raised.

'. . . fuckin' Hall of Mirrors . . . Let 'em get a look at themselves . . .'

He seemed to get lost in the thin crowd of early-birds, and wandered away behind the trucks. Luigi was managing to disperse the little demo, with some assistance from The Destroyer. Glancing up to make sure Tom was watching, the fighter pushed the vicar roughly away from the entrance to the tent. Voices were raised in protest, but the crowd began to back off. The Destroyer stooped and thrust his face into a woman's face. Throwing his arms into the air, he let out a ferocious, bellowing growl. The woman screamed and fell backwards.

'Baines,' said Tom.

'What?'

'Gary Baines. That was his name.'

'Whose?'

'His. The so-called Destroyer. He was always like this. Vicious. Deliberately nasty, in and out of the ring. The big show, all the time.' Tom spat. 'And you know what? Under that vicious exterior beat the heart of a cunt.'

Once the crowd had dispersed – amid dire threats of police and divine retribution – the show in the ring began. First Finn and Tobias would fight, then The Destroyer would come on and fight a fake match with Michael. He would have the boy on the canvas inside three, but in a way which showed that Michael wasn't at all hurt.

Jason wondered whether the big professional boxing matches were sorted out like this.

Finn and Tobias fought well, obviously enjoying themselves, and by the time they were finished a decent queue – headed by Michael – had formed to box.

Gary Baines, The Destroyer, stepped into the ring. The waiting queue seemed to shiver with sudden trepidation. Michael stepped up to face him. He towered over the small, blond boy. Luigi sounded the bell and the fight began. Michael danced around Baines, feinting skilfully. The Destroyer swung languidly. The idea seemed to be to give the impression that, for all his size, he was sluggish and slow – that the chances of a challenger actually having to take a blow were small.

Jason was suddenly aware of Tom, standing next to him.

'Who's on the Wheel?' asked Jason.

'Bob,' Tom replied.

The crowd suddenly roared. Baines had seemed distracted for a moment, and in that moment Michael had landed a solid uppercut on his jaw. The Destroyer staggered backwards, and struggled to regain his composure. He'd noticed Tom. For a split second their eyes had locked – Tom had tensed tangibly next to Jason – and Michael had hit home.

The Destroyer seemed more genuinely inept now. He seemed to be trying harder to block Michael's attacks, and failing consistently. His own punches were quicker now, but inaccurate. His eyes kept flashing on Tom.

Michael landed a second, identical jaw-strike. Again Baines reeled. Michael followed through. Baines narrowly avoided the canvas.

Recovering his footing, The Destroyer's face seemed to cloud. He looked icily at Tom for a long moment, then, snorting, turned to face his opponent.

Baines jabbed at Michael's head, fast and hard, effortlessly through the boy's defences. Michael flinched under the impact. Baines jabbed again. Michael staggered. Again. Again.

The Destroyer was batting the boy around the ring with vicious, cynical ease. He swung a wide hook, catching him on the side of the head. Michael bounced off the corner post and slumped to the canvas in front of Jason and Tom. His nose was bleeding profusely, his eye was swollen, his mouth broken and bloody. He appeared dazed. This had taken about thirty seconds.

'Cunt,' Tom whispered under his breath. He grabbed the ropes and swung himself over the top. He stood in front of Baines, his arms wide, hands out from his hips.

'Want to try that on me, Baines?'

Baines grinned noxiously. 'Jarrett. I'm scared.'

Tom's arms shot up, pushing Baines in the chest.

'What's it going to be, Jarrett?' The Destroyer taunted. 'Boxing or brawling? 'Cause I hear you're pretty good at both.'

Tom pushed again, his arms pistoning out. Surprised, Baines staggered and tripped, sprawling into the ropes.

Luigi scrambled into the ring and inserted himself between Tom and Baines.

'You go,' he said to Tom. 'Again you ruin –'

Looking past the fat man, Tom spat, turned and left the ring and the tent.

'OK!' Luigi turned to the crowd, grown restless and uneasy. 'Now, who next challenge Destroyer?'

A low murmur spread through the crowd. Those queuing to box suddenly melted away into the audience, which itself started to drain from the tent.

Jason was stooping over Michael, dabbing at his face with a handkerchief. 'Come on,' he said, 'let's get you out of here.'

He helped the boy from the ring and half-carried him from the tent.

'There's a first-aid kit in our caravan,' he said.

Michael was still unsteady on his feet. He held on to Jason as they walked to the caravan. Once inside Jason sat him down on the bed. He turned on the tap in the sink. All the towels were dirty, waiting to be washed. He stripped his T-shirt off and held it beneath the jet of warm water. Gently he dabbed the drying blood and the swellings on Michael's face. Michael winced.

'Sorry.'

''S OK,' Michael mumbled. He tried to smile, but winced again.

A pool of tepid water, dripping from the makeshift facecloth, was gathering in Michael's shorts. He shuffled uncomfortably.

'Let me get the box off,' he said. Painfully he slipped out of his shorts. Jason unstrapped the box and lifted it from Michael's groin. He lowered the boy's jockstrap. His golden-crowned cock flopped out.

Jason wet the cloth again, and dabbed at the bruises appearing on Michael's chest and shoulders. The memory of the day they did The Drop suddenly sprang into Jason's mind. In the garden shed, dabbing Paul's grazes with his handkerchief.

'Ow,' Michael winced.

'Sorry,' said Jason.

'He had a hard punch,' mumbled Michael, attempting a smile. Warm water trickled down his chest, trickled down his stomach, and wound in rivulets into his golden bush.

They heard Luigi's voice, crying among the caravans. 'Michael? Where Michael?'

They heard footsteps. He was right outside their caravan. Grinning, Jason placed a finger lightly on Michael's swollen lips. Michael looked shyly, wickedly into Jason's eyes. His lips twitched slightly, catching the furthest tip of the finger.

'Ah . . .' Luigi was talking to himself now. 'Two nights. Two nights and I am ruined. Ah . . .'

His footsteps faded into the distance. Jason continued running the wet cloth around Michael's chest. He moved lower, over his stomach. His face was close to Michael's now. Their lips brushed lightly. Dropping the cloth, Jason's hand wandered, fingers spread, down Michael's wet stomach and into his pubes. Jason tugged gently at the delicate bush. He brushed his lips against Michael's again, more deliberately this time. The tip of Michael's tongue appeared through his lips, catching Jason on the nose. Grinning, Jason extended his own tongue, darting at Michael's. Tongue touched tongue, nuzzled, broke and weaved like goldfish. Jason allowed his hand to drift down on to Michael's cock. As his palm rested on it, Jason felt it twitch and grow and harden, filling his hand. He squeezed it slowly.

Jason gently lay Michael back on the bed. Michael spread his legs slightly as he went back, lifting his hard cock into Jason's hand. Jason bore down on Michael and plunged his tongue into his mouth, all the time kneading his cock.

Michael spluttered a little. He seemed to have more difficulty adjusting to Jason's deep kiss than to being masturbated.

'Are you OK?' asked Jason.

'Yeah,' Michael replied. 'It's just . . . This is all a bit new for me. I've never . . .'

'Does the kissing bother you?'

'Yeah, I guess. I don't know. It was . . .'

'It's OK,' said Jason. 'No more kissing, if you want.'

'No,' said Michael. 'It was good.'

He thrust his mouth upward and clumsily caught Jason's lips. He pushed his tongue forward.

He was struggling to loose Jason's belt.

'Let me help you,' said Jason. He undid the belt and his fly. Michael's hands dived in, pulling the denim downward, now inside his pants, grappling with his painfully hard cock.

Michael pushed Jason backward onto the bed and unhooked his cock from the elastic of his briefs. He gazed at it, mesmerised for a moment, before running his tongue all over it like a child licking a lolly. Finally he stretched his mouth around Jason's helmet. Jason moaned with pleasure. He ran his fingers across Michael's pudding-basin-blond, bobbing head.

Jason felt like a teenager again – he was already close to coming. He pulled his cock from Michael's mouth.

'My turn for a bit,' he said. He slid down the bed, at the same time lifting Michael by the buttocks. Jason was sitting on the floor now, leaning back against the bed. Michael was straddling him, leaning over him onto the bed. Jason grabbed Michael's practically hairless balls and steered his cock into his mouth. Letting his head rest against the edge of the bed he took hold of Michael's buttocks and began rocking them backwards and forwards, pumping Michael's cock in and out of his own mouth. Michael soon got the rhythm. Bracing himself against the bed he fucked Jason vigorously in the mouth. Jason's hands circled Michael's pumping buttocks, playing with his sphincter, stroking the underside of his swinging balls.

'Shit, I'm coming . . .' he gasped, slamming his cock deep into Jason's mouth. Jason tasted quickly the hot, salty syrup before it slid down his throat. Michael slumped on the bed. 'Wow,' he said.

He turned to Jason and grabbed his head. 'Let's see what I taste like,' he said, pushing his tongue between Jason's lips.

They kissed for a long time, Michael's hands once more playing with Jason's hard-on.

'D'you want to . . . you know . . .' said Michael shyly.

'What?' said Jason.

'Fuck me,' said Michael, swallowing hard. 'D'you want to fuck me?'

'Have you ever . . .?'

'No,' said Michael. 'But I want to now.'

Jason kissed him hard and then crawled from the bed. Somewhere in his rucksack he had some rubbers. He'd got into them more or less in a panic when Spider had started doing rent, really just to make the point to Spider. He was glad now he'd hung on to a packet.

'Let me,' said Michael, snatching the condom from him. He ripped open the packet and rolled the latex over Jason's cock.

'Lay down,' said Jason. Michael flattened himself, face down against the bed, spreading his buttocks with his fingers. Jason spat onto his hand and rubbed the spittle into Michael's tight hole. He lined up his cock and pressed it gently forward.

'This might hurt a bit at first,' he said.

Michael nodded, teeth clenched as Jason eased his way in in the smallest of steps.

'No ... Ah ... Yes ...' Michael gasped. 'No ... Fuck, it hurts!'

'Nearly there,' said Jason. With one final push he felt his balls slap against Michael's cheeks. The boy's virgin arse was tight around his cock. Slowly he began moving his hips, drawing his cock in and out of Michael. He could feel Michael clenching and unclenching around his cock. Michael was rubbing his own cock against the bed in small, fast thrusts in syncopation with Jason's quickening strokes.

They came together, Michael pumping his seed into the bedclothes, Jason spurting into the latex sheath, deep in Michael's arsehole.

Michael laughed as Jason's cock slid out of his hole.

'What?' said Jason.

'That was just like having an enormous shit,' Michael said, grinning cheekily.

Jason and Michael lolled and loved in the caravan all evening. They chatted easily, they listened to the bustle of the fair, slowly rising and falling as the night oozed on, finally vanishing into silence.

'Tom will be back soon,' said Jason.

Michael was thoughtful for a minute. 'We can sleep in the boxing tent,' he said. 'There's loads of spare bedding in our trailer.'

He rolled out of bed, his cock still semi-hard. Jason gave it a playful tweak.

'Come on,' said Michael. 'There's plenty of time for that.'

Jack stood, naked, in front of a full-length mirror.

'I don't know why you fuss so,' said Laurent, passing behind him. He reached around Jack's side and ran his hand down his chest and stomach, over the bristles where his pubes were just growing back, and down onto his cock. 'I like you smooth.'

Jack's cock was growing in his hand. Laurent began running his fingers up and down it. Jack closed his eyes and let his head loll, languishing in the sensation. Smooth . . .

His eyes snapped open. Quite unexpectedly a decision had lodged in his head.

'Get dressed,' he said.

'I am dressed,' Laurent replied.

'We're going out,' Jack announced. 'It is time. We're going to town.'

Laurent had to run to keep up with Jack as he strode across the fairground, resplendent in purple bomber-jacket, announcing his return to the field.

'I have learned my lesson,' Jack declaimed. 'I have torn Northampton from the book. I have stricken it from the record. Sexually speaking, Northampton no longer exists.'

They reached the edge of the recreation ground and began the walk into town.

'I feel like a Jew after Ramadan,' said Jack, rubbing his hands. 'I have been spiritually cleansed. My fast has given me new insights. My appetite is Holy.'

'Ramadan's Muslim,' said Laurent.

They were in the pedestrianised heart of town.

'There's a little place around here,' said Jack. 'I haven't been there for years, but . . .'

They passed the mouth of an alley. The Nautilus Bar beamed a welcome.

'Here we are,' said Jack. He rubbed his hands again and marched down the alley. 'Christ, I've earned this,' he said.

Laurent shook his head and followed Jack.

'Nine days,' he said. 'You went without sex for nine days.'

'I know,' said Jack. 'I'm a fucking Sadhu.'

'What have we here?' the voice from the stage boomed. A six-foot drag-queen in sheer silver, hair all down her back, waved at Jack and Laurent as they entered the crowded bar. 'Don't be shy, boys, come forward. Don't skulk at the bar as if you're waiting for fucking rent.'

Jack pushed his way to a table in an alcove. Laurent skulked at the bar.

'Where you from, honey?' the drag-queen asked Jack.

Jack shrugged. 'Here and there . . .'

'Ooh,' the drag-queen cooed, 'a man of mystery. Hidden depths, girls. Don't you love a man you can really dig deep into?'

The audience whooped appreciatively.

'I'm from the fair,' said Jack.

'Ooooh!' This seemed to send the drag-queen to pussy heaven. 'He works at a fair, girls! A real roustabout! Hey, did anyone here watch the Canadian Lumberjack Finals? You know, two o'clock on a fucking Sunday morning after you've come home pissed and rejected on a Saturday night, you sit down, you stick the box on – and there's these dirty great lumberjacks shinning up wooden polls and balancing on floating logs. It's like *It's A Knockout* without the crimplene tracksuits. Christ, *It's A . . .* Now *there* was a show ahead of its time. Why the fuck did that show have to fold before the invention of Lycra?'

Jack relaxed back into his seat as the drag-queen rolled back into her act. Laurent returned from the bar with beers and company.

'Uh, Jacques, I would like to introduce to you Yousaf,' he said, 'and Suliman.'

'No,' said one of the men. 'I'm afraid you have it the wrong way round. May we sit?'

They were in their mid-thirties and Arabic, strikingly handsome, resplendent in tastefully expensive business suits, one of them carrying a briefcase.

'They're part of a trade delegation,' said Laurent. 'From Oman.' He turned to the men. 'Jacques has a very deep interest in your culture,' he said. 'Only this evening he spoke very earnestly about the Feast of Ramadan . . .'

The show rolled on and drinks flowed. 'No, of course one can get a drink in our country,' said Yousaf. 'If one knows where to look.'

'Weird idea,' Jack mused. 'Alcohol illegal. You drink, you're breaking the law. They could flog you.'

'But then, what is life without a little adventure?' Jack felt Yousaf's hand on his upper thigh. Jack spread his legs slightly. Yousaf's hand moved to his cock. Jack saw that he had unzipped the fly of his suit, and that his own large, straight, circumcised cock rose majestically from the folds of cloth. Jack reached across and wrapped his fingers around it. Yousaf was undoing Jack's fly, reaching inside, squeezing his cock through his pants. Looking across, Jack could see Laurent and Suliman, mouths clamped together.

'Shall we withdraw?' said Yousaf. 'There is, I believe, a back-room here.'

He pulled away from Jack and replaced his cock inside his suit. He stood and picked up his briefcase. Clumsily putting himself away, Jack rose to follow.

'There go two more,' boomed the drag-queen from the stage. A shout of vulgar encouragement rose from the audience. 'Randy as billy-goats, can't even wait till the end of my act. Ooh, and another two!'

Laurent and Yousaf were following them. They went through a door in the far wall, hidden in the shadows. 'Be safe, boys!' the drag-queen called as they left the bar.

The door must have been sound-proofed. They walked into a wall of sound – a bass-driven, pumping hardcore beat – and darkness. The only light came from a dull red bulb at one end of the black-walled room. It was like an oven. Shadowy bodies moved in and out of the red darkness. Dropping his briefcase Yousaf swung round and grasped Jack, pulling him forward. He jammed his tongue into Jack's mouth and ground his cock into his groin, rubbing it up and down in time to the frantic music. Jack picked up the rhythm with his own pelvis. The two of them ground together in a mad dance.

Jack's eyes were becoming accustomed to the dark. He watched Laurent slip to his knees and fumble with Suliman's fly. The Arab's cock stood out clearly, lifting the fine material of his suit. Laurent teased the fly down and Suliman's erection bounced into view. Laurent ran his tongue around the ridge of the circumcised head and then sunk his lips over the shaft.

Yousaf released Jack and took a step back. His hands parted Jack's bomber jacket and pulled the hem of his T-shirt outward, then he dropped to his knees in front of Jack and began kissing his stomach, probing Jack's belly-button with his tongue. He stretched the T-shirt over his head, freeing his hands to rake and scratch, pinch and caress Jack's bare torso. He moved his head up under the cloth, nipping at Jack's tits with his teeth. His tie flapped against Jack's belly.

Suliman looked as if he was about to come in Laurent's mouth. Jack watched the Arab ease the French boy's mouth from his cock and pull him to his feet. They kissed, Suliman's hands reaching for Laurent's jeans.

Yousaf was undoing Jack's fly, pulling down his jeans and pants. Jack's throbbing cock bounced against Yousaf's suit. Yousaf freed his head from the T-shirt and ran his tongue down the length of Jack's torso. He cupped Jack's balls, licking at the head of his cock, tracing a saliva trail down the underside of his shaft. He popped first one ball, then the other, into his mouth. Jack moaned with pleasure.

Without moving his mouth from Jack's balls, he reached for his briefcase. Jack heard the catches snap. A moment later Yousaf was fingering a condom. He thrust his head through the narrow space between Jack's legs and the constricting waistband of the jeans, now around Jack's knees. Craning his neck first one way then the other, Yousaf was able to lick around the insides of Jack's thighs, where the sparse hair of his legs began to bush at the groin, and the underside of his balls.

Laurent was completely naked by now; Suliman's tie was loose, his shirt was half-open, his trousers were undone. His cock and Laurent's were crushed together between his two slow-moving hands. Laurent, eyes shut, was feasting on the sensation.

Yousaf was on his feet again now, still immaculately suited, his cock standing out from his fly. He moved behind Jack, pressing his cock against Jack's bare arse. Jack felt Yousaf guide his cock into his ringpiece, felt his soft flesh yielding to penetration. Yousaf pushed his cock upwards in short, hard thrusts until Jack could feel the expensive suit against his arse. He almost stumbled. His jeans were still around his knees, keeping his legs together, making balance difficult. His T-shirt and bomber jacket were rucked up around his chest. Yousaf brought his arms up under Jack's, and gripped his shoulders, hugging Jack to himself as he continued to bang against Jack's arse-cheeks. Jack could feel the movement of Yousaf's cock inside him speed up. Yousaf brought a hand down onto Jack's cock and began drawing his foreskin deftly back and forth.

Yousaf fucked Jack urgently, as if driven on by the frantic, industrial soundtrack which boomed around the walls. Couples were sucking and fucking in the darkness the whole length of the room. Close by, Jack saw Suliman stoop, open Yousaf's briefcase and remove something. It sat about six inches long in his hand – a little black rubber cone, tapering conically to a blunt point.

He watched Suliman push Laurent gently to the wall. A stone shelf, like a narrow bench-seat, ran the length of the room. At periodic intervals along its length shadowy figures sat, or leaned, or otherwise braced, whilst other shadowy figures grunted and heaved against them. Suliman placed his toy, point up, on the sill, and squeezed a tube of KY around it. He kissed Laurent on the lips then, lifting him slightly, pushed him against the wall and gently lowered him onto the rubber cone.

Yousaf's grip tightened around Jack's cock. The Arab was breathing hard now, slamming into Jack's arse. With a moan Yousaf started to come – a final, frantic burst of thrusting followed by one, two, three slow, hard stabs. His head slumped onto Jack's shoulder, and his cock slowly slipped from his arse.

Laurent's face was buckled with pleasure, his breathing short and hard as he sank his arse onto the cone.

'You like watching your friend?' Yousaf whispered in Jack's ear.

'Butt-plug,' Jack replied. 'That used to be my nick-name at school. I've no idea why . . .'

Yousaf stooped and opened the briefcase. In amongst about a year's supply of condoms and lube were a half-dozen of the conical butt-plugs, clipped in a neat row in ascending order of size. One of the middle plugs was missing from its clip.

'Wow,' said Jack. 'Just like a socket-set.'

'Would you like to try one?' Yousaf asked.

'You bet,' said Jack, rubbing his hands.

'Which one would you like?'

'I don't mind,' said Jack, 'as long as it's bigger than Laurent's.'

Yousaf selected and greased up a shiny rubber plug, which he set on the sill next to Laurent. The French boy was fully impaled now – his sphincter had closed around the groove which ran around the plug close to its base; the flat rubber handle sat firm on the stone sill; Laurent's feet barely touched the floor. He was completely immobile. Jack allowed himself to be lowered onto his own peg. He'd taken some big cocks in his time, but this was something entirely new. He felt himself stretching painfully, dragged down by his own weight. He was drawing breath in fast, shallow gasps. Where was the groove? At last his ringpiece closed around it. Not that it offered much relief – it was scarcely narrower than the ridge of the cone – but at least his hole was no longer actually expanding. His buttocks touched the cold concrete. He clenched and unclenched various muscles, feeling the effect of the plug.

Suliman was kneeling between Laurent's thighs, his head bobbing up and down on his cock. Laurent wriggled and writhed, but the plug held his groin and hips motionless. Tantric sex the easy way.

Yousaf knelt in front of Jack and slipped his cock into his mouth. Jack felt Laurent take his hand. He smiled at his friend. They kissed lazily. Side by side, hand in hand, Jack and Laurent sat like boy-kings on their butt-plugs as their kneeling courtiers bobbed up and down in front of them.

Jack wasn't quite getting the same effect as Laurent. He was taller – his feet could get a purchase on the floor. He wasn't enjoying the same immobility. He lifted Yousaf's head, eased himself to his feet and walked awkwardly to the briefcase. His jeans were still around his ankles; his butt still plugged. He extracted a condom from the case and rolled it over his cock.

He shuffled across to Yousaf, who had risen to his feet, turned him to face the wall and bent him over so that he was leaning against the stone shelf next to Laurent. Jack lowered Yousaf's trousers and underpants. He placed his cock in the entrance to the Arab's tunnel and pushed. As Yousaf's sphincter closed tight around his cock, the sensation inside Jack's own hole was curious. Unexpected muscles kept butting up against the plug. As he began thrusting up and down with his hips the sensation was intensified. He felt the buzz of his prostate rolling against the hard rubber – it was rippling through him in waves. Panting, he soaked up the heat, the volume, the semi-dark. The distant, dim lightbulb flashed like a strobe as silhouette bodies jerked and writhed in its path.

Laurent was coming in Suliman's mouth, his legs kicking about in the air. Suliman himself, wanking, was not far behind. He jerked his head from Laurent's cock as his own began to spurt, arching his body backward, sending a great jet of spunk into the air and down the front of his suit. Jack himself was close to coming. The new sensations were just too much.

He groaned as he slammed his orgasm into Yousaf's hole.

The two friends watched their Omani lovers adjust their suits and close up the briefcase.

'Thank you,' Yousaf said. 'Most enjoyable. It has been a pleasure meeting you.'

'Uh, what about the butt-plugs?' asked Jack. He and Laurent were still wearing them.

'You have used them – they are yours,' said Yousaf. 'We should leave now, as discreetly as possible. Our position, you understand . . . It would not do to be seen with you.'

Jack nodded.

'Naturally, our paths must never cross again.'

'I doubt they will somehow,' said Jack.

The two Arabs solemnly shook hands with Jack and Laurent. Jack smirked to himself – they had been considerably less formal a few minutes ago. Pausing to shake hands with the trannie on the door, they left.

'Your round, I think,' said Jack to Laurent. 'You know, I might keep this thing in.'

It had been a long night for Tom, spinning the Wheel endlessly, bored with the screams and the lights, unable to take his mind off the boxing ring. At last the fair was empty. He had killed the engine and sat for a long time, watching the lit fronts of the other stalls and rides disappearing one by one, listening to goodnights from caravan doors, listening to the background buzz of the town at night. Only the Big Wheel was illuminated now. Tom switched off the lights. He rose from his seat and trudged across the fairground towards the glow of the caravans.

As he stepped past the Ghost Train a figure broke from the shadows in front of him.

'I should kill you for what you did,' said Gary Baines.

'Fuck off, Baines. Leave me alone.'

Baines stepped right in front of Tom. 'What's wrong, killer? This is how you like it. In the dark.'

His mind blank, Tom swung his fist into Baines's solar plexus. The Destroyer went down, gasping. Tom swung his foot into Baines's stomach. Baines curled himself into a ball. Tom kicked again, and again, until Baines lay motionless, trembling slightly.

'You know what I did out in Germany, Baines. You probably don't know why I did it. I was angry. Someone had fucked with my kid brother. You hear what I'm saying? If there's ever a repeat of tonight, if I ever see you fucking with a kid like that again, I'll kill you.'

Tom landed a final blow with his foot. Baines was motionless, moaning slightly. Tom gripped The Destroyer by the shoulders and dragged him across the show-ground. He dumped him at the steps of Luigi's mobile home and hammered on the door.

'Get this piece of shit out of here,' snarled Tom as Luigi opened the door. 'I see him round here again, he's dead.'

Luigi's fat jaw dropped.

'Destroyer,' spat Tom. 'You're not a boxer. You're just a fucking circus freak.'

He turned and strode in the direction of his caravan, then stopped. He heard movement in the shadows and swung around. It was Jason, trying to sneak away.

'What are you doing, creeping around?' Tom challenged.

'I heard voices,' said Jason. He was wearing nothing but a pair of red silk boxing shorts.

'You saw what happened?'

Jason nodded. 'He had it coming.'

Tom spat. 'Yeah,' he said. 'I guess he did.'

'What happened in Germany?' Jason suddenly asked.

Tom was taken aback. 'I, uh . . .' He licked dry lips and coughed slightly.

'I was posted out there,' Tom began. 'I liked it. It was a good life. I joined the army to get out of Newcastle. I hated Newcastle. My brother had got in with all the fucking street scum in the city. My parents couldn't cope with him. They were cracking up. I was the only one he'd ever listen to, and I didn't want to know. I joined the army and went to see the world. I was in Germany when the news came that David was dead. It was my fault. I could have saved him − kept him from the fucking delinquents he was running around with − but I abandoned him. I didn't want to know. When the news came I just lost it. I started drinking, getting into fights. My boxing went down the pan. Then one night some bloke, some lippy little mess sergeant, was winding me up. He kept going on about Geordie shit, taking the piss, doing the whole Up North bit. I lost my rag and put him in hospital. They put me in the glasshouse for three months, then booted me out. Baines just brought it all flooding back.'

'Yeah, well, like I said, he had it coming,' said Jason.

'Come on,' said Tom. 'Let's go to bed.'

'Um . . .' Jason was shuffling awkwardly from foot to foot. 'I'm . . . somewhere else tonight,' he said.

Tom shrugged. 'OK.'

He turned towards his caravan, fishing for the key. 'Goodnight then,' he called from the steps as he let himself inside.

Tom undressed quickly and climbed into bed. The bed felt strange. He'd got used to sharing the narrow mattress with Jason. The caravan smelt of sex. Tom guessed what must have happened.

He turned over and tried to sleep, missing having someone warm and still, breathing slowly next to him, someone to wrap his arms around.

Damned kids. Jason had got to him. He was coming to look upon Jason as he had his own brother.

He turned again, punching his pillow. Was he in danger of

losing Jason, as he had David? This was absurd – he had no claim
on the boy. But right now he felt very alone.

Jack and Laurent tumbled out of the Nautilus Bar and into the
alley.

'Careful, darling,' sang a voice from inside.

'I'm always careful,' Jack bellowed.

They tripped drunkenly down the alley, pushing through a
group of leather-jacketed youths, and out into the street of shops.
'Our Price Records,' sang Jack. 'God, I love this town.' Laurent's
butt-plug swung from his hand. Jack adjusted his jeans over its
partner, still buried inside him.

'Shall we now try to find something to eat?' said Laurent.

'OK,' said Jack. 'Let's go via the market.'

'The market?'

'The market,' said Jack. 'According to my system that should
be a good place to pull.'

'What? We have only just come out of the back-room. Haven't
you had enough yet?'

'Enough?' Jack shrieked. 'My appetite is barely dented.'

They turned into a poorly lit street and stopped. 'I don't think
this is right,' said Jack.

After a number of detours and false trails they spotted the
market gates. A group of youths in leather jackets were standing
around, smoking.

'There you go,' said Jack. 'Perfect.'

'I don't know,' said Laurent.

'They're fine,' said Jack. 'They were outside the bar.'

He minced up to the group. 'Hello, boys,' he said. 'Can I
interest you in a couple of used butt-plugs?'

One of their number stepped forward. 'You what?' he snarled.

'I . . . Ah . . .' Jack flannelled.

The youth pulled something from inside his jacket. A flick-
knife blade opened.

Nine

It was gone noon the next day when Jack and Laurent were missed. At first it was assumed that they were merely sleeping in after an excessive night. Perhaps they were not alone. When eventually Rex had volunteered to penetrate their caravan – regardless of what depravities he might witness in there – and discover the truth, the assumption had to be revised. They were not there. They had clearly not been there all night. Hence they had gone elsewhere – a party, a hotel, or whatever.

'The follies of youth,' Rex sighed. 'The follies of youth . . .'

Annie's response was less lyrical. 'I knew Jack wouldn't last,' she said. 'But I thought he'd do better than this. A month, maybe. That young man has no willpower and no ambition. He's determined to go wrong, and wants to take others with him. I think perhaps it's time to have a stern word with young Jack, mother to son.'

Only the normally phlegmatic Piper looked worried. He scuttled about, puffing hard on his pipe, scowling furiously and mumbling mournfully to himself.

Luigi and the boxers were packing up. Luigi was in a black mood. His Destroyer was gone. 'As the great Aristotle say,' the Italian moaned, 'two nights and I already ruined, three nights I mad to stay.'

Jason and Michael walked along the back of the line of trucks.

'Luigi's trying to sort out another fighter,' said Michael. 'He's talking about joining another fair, or doing some stuff around the clubs. I'm not sure . . .'

'Don't go with him,' urged Jason. 'Stay here. Stay with us. Stay with me.'

Michael looked at the floor, shaking his head slowly.

'You won't be able to box for a bit anyway,' Jason pleaded.

'I'm not going to box. I'm going home.'

'You're . . .?'

'I really enjoyed last night, Jason. It's got me thinking of a lot of things. Good things. Mostly it's got me thinking of you. But I'm homesick. What I really want is to go home.'

'But your home's shit.' Jason stopped walking and stood in front of the boy. 'You said so.'

Michael kissed Jason lightly on the cheek. 'It's still home,' he said, and smiled a bruised smile.

'Keep in touch, yeah?' Jason whispered. 'I'll miss you, mate.'

'Sssh,' whispered Michael. 'Don't say any more.'

Jason's lips closed over Michael's. They kissed, gently, deeply.

Tom watched the little marquee sag and fall and vanish into the trailer, the boxing booth break into its constituent parts and vanish after it. Luigi kept throwing him poisoned glances. The mood among the youngsters didn't seem at all subdued, but their boss was bewailing his luck to anyone — except Tom — who would listen.

Piper pulled on his pipe and stared at the ground as Luigi lamented.

'I am cursed,' said Luigi. 'This fucking fair — I am cursed. I don't know why always I come back here. As Plato say . . .'

Without a word Piper turned and walked away.

A policeman wandered into the fair and hailed Mavis. She looked about her, flapping her arms. Annie came over and spoke to the policeman.

Tom got up. He could see Piper hurrying across now. He could hear a babble of raised voices. As he broke into the group Annie swung to face him. Her mouth was open, but wordless.

'What?' said Tom. 'What's happened?'

'Laurent's in hospital,' said Annie.

The ticking of a clock drowned out the bustle of the ward. Tom and Annie sat in a corridor in Ward 5 of the Derby Royal Infirmary and waited. Neither spoke. A policeman emerged from a door and muttered a few words to a lady doctor. When he had left she addressed them with 'You can see him now. He was quite lucky.'

She stepped through the door into a single room. 'Laurent, you've got some visitors.'

Tom peered through the glass window in the door. Laurent was stretched out on the hospital bed, his head, shoulders and chest wrapped in lengths of white bandage. One arm was in a cast.

The doctor re-emerged from the room.

'He's taken a very bad beating,' she said. 'He's broken his arm and there's a lot of bruising to his face and chest, and also to his head. We're keeping him in for observation, probably for several days. There is a risk of concussion. Come in.'

They entered the room. Laurent gazed up at them through the bandages. Tom closed his eyes and ground his teeth.

'How are you, love?' said Annie, dropping to his bedside.

Laurent could only grunt.

'Bastards did this to you,' she said. Through layers of bandage she kissed him lightly on the brow. 'They want to keep you in for a bit, love. Do a few tests, and that. Just to make sure you're OK. They say you took quite a beating.'

She smiled weakly. Laurent grunted again.

'Hi, Tom,' said a voice.

Jack shuffled into the room in pyjamas, dressing gown and slippers. He was sipping at a mug of cocoa. 'Christ, you look like the Mummy,' he said to Laurent. He tugged at one of the pulley-lines which ran around the bed on a metal frame at standing-height. 'I expected your leg to shoot up in the air when I did that,' he said, sipping at his cocoa. 'Nice room. I didn't get a room.'

'You seem to be doing all right,' said Annie levelly. 'Cocoa . . .'

Jack smiled. 'You've just got to know which hearts to melt. Do a dying swan.' He threw his hand up to his brow. 'Flutter the old eyelids . . . Bingo.'

Annie was on her feet.

'Can I have a word with you outside?' She took Jack by the arm and pushed him through the door. Tom started to follow. 'Stay here, Tom,' Annie snapped.

He stepped back and closed the door. His eyes caught Laurent's in a moment of awkwardness.

'I don't give a shit if you think you can go through the world free of all care and all responsibility, troughing on your appetites day and night, but when you start dragging others into that black hole you call a life . . .'

Tom suppressed a smile as Annie's voice came through the wall. In his bandages Laurent was smiling too.

'. . . that's when it's got to stop, Jack!'

'Go easy,' Jack whined. 'I was beaten up too, you know.'

'Beaten up, were you? Where? Let me see.'

There was silence, followed by 'There's nothing there!', and a sharp crack. Laurent started to laugh silently. She had slapped him. Tom started to laugh too.

'You live at Gamlin's,' Annie lectured, 'not in the Land of fucking Do-As-You-Please. You've got responsibilities whether you like it or not. You're a gaff boy, for Chrissake. You run a ride. You're responsible for the safety of hundreds of people a night.'

'Hundreds of people,' Jack sneered. 'Have you seen the size of the crowds recently? No one's coming! The whole thing's falling apart anyway.'

'That may be true,' said Annie. 'That's why we need you, Jack. We need you with us. You're part of the family. If you're sick, we're all sick.'

'Which fair are you talking about?' shouted Jack. 'Have you looked around Gamlin's recently? We *are* all sick. All of us!'

Inside the room the laughter was giving way to embarrassment. Tom and Laurent's eyes met awkwardly.

'We pretend there's nothing wrong,' Jack's voice continued through the door, 'but the whole set-up's insane. Piper pulls a few good conjuring tricks and we act – though we never admit it –

like he's fucking Merlin. Tom in there: he goes round like a fucking penitent all the time and we pretend it's normal. We all pretend we don't know what he did to that geezer in Germany . . .'

Tom blushed. Outside there was another sharp flesh-crack. The boy in the bandages dropped his eyes.

'It's fucking thought control, Annie! It's the fucking Moonies!' Jack sounded close to tears. 'Well, not me! I go my own way. Christ, I didn't want Laurent to end up like that – what do you think I am? But I do what I do. That's what you always say about Piper, isn't it? Well, I'm like Piper, then. I'll take my own independent actions and I'll take the consequences, and none of you has a right to preach to me about it.'

There was silence, then the door of the room opened. Annie entered alone.

'That could have gone better,' she said.

Why did it have to be Piper? Jason was spooked enough in here as it was.

'Ha ha,' the old man cackled ecstatically. He grinned and mugged at the warped mirror in front of him. His legs were spindly, his body bloated like a balloon, his neck pencil-thin, his head flat and wide and ridiculous.

They were surrounded by such mirrors. Wherever Jason looked, grotesque parodies of himself leered out at him.

'All you got to do is call the pitch and take the money. It's easy. It's not like there's any moving parts. Hee hee . . .'

'Can we get on with it, please?' said Jason.

Piper led him along a twisting corridor of bent and crazy, laughing mirrors, and through into a large, empty space. The old man laid a hand on Jason's arm, and he stopped.

'Best look before you leap,' said Piper.

Jason smiled thinly and stepped forward. A dozen other Jasons stepped forward from all directions. He stepped to the left. A dozen more side-stepped into existence. These were not caricatures – these were perfect reflections. He stepped forward again. The army of reflections marched with him. He turned to look for Piper. He couldn't see him. He couldn't see him or his reflections.

He took a step back towards the entrance – and bumped into himself. He reached out and touched the mirror. Where the fuck was the entrance?

'It's a funny old place, the Hall of Mirrors.' The old man's voice seemed to come from very close by. He was still nowhere to be seen. Jason should at least be able to see a reflection or two of him. It was impossible to escape the reflections in here.

'Some people, they just see what's in front of them,' said Piper, invisibly. 'They see the surface, and they go on their way. Some see more. Some come here to meet themselves. Some, their selves is already in here, waitin' for them to come a-callin'. Waitin' in here to meet them.'

'I'm stuck,' cried Jason. 'I can't find the exit. I can't get out.'

'You'll find the way out,' the old man cackled from nowhere, before lapsing into silence.

Jason groped his way to the edge of a mirror. He stretched his hand forward, and encountered only air. He stepped into the gap. Twenty other Jasons stepped into the gap. Each looked pale and drawn, wide-eyed and thin-lipped. Ill at ease, panicky, mean. He heard a distant car horn, and the screech of brakes. He heard a dog barking itself into a fury. It was hot in here.

He stumbled forward. The barking grew louder. For a split second he swore he saw a light, the headlights of a car close behind him, bouncing off the mirrors, throwing him into a dozen silhouettes. Then it was gone, replaced by the Hall's pale, even light.

There was a sound – a single, distant footfall. Jason froze, sweating, listening hard. Behind the silence he was sure he could hear something. The sound was even, rhythmic and very, very soft, like someone breathing, just at the edge of earshot. The old man? No – he didn't breathe, he wheezed like a traction engine. Jason blinked. There was another subliminal flash in the mirrors. A face, gone in an instant. Someone was in there with him.

He started forward again, beginning to panic. He hit a mirror. He side-stepped and hit another, his reflected self lurching towards him. Startled, he twisted, tripped and fell to the floor.

Christ, it was hot. He could smell something acrid, like burning rubber. He groped his way forward, trying to ignore the images surrounding him. He looked small, wretched, rat-like, and frightened.

Something scuttled across his hand. A spider. He'd planted his hand on top of its web.

'Sorry, mate,' Jason whispered. He put the spider down on what was left of its web and got to his feet.

OK, calm down. Concentrate. A patch of darkness appeared ahead of him. He approached it cautiously. It seemed to remain constant as he moved forward. He could see what it was now – a door, a low door, open, set into one of the mirrors. He stepped forward and banged his head. It was just the reflection of a fucking door. Which was the real one? Groping from image to image, his hands finally closed on an invisible doorframe. The door was only three feet high. Beyond was the mundane back-of-ride storage space. Jason gratefully crawled through the little door.

He sat up and looked around. His hand closed on something next to the door. It was a clipboard. A single page of an official report was clipped to the board. Harpenden District Council. Across the paper had been scrawled a child's drawing in thick red crayon. It was a drawing of a woman – discernible as such by the polka-dot triangle of her dress and the tangle of curly string that was her hair and a pair of pendulous comedy breasts complete with nipples – her arms and legs splayed, too few fingers and great boots, grinning – or screaming – at the viewer.

Jason touched the drawing. The crayon-lines smeared easily against his fingers, leaving the tips red. He tested them with his nose, lips and tongue. He remembered the smell and the feel of the drag-queen yesterday. He was sure the drawing had been done in lipstick. He looked about the floor. Other, similar drawings lay scattered about. A house on fire. A man with his head cut off.

Jason had had enough. He threw the clipboard down and scanned the walls for the exit. He saw a door, open a crack, and daylight beyond. He lurched towards it.

Water from the shower-nozzle drenched him. It was deliciously warm. This should help him relax, get him fit for the night. One thing was for sure – he wasn't going into the Hall of Mirrors again. He'd stand outside and take the money, fair enough, but if anybody got the screamers inside, they were on their own.

He soaped himself briskly from head to foot. He blinked blindly. Water and soap cascaded down his chest and slalomed around his pubes, crashing over his cock and balls.

He tried not to think of the Hall of Mirrors. He thought of the recent, rich days. He thought of Michael. His cock loosened and swelled. He massaged soap into it, coaxing it upward until it was fully erect.

He thought of the sweet seduction of Michael. Through the semi-opaque plastic of the shower cubicle he could see, dimly, the bed where they had made love, the covers still scattered across the floor.

He leaned against the back wall of the cubicle, rubbing his cock with long strokes, his left hand caressing his chest, squeezing and pulling at his nipples. His mind drifted back . . . Battersea Park. He and Glen made love on the Peace Pagoda. Glen kissed him and turned him and leaned him against the Buddha statue. He felt his friend's cock prodding at his hole, squeezing its way in. He felt the deep, sweet pain of his arse being slowly forced apart by Glen's great, dark prick.

He moaned to himself. As he maintained the long, easy strokes with his right hand, his left moved to his balls, cupping and squeezing. He was in Newcastle again. He was naked on the grass at night in a park on the edge of town. Spider, also naked, rolled on top of him. They rolled and wrestled, tumbling down the gentle slope of the grass, their cocks erect and sticky and clashing together. Their clothes were scattered around them on the grass. The car they had boosted earlier that evening lay in shadow beyond the trees.

They rolled to a halt. Spider planted a deep kiss on Jason's mouth. He reached over to his discarded jeans and rummaged in the pocket. He pulled out a packet of condoms.

'Let me,' said Jason. He opened the packet and spread the latex mushroom over the head of Spider's beautiful cock. It tucked itself tight around the slightly bulging head. Jason lowered his lips and closed them around the sheath. Pushing with his lips he rolled it down Spider's shaft. Jason turned, on all fours now, offering

Spider his buttocks. Spider slid himself along Jason's back and, biting down on his neck, entered him.

Jason's feet skidded on the wet floor. He staggered and recovered, feet braced, leaning hard against the plastic door of the cubicle. He inserted two soapy fingers into his arsehole. His strokes were fast and hard now. His swollen cock pulsed. He, Michael, Glen and Spider rolled together, naked, kissing and biting, sucking, fucking, whilst the Buddha smiled down on them. Little Michael straddled Glen's huge cock, wincing as he slowly impaled himself on it. Spider bit and licked at Jason's balls, nibbling his way up the underside of his shaft, then swallowing the full bulb.

Then it all changed. He sucked on Spider, whilst Glen fucked him and Michael sucked . . .

He was coming. He slammed back against the cubicle, making it shake. He thrust his fingers high into his arse. He groaned. His cock heaved; his spunk erupted against the cubicle wall.

He stopped, breathless. He slumped. His cock still spasmed slightly every second or so. A final dribble of spunk peeped out. Jason let the water wash it away, then turned off the taps and opened the door. Water-blind, he stepped into the caravan and groped for a towel.

'Here you are,' said Tom.

'Aaah!' Jason jolted around. His hands shot to his groin and his still largely erect cock.

'How long have you been here?' Jason spluttered.

Tom smiled. 'You'd better clean up in there,' he said.

Jason was bored outside the Hall of Mirrors. Not many people seemed that interested, and custom was poor. Jason couldn't bring himself to call the pitch. He took the money from a group of girls without speaking or smiling.

'Cheer up,' one of the girls said. 'It might never happen.' She giggled and followed her friends through the mirrored swing-doors.

'I hope you're right,' Jason murmured. 'If it happens in there you're on your own.'

Jason felt a tugging at his sleeve. It was young Kevin Simpson.

'Jack wants you,' he said.

'Jack? Why?'

'I dunno,' the child replied. 'He's in the Tunnel of Love. Up on the top, where he goes.'

'Uh, right,' said Jason, 'but I can't really leave the ride.'

'I'm gonna do it,' said Kevin. 'Willow can handle the Tunnel of Love on her own.'

Reluctantly Jason followed Kevin's instructions. As he walked past the front of the Tunnel of Love he could hear Willow apologising for the breakdown of the machinery. The ride would be working again in a few moments.

This was a bad sign. He trudged around the side of the Tunnel of Love, into the open door and up the wooden stairs.

'Jason – c'mere, mate,' drawled Jack.

Jason picked his way across a floor blighted with a debris of empty bottles and makeshift ashtrays, overflowing. He kicked a bottle. It reverberated loudly as it clunked and rolled across the uneven wooden boards.

'Christ, what have you been doing? Living up here?'

Jack was again sprawled on the chaise longue. He was wearing a gaudy, lime green kimono, which looked faintly ridiculous on him. He rolled to face Jason. A flap of the kimono dropped to reveal his cock, dangling half-erect, a thick drip of spunk clinging to the end of it.

'Have some wine,' he said, swigging on a bottle. His words were slurred, his movements languid and imprecise. He was badly drunk.

'No,' said Jason. 'Seriously, Jack, how many nights are you spending up here?' He cast his eyes about the floor. 'How much are you drinking? I'm going.'

'Jason, wait,' slurred Jack. 'I brought you up here to see something. Down there.'

'No fucking way!' said Jason. 'I'm not getting into all that again.'

'Please,' said Jack.

'No!'

'Look, fuck what Annie's been saying to you. Or Tom, for that matter. They don't know shit.'

'They haven't been saying anything!' protested Jason.

'Bullshit. Are you seriously saying that they haven't tried to warn you about me?'

Jason didn't reply.

'I thought so,' Jack continued. 'Jack the debauchee. Jack the sad, empty fucking queen. Well, maybe they're right, but at least I'm out there. At least I'm interacting with the rest of the human race. Too many people use Gamlin's as a place to hide. Tom and Annie are the worst. And Doug, but at least he keeps his mouth shut.'

'Tom's . . . got his reasons,' said Jason.

'Yeah, yeah, I know you're sweet on Tom,' said Jack, 'but he's a prick. And Annie's worse.'

'Annie's all right!' Jason was getting annoyed. 'She's . . . genuine. She's down-to-earth.'

'Annie,' said Jack, 'is about as genuine as I am. That's what fucks me off. I might be living in cloud-cuckoo-land up here with my fairy grotto, but so is Annie with her fucking gypsy shawls and her crystal ball. Believe me, Annie's not what she seems. She's certainly not fucking Mystic Meg.'

'She's been good to me,' said Jason. 'She's —'

'*She's been like a mother to me,*' Jack sneered.

'That's not what I was going to —'

'She loves fucking playing mum. She even tried it with me early on, only I saw her for what she was.'

'Look, I'm going,' said Jason. He really didn't want to listen to this.

'No,' said Jack. 'Stay. Please . . .'

He placed his hand on the front of Jason's jeans and squeezed slowly on his cock. Jack's own cock was fully hard again, bobbing out from the kimono.

'Don't be like them, Jason. Don't be afraid to live. Don't be afraid to dream. Take a look down there.'

Jason moved closer to the edge of the platform, largely to put himself beyond the reach of Jack's hand. Something in his drunk friend's tone of voice was making Jason uneasy.

'There,' whispered Jack. 'In the blue boat.'

The blue boat was the only one to be seen — the grotto was

otherwise empty. A lone figure was lolling in the blue boat, head back, eyes closed. For a moment Jason was reminded of Jack himself. Like Jack, the occupant of the boat was wearing nothing but a kimono, long brown hair trailing over the sides of the boat. Jack was cute, sure, but this was one of the most beautiful figures Jason had ever seen – about twenty-five, Jason guessed, a perfect, unblemished face on a slender neck.

Who went into a Tunnel of Love on their own? Especially when they looked like that . . .

'Is that a man or a woman?' asked Jason. The visage was of the sort which would have made either beautiful.

'Guess,' replied Jack.

'I don't know. Pretty fucking fit, though . . .'

Willowy arms rested along the boat's wooden bow, fern-like hands stroked the surface of the water. One hand rose and sprinkled water lightly over the front of the kimono. The hand came down and separated the silk folds at the midriff. The garment slid to the floor of the boat, revealing a cock that rose, tall and swaying, plant-like from a rich, dark fuzz.

'*Pretty fucking fit?*' whispered Jack. 'I'll tell you about *pretty fucking fit. Pretty fucking fit* is the brick-shithouse navvy you pass on a road-gang in summer, bare to the waist with a sweat-line right down the crack of his jeans. *Pretty fucking fit* is the dizzy little disco-bunny who gobbles like a turkey and is happily working his way round the club, cock by cock. That down there' – he gestured wildly over the grotto – 'isn't your bog-standard *pretty fucking fit.* That, dear boy, is art. Look at that face, that cock . . .'

The young god was running his fingers up and down the shaft now, eyes still lightly closed. His other hand skated slowly around the outside of the kimono, circling the chest, massaging silk into skin.

'That's Ariel,' said Jack. 'Ariel was here last year. I was hoping for a repeat visit.'

Down in the boat, Ariel's hand was cupped around the head of his cock, pulling the foreskin forward with outstretched fingers, forward over the dark, swollen bulb, pinching the skin sheath into a tight bunch, letting it retract back over the head then pulling it forward again. His other hand was inside the upper folds of the kimono, rubbing his chest in hard, horizontal strokes.

'Look, I ought to get back to work,' said Jason. 'Kevin's on his own out there.'

'Wait,' replied Jack. 'Watch.'

Ariel's kimono spilled open. Silk billowed and avalanched down his honey-gold body. Two soft, round, full breasts bulged and bobbed beneath his moving hand. Women's breasts.

'He's . . .'

'Mmm,' said Jack. 'Amazing, isn't it.'

Jason was vaguely aware of Jack rising from the chaise longue and moving behind him, his garment open at the front, his cock waving in the air like an antenna. He felt Jack's body pressing against his back, his buttocks, his legs. He felt Jack's hand sliding around his hips and resting on the crotch of his jeans. He shifted, a little uneasily. Jack squeezed, his fingers massaging deeply through the denim. In spite of himself, Jason's cock was expanding. He felt Jack's own long, thick prick rubbing up and down against the cleft of his arse and the small of his back. Jack's fingers were inside Jason's fly-buttons now, trying to manipulate his cock free of the confines of his tight pants. Skimming through his pubic hairs, Jack's fingers curled around the base of his cock, and pulled. The engorged shaft bent painfully against the elastic constriction of the taut cotton, then sprung free, standing up and out, still wrapped in Jack's fist.

Fifteen feet below them Ariel's back was arched, his buttocks raised from the floor of the boat, feet squarely planted and neck and shoulders taking his body weight. That elegant neck looked as if it might snap. He was still pulling at his cock. His other hand was now between his legs – the heel of his hand was massaging his own balls and perineum, whilst his long fingers pushed apart his own buttock-cheeks, and slipped in and out of his hole. The fleshy, female breasts rolled like jellies.

Jason felt a familiar wave building in his balls. Jack's fingernails scraped along the underside of his ball-sac, whilst with his other hand he continued to piston up and down Jason's shaft, drawing the foreskin rapidly back and forth across the head.

He heard Jack moan, then felt the boy's lips and teeth sucking and biting on his neck. Jack's strokes up his back were getting faster and shorter. With a deep groan Jack's cock erupted up Jason's back, spunk splashing off skin and denim, exploding into cotton, soaking his T-shirt and his skin. At the same time Jason felt himself coming. He spat his spunk high, out over the grotto. It showered down through the net.

Both boys were silent. Jason could feel the warm, wet patch spreading over the back of his T-shirt.

'Christ, Jack,' he said, pulling away from the boy and testing the patch with his fingers. He wished that hadn't happened. 'This fucking place,' he muttered. 'This is so fucking unhealthy, Jack.'

'What is it with you, Jason?' Jack sneered. 'What is it that makes you so much better than me? What is it makes you the good son and me the spoilt little ingrate bastard? Is it that good old Northern grit, Jason? Like Tom? What?'

'I don't think you should come up here,' said Jason. 'It's not good for you.'

'Neither is booze,' said Jack. 'Neither are fags. Neither is any fucking addiction. But if you've got to have it –'

'This is just a fucking peepshow,' snapped Jason. 'D'you know how seedy this is?'

'You know what I'm talking about, Jason,' said Jack. 'Don't forget the last time you came up here. Your heart's desire Jason, remember?' He looked down. 'That's what I come up here for . . . My heart's desire.'

'And that's it, is it?' said Jason. 'Down there in that boat?'

'Look at it,' drawled Jack. 'Beautiful, serene, and utterly whole – complete and sufficient unto itself in every way.' He let out a heavy sigh. 'I bet it can even suck its own cock,' he said bitterly.

The boats were moving again. Below them Ariel bobbed out of sight behind a fake hill. Another boat appeared. A straight couple.

'Willow,' Jack called. 'What are you doing?'

'I'm going,' said Jason. 'This fucking fair, it eats into your head. Into your mind.'

'Don't go,' Jack whimpered. He grabbed Jason's shoulder. 'Don't leave me up here.'

Roughly, Jason pushed him off. Jack stumbled. His foot came

down on one of the empty bottles, which skidded out from under him. He sprawled to the deck. The bottle shot off the end of the platform and fell, bouncing through the net and exploding with a deafening crash into fake landscape fifteen feet below, smashing into thousands of fragments.

A girl in one of the incoming boats screamed.

Jack went white for a moment. Slowly his face pulled into a loveless grin. He picked up another bottle, and threw it hard over the side. It exploded close to its predecessor. Laughing, Jack picked up and launched a third.

Couples were abandoning the boats, running about the fairy dell in terror, looking for the way out.

'What the fuck are you doing?' Jason shouted. 'You fucking madman!'

'I thought you were going,' said Jack, picking up another bottle.

'No!' shouted Jason and made a grab for Jack's arm. Jack tried to push him away. The two of them struggled on the edge of the drop.

There was a noise of running footsteps on the stairs.

'What the fuck's going on?' Annie burst onto the platform, her face red. 'What were those explosions?'

Jack and Jason separated. Grinning, looking directly at Annie, Jack tossed the bottle over the edge. There was another deafening crash.

'What the fuck's going on up there!'

Tom's voice. Tom was below, in the Tunnel of Love.

'You little fucking psycho,' Annie hissed. 'You sick bastard.'

'Go fuck yourself, *Mum*,' snarled Jack. 'You could probably do that, couldn't you?'

'Jack,' Annie sounded concerned now, 'you're not well.'

'Who the fuck is, round here?' He was beginning to sound hysterical. 'You're not my fucking mother, Annie. Christ, everyone knows what a sick joke that would be.'

'Jack . . .'

'Fuck it! Fuck you all!'

Drunkenly he stumbled towards the staircase, his kimono flapping about him, and thudded down the stairs.

Annie placed a hand on Jason's shoulder. 'Are you all right?' she asked.

Jason nodded.

'What goes on up here?' Annie asked.

'Jack watches the boats,' said Jason. 'Sometimes they get a bit steamed up down there, especially the gays.'

'And who operates the ride?'

Jason was silent.

'Jason . . .' There was an urgent edge to her voice.

'Willow Simpson.'

'Willow . . . Come with me.'

She marched to the staircase. Jason followed. He followed her out of the painted wooden door and around the back of the ride. She was marching on Jack and Laurent's caravan. Jason could see Jack moving around inside, then suddenly slumping on the bed.

Annie hammered on the door. There was no reply. She tried to turn the handle. It was locked.

'Jack,' she shouted. 'I know you're in there. This is more serious than I thought, Jack. You've been letting a ten-year-old kid operate a complicated and dangerous ride, you've been drinking yourself into despair, and now this thing with the bottles. We must talk about this. We should talk to Piper!'

Still there was no reply.

'Jack . . . when you want to talk, I'll be ready to listen,' said Annie, and turned away. There was still confusion in the fairground. Frustrated lovers, *coitus interruptus*, were arguing with Tom and Doug. A few were crying. Most of the rest of the crowd was beginning to gather round the Tunnel of Love to see what was going on.

'Jesus,' muttered Annie, 'what now?' She marched towards the fray.

After the fair had calmed down, Jason returned to the Hall of Mirrors. Spurred on by guilt he even attempted to bark his pitch a bit. He sounded unenthusiastic, and only seemed to get customers when he shut up. He was glad when the fair finally closed. Returning to his caravan, he noticed a figure crouching in the shadows.

'Jason.' It was Jack. 'Come here,' he whispered.

'Jack,' said Jason. 'Are you all right?' He was relieved to see he had abandoned the kimono and was fully dressed again.

'Yeah,' said Jack bitterly. 'Never better, old mate.'

'D'you want to talk or anything?' asked Jason awkwardly. 'I really think you should talk to Annie.'

'Fucking Annie,' spat Jack. 'She's just so full of shit. She's a hypocrite! I'll prove it to you. Come with me.'

'Jack . . .'

'Trust me.'

Uneasily, Jason followed Jack. He stopped outside Doug and Annie's caravan. 'She's in Piper's van,' he whispered. 'No doubt making a full report about me. Doug's drinking in Rex's.'

He fished in his pocket for his key. 'One key opens all locks around here,' he said.

He opened the caravan door and slipped inside.

'Jack . . .'

'Come in,' said Jack.

Jason entered the unlit van. Jack was fiddling with the catch on the wardrobe door.

'Climb in here,' he said.

'What?'

'Get in the wardrobe, watch and wait. I'll prove to you that Annie's a fraud.'

Jack shot a glance out of the window.

'She's coming,' he whispered. 'I've got to go.'

He disappeared through the door. Jason looked around, his eyes slowly becoming accustomed to the dim light. What was Jack getting at? He'd been in here loads of times. Everything looked as it normally did – Doug's workbench-cum-dining table, the dense rail of clothes running the full width of the van, Annie's drapes and chiffons.

Jason felt a churn of emotions. He shouldn't be there: Annie was his friend; Jack was fucked in the head. And yet he was dying to know what Jack was getting at. What was wrong with Annie? Besides, he was getting some of the old adrenalin-rush, that childhood thrill of trespass. They had loved all that, he and Spider. Anywhere officially off limits was the place to be. Building-sites, offices, hotels. Even private houses once in a while, just for the thrill.

There was someone at the door. Jason glanced around rapidly. His Newcastle training took over. The wardrobe was a crap place to hide. He slid himself under Doug's workbench, pulling some propped-up, half-finished wood carvings around him. The door opened and Annie entered. She was humming tunelessly to herself, between mighty gasps on a cigarette.

She put the kettle on and began unbuttoning her loose gypsy-blouse. Jason crept from under the workbench and up to the clothes-rail. He crouched under a row of long, full-skirted, Spanish-looking evening-gowns, peering through red silk and black lace. Annie removed the blouse, and then the bra beneath. Her chest was flat – she had no tits whatsoever. The bra was all padding. She bunched her hair with both hands, and tugged. The whole thing lifted off in a clump, revealing a pancake of short, untidy grey hair, flattened beneath a hairnet. Jason shook his head. Was that all that Jack was getting at? He'd half-guessed Annie's shock of pitch-black hair wasn't her own. She ought to be grey at her age.

She slipped out of her shoes and eased down her jeans, stepping out of them as they touched the floor. Her legs were slender, and surprisingly smooth for her age. She was wearing what Jason's grandmother would have called a pair of bloomers, baggy things, extending down her thighs, finished with twin hems of frilly elastic. Jason had to stifle a laugh. Just like the fat old maid in *Tom and Jerry*.

The kettle boiled. Annie swung and lifted it from the gas. She had her back to Jason now. The bloomers came down. Jason's face creased in puzzlement. A heavy cloth strap ran around her waist, with another running down her buttock-cleft and disappearing between her legs. She turned to face the rail. What was that? Some kind of chastity-belt? A thick pad of webbing clung tight to her cunt. She pulled at a buckle on the side of the contraption and it peeled away, falling to the floor.

Jason's jaw dropped. Annie ran her hands languidly down her flat chest, over her stomach and into her grey bush, and on down the length of her dangling, semi-erect cock.

Jason scarcely had time to register the shock. The door of the caravan opened. Doug was standing behind him, staring down at where Jason's feet were poking out beneath the flowing dresses.

He jumped to his feet. Annie screamed and clasped her hands over the unexpected thing between her legs. Doug let out an oath.

'Jason,' Annie shrieked. 'What are you doing here!?'

'I . . .' He didn't know what to say. Cornered, aggression took over. 'Jack was right,' he said hotly. 'You're a fucking fake. All that Earth-Mother bullshit, and you're not even a woman!'

He pushed past Doug and ran from the caravan.

Ten

'D id you know?' Jason demanded.

Tom swung his legs out of bed and shrugged his shoulders. 'No,' he said. He pulled on pants, jeans and T-shirt.

'Doesn't it bother you?' asked Jason. 'Annie's a fucking man!'

'No,' said Tom again, lacing his shoes.

It was moving-day again. Jason had slept badly – he was awake before even Tom.

'I really liked her,' said Jason. 'I trusted her. You don't know . . . Listen – my own mum never gave much of a shit, right? She pretended to, when she could be bothered, but that wasn't very often. Dad was a boring cunt. All he ever did was work in some shitty office for fuck-all money, come home and sit there reading his Bible or watching wildlife documentaries. So Mum had affairs. Christ knows how many.' He laughed bitterly. 'She always tried to hide them from us, but she was crap at it. She'd disappear for days on end then come back and trot out some rubbish lie, and then give us some stupid, expensive present.' He shook his head, laughing, crying. 'She never bought us anything we might have wanted. She never had a clue what any of us were into. She bought me a Cabbage Patch doll once, because she heard they were all the rage.' He was crying freely now. 'I tell you, she never gave a shit about us. Annie was . . . more like a mum ought to be . . .'

Jason started as the door of the caravan clunked. He was alone. Through the window he watched Tom walking out towards the Wheel. Tom was talking to someone. A postman. The postman handed him an envelope. Jason sniffed and wiped his nose on his bare arm. Shaking his head clear, he rummaged about for his clothes.

In spite of the sunny weather, the atmosphere in the fair was chilly all morning. They were short-handed and the work was hard. Nobody was speaking much. Jack was missing, Tom seemed at his most distracted, barely saying a word. Annie seemed to be following Jason with her eyes, hurt, imploring, accusing. She was restored to her full feminine beauty – lush black locks, a flowing peasant-skirt, a shawl.

Jason avoided her studiously. He didn't want to talk to her. He was in a bad mood. The normal ambience of the fair seemed to be breaking down – Laurent was in hospital, Jack had blown a fuse and run off, Jason himself wasn't talking to Annie, and Tom wasn't talking to anyone.

He missed Jack and Laurent and the arch banter which Jack and Rex habitually fell into whilst working. Now a lone, loud voice, Rex merely sounded shrewish and irritable.

Jason thought about the infectious happiness of the young boxers. He missed them, too. Above all, he missed Michael.

The Wheel didn't seem to want to be broken down and packed away. Nuts clung to bolts, struts refused to separate, bulbs committed suicide, plunging from their sockets.

'It's old,' Tom grunted.

''Tisn't good for the rides,' mumbled Piper. 'All this takin' down and puttin' up and movin' about, year in, year out. They're like animals. They don't like it.'

'I've just spent the morning wrestling with this particular animal, twenty feet in the air,' said Jason. 'How about him going up there and having a go,' he added under his breath to Tom, 'instead of standing here spouting rubbish.'

Tom flashed Jason a quick, pained grin before returning to the job, his face once again a mask of concentration.

There was no rest after the Wheel was packed. The Tunnel of Love had to be broken down and stored for the journey. Jason was exhausted. He stood outside the ride, breathless, and looked to see who was in charge. Everyone still seemed busy. Making sure he was unseen, he stepped up onto the boarding platform and entered the tunnel-mouth.

It was dark and cool inside. He breathed deeply, enjoying the sudden relief from the day. Remembering the broken bottles, he scrabbled around until he found a light-switch.

Illuminated only by a couple of electric bulbs, the grotto looked tawdry and fake. Tiny, sharp fragments of glass lay everywhere. Jason jumped across the shallow stream. The bank groaned as he landed. He strolled up a hill to a clump of supposed trees. He grabbed a branch and tried to pull himself up. The tree bent alarmingly. He let himself drop back to the ground. It was somewhere back here he was so sure he had seen Spider. Another illusion. He looked for a silver spider, hanging by a thong from a tree. There was none to be found. Another lie.

'Here you are.' Annie's voice, sharp, behind him. 'We're waiting for you.'

Jason spun around. Annie was standing close to the tunnel-mouth. She/he looked strained and old.

Jason made no attempt to move.

'Are you coming?' Annie took a step forward. 'Look, we're at full stretch out there. First we get the work done, then I think we should probably talk. OK? I'll wait outside for you.'

Jason flashed Annie a frosty smile as she disappeared into the daylight. This feeling was too naggingly familiar. He was reminded of his mother, leaving strings of instructions – your dinner just needs warming, take the washing in when it's dry – and disappearing through the front door of their gloomy house, day after summer's day, swallowed by the sun. That was the year her affairs got completely out of hand, her behaviour completely flagrant, and the whole thing had come bursting out into the open. Jason was feeling now that same punch-in-the-gut sensation that you get when you find out that someone you thought you knew really well, and had come to love and depend on, you didn't actually know at all. That on some deep, fundamental level she was deceiving you. Watching Annie leave, that was exactly how he felt now.

Swallowing hard, trying to master his stomach, he came down the hill.

They worked silently and quickly, Annie, Rex, Tom and Jason, accompanied only by Rex, whistling the Dead March. It was annoying.

'Can't you give it a rest!' Tom suddenly snapped. Rex was too shocked to reply.

Jason was glad when the work was over. He began the slow walk back to the caravan.

'Pssst!'

He stopped and looked around. Piper was beckoning from the door of his battered old caravan.

Irritated, Jason went to see what he wanted. As he approached, the old man vanished back into the caravan.

'Come in, lad. Come in,' came the voice from inside the van. 'You've never been in here before, have you?'

Jason hadn't, and he was glad. The inside of Piper's van smelled of damp and food and old clothes. Boxes, cardboard and wooden, were stacked everywhere. And mirrors − mirrors hanging or leaning or lying wherever Jason looked. Dressing-mirrors, shaving mirrors, an actor's stage-mirror, surrounded by lightbulbs. Even in here the themes of mirrors and lightbulbs seemed to dominate. And clothes − old clothes − and coloured cloths. It was odd, but every mirror was covered, either with an item of clothing or a brightly dyed piece of cloth. Apart from the odd bright chink, not one single glass looked upon the room.

He couldn't see Piper. He groaned inwardly. Not the old man's disappearing act again.

'Whaa . . .' A strange, strangled noise came from the far end of the caravan, from a tall box covered in a red-and-white striped cloth.

'Hello, boys and girls!'

At last Jason realised what he was looking at. It was a Punch and Judy booth. Mr Punch was swaying and bobbing in front of him, his face red, grinning for all he was worth.

'Piper,' he said. 'I'm not in the mood. Is there something you want?' He fucking hated Punch and Judy shows. Always had.

'Where's Jack?' a high voice shrilled. 'Wheeere's Jack?' Judy bobbed beside her husband.

'He's in the cellar,' squawked Mr Punch. 'Eating coal.'

'He's not in the cellar. I've just been to the cellar.'

'He's asleep.'

'He's not asleep. His bed's empty. And Jack's bed's never empty, is it boys and girls? What have you done with Jack, Mr Punch?'

'Jack fell down and broke his crown,' sang Mr Punch.

'Ooh, I'm going to call a policeman.'

Judy disappeared into the wings and a policeman bobbed on.

'Now, Mr Punch,' said the policeman, 'what have you done with Jack? We need him to drive the Tunnel of Love up to Buxton. Don't we, boys and girls?'

'Get someone else to drive the lorry,' said Mr Punch. 'Let one of the boys and girls drive the lorry. Him!'

The puppet's beady eyes were staring dead at Jason.

'Ooh, you naughty Mr Punch!' Judy was back. The policeman had vanished. 'You can't ask that nice young man to do it. He probably doesn't even have a licence.'

'He's scared now,' said Mr Punch, 'but he didn't used to be. He used to nick cars all the time. He'll do it.'

'No he won't, Mr Punch,' said Judy.

'Yes he will,' said Mr Punch, picking up a big stick and striking Judy. 'Yes he will! Yes he will!'

'All right,' shouted Jason. 'What is it you want? You want me to drive the truck. You're right, the only things I have ever driven are boosted cars. We did it for the charge. I don't do that shit any more. But I'll drive your truck for you. And not because you scare me with your fucking parlour-tricks. Oh, and if I get pulled by the pigs it's on your head.'

Jason turned to leave.

'The keys are in the ignition,' said Mr Punch.

Jason stamped down the steps of the caravan. Behind him, inside, he was sure he heard a quiet 'That's the way to do it!'

* * *

Laurent stared out of the window from his hospital bed. He was unbelievably bored. He wanted to leave. It was pointless just lying there. He ached a bit, but his head which everybody seemed so worried about felt fine. He repositioned the cast on his left arm. Wherever he lay it, it got in the way.

A male nurse bustled into the room, humming quietly. 'How you doing, Laurent?' he asked.

'I feel OK,' said Laurent, grinning through the bandages. This was Steffan. He'd been nursing Laurent since his arrival. Steffan was about twenty-five. He was tall, with bright green eyes and an open, handsome face, over which his light brown hair fell to his shoulders in dense dreadlocks. He was nice.

'*Ah, mais c'est chiant*,' Laurent complained. 'It is very boring in here.'

Steffan was pushing what looked to Laurent like a too-tall bedside cupboard on wheels. On its flat top was a metal bowl filled with water and a large sponge.

'Time to change your bandages,' Steffan said. His voice was soft and friendly. 'I've got to give you a sponge bath, too,' he said. 'You'll enjoy that. Most guys do.'

He helped Laurent raise himself into a sitting position.

'Really, I am OK,' Laurent protested. 'I can do it on my own.'

'I'm the nurse,' said Steffan, smiling slightly. 'I know best.'

He slowly unwound the bandage from Laurent's face and head.

'How do I look?' Laurent asked.

'Drop-dead gorgeous,' said Steffan casually. 'Now raise your arms.'

He unpeeled the bandages from Laurent's chest and shoulders. They didn't come away so easily – several spots were stuck with dry blood, including one nipple. Steffan tugged sharply at the bandage, ripping it off Laurent's grazed, swollen teat. Laurent winced with the pain.

'There. Brave little soldier,' said Steffan. 'This'll be nice.' He pulled the bedclothes down, uncovering Laurent's striped pyjama-bottoms. 'Roll over on to your side,' he said.

Laurent did as he was told. Steffan dipped the sponge into the water and wrung it out hard. He pressed it gently between

Laurent's shoulder-blades. Warm, slightly soapy water trickled about his bruised back. He winced slightly, then giggled.

'Feels good, yeah?' said Steffan. He carefully sponged Laurent's back, then rolled him over onto it. He dipped the sponge in the water again and applied it to his neck and shoulders. Water trickled into Laurent's armpits, tickling him. Steffan chased the rivulets with his warm sponge, teasing it into Laurent's thick black armpit-hair. He moved the sponge across Laurent's chest, following the dusting of black hair to his nipples. Gently he dabbed the sore nipple, before moving warmly, damply down his stomach.

'Expecting any visitors today?' Steffan asked.

Laurent shrugged his shoulders, then winced. That hurt.

'How's your friend, by the way? The one who came in here with you?'

'Jacques,' said Laurent. 'I do not know. I have not seen him today.'

'Strange guy,' said Steffan, running the sponge over Laurent's belly-button, tracing the fine column of black hair which rose from his pyjama-bottoms. 'He was practically hysterical in casualty the other night. Swore he'd been knifed – swore he was dying – but wouldn't let anyone near him to take a look.'

Laurent began to giggle. He guessed why Jack hadn't wanted to be examined. It could only have happened to Jack.

'What?' queried Steffan.

'He had a butt-plug in his arse,' Laurent laughed.

'He . . . Jesus . . .'

Laurent cast his mind back to the Nautilus – the heat, the noise, he and Jack on their butt-plugs, Suliman and Yousaf on their knees. Warm water was seeping into the waist-band of his pyjamas, seeping down into his pubes, around his cock, over his balls. It felt alarmingly good. There was movement under the thin, striped cloth. There was no disguising the fact that he was getting a hard-on.

Steffan had seen it too. As the pyjamas stretched around Laurent's cock he soaked his sponge and let it drip freely, drenching the thin material, plastering it to Laurent's hard cock. The material clung – wet, it was practically transparent. Laurent could clearly see the outline of his shaft, his circumcised head, his balls.

The nurse undid the single fly-button and parted the front of the wet garment, peeling it away from Laurent's hard-on. He soaked the sponge again and ran it up the cock's hard underside. Laurent shivered with enjoyment, his prick twitching beneath the soapy sponge as it nuzzled around his cockhead.

Steffan gently removed Laurent's pyjama-bottoms, easing them out from under his butt. He ran the sponge slowly down Laurent's legs.

'Turn onto your side again,' he said.

Laurent turned. He felt the warm sponge gliding over his buttocks, squeezing into his arse-cleft, nestling in his hole. To his surprise he felt something else – a soapy finger snaking around the sponge, pushing its way inside.

'Relax,' said Steffan. 'I'm a nurse.'

Steffan's finger waggled and probed. Laurent squirmed and clenched around it. After a delicious moment Steffan pulled his finger from Laurent's arse and stooped to rummage in his cupboard-on-wheels. He pulled out what looked like a glass test-tube.

'This is an NHS butt-plug,' the nurse said, smiling. 'We call it a proctoscope.'

Laurent felt the tube, cold and hard, press against his buttocks, separating their soft flesh, burrowing its way into his pucker.

'This way I can see inside you,' said Steffan. 'I can see the walls of your arsehole clenching as I bring you off.'

Gently he eased one of the pillows from beneath Laurent's head and placed it by his buttocks. 'Onto your back again,' he said. Laurent rolled back. The pillow raised his buttock-cheeks and exposed his arsehole.

Steffan took a large mirror from his box-on-wheels and placed it at the end of the bed between Laurent's legs. 'Tell me when,' he said, angling the mirror until Laurent could clearly see his own arsehole, held open by the glass tube.

Knees bent, Laurent spread his legs wide. Steffan's hand cupped the underneath of his balls. He ran a fingernail up and down Laurent's shaft, around his cockhead and into his pisshole. Then he picked up the sponge again and, wetting it, wrapped it around Laurent's hard prick, squeezing soapy water out, rubbing hard. In the mirror Laurent could see the side-walls of his own arsehole clenching and unclenching against the tube as the nurse stroked and sponged his cock towards orgasm.

'Your hole's really going for it now,' said Steffan, looking in the mirror. 'You're gonna come pretty soon.'

He was right. The warm water, the sight and sensation of the tube up inside Laurent, the feel of Steffan's expert hand around his cock, all were pushing him over the top. He reached for the nurse's white trousers, bulging at the front, and tugged at the fly.

'Whoa . . .' said Steffan, but Laurent already had his hands inside the white cloth and around the nurse's cock. It sprang out from the uniform, short but thick, with an enormous head which poked beyond the end of the foreskin. Laurent tugged the foreskin back, then drew it forward again, back and forward. Steffan made a low moaning noise somewhere in his throat. Nurse and patient masturbated one another steadily. In the mirror Laurent's hips bucked rhythmically; his pink flesh-walls seemed to be trying to crush the glass tube.

He felt an orgasm welling up in his balls. He had quite forgotten his injuries. He twisted on the bed and pulled Steffan closer to him, stretching his mouth wide, sinking his lips over the nurse's cock.

It didn't take either of them long to come. Steffan bucked and his cock slipped from Laurent's mouth, spurting jism over his face and chest, splashing the bedclothes. Seconds later Laurent came too, his spunk arcing high over his belly. In French he mouthed a happy oath.

When their twin orgasms had subsided they sat and chatted. Steffan replaced Laurent's dressings and smoked an illicit cigarette, sitting on the edge of the bed. Almost as an afterthought he removed the proctoscope from inside Laurent. 'Nearly forgot that,' he said.

Jack tapped lightly at the door of the room and pushed it open. There was a male nurse in with Laurent, bustling about, looking flustered.

'Must go,' the nurse said. 'I have other patients to attend to.'

He grabbed a tall trolley and wheeled it hastily through the door, pushing past Jack.

'Hello, mate,' Jack whispered to Laurent, stepping into the room. 'Christ, you look awful.'

'I feel quite OK now,' answered Laurent.

Jack sat down awkwardly on the edge of the mattress.

'I fucked up,' he said. 'I know that. I'm really sorry about what happened.'

'Really, it is not your fault,' replied Laurent.

'Of course it is,' said Jack. 'I dragged you off to the Nautilus, I tried it on with those blokes. And then I ran off and left you. And now look at you . . .'

Laurent was smiling. He took one of Jack's hands in his.

'You want to know something, Jacques,' he said, 'I have never told you of this, but . . . you were my first. You remember how it was? Under the pier at Brighton? I was so scared for my family's reputation that I had to come to England to do it.'

'What d'you mean . . . *first*?'

'I mean that I was a virgin before the fair came to the town.'

Jack's mouth dropped. 'You . . . No!'

'Uh-huh. *Vraiment*. I was a good son and a good student and I never did anything wrong. And Jacques, I was so bored! Then I came to England and I met you, and you persuaded me to come with you, and . . . and I have discovered so much about sex and so much about life, and I have seen many places and enjoyed many unusual experiences. And now I have been beaten up. What I am saying is . . . *none* of this would ever have happened to me at home in France. I would still be studying business, or working for my father's company. My life now is very exciting, and I want it to stay that way. I like my life. I like my life with you, Jacques.'

Laurent tugged lightly at Jack's hand, drawing him down. They kissed gently, Laurent wincing slightly as Jack's lips met his.

Jack froze. His fingers were wrapped around the bedsheet. He raised them to his lips, tested them with his tongue. He sniffed the air. 'Wait a minute . . .' he said.

'What do your charts say about the Derby Royal Infirmary?' asked Laurent, smiling sheepishly.

'Well . . . nothing,' said Jack. 'What, you mean . . . him?' His eyes shot to the door. 'You little devil.' His voice was warm with approval. 'Virgin indeed . . .'

'But I was,' said Laurent. 'Then . . .'

His hand reached for Jack's fly, slicking the buttons open, squeezing his friend's fast-hardening cock.

'You know,' said Jack, 'I've never made love in a hospital.'

He stretched out on the bed next to Laurent and kissed him again, his hand tracing the fresh bandage across Laurent's chest. Laurent had his fist clamped around the distended head of Jack's cock, squeezing hard and pulling back Jack's snug foreskin. Jack peeled back the bedclothes. Laurent was hard again – his cut cock stood out proudly. Pulling down his jeans Jack rolled carefully on top of Laurent, their cocks and bellies slapping together. Jack began grinding his hips up and down, rubbing his cock against Laurent. Their cocks lined up side by side, and Laurent too began to move, pushing upwards from the bed.

They gradually became aware of a conversation outside the door; Steffan's voice, high now and panicky, and Annie's.

'I'll just see how he is,' Steffan warbled. He burst into the room. 'Your mum's here!' he hissed. 'Jesus, look at you two. You – get dressed.'

'Annie . . .' Jack was scrambling back into his clothes. He really didn't want to see Annie just now. 'Jesus . . .' he muttered. 'Jesus . . .'

He had an idea.

'Can I borrow your jacket?' he said to Steffan.

'You're joking,' said Steffan. 'It's part of my uniform.'

'Exactly,' said Jack. 'Just for a few minutes.'

'I told you,' said Laurent happily. 'He is mad. This sort of thing always happens to Jacques. You had better do as he says.'

'You'll get me fired,' said Steffan, allowing Jack to peel the jacket back from his chest and shoulders, down his arms and off. Underneath he wore a white T-shirt.

'Perfect,' said Jack. 'She'll never notice the difference. I'll leave the jacket on the bench by reception.'

Scanning the room, he grabbed the clipboard hanging on the end of the bed and buried his face in it, as if scrutinising the young patient's condition, and walked through the door and down the corridor. He turned his head in time to see Annie disappearing into the room. Cautiously he returned to the door and peeped through the glass window.

Annie was sitting down on the bed. She was rummaging inside a large straw bag, fishing things out and presenting them to Laurent. Grapes, chocolate, books to read. Just like mum. With touching sincerity she enquired how he was feeling, and how the hospital was treating him. She chatted lightly about the fair, how everybody sent their love, how he wasn't to worry about being laid up, they were coping fine. No mention of Jack's little explosion of the night before, he noted. No acknowledgement that anything was less than peachy. Then again, he hadn't mentioned his blow-up in the Tunnel of Love to Laurent either.

'Love,' she said, 'we're having to move on. We're in Buxton tonight. They want to keep you in a few more days. I can't stay, love. You know I would, but we are a little short . . .'

Laurent laid his hand on hers. 'That is OK,' he said. She leaned forward and kissed him on the head. Jack ground his teeth. It was a typical Annie trick, using duty to the fair as an emergency exit from her fantasy family world. As soon as the going got tough, she bailed. OK, thought Jack. Now we've seen what *you're* made of, let's see what *I'm* made of. The fair could fucking well do without him for a bit. He felt no inclination to go back there anyway. If Mother Annie wouldn't stay with Laurent, then he would.

He was resolved. And when Jack resolved to do something . . .

'Nurse . . .' he heard behind him. 'Nurse . . .'

A doctor was looking directly at him from inside the main ward-room. Another nurse was pulling the screens round one of the beds. Shit. He was still wearing Steffan's jacket. He tossed the clipboard across the floor and pulled open the jacket-front, his feet attempting to run.

'Nurse . . .'

He skidded round a corner in the corridor, saw the reception desk ahead, and sped towards it. The ward doors swung wildly as he hammered through them.

They were running hours late. Jason had been given money for petrol and a badly drawn map. The lorry looked like an old army truck, but painted an embarrassing shade of pink, with hearts on the side and Gamlin's Fair in baby-blue lettering. The whole effect was spattered with dry mud. Jack loved that truck. It suited him. Jason hated it. Quite apart from the appearance, the controls were all ancient, the seat was uncomfortable, there was no seat belt and no radio or – God forbid – cassette player.

He had only been going twenty minutes. At first he had been too tense to notice the lack of facilities in the cab. The size of the lorry didn't bother him, nor his lack of a driver's licence. It was the mere fact of being behind the wheel again. Christ, he was a bad enough passenger nowadays.

He slowed as he approached a junction somewhere on the outskirts of town. A car, a Ford Fiesta, was badly parked at the side of the road, its bonnet open. A young woman was staring uncomprehendingly at the engine. She must have been in her mid-twenties, about five feet five, darkly attractive with a mane of silky black hair reaching well down below her waist. She wore tight jeans and a blue mohair jumper, speckled with oil-stains. She looked in a state.

Spotting the truck she ran into the road, waving her arms in the air.

Reluctantly Jason wound down the window. 'Need a hand?' he asked, without much enthusiasm.

'Oh, thank Christ,' the woman drawled deeply. 'Fucking hire-car. I've got to be in Nottingham in a few hours.'

'Fraid I'm going to Buxton,' said Jason.

'That'll do,' said the woman. She retrieved a large shoulder-bag from the car and climbed into the cab next to Jason.

'Cute truck,' she said.

'What about the car?' Jason asked.

'I told you,' the woman replied, 'it's a hire car. Fuck it. They can pick it up. I don't know what my manager was playing at, sticking me in a fucking Ford Fiesta . . . me!'

'I know who you are,' Jason suddenly said. 'You're the drag-queen from the club.'

'Female impersonator,' said the drag-queen stiffly.

'I was in the other day. I danced with you.'

'Oh yeah! You kicked shit out of my ankles during "I Feel Love".'

'You looked taller then.'

'Heels, darling. You can call me Kim, by the way.'

'I'm Jason,' said Jason.

They drove in silence for a while. Kim was picking at his jumper, trying to pick pieces of congealed engine oil out of the long mohair strands. 'Fucking ruined,' he muttered.

'When I stopped I thought you were a woman,' said Jason.

'It happens,' Kim replied, still fiddling with his jumper.

'D'you always dress like that?' Jason asked.

'Like what?'

'Like a woman.'

'Do I dress like a woman?' Kim sounded puzzled. 'I suppose I do. I never really think about it. I just wear what I feel comfortable in.'

'But . . . what do you feel like? A man or a woman?'

Kim shrugged his shapely shoulders. 'Search me,' he said. 'What do you feel like?'

'A bloke, of course.' As if to emphasise the point, Jason pumped the accelerator and pulled hard on the steering-wheel. The truck rattled precariously past a Mini Metro.

'So, you . . . what? Play rugby and shag birds?' said Kim.

'No.'

'No, I thought not. Me, I found out what I liked and what I didn't like a long time ago. I've got no time to give a fuck about all this male–female bullshit. I figure this kind of life will be good for maybe another six or seven years – and I'm making hay while the sun shines. After that, it ain't going to be much fun. After that I'm just another burned-out drag-queen.'

'Female impersonator,' corrected Jason.

'Pull in here,' said Kim after a while. 'I can get a lift to Nottingham from here. I've been hitching these roads since I was a boy . . . girl . . . whatever.'

Jason steered the truck off the road and onto a huge, flat expanse of oil and gravel. Half-a-dozen lorries and vans were already parked there. At the edge of the rough lorry-park was an old prefabricated structure, painted a dirty green and sprawling by the roadside. A sign on the wall said CAFÉ.

'This doesn't look very you,' said Jason.

Kim smiled.

For the first time Jason noticed he was starving, and in need of a piss. Climbing from the truck he followed Kim into the café. Formica tables sat in rows like a school dinner-hall. Jason ordered a full breakfast.

'Bitch,' said Kim, peeling the top off a low-fat yoghurt.

A doorway led to TOILET AND SAUNA. They had a sauna! Jason found the row of urinals and stationed himself at one end of it. He was alone except for a man at the far end of the row – a trucker in checked shirt, jeans and boots. As he pissed a long, luxurious stream he was aware of the man's eyes on him. Jason turned his head. The man caught Jason's eye for a moment, then transferred his stare unashamedly down to Jason's cock.

Jason grinned to himself. This was the sort of thing that Jack claimed always happened to him, and Jason had seen enough to believe his claim. And now here he was . . . Everybody at the fair was fucking contagious. They carried their lives like fevers. He'd just caught a dose of Jack.

Unable to suppress a grin, he finished his piss, put himself away and strode back into the café. His meal was waiting for him on the table. Bacon, sausages, egg, beans, black pudding, mushrooms . . .

'I can't watch,' said Kim, rising from his seat. 'I'm going to take a sauna.'

Jason cleared his plate in under five minutes, slugged back a mug of tea and reclined in his metal-and-plastic chair.

The trucker was sitting across from him, still staring. Jason guessed he must be about Tom's age, or maybe a little older. He had untidy, blondish-brown hair, not unlike Jason's own, and a day's growth of beard. Jason could now see that the check shirt was open over a khaki vest, and that the sleeves of the shirt were ripped off at the shoulders, revealing bare, muscular, heavily tattooed arms.

Jason yawned languidly. It was hot and he was tired. His clothes were damp with sweat. Well, fuck the fair for a while. He rose from his seat, crossed to the counter and paid for his meal out of the petrol money.

'How much is it to have a sauna?' Jason asked.

'It's free, love,' the woman said. 'Go ahead. It's through there.'

Jason walked past the toilet and into an open area lined with white towels on hooks. Jason undressed and piled his clothes on a long bench. He slung a towel over his shoulder and pushed open a door marked SAUNA.

Jason clapped his hand to his eyes. They had to be joking. The sauna looked like a fucking converted coal-bunker. It was at least fifty yards away across the gravel car-park, and as far as Jason could see the conversion job hadn't gone any further than sticking a sign saying SAUNA on the coal-bunker roof.

He wrapped the towel around his waist, slipped back into his trainers and marched out over the gravel, trying not to imagine the looks he must be getting from the café windows.

The sauna consisted of no more than a single steam-room with benches rising in four short rows to the back wall, and one walk-through shower. A water-butt and charcoal brazier stood next to the door. The room was lit by a single fluorescent tube, set low into one of the walls. It looked eerie in the steam. The room was thick with it as Jason entered. A man was stretched out on the lowest bench, naked, his face covered with his towel beneath which he snored quietly. Kim lay face-up on the highest bench, his towel draped over his groin region, apparently asleep. Jason stationed himself on the bench below Kim, his towel still around his waist. He watched the man on the lower tier through the steam. The man looked fairly old, stocky and tanned; one of the hairiest men Jason had ever seen. Hair sprouted from under the towel in a thick mat, obscuring his chest and stomach, crowding in around his big, lolling cock and balls.

Jason continued to study him for five minutes or more, before the man suddenly woke, snorting, and got to his feet. He snapped the towel against his leg and walked out through the door.

A sound from the bench above made Jason turn over. Kim's towel had been discarded – he lay there on his side, hair spilling over the bench. Jason thought of Ariel in his boat in the Tunnel of Love – Kim's body was flawless: arms, legs, torso, even armpits were shaved smooth, limbs were slender, skin golden. The only hair on his body sat in a neat, black triangle around his cock, which hung, half-hard, over his upper thigh.

Jason scrutinised Kim's body openly. The drag-queen's exhibitionism excited him. He lay back on his bench and unwrapped the towel from his waist, glancing quickly down at his cock. Like Kim's it lay, lazy and heavy, across his belly. He could feel Kim's gaze. He closed his eyes and let his body soak up the heat.

He was half-asleep when he felt Kim's hand brush against his chest.

'What are you doing?' he exclaimed, startled.

'Making hay while the sun shines,' Kim replied.

He rolled from his bench and lay next to Jason. His cock was hard now; it nudged against Jason's hip.

Kim kissed Jason on the shoulder. 'The way I see it,' he said, 'we're none of us here for ever.' He kissed him on the nipple. 'We've all of us got just a few years to grab for ourselves and give out as much happiness as we can.' He kissed his stomach. '*Spread a little happiness as you go by . . .*' he sang softly.

Kim's hair fanned out over Jason's bare torso and cock. Jason's cock was hard. Kim gripped it in his fist, scooping up a handful of hair. He rubbed up and down the shaft, his silky hair sliding deliciously over itself between fist and cock. Jason was starting to sweat. So was Kim. Kim kissed him wetly, then peeled his body away. From somewhere he produced a condom.

'Where did that come from?' exclaimed Jason. They were both butt-naked.

'That's my secret,' said Kim. He rolled the sheath down over Jason's cock, then climbed to the bench above, placing his feet firmly on the lower bench and easing his buttocks to the very edge of the higher one. Jason saw what he had to do. He squatted between Kim's open legs and sought his arsehole with his hand.

Locating it, he guided his cock towards the dark ring until it was nestling in the entrance.

'Nice . . .' Kim cooed.

Perched on the balls of his feet, Jason drove upward hard between Kim's cheeks. Kim gasped. Jason drove again. Gradually he established a steady, hard rhythm. Sweat covered them now. Kim's hair was plastered to them both. Supporting himself with one arm, Jason took a handful of the endless black mane and closed his fingers around Kim's long, straight cock, wrapping it in hair, working the foreskin slowly back and forth over the leaking head.

'Oooh, yeah,' purred Kim. Jason thought he was going to start singing. His head was thrown back, his mouth open.

Sweat was making Jason's feet slip. He braced his legs and raised himself slightly, slowing and deepening his stroke inside Kim. Kim clenched and unclenched around him. Still massaging Kim's cock, he forced his lips against Kim's and pushed his tongue forward. Kim's hips began to jerk. His cock swelled suddenly in Jason's hand. He bit down on Jason's lower lip and sucked hard. His come flooded out over Jason's hand. It hung in strands from Kim's own hair. Jason caught a thick strand in his mouth and sucked, tasting Kim's salty jism and wet hair. Jason too began to come, slamming his groin against Kim's buttocks. Breathless, he shuddered as his cock discharged inside Kim.

He slumped down on the bench, letting his cock ooze out of Kim's passage, and peeled off the condom. Kim sat down next to him. 'There now,' he said. 'That wasn't so bad, was it?' He kissed Jason on the lips. 'I've got to go,' he said. 'Gig in Nottingham. Got to get a lift.'

'Try the bloke with the tattoos,' said Jason. 'He looked friendly.'

'Mmm. Yes, I noticed him,' said Kim thoughtfully. He kissed Jason again. 'Thanks, hon,' he said. 'I'll keep an eye out for your fair.'

'Gamlin's,' said Jason. 'You'd like it.'

Kim strode, naked, his towel at his side, down to the shower. He lingered in the broad jet for a moment, before disappearing.

At the same time an indistinct figure entered. The pair passed each other in the doorway, then the newcomer stopped. Jason wrapped his towel around his waist and lay on his stomach, watching. He tried to work out what the foggy shape was doing. There was a hiss of water-on-charcoal and clouds of steam billowed into the room. The figure moved into the path of the fluorescent light for a moment – and then the whole room was plunged into darkness.

There was a muted, dull sound from the bench immediately below Jason – the sound of someone lying down. Then silence, for long moments. Then a tiny, regular repeating noise, a slightly wet, rubbing sound, short, brisk strokes. The sound of wanking.

Lying on his stomach on the bench in the pitch dark, Jason listened, motionless, for several minutes. He felt his cock, so recently come, getting hard under his towel. The sound stopped. Silence again. Jason felt the towel twitch from his backside and flop down the sides of the bench. He felt a hand on one buttock. The hand, and his cheek, were wet with steam and sweat. They slipped slightly across one another. He felt the hand squeeze. He felt his other buttock being squeezed. Fingers clamped, the hands were prising his cheeks apart.

He felt a warm, slithery wetness moving down his arse-crack. A tongue. It stopped at his hole and pushed forward, slipping inside him. He wriggled appreciatively.

The tongue drove deeper. Jason could feel a pair of stubbly lips sealing around his arse, and the occasional grazing of teeth. The hands which had held him now moved freely on a sea of sweat and vapour, up around his hips and underneath him, forcing their way between skin and bench, tweaking and playing with Jason's slippery nipples.

One hand moved down his stomach and slid over his cock, still sticky with come, squeezing hard, running the length of his shaft, nudging his balls, squeezing the head again, drawing his foreskin out and away from his cock with tightly pressed fingers and letting it spring back, squeezing again. Jason raised himself slightly from the bench.

The mouth left his arsehole and moved up his body, all lickspit and stubble. He felt a long, thick, slightly curved cock snaking up his arse-crack. The cock drew back then sprang forward, back and forward, bobsledding up and down his crack on runnels of sweat.

The lips clamped his shoulder and sucked hard. Teeth bit down on the drawn flesh, twisting it painfully. A hard chest smacked against his back. The cock pumped faster between his cheeks. The hand on his cock moved in short, hard strokes now.

He heard a low grunting sound coming out of the darkness just behind his head. The stranger's cock shuddered to orgasm, spraying Jason's back. He let his face rest against Jason's shoulder for a moment, and slowed his stroke on Jason's cock, teasing his foreskin again. Then he lifted Jason from the bench, turned him and lay him down on his back. The room spun for a moment. Jason was disorientated.

The stranger lowered his mouth onto Jason's cock and moved his lips slowly, wetly down it – it felt by turns soft and stubbly – until Jason could feel his cock against the back of the stranger's throat. He drew his head slowly up, his tongue warmly, wetly tickling the underside of Jason's cock, then sank it down again, tightly, gradually increasing his speed. Jason could feel long, unruly hair brushing on his groin.

He felt the hands glide up his body, finding his nipples again, tugging hard, then moving on, tugging at the hair of his armpits.

He was coming already. He felt the delicious, building surge rise from his balls and out of his spasming cock, into the invisible stranger's mouth.

The stranger swallowed, and allowed Jason's cock to soften in his mouth. Then the mouth was gone, and Jason heard the light padding of footsteps. He lay back, tingling with the thrill of the anonymous encounter. The door opened and just for a second Jason saw again the steamy silhouette of his dark lover as he walked through the shower-arch and out. He dozed for a few minutes more, before stretching himself, groping for his towel. He got up and walked from the room into the shower. Wrapping the towel around his waist, he donned his trainers and plunged back across the car-park.

He dressed quickly, and strode back into the café. The tattooed trucker and Kim were standing together in the doorway. The trucker's hair dripped water onto the floor of the café. Kim crossed the room and put his arms around Jason. 'My lift,' he said, and kissed Jason on the lips. 'Remember,' he said, 'the songs say it

all. Spread a little happiness . . . Love the one you're with and . . .
er . . . Don't fear the Reaper. 'Bye, hon.'

He swung through the door, towing the trucker by the arm.

Back in the cab, Jason triggered the sluggish old engine and steered
for the road. A young figure was standing at the roadside with his
thumb stuck out into the traffic. A loose tangle of dirty black hair
sat on top of a Mediterranean head on a small, lithe, wiry body.
He reminded Jason of Spider. He stopped the truck and opened
the passenger's door.

'Where are you going?' asked Jason.

'North,' the boy replied.

'I can take you as far as Buxton,' said Jason.

The boy grinned and climbed nimbly into the cab. Thinking
about his own hitch-hiking days, Jason pulled into the road and
accelerated away.

'What's your name?' Jason asked.

'It don't matter,' said the boy. 'Funny truck, this.'

'It's old,' said Jason.

'No, I meant the paint job. All that hearts and flowers, and that
pink shit. Are you a faggot?'

'It's a fairground lorry,' said Jason, evading the question.

The boy's attention wandered out of the window to the passing
scenery, and then quickly back to Jason. He stared up at him,
unblinking. Jason rattled up through the gears.

'Is that a love bite on your neck?' the boy asked suddenly.

Jason was painfully aware of the welt that was already rising
where the stranger's teeth had bitten. He said nothing. They
stopped at some traffic lights and a deep vibration thrummed
through the truck, sending tingles through Jason's seat. He felt his
overworked cock hardening again.

The boy lifted his feet onto the seat, drawing his knees in to his
chest. He continued to stare at Jason.

'Are you, though?' persisted the boy. 'A faggot, I mean.'

Again, Jason didn't answer. He glanced down at the boy's lap.
The boy clearly had a hard-on inside his jeans. The boy was aware
of his eyes. He shifted position in the seat, moving his buttocks

forward and letting his right leg flop back to the floor so that his erect cock stood out against the denim.

'D'you want to get blowed?' he said.

'What?' Jason blurted, half-shocked, half-laughing.

'For the ride,' the boy said. 'I don't mind.'

He put his hand on Jason's crotch and began rubbing him through his jeans, pressing hard. Jason tried to concentrate on the road. His cock was still exhausted.

The boy fumbled with Jason's buttons and prised his fly apart. He ran his finger over the tight cotton of Jason's pants. The white lines of the road flashed under the lorry. Jason could feel the boy lifting the front of his pants over his cockhead, pulling them down and hooking them under his balls. He glanced down – his cock was still ruddy from the sauna. The boy moved his curly, scruffy head down into Jason's lap and steered Jason's cock into his mouth.

This had been a favourite game with Spider. Jason at the wheel of a boosted car; Spider's black mop bouncing up and down in his lap. Looking down, this could *be* Spider.

The lorry crossed the line in the middle of the road. Jason swung on the wheel, laughing to himself.

The boy's own cock, dark and slim, was poking from the front of his jeans. He pumped it as his head bobbed up and down in Jason's lap. Jason slipped a little way down the seat, reached across and wrapped his hand around his passenger's pumping fist, around his cock. Together they stroked it towards climax.

Jason shivered with nostalgia and pleasure as his passenger's wet mouth slipped up and down his shaft. The boy was drawing his teeth along the hard veined column on the up-stroke, sheathing them again with his lips as he reached the head, pausing occasionally to tease the eye with his tongue.

Jason could feel the boy's mouth tightening on his cock. He made a slight gagging sound in the top of his throat as he swallowed Jason again and again. Jason could feel the head battering the back of the boy's throat. The boy himself suddenly shot his load into the air, splashing the dashboard. He closed his eyes. The road vanished. He was coming.

* * *

Jason had forgotten the thrills of high-speed sex. It wasn't until his orgasm had subsided that the realisation of what they had just done had hit him. He had slammed on the brakes and the truck had juddered to a halt. He was pale and sweating.

'What's the matter?' the boy had asked.

Jason hadn't replied. Slowly he'd taken the lorry up to thirty miles per hour and stayed there, gradually relaxing and allowing himself to bathe in the lingering sensation of pleasure. The boy had curled up on the seat next to him like a dormouse, his cock still poking from his jeans, and appeared to sleep.

Jason didn't know where the lad wanted dropping off. At the moment he didn't mind. The road stretched lazily in front of him. He stretched himself, enjoying the drive. Broad fields lined the roads. Gamlin's always seemed to take the most out-of-the-way routes. They passed through villages. The boy eventually uncurled, yawning and rubbing his eyes. Sleepily, casually, he put his cock away.

'Where are we?' he asked.

'I'm, uh, not sure,' Jason replied. He looked around for Piper's inadequate map. He couldn't see it anywhere. 'I didn't want to wake you. You looked so . . . serene, I suppose.' Jason blushed slightly.

They passed a roadside café with trucks parked outside.

'This'll do,' said the boy. 'You can drop me here.'

Jason pulled in to the side of the road.

''Bye,' said the boy. 'Thanks.'

Without another word he slipped from the cab and trotted away. Jason watched him enter the café and pulled away into the road. The map was gone and he didn't know where he was. At the moment he didn't care. He let the road lead him, reflecting on the day. His cock felt sore. He wondered whether he was destined for a life of brief encounters. It wasn't so bad. He started humming to himself; a song he'd heard a drag-queen sing.

It was dark by the time Jason found his way to the Gamlin's site in Buxton. He was greeted with a mixture of relief and annoyance.

'Tom's gone off looking for you,' said Rex. 'He's not well pleased.'

'Sorry,' said Jason. 'I got lost. I picked up a hitch-hiker.'

'So did I,' Annie cut in. Jason met her gaze uneasily. He was starting to feel bad about what had happened between them. Annie was smiling, though. 'A nice young man from London, on his way to visit a friend. When he saw Gamlin's on the truck he jumped into the road. I nearly killed him.' She looked around her. 'Where is he?' she said. 'Glen!'

A figure stepped through the little cluster of people. 'Hi, Jase.'

Jason spun. Glen stood before him, grinning broadly, hands outstretched.

Tom tripped over a piece of scaffolding, and swore under his breath. He'd searched deserted roads for three hours without success. He was worried about Jason, and about plenty besides.

The lights in the caravan were burning. Jason was back. Creeping in, Tom stopped. Jason was in the bed with someone else. A black guy – sort of half-caste. They were curled up like hamsters, deeply asleep, smiling.

Tom sighed and shook his head. He switched out the light and, stretching himself on the narrow, padded bench-seat that ran under the caravan's main window, tried to sleep. He couldn't. He lay awake for hours, watching the dawn break, watching Jason and his companion, so peaceful in the first light.

It wasn't yet four. It was no good. He got up and strode across the fairground to the Wheel, dropping without pause into his morning warm-up routine. He drove himself hard, the army way. The only way.

Re-entering the caravan, he dressed and hunted out a battered suitcase. He took his one suit from the wardrobe. A black armband still hung around the sleeve. He folded the suit inside the case, and placed other clothes on top of it. When he was fully packed he sat on the edge of the bed, careful not to wake the entwined lovers, and quietly slid open the bedside drawer. He lifted the envelope from inside, ripped it open and pulled out the letter, scanning its even hand.

After long moments he put the letter back in the drawer, and took out a piece of notepaper and a pen. He scrawled a hasty note and closed the drawer. He gazed down at the sleeping Jason.

Gently he extended a hand and traced the scar beside Jason's eye with his forefinger. He leaned forward and kissed the boy gently on the head, then rose to his feet, picked up his suitcase and left the caravan, closing the door behind him.

Eleven

_____

Water washed over Jason's dreams, along with a voice. A great banshee-wailing in the distance. He struggled awake to the sound of the shower booming around its little cubicle, accompanied by some of the worst singing Jason had ever heard. Gilbert and fucking Sullivan.

'Mmmm . . .' said Glen, kissing Jason on the cheek. 'We should have done this back at the squat, instead of you sleeping on your own behind that curtain.'

They were tangled together, arms and legs hopelessly entwined. 'Who's that?' Jason asked. 'It's not Tom.'

'He said his name was Rex,' said Glen. 'He let himself in. His shower's on the blink.'

'Christ, what a voice,' said Jason, fishing around on the floor for something to throw at the cubicle.

'You were kind of wiped out last night,' said Glen.

'I was tired,' said Jason. 'It was a fuck of a long day.'

Tired and sore, he thought to himself. He'd dragged Glen off to bed almost immediately; only, it appeared, to fall asleep in his arms. 'Sorry,' he said, and kissed him on the cheek. 'I'm glad you're here.'

'I decided to get out of London for a while,' said Glen. 'Bit of a holiday. I'm heading for the Lake District.' He stroked Jason's un-tidy, dark-blond hair. 'That's a nasty bruise on your neck,' he said.

'Uh, that's a love-bite,' said Jason sheepishly.

In the shower Rex and Gilbert and Sullivan reached their climax and relapsed into silence.

'I'll say this,' said Glen, nodding towards the shower, 'he's got a ridiculous body, that bloke.'

'He was a strong-man,' said Jason. 'Let's get up. I'll show you round.'

'I kind of like it in here,' said Glen. He was lying on his stomach, twisting his head and craning his neck to see the shower-cubicle behind him. Rex's back and buttocks, wet and soapy, were pressed against the tiny chamber's thin plastic wall. Glen turned in the bed to get a better view. His cock, hard and pointing, bounced against Jason's leg. A moment later Jason felt Glen's hand trailing up the side of his thigh, rising to envelop his balls, fingers snaking up the shaft of his fast-expanding cock. Glen gripped the shaft and began running his fist up its length, squeezing hard on the swollen bulb at the top, then drawing down again, pulling Jason's foreskin fully back.

'We'll have to be quick,' whispered Jason. 'He'll be out any minute.'

They kissed hastily, and Jason began stroking Glen's huge, dark member, loosely at first, then more firmly. He looked down at the purple swelling emerging from the tight brown foreskin then disappearing again.

'Look,' Glen giggled.

They watched Rex's fingers, forcing their way back between his legs, tapping against the cubicle wall as they soaped his arsehole. They wanked each other hard as they watched.

'I reckon he's close to finishing,' whispered Jason.

'So am I,' said Glen. His foreskin was locked tight behind the ridge of his cockhead. Jason was rubbing directly on the glans. 'I'll just have to help you along a bit.'

He stretched his spare hand over Jason's hip and buttock. His fingers groped for Jason's arsehole. Swiftly he inserted two fingers and drove at Jason's G-spot. He rubbed the prostate hard as he continued to pump Jason's cock.

It was too much. Jason let out a long, low breath as he came.

Glen too was shooting. Their twin jets mixed and splashed over their bellies.

The sound of cascading water stopped, and the shower door opened. Rex stepped out, wrapping a towel around his waist and patting his moustache. Jason and Glen struggled to separate themselves on the bed.

'Oh, don't mind me,' said Rex. 'You two carry on.' He leaned over Jason. 'I like your friend,' he whispered, and strode through the door.

By the time Jason and Glen emerged from the caravan the fairground was already busy. They had set up on a patch of waste ground next to a school – a typical, modern, prefabricated-looking affair. For most of the morning teachers were shooing lines of small, staring children away from the railings which bounded the school playground.

Jason and Glen exchanged smiles. 'Rough on the kids,' said Glen. 'Having to look at this from your classroom.'

Most of the fair crew seemed to be clustered in small groups about the long trestle-table.

'OK!' Annie shouted. 'Shut up!'

Silence fell. People from other parts of the fairground moved in. Tugging Glen by one finger, Jason approached the assembly. Annie was standing at the head of the table. Piper sat in a chair next to her, his eyes closed, his chin rest ng on his chest. He looked fast asleep in the morning sun.

'Now you all know we didn't open last night,' said Annie. 'But we can't afford to lose any more days. The problem is, we're badly short of hands. Laurent's in hospital and Jack, it would seem, has gone. We've no casuals to help either, so you see what we're up against.'

'Where's Jack?' asked little Willow Simpson suddenly. She was standing with her brother and her grandmother Mavis, the hot-dog woman.

The crowd fell silent. Annie's face hardened into a scowl.

'I don't think we can include Jack in whatever future plans we might have,' said Annie. 'He's unfit to run a ride. He's a danger at the moment – to himself and to others.' Her eyes caught Jason's. He flinched from her gaze.

'That business with the bottles,' she continued. 'It's a miracle no one was killed.'

'That's a point,' said Doug. 'What are we going to do about the Tunnel of Love? Whatever happens we can't open it tonight. There's glass everywhere in there.'

'Can we afford not to open it?' Rex cut in. 'God knows, we're getting small enough crowds as it is, without closing down one of the main attractions.'

'We can't,' said Annie flatly. 'We'll have the police down on top of us. Now, who's going to do what? Jason, you're on the Hall of Mirrors.'

'No I'm not,' said Jason. He'd found Tom's note on getting out of bed. *Gone away for a few days on family business. Back soon, Tom.* Jason handed it to Annie with a shy smile. 'Tom's away,' he said. 'I found that this morning.'

Annie muttered something clipped under her breath.

'Tom?' said Rex. 'He never said anything to me. Where's he gone?'

Jason shrugged his shoulders. 'He didn't say. He hasn't said much to me for a couple of days.'

Rex fixed Jason with a hard stare. 'It's high time you came clean, young man. What have you been doing to Tom?' he said.

'He had a letter,' said Annie. 'It came yesterday morning, but I suspect he's been waiting for it for some time. Didn't you notice him, carrying it around all day – holding the envelope up and staring at it? He did that for hours. I guess he must have opened it.'

'A letter?' Rex queried. 'From whom?'

'I don't know,' sighed Annie. 'Jason?'

Jason shrugged his shoulders. 'I'm sorry, Annie,' he said. He reached out and squeezed her hand. She squeezed back.

'I had a really good chat with her on the lorry yesterday,' said Glen as they walked away from the gathering. 'Nice lady.'

'Yes,' said Jason. 'She is.'

* * *

The day was hard but enjoyable. Jason clambered about the Wheel, changing bulbs. Glen, who had agreed to help him, baulked at removing even one foot from the ground. He hated heights, and could only watch and wince as Jason swung and balanced high overhead.

The decision had been taken – the Tunnel of Love had to remain closed; Jason had to stay on the Big Wheel. Which meant Glen would have to take the money for the Hall of Mirrors.

'Me?' he shrieked. 'Why me? I mean – this is nothing to do with me. I can't –'

'Of course you can,' said Rex. 'A talented chap like you . . . I would be honoured if you would allow me to . . . give you a few tips . . .'

Rex had been all over Glen all morning. 'You shouldn't be greedy,' he told Jason. 'You've got Tom. *And* you had those boxers – and God knows who else with Jack and Laurent. Don't think I miss these things. Jack's sexual radar pales into insignificance next to mine.' The ex-strongman sighed. 'It's just that I've got no artillery to back it up.'

'That's the way to do it,' a familiar, tinny voice cut in, quiet yet razor-sharp.

'Like fuck it is,' said Rex. 'I've got to rip telephone books apart to relieve the sexual tension.'

The red and white Punch and Judy booth was standing in front of the Merry-Go-Round. Kevin and Willow sat on the grass, looking up at the little stage.

'Oooooh, hello, boys and girls!' called Judy.

A child Jason hadn't seen before sat down next to Kevin and Willow. Two more followed. It was the school's afternoon break. A trickle of curious under-elevens became a flood. A teacher shouted instructions at them, which they ignored. They came through the gates and over the railings, laughing, running. Most sat down in front of the Punch and Judy booth. A few of the boys ran and dodged around the fairground rides, shouted at by Rex.

Hand in hand, Jason and Glen moved into the crowd of kids and sat down.

Mr Punch killed his baby, beat up his wife, did the same to a policeman, and so on through the glove-puppet cast. A bloody, hysterical catalogue of madness and murder. All the time he squeaked his ebullient catch-phrase. Suddenly Jason thought of Jack. He was a bit like Mr Punch, restless, feisty, always pouncing on people. He hoped Jack was all right.

'That's the way to do it!' He thought of Spider. That grin like summer. Nobody ever told him what to do. Nobody killed his irrepressible lust for life. No way.

He thought of Glen. He too, in his quiet way, had a Punch-like defiance. He went his own way, did his own thing, and nothing ever stopped him. He looked into Glen's gentle, laughing eyes and smiled. Suddenly Punch and Judy seemed innocent, poking a child's tongue out at authority. That could have applied to him, too, in the past.

Mr Punch was engaged in a tug-of-war with a crocodile. The rope they pulled on was a long, indestructible string of sausages. The crowd shouted and squealed, and the contest raged. Finally Mr Punch pulled the string free of the cloth jaws and the sausages swung through the air and hung from the puppet's clasped arms over the front of the stage. A child from the crowd – one of the schoolboys, grinning wickedly – ran up to the stage, grabbed the sausages and pulled. He ran into the crowd, waving the sausages above his head.

'You little bastard, you little swine!' Piper crawled from the back of the booth and lurched into the crowd. Mr Punch still sat on his right hand, the crocodile on his left. 'Give me back them fuckin' sausages!'

He grabbed for the boy. The boy dodged, and passed the sausages to another, who ran from the flailing Piper. Suddenly the crowd was on his feet, running and screaming in delight around the cursing old man. The sausages passed from hand to hand. Kevin had them now.

'Kevin,' shouted Piper. 'I'll whip you, boy, I'll –' He aimed a feeble blow at Kevin, which went far wide of the mark. Kevin laughed and threw the sausages to someone else.

Jason and Glen stood motionless in the chaos, laughing hysterically. The sausages flew through the air. Jason caught them.

'Jason,' growled Piper. 'Give me them sausages . . .'

Jason grinned hugely.

'I'll sack you, boy . . .'

Piper sprang slowly forward. Jason tossed the sausages high in the air and the crowd surged.

Jason heard Rex, yelling. Boys were climbing over the Merry-Go-Round, sitting in the immobile Bumper Cars, vrooming and honking. 'Hey!' Jason saw three boys high up on the Wheel. Two were standing in one of the cars, twenty feet off the ground, fighting. The car swayed alarmingly. The third boy was out on the fuselage, swinging from a strut. 'Jesus!' yelled Jason, breaking from the crowd. 'Get down from there!'

Teachers were now marching across the fairground, blowing whistles and shouting. A stocky woman in tweeds collared Piper. 'You should be ashamed of yourself,' she lectured, 'setting up your *entertainment* here, luring my children from their lessons.'

"Ooo're you?" spat Piper.

'I am the headmistress of St Saviour's School, and I am responsible for these children.'

'Then you ought to be fuckin' ashamed of yourself, missis,' croaked the furious old man. 'Look at 'em! Little bastards, running wild across my fair. I'll have the fuckin' skin off their backs. And if there's any damage I'll have the police on you, missis!'

He stomped off to his caravan, swearing loudly. The headmistress stood, open-mouthed, her face reddening as the fury welled. Her fat right hand clenched and unclenched. She looked around for something to vent her pique on, and saw a little girl standing close by, sucking her thumb and looking shyly up at her. The headmistress clipped the child across the back of the head with a satisfied, genteel grunt.

The evening rolled in, bringing with it a small but enthusiastic crowd. Jason spun the Wheel and Glen, after a few more protests, manned the Hall of Mirrors. Reticent at first, as the atmosphere of the night drew on Glen was taking to this. He began bantering with people in the queue, and before long he was embarked on a long, wholly improvised pitch. It was an interesting variation of Piper's mad, spooky old man. Glen opened his eyes wide, flared his lips and nostrils, and went into a leering, grinning, dancing voodoo priest routine. *Them mirrors suck out yo' soul, bo'.*

Two grinning boys handed a five-pound note to Jason – the pair who had earlier been wrestling at the top of the Wheel. 'You two – no fighting up there,' Jason said to them. They smiled at one another and climbed aboard. Jason did a double-take – they were holding hands! He sent them into the sky.

It was a balmy, happy night – one of those nights when Jason was as swept off his feet by the tacky magic of the fair as the youngest of the punters. There hadn't been too many of these nights lately. Watching the last of the crowd leave, he wandered across to where Glen was standing outside the Hall of Mirrors. Piper was leaning against the ride and talking earnestly to Glen. He winked, patted the boy on the back and walked away.

Jason drew up beside Glen. Glen placed a hand on each side of his neck and drew him in close, kissing him softly on the lips.

'I've enjoyed tonight,' said Glen. 'It was a laugh.' Flashing a broad grin he slipped inside the entrance of the Hall of Mirrors.

'Hey,' shouted Jason, 'come out of there.'

'You come in,' came Glen's muffled response.

'Shit,' said Jason under his breath. 'Don't fuck about, Glen.'

No response. Swearing, Jason followed him through the door.

There was no sign of Glen on the twisted path that led to the interior of the attraction. Jason tried to ignore the grotesque distortions, the fat men, the beanpoles, the men without heads, which the bizarrely shaped rows of mirrors threw at him.

'Glen?'

'In here.'

Jason stepped into the maze. A dozen Jasons stepped into the maze.

'Glen?'

Glen stepped into view. A dozen Glens.

'Which one is you?' asked Jason.

'Here,' said Glen's voice. The Glens stepped forward, then vanished to one side. Jason's eyes darted about, looking for him.

There – he appeared again, twenty-fold, carrying his sweat-shirt in his fist, naked to the waist – then immediately was gone.

'Don't piss about,' said Jason.

'Strip,' said Glen from somewhere.

'Glen . . .' Jason was beginning to laugh, in spite of himself. He saw Glen's clothes in a pile on the floor. 'Right,' he said, ripping his T-shirt off. Garment by garment he dropped his clothes on top of Glen's.

He could see Glen behind him, bare-arsed, reflected in the mirrors. Glen kissed him on the shoulder, then stepped into nothing again. Jason could see the way he went. He followed. Something caught him by the hand and he swung round. Glen stood before him – and all around him – naked, his cock half-hard. He kissed Jason on the mouth, pushing his tongue between Jason's full lips, and reached for his cock.

They were close to the twisting passage which led to the entrance. Grinning, Glen took Jason by the hard cock and towed him along the passage. They stood in front of a curving, twisting mirror. Their heads looked flat, their chests bulbous, their legs thin and their cocks long. Jason stooped and took Glen's cock in his mouth. Jason's head looked long, bullet-shaped, as if Glen's huge cock was pushing his skull out of shape.

In the opposite mirror it didn't look as if Jason had a head – or Glen a cock – at all. Jason's neck seemed to taper to a point, vanishing somewhere between Glen's legs.

They heard muffled voices outside. 'Let's get out of here,' said Glen. 'Let's go somewhere quiet. I'll get the clothes.'

They dressed hastily and Jason peered out of the entrance to the Hall. A few of the fairground-folk were clustered close by, chatting quietly.

'Where shall we go?' he asked.

'Follow me,' said Glen, smiling. He took Jason's hand and led him around to the back of the ride and out of the fair. No one saw them leave. To their left was the school, dark and quiet now. Beyond that stretched the school's playing-fields, ghostly in the moonlight.

The two friends strolled hand-in-hand towards the neat green fields. White-painted lines shimmered slightly in the darkness. Rugby-posts cast long moon-shadows. They stood on a long grass bank which sloped gently down to the touch-lines. They embraced tightly, mouth finding mouth, tongues twining around each other like serpents. Kissing, they sank to the grass, fumbling with each other's clothing, tugging at belts and zips, lowering jeans and pants to reveal their twin erections. Still in each other's arms, trousers and pants around their knees, they rolled down the bank to the edge of the pitch, laughing, kissing and nibbling at each other's faces, ears and necks.

Jason ran his hands up inside Glen's T-shirt, following the contours of his chest, circling his nipples. Lowering his head, Jason opened his mouth and swallowed the swollen head of Glen's cock. The sharp taste permeated his mouth; his friend's musky cock-smell played about his nostrils. His mouth was full, his jaw stretched. He could feel Glen's cock against the back of his throat. He was only halfway down the shaft. Closing his eyes, willing himself not to gag, he opened his throat and sank his head until his lips were brushing Glen's pubes. Glen let out a groan. Jason began working his head slowly up and down the shaft.

Glen's cock turned in Jason's mouth. His friend was scuttling round on the grass. He licked all around Jason's cock with his tongue, then took it wetly inside his mouth, slurping slightly as his lips closed. Both started to respond with their hips, pumping their cocks into each other's mouths. Jason held Glen's head as he thrust; Glen's fingers spidered over Jason's balls and thighs.

They came together, each drinking the other's hot seed, and lay motionless in a tangle of arms and legs, clothes and cocks. Glen held Jason in his mouth, sucking and slurping and licking as Jason's cock softened. Jason was about half-hard now, and starting to stiffen up again. Glen was hard too, his cock bobbing against Jason's lips. He took Jason's cock from his mouth.

'I used to have a mate,' said Glen, 'bit of a philosopher. He always said when you have a feast, satisfy the appetite quickly and the palate slowly.'

He placed his lips against Jason's bush and kissed it gently. He kissed, licked and nibbled his way over Jason's balls and down his leg, easing his jeans down as he progressed. Jeans, pants and trainers came off. Jason squirmed with pleasure as Glen licked the soles of his feet, sticking his tongue between Jason's toes, popping each of them into his mouth.

He moved across to Jason's other foot, then up his leg and back to his balls. Cock, belly button, nipples, all were wetly probed and tested by Glen's mouth. Jason's T-shirt came off. Glen munched his way wetly over Jason's face and neck, then turned him over and continued his mouth-journey, around his shoulder-blades and down his spinal column to his arse-crack. His tongue plunged into the gorge, finding Jason's hole and pushing through the puckered sphincter.

His tongue still sponging the inside of Jason's hole, Glen removed his clothes. He took a condom from the pocket of his jeans and turned Jason onto his side.

Lifting his head, he said, 'Your turn, Jason.' He reached around Jason's hip and rolled the rubber down his cock.

Jason turned to face Glen, kissing his neck and shoulders. Glen wrapped his legs around Jason's waist and Jason felt with his fingers for his friend's arsehole. Locating it, he guided his hard cock towards it. He felt the resistance of Glen's butt-flesh, gradually giving way to his cock, taking it in, closing tightly about it.

He kissed Glen's windpipe as he fucked him, Glen's legs tight around his trunk. He pushed off the ground and raised himself upright. Glen sprawled back across Jason's thighs, his head and shoulders on the grass. Jason gripped his legs and guided them up onto his shoulders. He raised himself further, kneeling as if in prayer, pulling Glen's legs up with him. Glen hung from Jason's shoulders as Jason fucked him, feeling his cock swell inside him, feeling his climax building in his balls and erupting up his cock. 'Christ,' he croaked as he came.

They changed places. Glen fucked Jason. Then they lay together, naked, motionless beneath the moon.

'I've got something for you,' said Glen. 'Pass me my jeans.'

He fished into a pocket and pulled something out. It was small, and it swung and glinted in the moonlight.

'My spider!' He'd taken it off at the squat and never gone back for it.

'It had fallen down behind your mirror,' said Glen.

Jason kissed him wordlessly.

'Let me put it on you,' said Glen. He wrapped the thong

around Jason's neck and did up the little clasp at the back. The silver spider sat once more on his throat.

'Glen,' asked Jason, fingering the spider, 'why don't you stay here? With the fair.'

Glen thought for a moment. 'Nah,' he said.

'You enjoyed tonight – you said so – and everything seems more . . . normal . . . more sane, not so creepy when you're around.'

'I'm a city boy,' said Glen. 'I'd miss London too much, hanging about in all these backwaters. No, I'm off to the Lake District to get my head together for a bit, then it's back to town.'

'You stayed overnight,' said Jack. 'You're one of us now. You're a Lost Boy. Jack says once you've stayed overnight with the fair you never leave.' He laughed sadly. 'Then again, the number of men who stay overnight with Jack and then vanish without trace . . .'

'It's a long time since I really travelled,' said Glen. 'I've kind of got the bug. You're right, I *am* a lost boy. I'm lost in the English countryside, and it's great. I'll be through this soon . . .'

He began pulling his clothes on.

'No,' said Jason, getting to his feet. 'Let's stay like this for a while. Let's walk.'

And so, naked, arm-in-arm, the couple strolled across the ghost-lit playing-fields, silent, enjoying each other's presence and each other's nakedness.

'Why don't you come with me?' Glen asked suddenly.

'Come with you?'

'Yeah. I reckon you could use a holiday.'

'Well, I . . .'

Glen stopped, squeezing Jason's arm hard. 'Look over there,' he whispered.

A figure was standing under the far rugby-posts, watching them, bathed in moonlight, his long black hair and the swathes of his flapping coat swallowed by the dark. Beneath the coat a naked, hairy torso, crowned by a thick leather neck-collar, sat above a long, thin, red cock. The cock was hard and the figure was pumping on it with his hand.

'Who the fuck's that?' whispered Glen.

Jason walked closer to the figure.

'What are you going to . . .' Reluctantly Glen followed. 'Hold on, Jase,' he whispered.

Jason took a step closer. A deep, dark scar ran down the side of the figure's leathery neck. His mouth was stretched into a grimace or a snarl, which twitched slightly in time to his cock-strokes. Saliva dripped from his lips.

Glen caught Jason's arm. 'Don't go any closer,' he said. 'He looks dangerous.'

'It's OK,' said Jason in a low, even voice. 'I know him, sort of . . .'

Jason began to walk steadily towards the figure, holding out his right hand. He stopped before the figure and stroked its scarred neck and cheek. The figure extended a long, red tongue, and licked the open palm of Jason's hand.

'Jase, no!' Jason heard Glen's running feet behind him. He turned and caught his friend by the shoulders, pulling him to a halt.

There was a flapping sound behind Jason. He swung around. The figure had gone. He was nowhere to be seen. Jason scanned the dark, empty fields.

'You remember when you were a kid, and you'd fall or something and get a scab on your knee or elbow, or whatever?' said Jason slowly, his eyes still fixed on the monochrome dark.

'Yeah,' replied Glen. 'Why?'

'And you wish you could just put it out of your mind, the scab. But you can't. You can't fucking leave it alone. You've got to keep picking at it, working it loose, even though you know it's going to hurt like hell when it comes off, and what's underneath it is going to be all puss and raw skin.'

'Yeah,' said Glen 'What are you talking about?'

'Gamlin's is like that,' said Jason. He turned and kissed Glen. 'I can't come with you. Not yet.'

Twelve

The corridors of the Derby Royal Infirmary were becoming quite familiar to Jack.

'Morning, sister,' he called as he strode down the corridor. 'How is he today?'

'Much improved,' the sister replied. 'Your visits seem to be doing him a world of good, young man.'

Jack smiled. 'Healing hands,' he said.

He turned down a branch corridor, tapped on the door of Laurent's room and entered. Laurent was sitting up in bed. The bandages had been removed from his chest. Jack looked at the tender, puffy skin beneath.

'Poor baby,' he said, and sat down on the bed. Laurent grabbed him and pressed his lips against Jack's in a long, slow kiss. Jack ran his hands gently over Laurent's bare torso and arms. Laurent winced slightly.

'Sorry,' said Jack.

'It's OK,' said Laurent. 'Don't stop.'

The door opened behind Jack. He sprang away from Laurent. Sister was standing in the doorway, smiling knowingly.

'Healing hands. Hmmm . . . Perhaps I'll go.'

She turned and left the room. Laurent ran his fingers down Jack's long pony-tail.

'It's Steffan's day off today,' he said, 'so it's just you and me.'

'I'm glad,' said Jack. 'Do you know how long it's been since we made love together, just the two of us?'

'It's been a long time,' agreed Laurent.

They kissed again, Laurent wriggling down the bed until he was flat on his back, pulling Jack's head down with him. Jack felt his friend's tongue flexing and darting in his mouth. Jack reached for the grapes Annie had brought and lifted the bunch from the bowl. He bit a grape from the stem and held it between his lips, moving his face low over Laurent's chest and stomach, running the wet green fruit over his skin. He bit down, bursting the grape, running its juices over Laurent's chest with his lips. He burst another pair over Laurent's nipples, leaving a grape-skin cover on each bruised teat, and one more in his friend's belly-button. Grape-juice flooded the little crater, flowing over the sides and down into Laurent's black pubes. The French boy's circumcised cock was hard, standing out from his groin. Jack took another grape and burst it against the root of Laurent's shaft, where it joined his balls. Juice cataracted over the twin, hairy orbs. Jack's lips trailed the sweet liquid up Laurent's cock, working it into the head with his tongue.

Laurent's cock was slippy with grape-juice. The sugary taste mingled with the salt of Laurent's sweat and skin, filling Jack's mouth. He slid his lips down the shaft, feeling his friend's cock travel across his tongue to the back of his throat, then pulled back, lips tight around Laurent's twitching cockhead, then down again, as if drawing water from a well.

He pulled the blankets of the bed over his head. It felt as if he were in a tent, or a cave – just him and Laurent's hard cock. Laurent arched his hips, pushing deeper into Jack's mouth. Jack pulled a grape from the bunch and ran it up and down Laurent's buttock-cleft. Zeroing in on Laurent's arsehole, Jack gently pushed the grape past his anal sphincter and up into his soft tunnel. Laurent wriggled and giggled. Jack's mouth didn't break stroke on his cock. He picked another grape and again ran it under Laurent's balls and up his arse-crack. It settled in the entrance to his hole and, like its predecessor, Jack pushed it through the tight pucker.

Another followed it, then another. Sucking on his friend's cock, feeding his arsehole with grapes, Jack was pushing Laurent towards orgasm. The French boy began bucking his hips. Jack struggled to keep control of Laurent's cock with his mouth. His friend's arse was now full of grapes.

Laurent gasped something in French as his cock began to spurt its load down Jack's throat. His buttocks clenched and spasmed, sending crushed grape-juice squirting out over Jack's hand. Jack drank Laurent's load and lay with his cock in his mouth until it was soft, then lay with his head resting on his friend's groin, casually licking the sweet, spicy juice from his fingers.

'I can leave tomorrow,' whispered Laurent.

Jack smiled under the covers and kissed Laurent gently on the sugar-sticky groin. There was a creaking from the door of the room. He froze.

'How are you today?' he heard. Annie. Shit. What was she doing here? The fair had left town two days ago.

'I feel much better,' Laurent replied.

Jack felt the foot of the bed sink. Annie was sitting on it.

'You seem better,' Annie said. 'Laurent, is that a man in your bed, or are you just pleased to see me?'

Laurent giggled in embarrassment.

'OK, Jack,' said Annie. 'You can come out.'

Jack crawled to the head of the bed and poked his head out. 'How did you know it was me?' he said.

Annie smiled. 'Who else would ever be caught in that position?'

'Jack's been here every day,' said Laurent.

'I'm glad,' said Annie. 'How are you managing to live, Jack?'

Jack's shoulders sagged. He let his face relax into a rueful grin. 'I called my mum and dad,' he said. 'I just thought *Fuck it, why not?* I mean, they're loaded . . .'

'But you haven't spoken to them since . . .'

'Since I joined the fair. I know. I just thought . . . It was daft. I was cutting off my nose to spite my face, as usual. I'm through with all that, Annie.'

He took Laurent's hand and squeezed it. 'Ow!' gasped Laurent.

'Sorry,' Jack whispered. He turned to Annie. 'I owe you an apology too,' he said. 'Things have all been a bit . . . well, fucked-up recently.'

'I know,' said Annie. 'We've all been feeling it. It's not just the poor turn-outs. It's not even the . . . accidents and what-have-you. It's something else. I just can't shake this feeling that something big is going to happen any time now.'

'Maybe I should stay here,' said Laurent.

Annie looked at him and smiled. 'Piper got the puppets out yesterday,' she said, suddenly changing tack. Jack could see that beneath her light-hearted banter she was worried. He let her talk, saying nothing, just listening.

After a while she got up to leave. 'Do you want me to come down for you tomorrow?' she asked.

Jack shook his head. 'I'll bring him back safe and sound,' he said. 'I'm not leaving him again.'

Glen left as suddenly as he arrived. Jason walked him to the nearest motorway slip-road, where they said their goodbyes and kissed to the roar of passing traffic. Glen fished into his rucksack and extracted a handful of condoms, which he thrust into Jason's trouser pocket.

'Take care of yourself,' he said.

'I'll stay with you until you get a lift,' said Jason.

Glen laughed. 'How long were you on the street, mama's boy? I'll never get a lift if they think there's two of us. Get gone.' He kissed Jason once more, his thumb already extended.

There was a screech of brakes and a blaring horn. Jason started for a moment. A battered blur camper-van swerved onto the hard shoulder in front of them. Disco music was blaring within. The passenger door opened and a man in his mid-twenties, tanned, dark-haired, wearing only tie-dyed shorts and a pair of Lennon-sunglasses dropped to the roadside.

'Going north, *compadres*?' he asked, his accent thick and Mediterranean.

'I am,' said Glen. 'He isn't.' He turned back to Jason. 'Unless you've changed your mind,' he said, nodding towards the van.

'No,' said Jason. 'I'll see you round.'

'Damn right you will,' said Glen. 'Take care of yourself, Lost Boy.'

He gave Jason a final kiss and climbed into the van, ahead of the passenger.

Jason watched them roar off and turned wistfully back towards the fairground. He was sure he would see Glen again, but at the moment his friend's departure hurt. It always seemed to happen to Jason. Glen, Michael, Spider . . .

Fondling the silver spider at his neck, he walked slowly back towards the fairground.

There was a tense yet lethargic atmosphere across the fairground that afternoon. As Jason had walked back across town the sky had clouded over, and now it was starting to rain. A car was parked in the middle of the ground – a dark blue Mercedes, brand-new. Kevin and Willow Simpson were poking around the car. Kevin was trying to prise the Mercedes badge off the front grille. Jason smiled wistfully – how often had he and Spider done that? No car had been safe. The children's grandmother Mavis was hurrying towards them, shouting at the top of her voice. The old dear was always running after the kids and shouting, but today there was an edge to her voice which Jason had never heard before.

Almost all of the little community were standing about muttering together in tight little groups, when the first heavy drops of rain started to fall. Piper was nowhere to be seen.

'He's got visitors,' said Rex, peering in through the window of the old man's caravan. 'Piper never has visitors.'

Jason wasn't particularly interested. Black Shuck lay close by, tethered as ever to the Ghost Train. Jason looked down at the scar on the dog's neck. Slowly he lowered himself, hand extended, until he could cup the dog's muzzle. Black Shuck extended his long, pink tongue and licked Jason's hand.

There was a banging on the window of Piper's caravan. Through the glass the old man was waving Rex away angrily, shouting something.

'Touchy,' said Rex.

'What's to be done today?' Jason asked. He wanted to work, to be distracted. He didn't want time to dwell on his thoughts. It seemed to work for Tom, day after day.

'There's not much to do,' said Rex. 'They're hardly flocking in. We scarcely needed to do a litter-trawl today.' He scanned the rides. 'You could always have a go at clearing up the Tunnel of Love. It's still full of glass. I'll get someone to help you.'

'It's OK,' said Jason. He didn't want to think, but neither did he really want to talk to anyone.

The Tunnel of Love had sat there, erected but closed, since the morning after their arrival. Jason stepped into the tacky grotto, an empty plastic bin held in one hand, a thick builder's glove on the other. Tiny shards of glass gleamed in the harsh electric light.

Jason worked for hours, combing the fake hillocks. He laboured hard, stooping and gathering, working against his memories, trying to keep his mind focused on his task. He failed. In the aftermath of Glen's departure he felt terribly alone.

'How's it going? God, you've worked like a dog in here.'

Annie was standing at the edge of the grotto. 'Be careful,' she said.

'Oh, I am,' said Jason. 'I've made too many fuck-ups round here lately.'

'I've been to visit Laurent,' said Annie. 'He's coming out tomorrow.'

'Great,' said Jason.

'Jack was there,' Annie continued. 'He seems much better now. We've made our peace.'

Jason smiled weakly.

'I know you think I somehow betrayed your trust.'

'No,' said Jason. 'I was totally out of order.'

'We all behave like wankers from time to time,' said Annie. 'Forget it.'

'You swear like a man,' Jason said, smiling, stepping towards her.

'Stop!' Annie screamed. 'Don't move!' She stooped and pinned him to the floor of the ride. 'Look,' she said.

A spike of glass was protruding from the bottom of his shoe. Slowly she eased it out. 'Close,' she said. 'You take a break. I'll finish up in here.'

Jason strolled out into the daylight and looked around. A man was coming down the steps of Piper's old van, followed by Piper himself. The man was wearing a smart business suit, in contrast to

Piper's own filthy suit, and carrying a briefcase. He turned to shake Piper's hand, and for the first time Jason saw his face.

He darted back inside the ride. 'Annie!' he called. 'Annie!'

She hurried across to him. He didn't wait. Outside the man was walking away from Piper.

'What's wrong?' asked Annie.

'That man . . .' said Jason quietly.

'What about him?'

Without looking at Jason and Annie the man strode between the caravans and disappeared beyond the rides. Jason stepped forward. He could see the man getting into the big blue Mercedes. Two other men, each well over six feet tall, followed him into the car. A moment later it glided out of the fairground.

'D'you know who that was?'

'No.'

'I do,' said Jason, barely audibly. 'That was Victor Malcolm . . .'

Jason didn't understand anything any more. Why the fuck should Victor Malcolm turn up here?

He stared up the road after the long-departed Mercedes. What had Victor Malcolm been doing in Piper's caravan?

Jason pulled himself from the bed and strode out of the caravan and across to Piper's shabby living quarters. He could see the old man lying on his tiny bunk, apparently asleep. Jason tapped on the door.

He heard a muttering and shuffling from within.

'What?' Piper called.

Jason pushed the door open.

'Come in, lad. Sit down.'

Jason looked around for something to sit on. There was nothing.

'That man,' said Jason. 'The one who was here earlier. What was he doing here?'

'Him?' said Piper. 'He's a businessman. Comes from Newcastle.'

'Victor Malcolm,' said Jason. 'He's a crook.'

'A businessman,' Piper replied. 'A businessman. We were talkin' business.'

'About the fair?'

'Aye, maybe.' Piper's voice darkened almost imperceptibly in tone.

'What sort of business?' Jason was aware that he sounded agitated. 'You don't want him here, Piper, believe me.'

'Mr Malcolm's made me a fair offer. We've talked it through. We've been talkin' for months.'

'About what?'

Piper paused, looking at Jason. 'He wants to invest in the fair. Get in some new rides. Big stuff. The sort of stuff that gets the punters in.'

'New rides?' Jason was surprised. Piper had seemed, more than anyone else at the fair, to symbolise the unchanging life of the nomadic little community. 'Why would you want new rides? You won't even let the Merry-Go-Round go. When did you say it broke down?'

Piper sighed. 'I'm old, lad,' he said. 'You don't want to know how old. I'm done here. My ways ain't good for much any more. I'm packin' up, lad. Settin' me affairs in order, settlin' accounts.'

'Look, I know things are bad,' said Jason, 'but believe me you don't want to get involved with him. He's a gangster. He supplies drugs. He runs protection rackets. He runs prostitutes. Rent boys . . .'

'Now don't upset yourself, laddie,' said Piper. 'He's what we call a rough diamond. But he's fair. Always stands his round, like. If I'm any judge –'

'Well, you're not,' said Jason. 'Just look at the people you attract to this place.'

'Well, I'm not so sure as I can back out now,' said Piper. 'We made a bargain.'

'You signed a contract?'

'Not yet. He wants to put it in writin', and I've agreed, but we shook on it and drank a toast. As far as I'm concerned it's done.'

'It doesn't make sense,' said Jason. 'Malcolm's all flash and glitz. He likes the high life – cars, women, flash functions and the like. Why would he be interested in a shit-pile like Gamlin's? We all know it's going down the tubes! Whatever else he may be, Victor Malcolm's no fool.'

'Says he used to come to Gamlin's as a lad,' said Piper. 'Sentimental value, you might say.'

'Bollocks,' said Jason. 'Victor Malcolm doesn't believe in sentiment.'

'You know him then?'

'Oh, I know him,' Jason muttered.

'It's a pile of shit, boss.'

Victor Malcolm reclined on the deep, comfortable back seat of his car and lit a cigar. 'I know,' he said between puffs. 'I know. But Gamlin's and me, we go back a long way.'

'I mean, I've seen some pile-of-shit fairs in my time, but that one pisses on them all.' The driver pulled on the wheel and glided across lanes, cutting across the path of another car. Its horn blared.

'Keep your eyes on the fucking road, Vaughan,' said Malcolm. 'Let me worry about business.'

'I'm with Vaughan, boss,' said the front-seat passenger. 'Where's the profit in it?'

'It's not about profit,' said Malcolm. 'I grew up with that fair. Every year, as long as I remember, it's been coming to Newcastle. I probably smoked my first ciggy at Gamlin's. I probably got my first shag there, too. And I know I did my first mugging there. Some old bloke. Bit of a tramp, really. Bad choice. But the old bastard had nearly seventy quid on him. And that was a lot of money in those days, boys, believe me.'

'But –'

'Crabb, I don't pay either of you to think,' said Malcolm. 'I pay you to do. I know you've been restless, but I promise there'll be work for you soon. You know we've had to lay low until we were sure the inquest wouldn't turn anything up.'

'I thought you might be going soft,' said Crabb. 'That's what they'll say when word gets out about this fair business.'

'No one's going to know,' snapped Malcolm. 'Boys, think about it. It's a good way of moving stuff in bulk up and down the country. Abroad, even. I'll get them on the Continent. It might sound daft, but there's something about that fair. They're like a bunch of holy innocents, rambling up and down with their tame little rides. I don't think the police would ever suspect them of anything. You wouldn't know unless you'd grown up with it like I did. Trust me. I'm not going to push much money into the place. I bullshitted the old man – gave him a load of flannel about new rides, got him pissed in some flash hotel in Northampton, had him eating out of my hand. It'll be a pushover.'

'As long as I don't have to get involved,' muttered Vaughan. 'I'm no fucking candy-floss seller.' He wound down the window and spat at a passing car.

It was getting dark. Jason lay on the bed, running the same thoughts endlessly through his mind, mangling them, wringing them dry. Victor Malcolm. Geordie fucking Godfather. It was Spider who had run across him first. One of Malcolm's dealers had made the introduction. Spider and Jason had then been invited to a party of Malcolm's. It had been like something out of the Roman Empire. Girls, boys, booze, cocaine.

Jason had been a bit overwhelmed by it all. He'd ended up puking in the toilet. Spider had loved it. He'd talked about nothing else for days afterwards, until Jason, pissed off, had turned on him. They'd quarrelled. It was their first quarrel. Spider started hanging around with some of Malcolm's lesser minions. Half of them were rent boys – Malcolm ran a lot of rent boys. It was only a few weeks before Spider himself was doing rent.

Jason had freaked when he found out. They'd had a blazing row . . .

The lights were coming on all over the fair. The music was starting up.

He should get to work. He'd have a word with Rex during the show. Warn him, try to get him to talk to Piper.

There was a tap on the window of the caravan. The door opened.

'Ready, love?' said Annie, leaning in. 'You're definitely on the Wheel tonight. Kevin and Willow are helping out.' She smiled ruefully. 'I'll say this for Jack, at least he prepared them for this sort of thing.'

'Annie, there's something I've got to tell you,' said Jason. 'Piper's about to do something really stupid.'

'So what's new?' said Annie caustically. 'Listen, I've got to go, love. We can talk after the show, OK?' She blew him a kiss and left.

Christ, if even Annie wouldn't listen . . . Maybe if Tom had been around – Tom would almost certainly know about Victor Malcolm. In fact, Jason was worried that Tom might know too much about Victor Malcolm. Too many skeletons . . .

He leaned across the bed and opened Tom's bedside drawer. A letter was lying on top of the photo-pile. He snatched it out and read it.

It was from Tom's mother. *Dear Tom, Hope this letter reaches you . . . so hard to contact . . . time you stopped all this nonsense and settled down . . . Darling, the main reason for writing to you is to let you know that David's inquest is on Thursday 29th at the Coroner's Court here in Newcastle. We don't expect them to say much, they still haven't turned up the driver, and the talk of a second car being involved never came to anything, but at least it will all be over. We guessed you would want to be there. Your father and I are looking forward to seeing you again, darling, and we would love it if you would spend a couple of days . . . miss you . . .*

Jason groped in his rucksack and pulled out the now-battered photo from Tom's collection. The whole family on holiday, happy together. He lay back and placed the letter and the photo on his chest.

He slept. He knew he must have slept because he dreamed. He was running down an alley, dwarfed by high, blank walls. It was night. A car roared down the alley after him at full speed. A dark blue Mercedes. The engine snarled at him. The car was practically as wide as the alley. It glanced off the walls as it bore down on him, creating sparks like fireworks.

A dog was barking somewhere. Darkness up ahead. A wall. He had run into a blind alley. The car roared and sparked towards him. He turned to face the wall, looking for a purchase. Jamming his fingertips into cement-holes between the bricks, Jason began to haul himself upward. This wall wasn't as high as the side-walls. Jason reached the top and balanced for a moment before dropping down the other side.

Falling. The drop on this side was far greater. The barks of the dog were loud now. He hit something, which broke beneath him. There was a crashing of glass all around; it sheeted and splintered on every side. He didn't know what he had fallen into. He hit the ground hard. It was hot. There were flames everywhere. Flames and broken glass. He heard the slobbering breath of the dog grow into a deep snarl. It burst through the flames, huge and black, eyes like burning gold, mouth red, teeth wet and dripping with saliva. The red mouth darkened as it closed over Jason's eye. He felt flesh tearing. The eye filled up, crimson with blood.

He snapped awake, unrefreshed. Naked, but for the thong tight around his neck. He could barely remember having undressed.

Someone was moving around outside the caravan. The door swung open. Tom stood, swaying in the doorway. He was still wearing his suit, but it was stained and crumpled. His shirt was open, his tie gone. He stumbled into the caravan, holding on to the wall for support. His breath stank of booze.

'Tom . . .' Tom never drank.

He stood over Jason, looking blankly at him. Jerkily he turned to the bedside drawer and yanked at it. He didn't seem to notice that it was already open. He picked up the stack of photographs and began shuffling clumsily through them, growing increasingly agitated.

'Not here . . .' he muttered. He began scooping handfuls of stuff out of the drawer and onto the floor.

'It's not fucking here!' he bellowed.

He turned to Jason, his eyes blazing. He pointed an unsteady finger at him.

'There's a photo,' he slurred angrily. 'A photo of me and my brother, on holiday. It was in this drawer. It's not there now. Where is it?'

Jason's eyes darted about. Tom's letter was still lying on the bed, half-crumpled under Jason's body. The photo was on the floor, creased and torn. He prayed Tom wouldn't see it.

'Have you got it?' said Tom.

'No,' Jason pleaded.

'Oh, come on,' snarled Tom. 'I know you've been through my stuff before now.'

'No!' Jason lied desperately.

'Fucking Newcastle street trash. I should never have . . .'

'On my life, Tom —' Jason tried to turn, to cover more of the letter with his body.

'On your life . . .' Tom hissed. 'If I find you're lying . . .'

His anger seemed to well over. He slammed his fist into the wall of the caravan. The wood veneer dented and cracked under the impact.

Tom lurched unsteadily to his feet, gripping the wall for support. He swallowed hard, trying to suppress a sob. Another followed it, then another. Jason watched, motionless, unable to move, as his friend cried. Jason felt like crying too.

'Jason . . .' Annie poked her head round the door of the caravan. She fell silent, looking at Tom. Clumsily he pushed past her and out of the caravan.

'What's wrong?' Annie croaked.

Jason looked imploringly into her dark eyes. Tears flooded his vision.

'I killed his brother,' he whispered.

His face creased. He rocked forward into Annie's arms and pressed his head against her fake chest, crying freely. She hugged him to her and stroked his hair as he cried.

'Ssssh,' she whispered.

'I fucking killed him, Annie.'

There was movement from the door. Tom was once more standing there. Annie rose to her feet.

'Tom.'

'I'm OK, Annie.'

'I'll go,' she said. 'If you need anything . . .'

'Yeah, thanks.' Tom was almost brusque. Annie slipped out of the door.

Tom sat on the edge of the bed. 'Jason, I said some things . . . I didn't mean them. I'm sorry.'

Jason sat up and put his arm around Tom, hugging him tightly. 'Tell me about Newcastle,' he ventured after a pause. 'Tell me about the inquest.'

There was a long moment of silence.

'My brother was a passenger in a car,' Tom said eventually. 'A stolen car. After I went abroad David went completely off the rails. He was running with a pack of toerags. At some point he got into stealing cars. One night, there was a crash. My brother was killed. The driver got away.'

Tom sniffed loudly.

'Death by misadventure,' Tom intoned. 'Death by fucking misadventure.'

'Who was the driver?' asked Jason.

'That's the trouble,' said Tom. 'He never came forward. They don't know.'

He sniffed again.

'I think I'd better sleep now,' he said. 'I don't usually drink. I've had a skinful.'

He rose to his feet. 'If you want me to sleep somewhere else . . .' he said.

'No,' said Jason. 'Come to bed.'

Jason watched as Tom discarded his suit, leaving it in a crumpled heap on the floor. This wasn't the Tom Jason knew. He slipped out of his shirt and pants and turned towards the bed. Jason could see that his cock was slightly engorged, thick and long, the main vein clearly visible, the whole surrounded by a thick black pubic bush. Jason rolled onto his side as Tom slid beneath the bed-covering. He pressed himself against Jason's back and put an arm over his shoulder.

'If I ever find the driver of that car,' Tom said in a quiet, hollow voice, 'I swear to you I'll kill him.'

Thirteen

J ason awoke at nine to the hiss and the smell of frying from the
stove. Tom was standing with his back to him.

'You're not eating enough,' said Tom without turning around.

He deftly tipped the contents of the frying pan onto a plate and
handed it to Jason.

Jason was starving. He flashed an appreciative glance at Tom
and began shovelling breakfast into his mouth.

'Aren't you going to have any?' Jason asked between forkfuls.

'No,' said Tom. 'I don't eat breakfast.'

He turned and left the caravan. Jason watched him go. He must
have been into town already this morning. Jason returned his
attention to the meal, clearing his plate in less than a minute.

He dressed and strode out into the fairground. It was a windy
morning. The Wheel swayed in the gale. Tom was already up
there, changing bulbs. Jason began to ascend.

'I can manage up here,' Tom shouted over the wind.

'What d'you mean?' Jason shouted back.

'I mean, it's blowing a gale up here! You're not used to these
conditions.'

'Yes I am,' said Jason. He'd climbed in much worse than this.

'Get down,' said Tom. 'I won't tell you again, Jason.'

'OK, OK.'

Jason returned to the ground.

'You can help me for a minute, if you like,' said Rex. 'It's only a small job. You can help me to adjust the spring.'

'The spring?'

'In Bertha.' The Test-Your-Strength machine. 'It needs tightening. Too many people have been winning lately. It's bankrupting me.'

'Isn't that a bit dishonest?' asked Jason.

Rex shrugged and began unscrewing a plate on the back of the machine. 'Stick your hand in here,' he said. Slightly alarmed, Jason did as he was told. 'Have a grope around in there,' said Rex. 'You should be able to feel a cock. Grab it.'

'A what?' queried Jason.

'A cock. A stop-valve. A tap. It tightens the spring.'

'Got it,' said Jason.

Rex picked up the hammer and walked up to the peg. He swung the hammer high and brought it down hard. The vibration travelled down the machine and up Jason's arm. The bell at the top of the machine clanged loudly.

'OK, turn it clockwise,' said Rex.

Jason turned the wheel, and Rex struck the peg again. Again the bell clanged.

'More,' said Rex. 'Much more.'

Jason turned the wheel several times. Rex struck a third time. This time the bell was silent.

'That'll do,' said Rex. He sat down. 'I'm losing it,' he sighed. 'I used to be able to ring the bell on the hardest setting.'

Jason sat down next to Rex. Rex rummaged inside the wooden box where he kept his telephone books. He fished one out, and tugged limply at it. 'Even the phone books have been getting harder of late.'

He tugged at it again. It refused to rip. With a mournful expression, mouth drooping glumly beneath his preposterous moustache, the strong-man opened the book, tore out a single page and then, closing the book, tore it in two.

He tossed the two halves to the ground. 'I rip directories. I blow up hot water bottles. I practically bend lamp-posts and eat cow pie. That's who I am – I'm Desperate Dan. I'm old. I'm obsolete. And a bit desperate.'

This wasn't like Rex at all.

Not that Jason was particularly interested at the moment. Too much had happened. He was still preoccupied above all with Victor Malcolm's sudden reappearance in his life.

'Rex,' he said. 'D'you talk much to Piper?'

'Now and again,' Rex said. 'Why?'

'He won't listen to me,' said Jason. 'He's got involved with a businessman called Victor Malcolm. I say businessman – he's a crook. He's really, really bad news.'

'Piper usually knows what he's doing,' said Rex.

'Piper *never* knows what he's doing,' spluttered Jason.

'No . . .' Rex replied. 'But things tend to work out anyway.'

'So you're not going to do anything?'

'Why don't you ask Annie?' said Rex. 'Or Tom. Ask Tom. I'm not really feeling myself today.'

That was what Jason wanted to do – ask Tom. But he couldn't ask Tom. Not now.

He'd try Annie again. 'Are you through with me?' he asked Rex.

Rex nodded. Jason trotted across the fairground to where Annie was polishing her cars.

'Need a hand?' he asked.

'I'm fine,' Annie replied. 'You look restless.'

'I need to talk to you,' he said, and repeated his account of Piper and Victor Malcolm. Annie listened in silence. When he had finished she nodded slowly and said, 'Piper usually knows what he's doing.'

'That's exactly what Rex said,' Jason cried. 'And we all know it's bullshit! This bloke's really bad news, Annie.'

'Piper can't really do anything. He doesn't own the fair,' she said. 'Nobody does.'

'No, but you treat him like he's fucking Gandhi, when anyone can see he's senile. If he jumped over a cliff, you'd all jump after him. And that's what you *are* doing!'

'Sometimes things get a bit rough at Gamlin's,' said Annie. 'We've had our ups and downs lately, and I half-expected things to get worse. They usually do.'

'What is it with this place?' Jason grumbled.

'It's always been a place of outsiders,' said Annie. 'People who are a bit lost, or just different. Sometimes that makes us a target. Sometimes we get crap from the outside. And sometimes we bring crap from the outside in with us.' She smiled. 'But don't worry – we'll survive. We always do.'

'So you won't talk to Piper either.'

She sighed. The smile slipped a bit. 'I'll have to think about it. It's not really the way we do things, love. We tend to throw our fortunes to the winds here.

'I'll do a horoscope,' she called after him as he trudged away.

No one seemed to want to know. He wandered about doing odd jobs, but no one really seemed to have need of him. They had acquired three new casuals that morning – all not-so-old friends of Piper's – who had sailed through the work. By the time the wind had died Tom was finished on the Wheel.

Jason was sick of killing time, ploughing endlessly through his thoughts. He decided to sit in the sun and watch his friends work. The same routine today as every day. The same banter, the same calls-and-responses.

When the blue Mercedes had first pulled into the fairground they'd been only too curious. Piper with a visitor. They'd been worried. Now suddenly they didn't want to know.

OK, if he had to he'd sort this out on his own. Victor Malcolm had fucked with those he cared about once – he'd never do it again.

He was aware of a buzzing in his ears, slowly getting louder, becoming a roar. Two motorbikes swerved to a halt in between the rides. Each was ridden by a leather-clad Hell's Angel. Behind them sat two less imposing figures – Jack and Laurent. The fairground-folk were starting to congregate around the bikes, Annie to the fore. Hands reached out to help Laurent, laughing and breathless, from the pillion. Jack stumbled from his seat, his legs gave way and he slumped into the mud. Nobody paid him any attention.

Annie fussed over Laurent. When Jack was on his feet again she turned to him. 'Welcome back,' she said, kissing him on the cheek. 'We've missed you.' She gathered herself. 'But where in God's name did you get the retarded idea of bringing Laurent back from Derby Royal Infirmary on a fucking *motorbike*?'

The bikers exchanged glances. Laurent was laughing uncontrollably. '*Mais non!*' he chortled. 'We came by taxi and by the train, Annie. Jacques only picked up those two at the railway station.'

Annie's face relaxed into a reluctant smile. 'Welcome back,' she repeated warmly.

Jason moved into the crowd. When the boys had recovered their breath and the bikers had ridden off, the fair workers one by one welcomed each boy back. It seemed almost ritualistic. Jason hugged each boy in turn.

'You look fucking awful,' he said to Laurent.

'It is good to see you too,' said Laurent, grinning.

Jason was pushed aside by Kevin and Willow, who had just been told the news. Behind them their grandmother shouted and flapped her arms in vain.

The day's work seemed to rush happily by. Lunch was called early, with nothing but a lazy afternoon ahead. After they had eaten Piper vanished and reappeared rolling a beer barrel. Some of the younger men hefted it onto the table, pegged and spiked it. Somebody hunted around for glasses.

Three hours later the beer was still flowing. The barrel never seemed to end. Tom, who had lined up with the rest and murmured his brief greeting, sat slightly apart from the others. He had eaten in silence. When the barrel was opened he slipped quietly away to his caravan.

Jason noticed Rex watching him go. Rex too had been unusually quiet. Jason had expected more on the return of his old sparring-partner Jack. It seemed his melancholic mood of this morning hadn't lifted. As Tom disappeared into his caravan Rex too got up and slipped quietly away.

The day wore drunkenly on. Piper's new casuals had found their way to the Test-Your-Strength machine and were trying to ring the bell. The projectile flew high, but none actually made contact with the bell. Jack tried – and did pitifully. Laurent, in his condition, did considerably better. Doug did pretty well for a small guy. Jason himself had a swing. Not even close (though better than Jack).

'This is impossible,' complained one of the roadies. 'It's a fucking fix.'

'I bet Rex could do it,' Jason blurted out. Yeah. It would be good for Rex. Cheer him up. 'Wait here,' said Jason, and ran towards Rex's caravan.

'Come in,' said Rex forlornly.

The walls inside Rex's caravan were covered in framed posters. Circus tours, mostly. He stood in front of an open mahogany drinks cabinet. His hand was extended around a large, full brandy-glass.

'Chin chin,' he said without turning around, and downed the glassful.

'Rex,' said Jason, 'the new boys were trying out Bertha. None of them could do it. None of us could. Why don't you come and show us how it's done?'

Rex didn't reply for a moment.

'Perhaps you'd like me to rip a telephone book in half too?' he enquired with studied politeness. 'Anything to oblige.'

He refilled his glass.

'Do you know how old I am, Jason?'

Jason shook his head.

'I'm fifty,' said Rex.

'You don't look it,' said Jason.

'The hair is dyed,' said Rex solemnly. 'And that's not the worst of it.'

'Don't tell me,' teased Jason. 'Your moustache is false. So you're fifty. So what?'

'*So you're fifty. So what?*' Rex repeated slowly. 'I see. Not even a happy birthday.'

'You mean . . .'

Rex nodded glumly. 'No,' he said. 'Please don't congratulate me. I'm not really in the mood for congratulations. And please don't tell anybody.'

'Are you coming out?'

Rex shook his head. 'I'm too old to come out to play. I want

to wallow in self-pity for a while. It's an annual tradition for me.
I'll be perfectly fine. You go.'

Jason flashed a smile and left. In any event, he could see the
party by the Test-Your-Strength machine was breaking up.

He knocked on the door of Jack and Laurent's caravan and
entered. The two were lying side by side on the bed.

'Christ, I'm drunk,' said Jack. 'I'd more or less resolved to give
up.'

'Guess what?' interrupted Jason. 'I'm not supposed to tell you
this.'

He recounted Rex's news. Jack sat up on the bed.

'We need to think,' he said.

Half-an-hour later Jason left the couple.

'Get some sleep,' were Jack's parting words. 'I've got work to
do now, and not much time. You be ready for action after the
show tonight.'

But Jason couldn't sleep. He wandered restlessly about, willing
the punters to arrive. The fair was deserted now except for Piper,
unconscious in one of the Ghost Train's cars, and Black Shuck,
tethered, snoozing in the late-afternoon sun.

At last faces appeared from inside the caravans and Gamlin's
started to wheeze into life. Jason joined Laurent on the Hall of
Mirrors, where they plotted and conspired all night. Jason was
happy with his decision over Victor Malcolm – he would deal
with him when he had to – but nevertheless wanted to keep his
mind busy. This was perfect. Jack was a genius.

The show closed gradually, as it had opened. Jason watched the
last punters go.

'Jason,' Annie was standing outside her caravan. 'Fancy a cup of
tea?' she asked.

He walked across and followed her inside. She lifted a large
china teapot from the workbench and poured tea into porcelain
cups. They sat down.

'It's good to see Jack and Laurent back,' she said. 'This really
seems to have changed them. Jack especially.'

'They can't keep their hands off each other,' smiled Jason.
'They sloped off a good ten minutes before anyone else tonight.'

He drained the cup.

'Want to read the tea-leaves?' he teased, still a little drunk.

'Mock if you want to.' Annie shrugged. 'Some believe, some don't.'

Jason leaned back in his chair and fingered one of Annie's dresses, hanging in the rail.

'I know you think I'm a bit of an old fake.' she said.

'No I don't,' he said, smiling. 'Not at all.'

She smiled and hugged him.

'Can I ask you something?' Jason asked.

'Of course, love,' Annie replied.

'What does Doug think of it? Of you, I mean. You, not really being a . . . I mean, sharing this caravan, him being your brother and all.'

He stopped. For some reason Annie was laughing.

'Doug *is* your brother . . .?'

She was shaking her head in great sweeps, chortling silently.

'No,' she said, breathlessly, 'he's not. Another lie, I'm afraid, Jason. Doug's not my brother. Doug's my sister.'

There was a tapping at the door of the caravan.

'No . . .'

Annie nodded. 'Twins. Same problem. We just swapped birth certificates.'

The tapping grew louder.

'Jason,' Jack whispered through the door, 'it's time.'

The door opened a crack and Jack peered round it.

'I've got to go,' said Jason, rising to his feet. 'It's something we're doing for Rex. It was his fiftieth birthday today.'

'Rex!' Annie jumped to her feet. 'Oh, I had no idea.'

'None of us did,' said Jack. 'But don't worry, we've sorted something out for him.'

'Am I invited?' asked Annie.

Jack and Jason exchanged a hasty glance.

'It's sort of a men's thing,' said Jason, smiling sheepishly.

'Ah,' said Annie, her face breaking into a grin. 'I understand. If you see that brother of mine, send him home, would you?'

* * *

Jason could see Rex and Laurent coming out of the strong-man's caravan.

'Laurent's slipped a little something into Rex's drink,' whispered Jack. 'It should kick in soon. He'll enjoy this.'

They were standing beside Jack and Laurent's caravan. The long trestle-table stood against the back of the van, running its full length. Jack scrambled onto the table and beckoned to Jason. Jason joined him. There were no curtains in the windows of the van. The two of them peered inside. Lounging around on a bed of cushions which covered the floor were two young men. One, about twenty, was small and pale-skinned, with a delicately sculptured face beneath an almost-black crew-cut. The other was older by a few years, handsome, muscular and black.

'I found them in the town. My system actually worked for once!' whispered Jack. 'Simon and Chris. What d'you think?'

'Mm,' said Jason. 'I've never seen your van looking so clean.'

'Sssh,' whispered Jack. 'Here they come.'

Through the glass they watched the caravan door open and Rex step through it. Laurent was standing right behind him. As soon as Rex was fully inside, Laurent stepped back and slammed the door. Rex spun and tugged at the handle. The door was locked.

'Not the most subtle approach,' whispered Jason.

The two men were advancing on Rex, smiling, holding out their hands. Rex backed away. He was talking fast. Jason couldn't make out the words.

Each youth took one of Rex's hands in his, and they began to pull him, still protesting silently, towards their cushion-bed.

'It's like a tide!' Jack suddenly shouted. 'Give in to it!'

'Ssssh!' Laurent hissed, scrambling onto the table beside Jack.

Rex didn't seem to have heard. The black lad said something to him – it might have been *Happy Birthday* – and kissed Rex slowly on the mouth. Lips engulfed, Rex allowed himself to be drawn down onto the cushions.

The white youth began undoing Rex's bootlaces and belt. He prised the strong-man's boots and socks off, then eased his trousers down, revealing a pair of striped, seaside-postcard underpants coming down nearly to Rex's knees. The strong-man's cock bulged, thick and long, against the material.

'Jesus,' said Jack, laughing. 'Look what Chris has found. Those underpants – whatever next?'

The white youth removed the rest of Rex's clothes, then peeled away his own shoes, shirt and trousers. He unhooked a long, pale cock from beneath a pair of tight red briefs. Rex flexed his buttock and stomach muscles. His cock did a little dance in the air.

The black youth – Simon – was still kissing Rex passionately. He lifted his head and yanked his T-shirt over it. His body rippled with muscle. He came down on Rex again, hard, nipping and tonguing at the strong-man's ear. His muscular body strained against Rex's. Rex had a superb body for his age – for any age – a great, sculpted knot of muscle-on-muscle, bulging and flexing as the pair wrestled together.

Rex pushed Simon away for a moment. He took hold of one end of his waxed black moustache and pulled. The proud growth peeled from his lip and hung limply in his hand.

Jason let out a shout of delight. 'It *is* fucking false!' he blurted.

Jack and Laurent didn't seem to be listening. He turned to see them next to him on the long trestle-table, clasped in each other's arms, kissing passionately.

Inside the caravan Simon was struggling with Rex. Their mouths dodged around one another, striking at each other's flesh like diving birds. Their bodies forced against one another. Their hard cocks, dripping pre-come, smashed and slipped together. Chris inserted his head between the legs of the others and began nipping and licking at their bouncing balls and taut, hairy perineums.

Jason heard a long moan next to him. Jack and Laurent were tightly embraced, struggling to remove each other's clothes whilst maintaining maximum body-contact. Jeans and pants were clumsily shuffled off. The table began to rock beneath them.

Through the glass Simon was vertical, holding his buttocks apart, squatting over Rex's now-sheathed cock. Slowly he lowered himself onto it. Chris had moved too, and was squatting over Rex's mouth, facing his friend. As Rex's cock disappeared into Simon's arse, Rex arched his head back and sucked one of Chris's balls into his mouth. He opened wider and the other one went inside too. Chris started wanking as Rex sucked and pulled at his scrotum.

Next to Jason, Jack and Laurent were still kissing passionately, clothes half-off, tugging at one another's hard cocks. Holding on to the side of the caravan to steady himself, Jason's eyes darted between the birthday orgy going on inside and Jack and Laurent's little side-orgy on the table.

Through the window Jason saw Chris pull his balls from Rex's lips and twist around, plunging his long, pale cock into the strong-man's mouth, thrusting it in and out. By the look on his face he was already close to coming. His eyes closed, his mouth contorted into an ecstatic rictus and he slammed his juddering groin against Rex's face.

Simon was still pumping up and down with his whole body, driving his arse on to Rex's cock. When he had drunk all of Chris's jet, Rex eased his head out from between the boy's legs. He lifted Simon from his cock and lowered him onto his back. Kneeling, lifting Simon's buttocks, he re-inserted himself, pushing forward, thrusting slowly. Simon wrapped his legs around Rex and hooked his feet around one another. Chris was behind Rex, kissing his neck and back and biting Simon's toes. Rex's stroke became more vigorous.

Biceps bulging, Rex lifted Simon's shoulders from the floor, thrusting his own head and shoulders out behind him, rocking back onto the balls of his feet. Still impaled on Rex's cock, Simon rose into the air. He leaned back in Rex's strong arms. Holding him under the back, Rex continued to thrust his big cock into Simon. He swung him around like a pendulum, knocking hastily placed ornaments off the telly.

Simon's head banged against the window. Rex stopped turning and fucked him hard. His head banged on the glass with every stroke.

Rex moved slightly back from the window and Simon let his head dangle. Upside down, he was looking through the glass directly at Jason. Jason instinctively retreated from the window, but the black boy's face merely winked and smiled.

Jason looked around for Jack and Laurent. They were gone — slunk off somewhere more intimate, he guessed.

Rex let out a great bellow. He was thrusting like a berserker now. Simon was shaking like a pillow. Rex sank to his knees as he came, smiling, panting. Chris was already moving in, sinking his head over Simon's cock . . .

Happily, Jason slipped from the table and into the shadows. Let them have their privacy. He wandered back to the caravan he shared with Tom and entered quietly. Tom was already asleep. Jason undressed quickly, his cock still stiff with the memory of what he had seen.

He slid into bed next to Tom and snuggled against his back, letting his hard prick rest in the sleeping man's arse-crack. Almost involuntarily Jason's hand drifted down onto Tom's lolling cock.

He must have fallen asleep like that. He woke with a start – it must have been hours later – to the clanging of a bell, echoing around the fairground.

He sat up. Someone was mucking about with . . .

His anxious face relaxed into a smile. It was Bertha's bell. The Test-Your-Strength machine. The triumphant echo lingered in the night.

Fourteen

The fair moved on, skirting the village edges of Manchester, hitting the heart of Bradford, climbing the Pennines to high Harrogate, then to York, then across to Scarborough on the coast. Darlington . . . Durham . . . The crowds were small, the atmosphere dogged.

Tom remained distant, but continued to punctuate his aloofness with acts of silent consideration. Breakfast became a ritual – Tom cooking, Jason eating – and Tom always seemed to be on hand when Jason encountered any difficulty in the day-to-day running of the fair. In Bradford Jason got hassle from some yob posse, all drunk. Virtually before he had even realised what was happening Tom had appeared and pinned the ringleader to the side of the Bumper-Car rink. He had said something to him in a low growl – too low for Jason to make out the threat – and tossed him into the path of one of the cars. The car had been hit with a sickening thud. Jason had winced. Tom had turned in silence and walked back into the crowd.

At night they would still sleep together, naked. Tom would mutely acquiesce as Jason put his arms around him and hugged his strong chest. Slowly Tom's arms would fold around Jason's shoulders. They would lie like that, in silence, until they fell asleep. On more than one night Jason awoke screaming from his dreams. Tom had stroked his sweat-moist hair and gently kissed

his tears away, then hugged him tight to his heart until Jason slept
once more. It was as if by night each was comforting the other in
some shared, unspeakable grief.

Jason was glad of the silence between them. He was sensing a
growing tension in Tom, and also in himself. He knew the reason
only too well. All the time they had been getting nearer and
nearer to Newcastle; now they were practically there. Jason's mind
was a whirl of apprehension and anticipation. He was afraid of
what he might reveal in this state to Tom. He couldn't forget
Tom's state when he had come back from the inquest. His fury,
his grief and finally his chilling oath of revenge.

Jason was also beginning to dread once more the return of
Victor Malcolm. Newcastle was his city. If he was going to strike
anywhere, it would be there. They were walking into a fucking
lion's den, and no one seemed to care.

The last night in Durham they closed early. Practically no one
came. With all the rides now manned, Jason wandered about,
trying to avoid conversation with anyone. Tomorrow they set up
in Newcastle.

Neither Jason nor Tom slept well that night. They lay awake,
side by side in the darkness, for over an hour.

'Newcastle tomorrow,' Tom said at last.

Jason said nothing. He wrapped his arms around Tom, hugged
him hard and held him all night.

They were up early the next day, breaking down the equipment. It was only a short drive to Newcastle – the fair was
assembled by two.

They had pitched on a stretch of derelict land next to the river.
Tom was about to give the Wheel a test spin.

'Hang on,' said Jason. 'I'm going up.'

He climbed into a car and rose slowly into the air.

Newcastle opened itself below him. Jason watched the Tyne's
waters spilling over the horizon in a great, broad belt. He saw the
bridges hot in the sun, the great sprawl of the shopping centre, the
Civic Hall, big on the inside, pokey on the outside, the university,
the great tower – Insurance Tower, they'd called it – with the ball
on the summit. They'd climbed that.

When he had reached the top of the Wheel he felt the great contraption shudder to a halt. He smiled. Tom knew. Another of his silent gifts to Jason.

The city shimmered in a heat-haze. He watched miniature people scurrying along miniature streets, the cars like toys on an impossibly detailed model. He had seen the city from on high hundreds of times, but from this spot the angle – the perspective – was quite different. The town looked weird – familiar yet not so. Somewhere down there was his mother, probably having her hair done. Somewhere down there his father would be sweating and sweltering at his desk, getting shit from some twenty-year-old junior manager. And somewhere down there Victor Malcolm was sitting like a spider at the centre of his city-wide web.

'Take me down, Tom,' he called at last. The car began to descend. The city rose up as if to swallow him.

He returned to the caravan and reached into his rucksack. He didn't want to face this alone. He lifted out the leather thong with the little spider perched on it. He'd only worn it a couple of days before removing it. Tom hadn't been able to stop staring at it – and Jason had woken one night to find Tom lying next to him, gently fingering the little pendant. He had removed it the next day.

Now he put it on again. Spider had always worn it for luck. He had given it to Jason as a peace offering. No more rent. No more Victor Malcolm. Like foolish children they had planned their revenge on the tycoon.

He had given it to Jason just before the accident. Maybe it had saved his life that night.

It was late afternoon before the blue Mercedes pulled into the fairground. Practically everybody had retired to their caravans. Jason was too agitated to rest. He watched Victor Malcolm disappear into Piper's caravan, and his two big henchmen wander back towards the town.

He had to act fast. Scanning the rides to make sure no one was about, he crept up to the Mercedes and looked inside. A briefcase lay on the back seat. The door was unlocked. Jason slipped into the car and triggered the clasps on the case. Inside were papers.

Tons of papers. There had to be something in here to incriminate Malcolm. Something he could show Piper.

He began leafing through them. Figures, mostly – Jason couldn't make sense of them. He decided to take the lot. It was then that he heard a fatal footstep outside the car. A shadow fell across Jason. One of Malcolm's goons was standing over him.

'Out,' a voice said flatly.

Jason scrambled from the back seat. The man towered over him – an ugly, broken face, an untidy ginger crew-cut. He grabbed Jason hard by the shoulders.

'Planning a ride?' the man asked. His hand flashed hard across Jason's face. 'Stupid. Very –'

The man froze in mid-sentence. His face creased in thought, then cleared into a smile of astonishment.

'Well, well,' he said. 'Small world.'

Jason looked hard into the face. Did he know him?

'Vaughan,' a voice called across the fairground.

'Over here, Crabb,' Jason's captor barked.

The other man lumbered up beside Vaughan. Crabb was also well over six feet tall, with a long face and greasy, dark, thinning hair.

'Who's this?' he asked.

'An old friend,' replied Vaughan. 'Sorry, I've forgotten your name.'

'Jason,' mumbled Jason.

'Jason, that's right. Spider's woman.' Vaughan nodded slowly, happy with the world. 'This is a very neat coincidence,' he said. 'Too good to pass up, really.' He cast his eyes about. 'Let's see . . .' he said. 'Aha!'

He began dragging Jason in the direction of the Big Wheel.

'What are you doing?' asked Crabb.

'Just attending to a little unfinished business,' Vaughan replied. 'You're good with machines, aren't you, Crabb?'

'Who are you?' Jason shouted. 'I've never fucking seen you before in my life!'

They reached the Wheel. 'Show my colleague here how to start this thing up,' said Vaughan, twisting one of Jason's arms hard behind his back. With his free arm Jason indicated the simple controls.

'Right, get in,' said Vaughan. He thrust Jason into one of the cars and got in beside him. 'OK, Crabb,' he called, 'start her up.'

The Wheel gave a small lurch and crawled into the air. Once again Newcastle lay below Jason. This morning he had felt some of his old invulnerability – now he felt the city had reached up and grabbed him by the throat.

Down below Jason heard barking. Black Shuck, tethered to the Ghost Train, was leaping in their direction, straining at his leash, barking furiously.

'Look, please,' said Jason, 'I don't even know who you are.'

'Brain a bit scrambled, I suppose,' said Vaughan. 'After the . . . accident. Perhaps this will remind you.'

He raised his fist beside his head. On one finger sat a huge brass ring. A cold lump of metal, shaped into the head of a savage dog. Even the teeth had been carved in.

Vaughan brought his fist down. The dog sprang into Jason's face, crunching bone, tearing skin. Blood and memories flowed. The dog. The wrecked car. That ugly face grinning down at him, hitting, punching him into oblivion.

People were starting to emerge from their caravans in response to the dog's barking. Tom was the first. The Wheel was in motion. He could see two figures high in one of the cars, beginning their descent. They were fighting – or at least one was. The other just appeared to be slumped there.

With a lurch of his stomach Tom recognised Jason. He ran forward. A large figure moved towards him. He felt a blow to his shoulder which sent him reeling to the ground. His tall, balding assailant stood over him. Fists clenched, he strode forward, aiming a kick at Tom's crotch. Without rising, Tom spun on the dried mud. His heel pistoned out, hitting his opponent's knee like a bullet. The man staggered backward in pain.

'Crabb,' a voice called from above. 'What the fuck's happening?'

'Get down here, Vaughan,' the man shouted back.

Tom looked up. Jason's car was rising again. His companion

appeared to be trying to pitch him out. Jason had his arms and legs wrapped around the safety bar. Tom strode forward. His army training kicked in – he barely thought about what he was doing. The army takes all the effective bits from the martial arts in all their variety and colour, and discards the art. Tom stood for a second in front of the recovering Crabb, then brought his knee up under the man's balls. Crabb crumpled. Tom gripped him by the back of the head and drove his face down into his still-raised knee. He didn't wait to see Crabb fall – he killed the Wheel's engine and swung himself up into the giant fuselage.

The Wheel juddered to a halt, but Jason barely noticed. His grip was loosening. There was only air below much of his body. They say your life flashes before your eyes at times like these – Jason was limited to certain endlessly repeating scenes. Lights. A screeching of brakes and tyres. The crash. Jason being flung against the steering wheel. Pain. Blood. The smell of petrol. Vaughan leaning through the broken window, hitting him.

He felt himself falling – back into the wooden seat. Vaughan had released him. Vaughan had a gun in his hand. A shot cracked out.

Jack and Laurent had been among the last to emerge from their caravan. They saw Tom drop a man with cruel efficiency, stop the Wheel and begin climbing it. There was something going on in one of the cars.

Black Shuck was barking himself hoarse. The Ghost Train juddered as he threw himself against his leash.

Laurent trotted closer to the Wheel. With some reluctance, Jack followed. Annie, Doug and Rex were already clustering around the man. He was hunched over the motor controls of the Wheel now, one hand clutching his balls. Jack could sympathise. Rex stepped forward, then stopped. The man had drawn a gun.

For a frozen moment no one moved or breathed. The man was shaking.

A volley of shots rang out from above. The man looked up with an expression of blind panic, then began looking wildly from one to another of his accusers. His finger trembled on the trigger. There was another shot from above.

There was a mighty ripping and roaring from the Ghost Train, and something dark streaked across the fairground. Black Shuck had finally broken his bonds. The man stared in momentary horror at the giant shadow moving as if to engulf them all, before his nerve broke. One shot was all he got. The dog flew at the man, crushing him back against the motor, sinking his fangs into his shoulder. The man screamed and thrashed against the controls. There was a muffled shot, and a deep howl from Black Shuck. The dog released its grip. The man staggered to his feet and ran, stumbling across the wasteland along the river's edge.

The fairground-folk clustered around the slumped body of the dog. Its breathing was shallow, its eyes half-closed, its black coat dimming with blood. The bullet had gone through the dog's chest.

It was Rex who broke the spell. 'Look at the Wheel!' he shouted. The Wheel was moving again, gaining speed at an alarming rate.

Jack peered at the controls. The main switch was broken, the gear lever was bent in half and the governor was smashed off. It was a miracle the dog hadn't broken the man's neck.

Another shot rang out. Tom clung to the moving Wheel. Its sudden lurch into life had almost thrown him from his perch. Something was wrong – it was picking up speed much too fast.

He was close to Jason's car but was being carried downward with a momentum which threatened to hurl him off the Wheel at any moment. He could barely hang on, let alone climb. He had somehow to anticipate the changing relative positions of himself and the man shooting at him – one moment he was sheltered by the Wheel, the next he was a sitting duck.

An idea flashed across his brain. He could use their rotation to his own advantage. If he could just keep out of the line of fire until they had passed the lowest point . . .

He swung behind one of the Wheel's great spokes. The angle of his descent was lessening. He was bottoming out. The gunman appeared almost gracefully before him, descending from above, aimed and ready. They were level now. A bullet cracked past Tom's head and ricocheted off the Wheel.

Tom was rising into the air again. The gunman vanished beneath him, obscured by empty cars and metal cross-struts. Tom could see him through the cracks, peering upwards, pointing his gun uncertainly.

He had to time this just right. He dropped into a car and balanced himself carefully, facing into the Wheel. There were two empty cars below him, then the gunman and Jason. He turned his back on the drop and let his feet slip.

Now . . .

Tom dropped lightly from the car, his body as straight as a poker, his arms slightly apart. Moving metal girders flashed past his face. If one of them caught him . . .

He fell through the air.

The car lurched badly as he landed. He struggled to regain his balance. The man seemed paralysed by surprise. Tom made a snatch for his gun-hand, but he snapped it back. Tom jabbed a palm-heel into his solar plexus and he staggered back, teetering on the edge of the car. It wasn't a good blow – it should have dropped him. The man recovered fast. He suddenly ducked and grabbed Jason by the collar, hauling him up, the gun pointed at Jason's head.

'Vaughan,' said Tom. 'Leave him alone.'

'Well, well, well,' sneered Vaughan. 'What a day. The world gets smaller by the minute. So you're into your dead brother's hand-me-downs now, are you?'

'What?' spat Tom.

'Him here. He was fucking your kid brother.'

'My brother . . . David . . .'

'David. Was that his name? Never knew that. Spider, we called him. Best little whore-boy the boss ever had.'

Tom took a step forward. Vaughan jabbed the end of the pistol into Jason's head.

'I'll tell you something else,' he said. 'It was your little bum-chum here that killed your brother. He was the driver of that boosted car.'

Tom's lips moved slightly, but no words emerged.

'Ask him,' said Vaughan.

'Jason . . .'

Jason didn't reply. He was staring into space, trembling violently.

'Jason . . .'

The voice sounded far away.

'Jason . . .'

Cold metal against his ear. The car has turned over, wrecked. Spider is next to him, his head smashed through the windscreen, dead. A man is leering in at him, his fist raised, eerily illuminated by the lights of his car. Blow after blow. A ring carved into the head of a dog. Jason blacks out. The last thing he hears are the man's retreating footsteps, then his car pulling away. He comes to again – his face is wet. An old man is pissing all around him. Pissing into the wrecked car. The old man finishes his piss and pulls Jason from the wreck.

The other car has gone.

The other car . . .

'There *was* another car!' Jason blurted out. 'It was him! He came out of a side road. He ran us off the road! I –'

'I thought I'd left you to die in that car,' snarled Vaughan. 'Little shits, stealing cars, doing dodgy drug deals, threatening to bring the law down on all of us. And Mr Malcolm was very fucking unhappy with your little bum-chum. First he says he won't do any more rent, then you and him decide to take Mr Malcolm's car for a little run.'

'So you decided to kill us!'

'We watched you. Next time you boosted a car, we followed.'

'And you ran us off the road.'

'I thought I'd been thorough,' said Vaughan. 'There was petrol everywhere. I chucked a fag in.'

'An old man pissed on it,' said Jason.

Vaughan laughed loudly. 'You've got a bit of spunk, lad, I'll give you that. Shame I've got to finish the job, really. A nice, clean fall from this death-trap.'

Jason looked at Tom. Tom seemed paralysed – his face ashen.

The Wheel passed its summit and they began the plunge down

the other side. The lurch to the stomach seemed to shake them all.

'None of us are going to get off this thing,' said Tom. 'Can't you see how fast it's going? Someone's removed the governor. The thing that regulates the Wheel's speed. If it goes much faster it'll shake itself apart.'

'I'll worry about that after I've disposed of him,' said Vaughan. 'And you. You heard my name.'

He raised the gun to Tom's head.

'*No!*' screamed Jason. He threw himself backward into Vaughan with his full weight. The gun went off and Vaughan let out a shout. They were tumbling in space, the two of them, falling. Jason felt hands clamp around his legs. He jerked to a halt and felt himself being dragged upward.

He heard a scream below him. Vaughan bounced off a strut. The rebound lifted him high into the air and down into the wide, grey waters below. The Tyne swallowed him in a second.

A confusion of metal and sky filled Jason's vision, then Tom's face sprang into view.

'You're OK,' said Tom. 'Now we've got to stop this thing.'

They were nearing ground level again, but far too fast to jump.

'Kill the motor!' shouted Tom to the onlookers at the Wheel.

They were still arguing about what to do. The brake wasn't working – the speed of the Wheel was just too great. Jack had sent Laurent off to get some sugar, which he wanted to pour into the fuel tank. He was arguing loudly with Doug.

'They haven't got much time,' said Rex. 'You heard Tom – we've got to stop this motor.'

He walked around to the other side of the engine. 'OK,' he said. 'Let's see if I can really still cut it.' He braced himself against the engine and gripped the fuel supply pipe where it entered the engine's bulkhead.

Jack moved closer, to see what he was doing. The others followed.

'I shouldn't get too close,' said Rex. 'There might be some spillage.'

Muscles bulging, he strained against the pipe. It was made of metal, and securely bolted to the engine; the whole thing had long since corroded into a solid mass.

'They built these things to last for ever,' he gasped. 'That's why the company went out of business.'

He re-anchored his feet and braced himself once again. He let out a low moan as his mighty muscles locked. And slowly, with a rending, wrenching sound, the pipe came away from the engine. Rex slumped forward, smiling as the engine spluttered and died.

'The brake!' shouted Jack. He sprang forward and pulled the hefty metal lever across. Sparks flew. Rex appeared behind him, and threw his weight against Jack's back, against the Wheel. His crotch pressed into Jack's buttocks.

'Rex, are you getting a hard-on?' asked Jack.

Rex tutted. 'Trust you to think about something like that at a time like this,' he said.

'Besides,' he added, 'I expect it's just the adrenalin rush.'

The Wheel slowed rapidly now. As they drew level with the ground Jason stumbled from the car, followed by Tom. The crowd fussed around them.

'What happened up there?' asked Annie. 'Are you hurt? Jason, you're bleeding. You're a mess, boy.'

They half-carried Jason and Tom down the steps of the Big Wheel.

Jason was standing in a pool of blood.

'What's this?' he asked.

'Black Shuck,' said Annie sadly.

'Hey,' shouted Laurent, 'where is Black Shuck? We left him here. He can't have crawled off.'

Annie smiled softly. 'Black Shuck won't stay here to die,' she whispered.

'Where's Piper?' Jack suddenly asked. 'Someone should tell him. Surely he can't have slept through all this?'

Shit, Piper.

Jason pushed his way through his friends and ran unsteadily across the fairground. He had to stop Piper signing that contract.

The light was on in his caravan. Jason ran up to the window and peered in. Piper and Malcolm were sitting on boxes, facing one another across a rickety old card-table. He hammered on the window and shouted. They ignored him. They didn't seem to hear him at all. As he watched, Malcolm took out a pen and flourished his signature across a piece of paper. Piper's spidery scrawl was already on it. Malcolm and Piper shook hands.

Jason ran around to the door and yanked at it. It was locked. He hammered again.

The door opened, and Piper and Malcolm came down the steps. Piper beamed at Jason. Malcolm puffed benignly on a cigar.

'Don't do this,' Jason pleaded. 'Piper, please.'

'Now, young man,' said Piper, 'I thought we'd sorted this out. Mr Malcolm and myself have signed an agreement. We have certain . . . obligations to each other now.' He winked at Jason. 'Trust me,' he said.

He put his arm around Victor Malcolm's shoulders and steered him into the fairground. 'Now,' he said, 'a ride on the Ghost Train first, wasn't it?'

Jason watched as the crook climbed into the front car of the little train, chomping on his cigar and smiling broadly. Piper powered up the ride and watched the cars move off, then shuffled back towards his caravan.

'People should always read what they sign,' said Piper. 'Always remember that.'

Victor Malcolm sat in the tacky little car at the front of the train, painted midnight blue and dotted with Caspar-style-friendly-fucking-ghosts, and chuckled to himself. *Same colour as my car*, he thought. He lounged back as he was carried through the black, swinging doors into the Hell beyond. Klaxons howled and hooters hooted. Cardboard skeletons wobbled on every side. He laughed out loud and threw his dying cigar into the darkness. The car lurched to the left and through the gaping mouth of a monster. Cobwebs brushed his face. Sheet-ghosts and more skeletons wobbled about him. Frankenstein's monster. Lights flashed on and off. Something went 'Whooo.'

There was a jolt, and the car stopped.

Fucking rubbish electrics. The whole place was falling apart.

Not that that bothered Victor Malcolm. He knew how effective health and safety executives were.

It was getting hot. Someone had better get a fucking move on.

There was another jolt, bigger. The whole floor seemed to heave for an instant. The car dropped, maybe a foot.

Smoke. There were flames flickering behind the skeletons. The car gave another lurch downward. The skeletons swayed towards him. They seemed to dance in the flames. The ghosts flitted and flapped around him. The Frankenstein monster lumbered from the smoke, jacket smouldering, arms extended. This was ridiculous. This was fucking . . .

The car pivoted forward and down. Victor Malcolm clung on. The smoky darkness seemed to extend for ever below him. Torn rails hung like broken fingers over the precipice. Clinging to the car he looked around. The other cars teetered above and behind him, but they were no longer empty. People, figures, young, old, incorporeal, barely there at all. They held out their hands to him, moaning and muttering. Villains, innocents . . . All dead. All dead by his hand.

The flames were on top of him now, setting light to his clothes. In vain he flapped and screamed. The car tipped forward one more time, left the rails and Victor Malcolm fell, screaming and burning.

'Jason . . .'

Tom was looking for him. He didn't want to face Tom. It was all out now. He had loved, and killed, Tom's brother. He ran.

He scarcely knew where he was. Tom was close. He dodged around the side of one of the rides and slipped inside.

The corridor twisted crazily away ahead of him. Mad, mocking mirror-faces lined up on every side to jeer and throw stones.

Why here?

He ran the crooked length of the corridor and into the reflecting labyrinth beyond. A dozen Jasons appeared around him, all pale and dirty and bloody, wide-eyed, frail and friendless.

Piper was right. Here he was, the real him, waiting all his life to confront him. The masks were down. For the first time Jason knew himself. His father had once told him he had the Mark of

Cain on his brow, and gone into some detailed biblical explanation. 'You shall dwell in the Land of Nod for ever, if you're not careful, Jase,' he had whinged.

Jason had never seen it before – the Mark of Cain. He saw it clearly now, etched in blood into his forehead by Vaughan's ring.

'Jason . . .'

Tom suddenly appeared from nowhere. Twenty Toms.

For a moment neither of them spoke.

'So now you know,' Jason said at last. 'What are you going to do to me?'

Tom was silent, staring.

'I killed your brother,' said Jason in a hollow voice.

'What he said's all true then . . .'

Jason barely heard him. 'I was driving the car,' he continued. 'He came at me from a side road. I wasn't sure until tonight. It was all confused. There were . . . gaps.'

'Gaps . . .' said Tom hoarsely. He stepped towards Jason. 'Gaps . . .'

He grabbed Jason by the shoulder and pulled him roughly forward. His eyes looked blank, expressionless. His fingers closed around Jason's throat, lifting him slightly from the floor. His other hand was raised in a fist above his head, poised to come down hard. Jason choked and kicked. Tom's grip was driving the silver spider into his windpipe. He pulled Jason closer. His eyes seemed to focus on the little arachnid.

'I loved him, Tom,' Jason croaked. 'I really loved him.'

Tom's grip relaxed. Jason slumped forward against Tom, sobbing, gasping for breath.

Tom was crying too; great, rolling tears. He buried his head in Jason's neck. His hands hugged Jason roughly to him. Jason lifted Tom's strong, tormented face and hugged it to his own. Their tears washed together. Gently Jason kissed a tear from Tom's cheek. Tom turned and kissed gently, haltingly back. They kissed again. Their kisses became harder. Slowly they found one another's lips.

Jason's arms were around Tom now. His hands slipped without thought up under his vest and began running backwards and forwards across his twin columns of muscle. Their bodies strained together. They stank of sweat. Jason could feel Tom's cock, hard beneath his jeans, pressing against his own swollen member. They kissed each other deeply, clumsy with emotion. Jason pulled Tom's T-shirt up his back. Tom raised his arms to allow Jason to remove it. Jason pulled his own filthy, bloody T-shirt over his head and dropped it to the floor. He reached forward and undid Tom's belt, then one by one released his fly-buttons. Tom kicked his trainers off, and allowed Jason to pull his jeans and pants down and off.

Jason stepped back. There was a breathless pause as Tom stood, naked and erect, in front of him, reflected twentyfold in the mirrors. Slowly Jason removed the rest of his clothes. The two stood, staring at each other's unclothed, openly sexual bodies. Jason stepped forward and gripped Tom's head again, pressing it against his own, tongue lashing tongue. Jason lowered a hand to Tom's buttock and pulled it forward. Cock collided with cock. Jason ran a frenetic hand over Tom's muscular chest and lean stomach, combing through his pubes, cupping his balls and running up his thick shaft.

Tom fumbled for Jason's cock and ran his fingers roughly across its shaft, prodding and pinching at his balls then squeezing his cockhead, skinning the hood back, testing the loose flesh between his fingers, exploring with all the awkward curiosity of a teenager. He dropped to a squat, prising his mouth from Jason's, dragging it down his chest to his nipples, biting hard, suckling like a babe. He dropped to his knees, nuzzling Jason's cock with his nose and mouth. His stubble tickled. His teeth bit Jason's shaft. He closed his lips over Jason's cock and drew it into his throat. Jason began slowly moving his hips, at the same time scanning the mirrors, watching Tom's head sucking his cock from a dozen angles.

He pulled Tom slowly to the floor and laid him down. Jason lay beside him as he had lain so many nights. They kissed again, tearfully, then Jason brought his head down over Tom's cock, tasting his meat for the first time, Tom's rich juices seeping on to his tongue. He drew back slowly, then plunged again, drew and plunged.

'Is this what you and David used to do?' gasped Tom.

'And other stuff,' said Jason, lifting his head.

'Show me,' said Tom. 'I want to feel what David felt.'

Jason reached into the pocket of his jeans and extracted a condom, which he spread over Tom's thick shaft. He reclined on his back and opened his legs, raising his buttocks and pulling his cheeks apart, offering Tom his arsehole. Tom rolled his body forward and through Jason's open legs, guiding his cock towards the offering. He butted around the entrance for a moment, before sinking the tip of his bulb into Jason's arse. Jason felt the bulb easing through his tunnel, pushing the walls apart, grazing his prostate.

Tom began to rock his hips, moving his cock in short, round strokes that seemed to roll through Jason's tunnel walls and across his cock and balls in a wave. Tom's stomach rippled like when he was exercising, doing his slow sit-ups. Jason looked up into Tom's eyes. They could almost have been Spider's eyes. Jason had never before seen the depth of the resemblance. A dozen Toms with Spider-eyes fucked him in the mirrors.

Tom's movements were becoming more rapid and jerky. His big cock was soon driving up and down Jason's passage, battering the walls. His face had clouded over. His mouth was clenched, his eyes were wide and wet. He made a little noise with his mouth to accompany each thrust. Little sobs. He seemed angry as he drove his great prick home. Jason was beyond tears. The events of the day were just too overwhelming. They seemed concentrated in the mirrors. Voices seemed to whisper; eyes seemed to peer. His friends, his enemies, his lovers . . .

From nowhere an orgasm hit him, spasming through his cock, which erupted in a cataract of white, all over his chest and stomach. He could tell Tom was coming too, grunting his sobs, his cock inflating in Jason's arsehole, his balls slamming into Jason's butt.

Tom collapsed on top of Jason, sweat and spunk sliding between them. Both were sobbing.

'Thank you,' said Tom after a while. Jason smiled – he knew plenty of straight blokes who didn't mind a bit of arse-fucking if there were no women about. Provided it was they who were dishing it out.

Tom kissed him again on the lips. 'Would you do that to me?' he asked.

Tom whimpered slightly as his friend penetrated his tight butthole. Jason inched his cock in, feeling the reluctance of the tight flesh to part.

When his cock was fully embedded he fucked Tom in an easy, relaxed manner, long, slow strokes. He felt warm and safe against Tom's back as he rode him, kissing and biting, arms wrapped around his broad shoulders, cock pumping in and out of his arse.

Even the mirrors seemed to smile now. Spider, watching from behind the glass, whispering and teasing.

He ran his hands down Tom's outstretched arms until their hands touched, fingers interlocking, tightening as Jason approached his climax. He shuddered against Tom as his cock started to discharge.

The mirrors were empty. Spider was gone. They lay there for a long time, Tom stroking Jason's head. 'Be showtime soon,' he said.

That night the punters came in their droves. 'As numerous as the fish of the sea,' as his father would say. The fair lit the river and made it look like an oil-slick. The Wheel, of course, was closed, as was the Ghost Train (although nobody seemed quite sure why), but that didn't stop half of Newcastle flooding over the little show in great shoals, straight into their nets of coloured light and bright hoardings, laughing, drinking, screaming and shouting. Jason had never known a night like it.

Fifteen

Nobody noticed the Ghost Train fire until the next day. The exterior of the structure had sustained surprisingly little damage. The inside was gutted. Jason didn't mention the man who was probably in there when it happened.

More worryingly to Jason, Piper was missing. Nobody was sure whether they had seen him last night. The last positive sighting was Jason's, just before the fire.

Nobody else seemed unduly worried.

'He'll turn up again,' said Annie. 'One way or another. He always does. There have been others before Piper . . . before Gamlin . . .'

'He said something to me about packing up,' said Jason. 'Settling accounts . . .'

That day Tom and Jason went into Newcastle together. They wandered the streets, spotting old landmarks, sharing memories, talking freely for the first time about their common past. They talked at length about Spider. They talked about the crash.

'You didn't kill David,' said Tom. 'He did. Vaughan. Him and his boss.'

'It was my idea to boost the car,' said Jason. 'Spider didn't want to that night.'

'That night,' said Tom. 'Whose idea was it the time before that? Whose idea was it to boost Victor Malcolm's car?'

'Spider's . . . David's.'

'Jason, I don't blame you for what happened to my brother. I did, for a short while, but . . . David was crazy. No one could stop him. He was the most over-the-top, crazy, full-of-life guy . . . I suppose really that's what killed him.'

Jason lowered his head.

'What made you come looking for me?' Tom asked.

'I didn't,' said Jason. 'That first night, when I tried to rob you, I had no idea who you were. Then when you locked me in the caravan and I found I couldn't get out, I went through your stuff. Looking for a key, I suppose. I went into your drawer, and saw your family photographs. I nearly died on the spot. I was looking at Spider. I didn't believe it. I was half-convinced it was a coincidence. Someone who just looked like him. I mean, they weren't particularly good photos. I wasn't sure for a long time. The name threw me.'

'David changed it when our mother remarried,' said Tom. 'My step-dad's name is Mann. David wanted to be Spider Mann. Crazy kid.'

'But I couldn't put it out of my mind, so I watched you. I followed you out of London. I wanted to tell you, I really did. But I couldn't.'

'No,' said Tom. 'It's probably a good thing you didn't try.'

'There were times I was really scared,' said Jason. 'When you spotted the photo was missing . . .'

Tom shook his head, smiling sadly. 'My God, I might have killed you. Over a nicked snapshot.'

'I never had a photo of Spider,' said Jason.

The fair was to stay four days in Newcastle. On the afternoon of the third day Tom travelled across the water to Gateshead. Jason knew what he was going to do.

He was in bed when Tom returned. Tom stripped and slipped in beside him. They had not made love since the Hall of Mirrors, and now they lay comfortably in each other's arms. Tom had been a little embarrassed the next day, but Jason had teased him into talking about it.

'Don't worry, I know you're not really gay,' he had said.

'It was . . . strange,' Tom had replied. 'It was good, but strange.'

'Pity really,' Jason had mused. 'You were terrific. I'd better not tell Jack.'

Now Jason huddled against his friend, enveloping him in bed-warmth.

'I went to see my mother,' said Tom.

'I know,' said Jason.

'It was . . . all right.'

'I went to see my mum and dad too,' said Jason. 'They're back together. Just like before. I don't know if she's still messing around, but I reckon she's being a bit less blatant now, and Dad manages to miss most things anyway.'

'And how was it?'

'Like you said,' Jason replied, 'it was all right.'

'Jason,' said Tom after a pause, 'I've decided to take a break from the fair for a while. Stay here for a bit. In Newcastle. The Wheel's out of action, and for now there's no money to repair it, so I'm sort of out of a job anyway.'

'You know that's not the way Gamlin's works,' said Jason.

'I know,' said Tom. 'It's just that . . . I actually felt at home here today.'

'So did I,' said Jason.

'Stay with me then,' said Tom.

Jason shook his head. 'I'm not ready for Newcastle full-time yet. There's more I want to see. I've never been to Scotland . . .'

'You'll have my address,' said Tom. 'Any time you change your mind, there'll be a roof for you.'

'You haven't seen the last of me,' said Jason. He hugged Tom's strong chest, listening to the reassuring, deep rhythm of his heart.

On their final night in Newcastle Jason stayed up late, long after his friends had gone to bed. He wandered far along the bank of the Tyne. The river was low, and for much of the way he could slosh through the mud of the river-bed. He hadn't done this since he was a kid.

He stopped. A figure was standing in the shadows in front of him. Long black hair. Naked, but for a great, flapping greatcoat which looked like leather but gleamed like fur. A gaping wound in his bare chest.

The figure stood motionless in front of Jason. Slowly Jason raised his hand and touched the figure's coarse cheek. The figure turned his head, extended his long tongue and licked Jason's palm slowly.

'That's twice you saved my life,' Jason said quietly.

The figure stepped back and looked steadily at Jason for a moment. Then he turned, his long coat describing a great arc against the darkness, and vanished back into the shadows.

Jason was alone. He turned and watched the lights of Newcastle, twinkling in the distance. It looked like a Christmas decoration. He smiled to himself and began walking towards the light.

The whole fair lined up to bid Tom farewell the next morning. Rex was in tears, and Jack wasn't far behind him. Annie gave him a cake in a tin. 'Make sure you eat properly,' she said, kissing him.

Tom picked up a big old suitcase. 'Walk with me a little way,' he said to Jason.

They walked through the little collection of rides, packed on their lorries, ready for the next pitch. Victor Malcolm's Mercedes still stood where it had been parked on rough ground at the edge of the fair. Now that the rides were broken and stored it looked quite alone and forlorn. Even before they had fully packed up the fair, Jason noticed, local kids were beginning to pick their way like weeds over the car. The grille badge was missing and the lights were all smashed. Jason watched a kid of about thirteen hacking at one of the tyres with a spiked metal railing, laughing and joking with his mates.

Jason took Tom's hand. They walked in easy, sad silence, hand in hand, as far as the main road.

'This is where I get my bus,' said Tom. 'To Gateshead.'

'OK,' said Jason hoarsely.

'I'm . . . really glad that you and David were so in love,' said Tom. 'And I think he did love you. He gave you his silver spider, for a start. Normally he wouldn't let anyone touch it.'

Jason smiled.

'You took it off for a while,' said Tom.

'I could see it had you rattled,' Jason smiled tearfully. 'I'll never take it off again.'

'Whatever David's faults, he was always a happy kid,' said Tom. 'And I guess a lot of that happiness was down to you. He loved you. I see that now.'

'There's your bus,' Jason whispered.

They gazed at one another for an everlasting instant, then Tom engulfed Jason in a great, crushing bear-hug, holding him madly. Jason hugged back. They kissed briefly and hard on the lips, then hugged some more.

At last they drew apart. A queue of women was filing on to the bus. Grinning, Tom picked up his case and took his place at the back.

'I saw Black Shuck last night,' shouted Jason. 'He's all right.'

'You saw him?' Tom shouted back, jostling forward with the queue. 'Where? How? I thought he was dead.'

The bus doors began to close around Tom. Jason smiled and shook his head.

'It doesn't matter,' he said. 'It's a sort of dream I have . . .'

Epilogue

Rain at night, beating on glass, driven by the wind. His favourite sound.

Jason Bradley peered through the glass of the railway carriage at the houses and gardens flashing darkly by. The first of the dawn-light was creeping across the sky.

They had set up last night on the Greenwich Marshes. The Gamlin's routine never changed − same time, same place, year after year. It was a year since Jason's first encounter with the fair.

It was just gone five in the morning. He had caught a ridiculously early, empty train into Waterloo, then another near-empty train out again. London was just waking up.

The sky was definitely lightening. He was late. The dawn cast long, pale shadows across trees and houses. Jason peered into the shadows − he was sure he could see something darker moving in the distance, behind the buildings − a great, loping shadow, keeping pace with the train. It sort of looked like a huge dog. Or the shadow of a huge dog.

He smiled to himself. Much had happened to him in the last year. He fingered the dog-scar above his eye. The wound had healed completely, leaving yet another battle-trophy. He felt like a veteran. One who has served in his wars and come home, and for whom it's time to embrace the peace. That's what he was going to do.

The train was drawing to a halt. Queenstown Road. Jason alighted and trotted down the stairs of the empty station and out into the street. Battersea Park was close. He crossed the scruffy, empty roads and found the park gates. They were still shut. He climbed over them with ease and trotted past the café, the bandstand. He thought about Jack and his ledgers and charts. Jason didn't need such an elaborate system – not today.

He was late. He broke into a run, across the grass, over a narrow bed of flowers.

Falling up the steps of the Peace Pagoda he stopped, leaning forward on his knees, gasping for air. Recovering his breath, he walked around the Buddha-column. He was alone up here. The whole park was deserted. Out on the river a cargo-barge chugged past. On the far bank Jason could see the first stirrings of life – a few cars, blinds being raised on the day.

He had been so sure . . .

He watched the barge motoring upriver.

He felt a warm breath at his ear. Unseen hands caressed his shoulders. Lips closed about his earlobe, teeth nipping lightly.

'Lost, boy?' a familiar voice purred.

Jason spun. Glen, like a black madonna, haloed by the early-morning sun, drew him into his arms.

'No,' Jason whispered.

IDOL NEW BOOKS

Also published:

THE VELVET WEB
Christopher Summerisle

The year is 1889. Daniel McGaw arrives at Calverdale, a centre of academic excellence buried deep in the English countryside. But this is like no other college. As Daniel explores, he discovers secret passages in the grounds and forbidden texts in the library. The young male students, isolated from the outside world, share a darkly bizarre brotherhood based on the most extreme forms of erotic expression. It isn't long before Daniel is initiated into the rites that bind together the youths of Calverdale in a web of desire.

ISBN 0 352 33208 5

THE KING'S MEN
Christian Fall

Ned Medcombe, spoilt son of an Oxfordshire landowner, has always remembered his first love: the beautiful, golden-haired Lewis. But seventeenth-century England forbids such a love and Ned is content to indulge his domineering passions with the willing members of the local community, including the submissive parish cleric. Until the Civil War changes his world, and he is forced to pursue his desires as a soldier in Cromwell's army – while his long-lost lover fights as one of the King's men

ISBN 0 352 33207 7

CHAINS OF DECEIT
Paul C. Alexander

Journalist Nathan Dexter's life is turned around when he meets a young student called Scott – someone who offers him the relationship for which he's been searching. Then Nathan's best friend goes missing, and Nathan uncovers evidence that he has become the victim of a slavery ring which is rumoured to be operating out of London's leather scene. To rescue their friend and expose the perverted slave trade, Nathan and Scott must go undercover, risking detection and betrayal at every turn.

ISBN 0 352 33206 9

WE NEED YOUR HELP . . .

to plan the future of Idol books —

Yours are the only opinions that matter. Idol is a new and exciting venture: the first British series of books devoted to homoerotic fiction for men.

We're going to do our best to provide the sexiest, best-written books you can buy. And we'd like you to help in these early stages. Tell us what you want to read. There's a freepost address for your filled-in questionnaires, so you won't even need to buy a stamp.

THE IDOL QUESTIONNAIRE

SECTION ONE: ABOUT YOU

1.1 Sex (*we presume you are male, but just in case*)
Are you?
Male ☐
Female ☐

1.2 Age
under 21 ☐ 21–30 ☐
31–40 ☐ 41–50 ☐
51–60 ☐ over 60 ☐

1.3 At what age did you leave full-time education?
still in education ☐ 16 or younger ☐
17–19 ☐ 20 or older ☐

1.4 Occupation _____

1.5 Annual household income (if you don't mind telling us)
under £10,000 ☐ £10–£20,000 ☐
£20–£30,000 ☐ £30–£40,000 ☐
over £40,000 ☐

1.6 We are perfectly happy for you to remain anonymous; but if you would like us to send you a free booklist of Idol books, please insert your name and address

_____

_____

_____

_____

SECTION TWO: ABOUT BUYING IDOL BOOKS

2.1 How did you acquire this copy of *Hall of Mirrors*?
I bought it myself   My partner bought it
(from a bookshop) ☐   (from a bookshop) ☐
I borrowed/found it ☐   It was bought through ☐
mail order

2.2 How did you find out about Idol books?
I saw them in a shop ☐
I saw them advertised in a magazine ☐
I read about them in _____
Other _____

2.3 Please tick the following statements you agree with:
I would be less embarrassed about buying Idol
books if the cover pictures were less explicit ☐
I think that in general the pictures on Idol
books are about right ☐
I think Idol cover pictures should be as
explicit as possible ☐

2.4 Would you read an Idol book in a public place – on a train for instance?
Yes ☐   No ☐

SECTION THREE: ABOUT THIS IDOL BOOK

3.1 Do you think the sex content in this book is:
Too much ☐   About right ☐
Not enough ☐

3.2 Do you think the writing style in this book is:
Too unreal/escapist ☐   About right ☐
Too down to earth ☐

3.3 Do you think the story in this book is:
      Too complicated   ☐   About right   ☐
      Too boring/simple   ☐

3.4 Do you think the cover of this book is:
      Too explicit   ☐   About right   ☐
      Not explicit enough ☐
Here's a space for any other comments:

SECTION FOUR: ABOUT OTHER IDOL BOOKS

4.1 How many Idol books have you read?

4.2 If more than one, which one did you prefer?

    _____

4.3 Why?

SECTION FIVE: ABOUT YOUR IDEAL EROTIC NOVEL

We want to publish the books you want to read – so this is your chance to tell
us exactly what your ideal erotic novel would be like.

5.1 Using a scale of 1 to 5 (1 = no interest at all, 5 = your ideal), please rate
    the following possible settings for an erotic novel:
      Roman / Ancient World   ☐
      Medieval / barbarian / sword 'n' sorcery   ☐
      Renaissance / Elizabethan / Restoration   ☐
      Victorian / Edwardian   ☐
      1920s & 1930s   ☐
      Present day   ☐
      Future / Science Fiction   ☐

5.2 Using the same scale of 1 to 5, please rate the following themes you may find in an erotic novel:

Bondage / fetishism ☐
Romantic love ☐
SM / corporal punishment ☐
Bisexuality ☐
Group sex ☐
Watersports ☐
Rent / sex for money ☐

5.3 Using the same scale of 1 to 5, please rate the following styles in which an erotic novel could be written:

Gritty realism, down to earth ☐
Set in real life but ignoring its less pleasant aspects ☐
Escapist fantasy, but just about believable ☐
Complete escapism, totally unrealistic ☐

5.4 In a book that features power differentials or sexual initiation, would you prefer the writing to be from the viewpoint of the dominant / experienced or submissive / inexperienced characters:

Dominant / Experienced ☐
Submissive / Inexperienced ☐
Both ☐

5.5 We'd like to include characters close to your ideal lover. What characteristics would your ideal lover have? Tick as many as you want:

Dominant ☐ Caring ☐
Slim ☐ Rugged ☐
Extroverted ☐ Romantic ☐
Bisexual ☐ Old ☐
Working Class ☐ Intellectual ☐
Introverted ☐ Professional ☐
Submissive ☐ Pervy ☐
Cruel ☐ Ordinary ☐
Young ☐ Muscular ☐
Naïve ☐
Anything else? _____

5.6 Is there one particular setting or subject matter that your ideal erotic novel would contain:

5.7 As you'll have seen, we include safe-sex guidelines in every book. However, while our policy is always to show safe sex in stories with contemporary settings, we don't insist on safe-sex practices in stories with historical settings because it would be anachronistic. What, if anything, would you change about this policy?

_____

_____

SECTION SIX: LAST WORDS

6.1 What do you like best about Idol books?

_____

6.2 What do you most dislike about Idol books?

_____

6.3 In what way, if any, would you like to change Idol covers?

_____

6.4 Here's a space for any other comments:

_____

_____

_____

_____

Thanks for completing this questionnaire. Now either tear it out, or photocopy it, then put it in an envelope and send it to:

    Idol
    FREEPOST
    London
    W10 5BR

You don't need a stamp if you're in the UK, but you'll need one if you're posting from overseas.